T0365254

Dog Days
of Summer

Dog Days
of Summer

Rick Milone

Dog Days of Summer

iUniverse books may be ordered through booksellers or by contacting:

iUniverse LLC
1663 Liberty Drive
Bloomington, IN 47403
www.iuniverse.com
1-800-Authors (1-800-288-4677)

ISBN: 978-1-4917-4400-0 (sc)
ISBN: 978-1-4917-4402-4 (hc)
ISBN: 978-1-4917-4401-7 (e)

Library of Congress Control Number: 2014914638

Printed in the United States of America.

iUniverse rev. date: 08/13/2014

I'd like to thank my dear sister Tracy, my long time and dear friend Susan and my wonderful wife Mary-Jo for helping me edit this book.

Chapter 1

Page 231.

Her white, palomino-tipped breasts were heaving, as her breathing became heavy. She clutched at the sheets tightly as a shiver of pleasure passed through her passion-filled body. She felt she would explode. As she was about to...

"Randy?"

Almost jumping out of his skin, Randy dropped the rain-stained paperback book he was reading as quickly but nonchalantly as he could. He read the book by his screenless window just for this reason. He didn't want his mother to know that he had the book. He didn't want her to know he was reading *that* kind of book.

His bedroom was perfectly suited to help him disguise his secret behavior. The ceiling slanted down over his bed from the middle of the room down toward the floor. The people who had the house constructed had placed a window in the four feet of wall space, which hinged to swing outwardly. The window was near the foot of Randy's bed.

Randy would lay across the bed with his window propped open. He did this on cold winter days as well as hot summer days so that he would be consistent in his behavior. He didn't want the open window to be out of the ordinary. He had knocked the screen out long ago and broken the screen's frame in order to keep the screen from being replaced. The window was truly such an odd size; it would be nearly impossible to replace the screen without constructing an entirely new frame.

Randy didn't want to build a new one and his stepfather didn't really care if Randy's window had a screen or not. The window wasn't in Randy's stepfather's room.

Randy Harrison had read and reread the sultry novel many times. Quite often he had to drop the book out of the window when anyone would enter his room. Once he had dropped it and it had fallen onto his sister's head. She had brought the book back to him, but not without a few comments. He didn't know how many times he had dropped it. He dropped it in the rain, the sunshine and even in the snow. The two-story fall had not hurt the steamy paperback as much as the weather had discolored and aged the pages.

Despite being stained by standing water, melting snow and raindrops, and the harsh sun-discolored pages, it still had the thrills Randy was looking to find. He didn't always remember to pick it up the same day or the next day. Then suddenly he would remember and scurry to retrieve the book before anyone could find it.

Once or twice he had remembered in a panic while sitting at his desk at school. He prayed all day that his mother had not discovered the tawdry pulp novel when she had gone outside to the clothesline to hang up the daily wash. Luck had been with him so far.

"Randy!" His mother called again a little bit louder.

He turned his head and said, "Oh, sorry Mom. I was daydreaming about how nice it would be to be outside on this fine summer's day."

"Well you wouldn't have to be daydreaming about it, if you learned to behave yourself once in a while," his mom retorted in her condescending way.

"I didn't do anything wrong for Dad to have to send me to my room. Sometimes I think he doesn't like me." Randy stated trying to pull his mother to his side of the discussion.

"He likes you just fine," she said. "You should try and get along with him a little better."

"He likes me when I'm not bothering him. And believe me... I try not to bother Mr. Warmth."

"Okay, that's enough," his mother scolded. She didn't want to become involved in a long discussion about her son's relationship with his stepfather. But she made a mental note to speak to Harlan later. She felt he could be cranky around the house.

"Harlan said you could go to your Aunt Carrie's if you want to go," his mother offered.

"Great... it'll be nice to smell the fresh air and feel the warmth of the sun," Randy replied sarcastically. "How long can I stay for?"

"A couple of weeks, Mr. Smart Aleck," his mother said. "You know this was brought on by yourself. You're lucky we're letting you go to Carrie's. Now put your things together while I go and ask your sister if she wants to go with you."

"Okay. Okay," Randy muttered. He watched his mom wag her finger at him as she turned to leave his room.

He knew he had caused his own problems this time. Things just sort of snowballed the last few days. He was thankful for the chance to go to his Aunt's house down in Colmboro. The country air would do him good and he would have a chance to see his friends... especially Mary Jo.

Trouble was not something he usually aimed for on a day to day basis, but it seemed to be around him on a constant basis. He and his friends had been hanging out on the other side of the railroad tracks at Eugene Jones house when they had decided to play baseball. They always played their games on a vacant field two blocks down from Randy's house this side of the railroad tracks.

As they made their way towards the tracks, a huge mile-long freight train began to amble by clattering on the tracks and blocking their path over the crossing. This would not have been a problem had the train continued on through town, but as trains sometime do; it came to a complete stop blocking the way of the anxious baseball players.

One thing led to another about how to cross the tracks with the freight train in the way. Boys were bragging about how they could climb over and under the train. His hotshot rival among the gang, Dean Pringle, called out Randy's brag. Both boys constantly vied for the unofficial leadership of the group – always trying to outdo one another.

Randy had boasted himself into a corner. He could sense a part of the group wanted him to crawl under the train as he stated he would, and he felt another part of the group didn't think he had the foolhardiness to do it. The girls were trying to talk him out of it. Dean was egging him on with his smug, smarmy taunts about his manhood. Randy could read in the eyes of the boys that shone bright with anticipation of the confrontation if he failed to deliver on his boast.

Randy wanted to crawl under the train to shut Dean up. He wanted to do it so that his prestige would raise high among his friends. He wanted to really impress the girls even as they were asking him not to do such a simple-minded dangerous act. But all that Randy could think of was the social status of a fifteen-year-old gangly black-haired boy would be greatly enhanced by this daring but foolish maneuver. His thoughts of popularity among the girls pushed him over the top. He mustered his courage and moved forward to crawl under the heavy steel railroad car.

Randy had to squat with his hands touching the hot pavement and steel rails for balance. He ducked his head so as not to bump it on the mechanical metal protrusion underneath of the car. As he folded his body halfway under the car, the train jolted to move forward ever so slowly. He reached the halfway mark to the screams of the girls shouting to him that the train was moving. The boys shouted encouragement but not without a tinge of fear. Randy felt a huge wave of adrenaline rush through his body. No panic, but he felt the need to hurry and clear to the other side of the train.

As he exited to the other side of the train, he raised his hands high in the air. He shouted a primal scream. He could hear the cheering from his friends on the reverse side of the train.

What happen next caused Randy's jaw to drop. It must have looked like a cartoon jaw dropping to the hot black macadam. He had spied his mother on the front porch of the McCalister house. He was doomed.

Randy could see his mother's face very clearly. She was only about one hundred feet from where he stood. She was being very calm- saying something to Mrs. McCalister who was pointing into Randy's direction. Randy could see the apprehension mixed with fury stamped upon her visage. He wanted to run, but he didn't dare. He had too much respect to flee his mom. He would have to face the music.

His mom, all five feet two inches of her, was a force to be reckoned with. Her black hair and dark brown eyes accented her pretty face when she was passive and funny, but the dark features transformed her into something much more ominous when she was angry. She always tried to be fair with her children. Sometimes they just crossed the line.

Randy's mom, Sylvia, held that deep seeded, gut-wrenching fear that something was going to happen to her children one day. While she wasn't overprotective, she was very cautious and knowing when it came to her children. To think he may have be hurt, maimed or killed made her want to severely punish him for his stupidity.

Randy walked over to his mother and they had walked home in silence. Randy's friends stared silently as they watched the two of them saunter toward Randy's home. They knew he was in deep trouble. They were glad they were not in his shoes at this moment.

Just before they entered the house, Randy's mother motioned for Randy to sit on the porch. He sat on the steps and his mom sat in the chain-hung, wooden-slatted swing.

"Mom, I'm sorry..." Randy started, trying to break the unbearable silence.

"Wait a moment until I've calmed down and collected my thoughts," Sylvia said as she held up her hand to stop him from speaking.

"Yes ma'am," he said softly and politely.

Randy toyed with his shoes, pulling on the rubber striping that wrapped around the outside of his Converse sneakers. A million thoughts were running through his head. Just his luck to be caught when things were going so well lately. He had not been in trouble since school had let out for the summer. But this appeared to be big-time trouble.

"Randy...I've no idea what you were thinking about. Why on earth did you crawl under the train? Don't you know you could've been killed or maimed?" His mother continued speaking but talked so fast Randy didn't have a chance to volunteer any answers.

"I don't know what on earth I'm going to do with you," she continued. "As of now, you are grounded. You can't leave the yard for another three weeks. I should really beat the tar out of you, ya' know."

"Mom, I'm really sorry. I didn't mean to scare you. The train wasn't even moving. I..."

"That's enough young man. There is no excuse for what you did. Even if the train wasn't moving—and I believe I saw it moving, you could've caught your foot or bumped your head. Then who knows what would have happened. You're going to drive me to an early grave. Between you and your sister, I'm going to have a nervous breakdown."

With that said, his mother rose and walked over to the screen door and held it open waiting for Randy to go through ahead of her. As he passed, she lightly rapped the back of his head with a slap of frustrated affection. He was a pain, but she loved him.

"Ouch. That really hurt," he said feigning pain.

"Sure it did. I should beat you more often."

"Mom, are you going to tell Harlan?" asked Randy.

"I've really no choice. He'll wonder why you're staying around the house, "she replied.

After she told Harlan what had happened, he added to the punishment which is when the rest of Randy's trouble began. He was sentenced to sitting on the floor for two solid days. He couldn't leave the house or his position on the floor without permission. He was only allowed to visit the bathroom, go to bed and eat his meals.

Randy would have rather had a whipping so that the punishment would have been completed, but he never received corporal punishment. He always had privileges and freedom of movement taken away. Sitting on the floor for two days was totally embarrassing for a fifteen-year-old boy. So when the chance for revenge struck, Randy took advantage.

Harlan Finewick was the most sullen man Randy had ever met. Randy knew there wasn't a man alive, who could match up with his father, but his father was no longer at home, and he had to accept the fact that Harlan was the self-imposed lord and master of the house.

Harlan had not really been that mean to Randy. He just didn't have any humor to him. He did little when he was not at work; He sat in the frumpy old chair he brought with him when he moved into the house. He read cheap paperbacks by the hundreds. He read his monthly Playboy magazines at the beginning of each month. Randy was sure he read the articles and ignored the pictures. He was equally sure that Harlan never read the comics in the magazine, because he had never heard him laugh or seen him crack a smile.

Randy also didn't like the way Harlan would look at his seventeen-year-old sister. He hated the way Harlan would sneak a peek at his sister's rear end as she was exiting the room. A few times Harlan had sensed Randy was watching him. Harlan would hold the eye contact momentarily and then retreat back to his current paperback. Randy would not look away. He had spoken to his sister about the surreptitious leer, but she shrugged it off. She said all men were alike—sex-maniac scum.

If there was any other constant in Harlan's life, it was his desire and obsession for coffee. The man drank cup after cup after cup. Randy estimated the man drank at least ten cups of coffee a day and that was just while he was at home; who knew how many cups he drank at work on the second shift during the evening at the luggage factory. Everyone else in the house was a slave to the master in this regard. They were all called upon to deliver the coffee to Harlan as he sat in his tattered old chair reading his paperback novels. Randy felt the urge to produce a restaurant check for his services, but he didn't want to cause any waves of dissatisfaction for his mom.

Randy was counting on Harlan's obsession with coffee for an opportunity to stretch his legs. He watched Harlan with casual glances, discerning when the coffee cup was empty. Randy knew it would only be minutes before the call to refill the cup would be ringing from his stepfather's lips. Randy knew his mom and sister were outside with the laundry. He would be the logical choice to refill the cup with coffee.

"Do you want me to get you another cup of coffee? " Randy asked. He could wait no longer. He wanted to walk around for a while.

"No, I'll get it myself. You stay there and think of how you can learn to be a more responsible person," Harlan answered.

A few seconds later, Harlan stood up, picked up his coffee cup and headed out to the kitchen. At this point Randy was simmering slightly. He was miffed. This man really tried to aggravate him when his mother wasn't around, Randy could've have sworn he saw a smirk on the man's face as he walked past. Randy stared straight ahead at the television. He didn't say anything in response to Harlan.

Randy could hear the muted conversation of his sister and mother as they entered the house through the kitchen door. His dog Dodo came into the house at the same time. The dog raced through the house until he found Randy. Randy gave him a hug, a few pats on the head and a teasing hold of the muzzle. They played a few moments before Dodo found the throw rug under the coffee table and laid down.

Harlan reentered the room with his coffee. Randy replaced his happy expression his dog had given him with a dour one for his stepfather. Harlan placed his coffee cup on the end table beside his chair. The coffee cup was strategically placed to the right side of the chair on its coffee-stained doily. Harlan used his right hand to drink the coffee even though he claimed to be ambidextrous.

"Now I've got to go to the bathroom," Harlan said to no one in particular. Besides, Randy was the only one in the room and he ignored the comment.

Dodo picked himself up and walked over to Harlan who rubbed his head and left for the bathroom.

Harlan had given Dodo his name, albeit the dog was Randy's dog. Harlan had said the dog was stupid as a puppy and reminded him of a Dodo bird. The name stuck and he's been called Dodo ever since the statement had been made. He seemed to live up to the moniker on occasion, like when he stood outside of his doghouse when it rained rather than go inside. But he was cute and cuddly and loved by the family – especially Randy.

Harlan left to go to the bathroom; Dodo remained on his feet and watched Harlan leave through the door. Dodo waited a moment or two and then went over to Harlan's chair. He stood up on the worn seat cushion and smelled the cup of coffee. He turned his head toward the door as if to see if Harlan was returning, It seemed to Randy as if Dodo had done this on other occasions. Once he was satisfied Harlan wasn't coming back; he lapped a few laps of the coffee from the cup.

"Get down!" Randy barked at the dog in a harsh low whisper.

Taking one last lap, Dodo plopped his paws down onto the hardwood floor and resumed his place under the coffee table on the rug. Harlan reentered the room a few minutes later.

Randy pretended he had an interest in the baseball game on the television. He could hardly contain himself. He waited for Harlan to take a sip of the coffee.

Harlan picked up his paperback book and began to read. He reached for his coffee cup; bringing the cup up to his nose for an instant, feeling the steam, savoring the smell before he downed another sip or two.

"That's some good java," he said. Then he took a few more sips. He held the cup with both hands feeling the warmth of the coffee.

"Hey... you didn't drink that coffee did you?" Randy asked in a mockingly alarmed tone.

"What...what do you mean?" asked a puzzled Harlan.

"I asked you if you drank from that coffee cup," Randy answered a little louder.

"Don't shout. I heard you. Why shouldn't I drink the coffee?" Harlan asked feeling annoyed with this game.

"Because the dog drank from the cup."

"What?! Why didn't you tell me?"

"I *am* telling you."

"Why didn't you tell me before I drank it?"

"I don't know. I guess I forgot. I was watching the ball game on TV."

"Why didn't you throw out the coffee and get me some more?"

"I'm not allowed to move, remember?"

Harlan was silent. He scowled at Randy. Dodo picked himself up and went into the kitchen. Randy tried not to grin. He focused his full attention on the television. Harlan realized he had been had.

"I think you didn't tell me on purpose," Harlan stated.

Silence from Randy.

"Answer me boy," Harlan was becoming very angry.

"I *told* you as soon as I remembered."

"I'll tell you what. Why don't you spend the next two days in your room? No television. No radio. If it were up to me you'd have no supper. Now go on. Cool your heels up there until you learn a little consideration and respect."

Randy stood up. As he turned his back to enter the hallway where the stairs began, he could hold his smile no longer. Harlan couldn't see him. The added punishment was worth it. He couldn't wait to tell Karen. His sister would laugh long and hard on this one.

Randy was delighted his punishment had been cut short. He was so bored even his revered steamy paperback was unable to hold his interest as it usually did. He hoped he would find a way to pick it up before he left for his Aunt and Uncle's farm in Colmboro. He enjoyed his visits there. He had been going to the farm since he was able to walk.

Randy and his sister Karen had quite a few friends in his Aunt's neighborhood even though the houses were spaced far apart. They would meet at the millpond, church socials or at the small rodeo center down by the big curve next to the millpond. He and his sister had spent many summers and weekends at the farm.

"Randy, you ready?" his sister asked.

"Almost. I just need to pack a few more things. What's hanging on the clothesline? Any of my stuff?"

"I don't know, look out of the window."

Randy went to peer out of the window. He saw a pair of his favorite pants flapping in the light breeze. Good. He would use this as an excuse to retrieve his book.

Standing up he said, "I'm surprised you're going. I thought you couldn't stand to be away from *Gregory*."

"Very funny. You know I'm restricted. Harlan found out I missed curfew and I'm not allowed to see Greg for a couple of weeks."

"Yeah I know. Just thought I'd rub it in a little. Call him from Aunt Caroline's house."

"I can't. He's out of town on vacation with his folks. That's why we missed curfew...saying good bye."

"I see. It's all coming clear to me now. This'll give you a chance to see Chuck Bailey at the pond and Harlan has no idea he's not really punishing you. You're a very clever little girl."

"Mind your own business, pud puller. You'll have your hands full of Mary Jo Magurk anyway. Don't worry about me."

"I hope I get my hands full. Besides the pud pulling has never and I repeat never been proven."

Karen laughed. She left the room with her suitcase and Randy could hear her going down the stairs. He was very close to his sister. They were best friends. He felt as though Gregory was splitting them apart a bit. He was glad to hear she was going with him to the farm.

Randy pushed the last few articles of clothing into his duffel bag. He rarely used his suitcase—it was too bulky. The duffel was easier to carry. He threw the bag over his shoulder and descended the stairs.

He entered the living room and set the duffel bag down beside the chair closest to the front door. Harlan was in his chair peeking over his paperback at Randy. Randy could feel the watchful eyes of his stepfather. Harlan had it in his head that Randy was sneaky. He had told Randy that on many occasions—always out of Randy's mother's presence. Randy shrugged it off.

Randy had to go outside to pick up his book, but he didn't want to leave his duffel bag unattended. He had placed one of Harlan's old *Playboy* magazines at the bottom. He didn't want Harlan to go through the bag. Unfortunately he had already set it down and he didn't want to bring too much attention to it. He decided to gamble. Nonchalantly he kicked the bag back toward the wall and walked back though the living room to exit into the kitchen.

He left through the back door. Once he was outside he sprinted to the book. He didn't pick it up yet. He just wanted to know where it was located. He grabbed the trousers from the clothesline and sped back over to his book. He picked it up and stuffed it in the rolled up khaki pants.

Randy reentered through the back door. He was out of breath. He needed to be near his duffel bag as soon as he could to slide the pants inside of it. He was hoping to avoid his mother, but she walked into the kitchen from the dining room just as he came into the house.

"What have you got there?" she asked.

Befuddled for a moment, he asked her, "What do you mean?"

"What do you have in your hands?" She said deliberately and slowly.

Randy thought that she was on to him. With no choice he said, "My pants."

"Really you could've fooled me. It looks like a pile of rags the way you're treating them."

Randy breathed a silent sigh of relief. He was going to have to dispose of this book one of these days. The anxiety was killing him.

"Funny, Mom." Sarcastic, but not too sarcastic was the tone.

"Give them to me and I'll show you how to fold them neatly."

"No...I'll do it. I swear."

"No I insist you give them to me and I'll fold them for you. Don't be obstinate."

Randy was beginning to panic. He didn't want her to find the book. Those heaving white palomino-tipped breasts were causing him quite the heart attack. The situation would be entirely too embarrassing. He looked at his mother with her outstretched hand. He wondered if he could make it past her and run upstairs. He would look foolish and probably get into trouble once again, but he thought he would take the chance. If she managed to snatch the pants from him as he went by her, the book would fall out. *Christ.* He should just as well give up and take the verbal lashing.

"Mom!" Randy heard his sister call. He looked at his mother as she turned her head to listen.

He bolted past her.

"Randy!" His mother exclaimed.

"Mom!" Karen called again.

"I'm in the kitchen," his mother called back. Then she said to herself, "I don't know what I'm going to do with that boy." She chuckled to herself and went to find her daughter.

Randy raced up the stairs, where he placed his paperback in its hiding place. He dropped the pants on the bed and hurried back down the stairs to the living room to baby sit his duffel bag.

Sylvia and Harlan were sitting in their usual chairs conversing about something. Randy hoped he wasn't the subject this time.

"He's lucky I'm letting him go," Randy heard Harlan say.

"I'm sure he's grateful," Sylvia said. "I want him to get away from some of the boys around here. I don't think they're a very good influence on him."

Sylvia turned her head as Randy went to sit by his duffel bag.

"Where are the pants?" his mom asked.

"I decided not to take them with me."

"I guess you folded them up and put them away, did you?"

"Well no...I left them on the bed. I was hoping you would iron them for me."

"You shouldn't cause your mother so much work, Randy," Harlan said sarcastically.

"It's no trouble," Sylvia said deflecting Harlan's criticism.

"I hope you learned a lesson here boy," Harlan said unrelenting. "That was a mighty foolish thing you did...crawling under that train. You worry your mother and me to death with stunts like that."

"I did. I'm really sorry. I know it was foolish. I promise to use my brain from now on."

"I hope you appreciate the fact we're letting you go to your Aunt Caroline's house. We didn't have to let you go ya' know," Harlan said ignoring Randy's apology.

"Yes I do," Randy said. "Sometimes you're just too good to me."

Harlan stared at Randy.

"You're a smart ass, boy," Harlan began, "one of these days I'm gonna..."

"Harlan don't over react," Sylvia interrupted. "I'm sure he was being very sincere."

"I am! I am!" Randy replied with a mock look of surprise.

"I don't know. He's got such a smart mouth. He should have a little more respect for his elders."

"Harlan, what do you want from me? I said I was sorry about the train. I complimented you on being nice to me. I'm not trying to be a wise guy. I mean what a *d*!"

The last sentence came out of Randy's mouth before he had a chance to think about what he was saying. It was a saying that he and his friends used to designate a person or situation that was contrary or problematic. *What a d* was really short for *what a dick.*

It was shortened to escape rebuke by any adults who overheard any of their conversations. Now he had said it to Harlan.

"What's that mean? What did you say I was young man?" Turning to his wife he said, "You see, Sylvia, the boy has no respect for me or anyone else. Perhaps he should stay home in his room for two weeks. Maybe that will teach him a lesson."

"Harlan. Harlan. Give me a chance to explain. It means *What a Dad.* It's a compliment; I'm thanking you for leniency and understanding." Randy rushed to explain trying to sound as sincere as he could. "You see what I mean?"

Harlan stared at Randy. He was gnawing at his lower lip. He had both hands on the armrests of his chair as if he was going to spring up at any moment. He was steaming, but he knew he was in a no win situation. He would be glad to be rid of the boy for a while.

"Harlan?" Sylvia asked, "Do you see what he means?"

"I guess so. Sometimes it's just the way he says it."

There was a knock at the door. Randy's aunt had arrived just in time.

Chapter 2

After all the pleasantries had been said, spoken and bestowed upon each other, Randy's mom and step dad said goodbye to Randy and his sister Karen. The two siblings accompanied their aunt across the porch and down the steps to her car. Sylvia and Harlan stood at the door calling out instructions to the children to behave themselves and to stay out of trouble.

Randy and Karen stopped at the trunk of the car with their suitcases waiting for their Uncle Harvey to exit the car and unlock the trunk. They could see the back of a man's head sitting in the back seat. Randy immediately recognized it as his aunt and uncle's neighbor. Randy knew he would have fun with his sister because she loathed the man for the drunken lecher that he was.

His nickname was Pup - shortened from Puppy Dog. Pup lived down the country road to the east of his aunt and uncle. He lived with his pious wife, who had a difficult time keeping her nose out of other people's business. Rumor around the neighborhood was that Pup and his wife Arlene stayed together because he owned the farm and she had signed a prenuptial agreement when they married thirty years ago. Pup's dad was influential in the county and held a great deal of wealth. He was looking out for his only heir. One that was quite a ne'er-do-well.

Pup didn't stay home very much. He ambled about the neighborhood going from house to house with his ever-constant companion of a Mason jar half full of homemade peach brandy. When he finished off his jar of brandy, he would head home and sleep through the night. Pup had an allowance from a trust fund, which he usually used up in town at his favorite watering hole the first couple of nights during the month. Arlene doled out Pup's share of the trust fund allowance. The rest of the month he stayed around the neighborhood drinking his homemade brew.

A short man, who was extraordinarily thin, Pup sported tattoos all over his sun- bronzed arms. The sun and alcohol had taken its toll on his weather-beaten face. His thinning hair was Brylcreemed back in 1950's styling. He fashioned himself a ladies' man, but the illusion was in his own mind.

When he was through with half of his Mason jar full of peach brandy, he tended to laugh at his own ramblings, while others found his utterances more annoying than humorous. The brandy caused him to slur a good deal of his words. His lecherous approaches to the opposite sex were openly brash, but he felt as though he was being as subtle as a soft rain

Why the neighbors stood for such nonsense from a known drunk was just an affirmation of the nature of the people who lived in the area. Most people accepted the people they had known for a long time for what they were. If judgment was passed, it usually stayed within the households or within the circle of friends. Everyone had crosses to bear and everyone in the neighborhood was aware of their own closets full of burdens.

Caroline and Harvey had known Pup all of their lives. There were times they were angry with him and there were times when they immensely enjoyed his clowning. Pup had a penchant for telling stories about everyone by taking generous liberties with the truth. The couple tolerated him even though they knew he would probably be telling stories about them as soon as he had settled down in someone else's living room. Carrie liked the attention Pup lavished on her and Harvey liked to listen to Pup tell about his fabricated exploits around town.

Karen was not of the same mind. Pup was a smelly old man to her. He had tried to touch her intimately far too many times for her liking. He tried to make the inappropriate touching look like an accident and then laugh off the moment with an apology. She detested his touch and wouldn't venture near him for any reason. She had told her brother of his advances, but never bothered to tell her Aunt or Uncle. She felt he was harmless, but she also felt better knowing her brother would watch out for her.

Once the suitcases were in the trunk, Randy watched as Pup moved to the center of the back seat. This way Pup was assured of

Karen sitting next to him on one side or the other. Randy raced to the back door and held it open.

"Hop in Sis," Randy said nonchalantly.

"No," Karen said. She glared at her brother. He smiled back mischievously.

"C'mon-- hop in. I was here first. I want to sit by the window."

"I want to sit by the window. You know I get carsick," his sister replied.

"Then go round to the other side and sit behind Uncle Harvey," Randy teased.

Karen stood still with her hands on her hips. She was going to kill her brother when she had the chance.

"C'mon in - the water's fine," Pup semi-shouted from inside of the car.

"Go ahead," Randy laughed.

"Let's go. Let's go." Their uncle was losing his patience with the tomfoolery.

"OK, OK," Karen said with resignation in her voice. She was truly disappointed to have to sit next to Pup; she could just imagine the trip to the farm, Pup spouting his drunken philosophy and stale unfunny jokes trying to touch her as much he as dared with everyone in the car.

When she moved to enter the car, Randy placed a hand on her head and pushed her backward away from the car. She almost toppled over onto the driveway.

"OK, you baby. Sit next to the window. I don't want you tossing your cookies on me. You owe me big time. I mean big time," Randy said with a wink of his eye.

"Oh—you'll get yours all right. I just don't know when. But you'll get yours," his sister stated.

"C'mon let's go. Let's go." Harvey was rattled and shook his head at the delay.

The brother and sister sat in the car with Pup pushed to the left. Randy turned to him and nodded. He could see the disappointment on Pup's face. Pup was undaunted he placed his arm across the back of the seat and tapped Karen on the shoulder. When she turned to look at him, he smiled. Karen just sighed again and sank closer to the car door out of his reach. Randy laughed. He pulled his arms down to his sides intentionally striking Pup in his bony ribs with his elbow. Pup groaned and pulled his arm back down to cover his exposed ribs.

"Sorry," Randy said.

"That's okay," Pup replied. Then he took a sip from his Mason jar.

"Let's fly Uncle Harvey," Randy said. "I've got some swimming to catch up on down at the pond."

"Alright, alright," his uncle answered shaking his head. Randy puzzled his uncle with his carefree attitude.

Randy sat back the best he could, the hump under the seat caused by the transmission made it a little awkward, but he was pretty comfortable. He listened to Aunt Carrie and his sister prattle on about things surrounding the family. He could not wait to arrive at the farm.

Karen and Randy had been going to the farm without their parents since they were toddlers. Aunt Carrie and Uncle Harvey were surrogate parents to the two of them. Aunt Caroline was their real father's sister.

She was a short, rotund, fun-loving woman. Her affection for her niece and nephew was shown in such a demonstrative manner that it embarrassed Randy to no end in front of his friends. She was always hugging and kissing them whenever they came into her reach. The daughter of immigrant Italians, Aunt Caroline could cook up the best-flavored meals this side of the Atlantic. She made sure everyone ate their share and was insulted when someone entered the house and refused her food. With no children of her own and little chance of having them, she informally adopted the daughter and son of her brother.

Quick with a laugh and a giggle and a love for a good time, she made it easy to be around her. On the rare occasion when she would have a Rolling Rock beer she became even more giddy and riotous. Laughing so hard sometimes she would wet her pants, holding her belly from the beer-induced gas. She was well known in Colmboro having lived there since her early teens. Her dad and mom had passed away while she was still in her early twenties. Just after they passed away she had married her high school sweetheart Harvey Kearney.

Harvey was a tall man. He was very quiet and had very little to say. It was said that lightning had struck the ground near him when he was a child, causing him to be just a bit slower mentally than his peers or it could have been caused by the mule kicking him in the chest and knocking him out for a few hours when he was young. Whatever the reason for his one-step-behind mentality, it didn't stop him from being a kind and loving uncle. Sometimes Randy tried his patience, but he adored his nephew nevertheless.

Karen and Randy had great times with their aunt and uncle. They were taken to the County Fair in Rosemont every year and given almost anything they wanted within reason. The one thing the elder couple asked of their niece and nephew was to help around the farm.

Randy had trailed behind his uncle since he had been at least five years old, cleaning chicken troughs, filling water jugs for the newly-arrived biddies and shaking down feeders for the fast-growing chickens. Randy loved to help fill and push the hanging feed cart down the chicken house from gated room to gated room. He would wait by the cart while his uncle dipped the metal feed bucket into the round, brown pellet feed, digging out enough to fill five or six of the hanging feeders which nourished the ever- growing chickens.

The smell of the chickens coupled with their deposits on the sawdust created a smell that when first encountered would cause anyone to bring their hand to their noses. As the chickens grew and the weeks went by, the smell became more overwhelming. The mixture of ammonia from the excrement produced by the chickens and dirtied sawdust was caustic to the senses. The chickens had to be kept at a warm temperature in the winter and a bearable temperature during the summer. In any season, the closeness of the chicken house pushed up against the feeling to leave immediately upon entering the building.

Fryers they were called. The big chicken plant owners would place the freshly-hatched chicks in the chicken house for his uncle. They would then supply feed and nutrients for the nine-week period they would take to grow. At the end of their term, the chicken plant would sell the chickens for so much a pound and give Uncle Harvey a percentage of the money, less the cost of the feed, nutrients and baby-chick costs.

Randy even liked to be awakened when it was time for the chickens to be captured and placed into crates when they had matured. He enjoyed watching the deft black men come in around three in the morning with their big tractor-trailer full of empty wooden chicken coops. The chickens would be at rest in the chicken house unsuspecting of their fate.

The catchers would swoop into the chicken house room by room snaring the sleepy chickens, tossing them in their wooden, round dowel cages, which would be their prisons on the way to the processing plants near Jamestown. Randy loved to watch how skillful and jovial the men were. It was hard, undesirable work, but the men had to earn a living. They were always nice to him and occasionally prodded him to try his hand with the long metal catch hook they used to snare the chickens by their legs. He sometimes practiced when his Uncle Harvey was not around and found he was getting better, but not nearly as good as the professionals.

It was all over in about two hours. Between fifty- and one-hundred thousand chickens were caught, cooped and placed on the truck bed ready for transport. It was an amazing feat to see. His sister thought he was crazy to rise so early to watch, let alone to enjoy the process, but Randy truly enjoyed it.

He loved helping on the farm. He enjoyed driving the tractor that plowed the field when his uncle would let him. He enjoyed tossing the baled hay onto the slow-moving cart being pulled by the tractor that his uncle was driving. He enjoyed picking the vegetables from his aunt's garden by the house. He just enjoyed being outside in the country air.

Karen worked inside with her aunt. She learned how to cook Italian food, how to can vegetables, how to pickle cucumbers and how to make jelly and preserves.

The farm was fun. Randy loved the freedom. He was especially fond of the woods behind the farm. He enjoyed walking through the trees be it winter or summer. The summer because of the beautiful green foliage, the sweet singing of the birds, the ever-flying and populous insects like the Monarch butterflies and the wild blackberries on their thorny bushes.

He liked the woods in the winter when nature stripped the denizens of most of their leafy camouflage. He saw more deer, rabbits and wildlife in the winter. His friends loved to hunt the squirrels, rabbits and deer, but Randy always pretended, because he really didn't have the heart to kill any of God's creatures. Until recently his friends weren't skillful enough with their firearms to kill much of anything anyway, so his reluctance was overlooked, but last winter he heard a comment or two about him being soft-hearted. He ignored the comments and thought they could think whatever they wanted to think. He didn't really care as long as he didn't have to kill the little forest animals. Besides, Picker, one of his best and most unique friends was as opposed to killing animals as much as he was only much more openly.

At the edge of the woods where his uncle's property ended, there was a creek, which fed down to the milldam where everyone in the area went swimming. Randy loved to sit by the creek on the bank fishing and thinking. He had found a rock formation in the shape of an easy chair.

The back and seat of the chair was smooth flat rock with a little tilt at the crease where the back and seat met creating a comfortable reclining effect. The rocks were imbedded in the roots of a huge weeping willow tree. The roots came out from both sides, rising up slightly forming almost perfect arms. The huge tree above provided shade as well as protective cover from light rains. This was Randy's thinking place.

No one else usually frequented this spot that Randy could tell. He kept a small amount of tackle in a box near his nature-produced chair, along with a cane pole given to him by a local old man named Foster. He would fish with dug up worms from the soft dirt in the woods and toss the occasional perch or pike back into the creek if he caught one.

He could see the outline of the Magurk's roof from his easy chair as he sat in it with his fishing line in the water; he always hoped Mary-Jo Magurk would wander through the trees so that he could see her. Randy had fantasized about her for about six years now.

He had met her at the Methodist Church during a church potluck social. The church served as a social gathering place as well as a place of worship for the surrounding community. Most people in the area went to the Methodist Church despite their original religious affiliation. It served everyone well and kept the community spirit intact.

The Magurks had moved into the area when Randy was nine. He fell in love with the brown-haired, brown-eyed girl the moment he had seen her. He was infatuated with her and hardly heard his Aunt Caroline introducing him and Karen to the entire Magurk family at the potluck dinner. He remembered when the whole gang played and how satisfied he felt whenever he had a chance to touch her skin during a game of tag or hide- and-go-seek. He couldn't control the butterflies in his belly or stammers in his speech when he was speaking to her. Nor could he feel secure in what he said. It all sounded stupid to him as soon as he said it. No one knew of his feelings except his sister.

The farm was a place of fun and solitude. It served both portions of Randy's personality. Sometimes he loved the socialization with his friends and the quirky characters that populated Colmboro. But he also loved the quiet noise of the woods and the creek when he needed the time to be alone with his thoughts. If he did not think he would miss his sister and mother so much, he would have loved to move in with his Aunt Caroline and Uncle Harvey after his father had left the family.

Chapter 3

Uncle Harvey's slow, methodical driving was painful and even more unendurable while Pup was in the car. Uncle Harvey never exceeded the speed limit and Pup never shut his ever-running mouth on the entire journey to Colmboro. Randy could not wait to be free of this rolling prison and stretch his legs in the open air.

The car rounded the curve into Colmboro. Just around the curve was the millpond. Randy and Karen both turned their heads to see if they knew anyone who was swimming; they only saw a couple of younger children that they did not know. They thought it was a bit early for the teenagers to be here and they were right. Chores needed to be done before play could commence but it would not be long before the area was full of activity.

Uncle Harvey slowed the car down as he neared his house. Randy could see the hand-painted sign some jokester had nailed to his Aunt and Uncle's mailbox support. Dogville, it read. The sign had been there about a year now. The big joke in the neighborhood was about the number of dogs that lived at the Kearney's farm. In fact, Uncle Harvey had to slow down until three of the year-old puppies picked themselves up off the road and moved out of his way.

"Those damn dogs are going to get killed," he said to Aunt Carrie.

"Well, teach them not to go out and lie down in the road," she snipped.

"I've tried, Carrie. I've tried. They are just hard-headed".

"It won't hurt your dog population, if'n they did git run over," Pup offered with little sincerity.

"Be quiet, Pup," Aunt Carrie snapped. "They're our dogs not yours." She was a little sensitive to the comments, as some of the neighbors had been complaining behind the Kearneys' backs about the number of dogs at their farm.

"Now, now, Carrie. Just a little joke," Pup consoled. "Where's your sense of humor?"

Aunt Carrie ignored him. Pup slumped back into his seat and drank from his almost empty jar.

"Not funny, Puppy dog," Randy pressed.

"OK, Randy. That's enough, by golly," Uncle Harvey admonished.

Randy and Karen laughed as Pup scowled. Uncle Harvey waited for the dogs to clear and pulled into the gravel-laden driveway. The rest of the Kearney dog pack greeted the car with a cacophony of barks. The wind created from their wagging tails was enough to pull the dust up and off the small rocks that acted as the driveway.

The passengers and driver stepped out of the car and into the midst of the surrounding furry chaos. Randy recognized most of the dogs but there were a few new additions.

Bessy, the white longhaired shepherd, ran to him and he rubbed her on the head. He could see Queenie, the mother of his dog Dodo, sitting on the outskirts of the pack. She was a relative to most of the other dogs, which were a breed of terrier not officially known by name. His Uncle Harvey claimed they were rat terriers. Randy thought because they caught the rats that tried to infiltrate the chicken houses to feast on the chickens when they were young. No one disputed his Uncle, so whenever anyone asked what breed of dog they were, they were told rat terriers.

Everyone in the rural setting in and around Colmboro had a dog or two wandering about their farm or homestead. The dogs served many purposes such as a warning of approaching strangers, a pet for the family or perhaps they were used in a hunting capacity. The difference between the Kearneys and their neighbors was not the love or function of the animals; it was the amount of dogs. With the exception of the Kearneys and Taylors, no one had more than three dogs. The Taylors' dogs were bird dogs and they were kept in a dog pen at the rear of their property. The Kearneys' dogs were loose in the neighborhood and numbered not less than five on a constant basis. Presently there were ten dogs on Aunt Carrie's and Uncle Harvey's farm.

It was the Kearney's contention the dogs hurt no one and stayed on their property for the most part. Aunt Carrie loved the dogs. Usually any criticism of that sort rolled off her back. She usually shrugged it off with a laugh or a giggle, recited an Italian proverb in English and Italian and dismissed the busybodies with a wave of her hands. Recently though she had had her fill of people constantly referring to the subject and was building up a head of Italian steam which would finally break on someone who pushed the envelope a little too far.

Uncle Harvey was quiet on the subject and not nearly as volatile as his wife. Once he became fed up with the unrelenting pressure, he would simply ask the offending party to kindly mind their own business and then ask his usual farming questions to change the subject.

Ten dogs seemed like a hundred when they were all milling about. Randy shooed them out of the way and walked to the trunk of the car to stand beside his sister. Uncle Harvey opened the trunk and handed Randy his duffel. Karen tried to take her suitcase from him, but he would not let her, so she followed the two of them up to the side porch where the entrance was.

"Karen!" someone shouted from across the way.

Everyone looked toward the shouting. Rhoda Powell and her little sister Carol were running across the lawn up to the two lane blacktop road which separated the Kearney and Powell properties. Karen turned away from her uncle and brother and walked across the road to chat with her friends.

"Hi, Randy," cooed Carol. She was only twelve, but she had a crush on Randy.

"Hi, Carol. Hi, Rhoda. Where's Lee?" Randy asked.

"He's back at the old house with Vern," Rhoda answered.

"Tell him I'll be over in a bit," Randy said.

She nodded. Randy followed his Uncle Harvey into the house. He deposited his duffel upstairs in the annex room where he slept. He ransacked the bag until he found his freshly pilfered Playboy. He secured it under his shirt in his pants behind his back. The room had been built onto the entry way a few years ago. It sat on top of the kitchen.

Randy liked the room most of the time, because the aromas from the kitchen usually filled the room. They filtered up through the register cut in the floor, which provided heat and ventilation from the bottom floor. When he was smaller he would lay down by the register and listen to the conversations from the older folks who were sitting at the kitchen table after he was sent to bed. He fell asleep many a time while he was on the floor.

Occasionally, the room was a little scary; especially when everyone else was asleep. He would hear all kinds of creaks, squeaks and cracks as the wind blew or the sounds from the settling of the house. The attic door was adjacent to the doorway entering the annex. As a little child he often imagined huge monsters living up there. At least a vampire or two had surely taken up residence there just waiting for everyone to go to sleep so that they could begin their nightly blood feast.

Randy bounded down the stairs. He stopped and peered out the window in the front door. He could see his sister and her two friends sitting under a shady maple tree. They were talking about something exciting because he could see his sister gesturing wildly. He wanted to visit his stone easy chair before he went over to Lee's house.

He made his way through the living room. As he entered the kitchen he could see Pup sitting at the kitchen table with his aunt. Pup eyeballed him but said nothing. Randy had the Playboy tucked in his pants under his shirt and felt as though Pup knew what he was up to so he averted Pup's eyes. Randy assumed his Uncle Harvey was in the chicken houses tending to his charges.

Randy bent to kiss his Aunt Caroline on the cheek. "I'm going out to the creek and then over to Lee's House. I'll be back for dinner."

"Be back for lunch," she said.

"Lunch time is over", Randy replied.

Aunt Caroline looked up at the clock. "So it is," she said. "So it is."

"Bye, Pup," Randy said.

Pup nodded his head slightly.

Randy ran out into the sunlight. He squint his eyes and waited a moment for his pupils to adjust. Two or three of the dogs ran up to him. Randy ignored them, but they stayed with him anyway on his walk to the woods.

The chicken houses were directly to the rear of the house down a dirt lane about fifty yards from the house. To the right of the chicken houses was huge plowed field of young watermelons. Randy could see Uncle Harvey's father hoeing down a long row of watermelons. The man worked from sun up to sundown hoeing the weeds from his watermelon crop. Randy liked him better now that he had gotten older. When Randy was younger, the old man scared him silly. Because he was so gruff, Randy and Karen had many an amusing laugh at the kindly old man's expense.

To the left of the chicken houses before the woods was Aunt Carrie's garden where she grew vegetables to be eaten, canned and given away. It was well maintained by Uncle Harvey and had many satisfying treats for the family. There was even a short row of popcorn this year.

Randy made his way toward the woods crossing a field that was used for winter wheat. It was overgrown with leftover wheat stalks and high grass. The grasshoppers and flying bugs were jumping and flying out of his way by the thousands. He could feel the long tentacles of the grass grabbing at his feet and legs. The crunch and snap of the grass pleased him as he trudged through the field closer to the woods. He watched as butterflies hovered over the tips of wheat stalks moving only slightly as he passed by.

His dog companions stopped and ran back to join the dogs at the house when they began to bark at something near the road. He picked up his regular trail, more from familiarity than from actual visual recognition. The undergrowth had covered up the beaten path near the beginning of the woods. A short jog into the trees and Randy was following the narrow dirt trail that would lead him to the creek.

He felt the bark of the trees with his hand grabbing young trees for balance as he made his way along the trail. He was cautious to avoid the devil's walking stick that had scraped his skin on more than one occasion. The sun sparkled down through the tree canopy made up of huge maple and sycamore trees. Randy made a stop at a cherry tree and plucked a few of the ripe berries off for a snack. They looked riper than they were and Randy spit the tart cherries out and wiped his tongue on his shirt.

The beauty of the green foliage and tranquil sounds of chirping birds had a hugely satisfying effect on Randy. He was at peace with the world here. He could forget his differences with his stepfather and his unexplained unhappiness with his mother's decision to marry the man. Harlan didn't seem to be such a bad guy, but Randy couldn't reconcile the differences in the way life had been and the way it had become.

He did not know if he was just growing up or if the profound difference in his father's way of doing things and the way Harlan did things really caused the insecurity he felt in his life at home. Randy wished he could close his eyes and wake up to the time when he was in second grade; a time when his bedroom was a cozy place. He would be snuggled under his huge goose down comforter waiting for his father to come and wake him up so that they could go fishing at the pond down the road.

He wished the dream often, but the dream never came true. Perhaps he figured at least here in the woods near the creek he was near his father. He knew however he couldn't stay in the woods forever. Eventually he would come to the clearing and leave his comfort zone behind.

The small cluster of birch trees on the path signaled to Randy that he would be at the creek's edge in a few steps. He rounded a small turn and the creek came into view. He could see the weeping willow trees draping their long willows down into the brown tannic water of the creek. The jagged stumps of a few broken down cypress trees protruded from the surface of the water near the middle of the slow moving creek.

Once out into the sunlight he turned to the left and found his made-from-stone chair. He could see his cane pole leaning against the tree. On the side where he kept his box full of tackle, the leaves looked untouched. No one had disturbed his sanctuary

Randy picked up his cane pole and tested its resiliency. It worked fine. He wouldn't fish today, but he probably would come down early in the morning and fish for an hour or two. The feel of the pole left him warm inside. He sat down in his stone chair and fondly remembered Old Man Foster.

He was a gnarled old black man who did odd jobs around Colmboro. Randy had known him most of his life. The house he lived in was down the creek bank a few yards from where Randy's stone chair sat. On a small piece of land Mr. Foster grew some vegetables for himself and his wife.

Mrs. Foster cleaned houses in the area and took in ironing to help make ends meet. Mr. Foster would fish in the creek for supper on occasion. Randy would watch in amazement at the ease the friendly, gentle, man would bring in fish with his over-long cane pole. Mr. Foster had a taught Randy how to use the cane pole and one summer gave Randy his special pole that still had lots of fish=catching ability.

Randy revered the old man and his wife. His pole was one of his most prized possessions. It was truly a sad day when Mr. Foster had passed away. Randy was broken- hearted for very long time.

He had been invited into the Foster home for dinner many times. At first he was taken aback at the sight of a fish cooked with its head still connected to its body. But Mrs. Foster explained the flavor and juices were enhanced when the fish was prepared that way. After Randy had eaten his portion of the fish he had to agree with Mrs. Foster. He ate many things at the modest home he would have never been offered anywhere else and he was grateful for the experience.

Sometimes when Randy had visited the Foster home, Donzella, their niece, had come for short stays at their home. The elder Fosters never let on as to why Donzella showed up for frequent visits, but she had confided to Randy and Karen, that when her dad became mean and abusive to her mom, her mom sent her to her Aunt's and Uncle's house until they cooled down.

Randy recalled that Donzella was a feisty girl. She was the most competitive girl Randy had ever encountered and they held contests all the time. Racing was their favorite contest and Donzella was very fast. In fact, she was faster than Randy was up through the third grade. At this time Randy had developed physically quite a bit and had beaten Donzella three times in a row on a race from Aunt Carrie's to the Negro Gospel Church down the road.

Donzella was so incensed when she had lost the third and final race to Randy, that she had stomped her feet and shouted into the air. The realization came to her that Randy was now faster than she. After she had calmed down, she put her arms around Randy to congratulate him. Putting her face close to his, she took a quick bite of his lip, leaving him howling.

Randy chased the laughing sprite through the fields to her Uncle's house. Randy was so mad, he cried all the way. Donzella arrived just ahead of him as he had closed the gap to be near her, she had raced up on the porch and slammed the screen door in his face. Randy knocked and yelled at the door.

Mr. Foster opened the door. "What the hell is going on?"

Donzella stooped behind him laughing and panting for breath.

"I beat you here," she sputtered breathlessly.

"You cheated with a head start," Randy countered. "Mr. Foster, she bit my lip!"

Randy pulled his lower lip out so that Mr. Foster could see the damage Donzella had done.

Mr. Foster chuckled and bent to look at the young boy's lip. "Don't see no blood. But I do see a few indents from someone's teeth."

"I told you she bit me," Randy said smugly thinking he had Donzella where he wanted her- in trouble with her uncle.

"So what," Donzella retorted.

"Now, now, children. Why don't we just relax and see if'n we can straighten this out."

"Donzella, why did you bite Randy?" Mr. Foster asked in a semiserious tone.

"Because I beat..." Randy tried to interject. But Mr. Foster held up his hand for Randy to be quiet.

"Because I thought he would taste good," she teased.

Mr. Foster snickered at the comment. Randy's face went to shock. He didn't know how to respond to Donzella's comment.

"Well...Donzella, go out to the kitchen and help your Auntie. I'll deal with you later. Right now I need to speak with young Randy here."

"Bye, Randy," Donzella said coyly.

"Bye," Randy said weakly averting her eyes.

Mr. Foster sat on the weathered piece of wood serving as a step to the front door along side of Randy.

"I beat her in a race and she got mad. That's why she bit me," Randy said. He had other thoughts running through his mind.

"Well she don't like to lose I know that. But don't take it so bad. She didn't do you no harm. Hell it's good to get bitten by a woman now and then." Mr. Foster spoke in a tone of a confidant.

Randy opened his eyes wide in surprise. He didn't understand a lot of things about what had just happened and this was the first time Mr. Foster had spoken to him in this manner regarding girls.

"Well I didn't like it. It hurt."

"I don't want to cause no hard feelings, but there is something I got to tell you, boy. Something you must keep to yourself for awhile. How long... I don't know. I guess you will know when the time is right. But I can tell you now is not the time.

"What happened to you today has changed your life. It will be forever different. How you handle it will be up to you. But I know you, and you is really good people, proud of you already, boy."

Randy looked at Mr. Foster with a mixture of pride and apprehension.

Mr. Foster paused and then he continued, "Randy today you have been initiated into the Negro race. That little bite given to you by Donzella has raised a part of you called... *soul.* You've eaten our food, fished our way and been welcomed into our home. Donzella's done something she shouldn't have done without your permission, but what's done is done. It's up to you to accept the privilege."

Mr. Foster was quiet. He leaned back against the post of the porch railing and sneaked a look at Randy from the corner of his eye. Randy had his head in his hands resting his elbows on his knees. He was confused. All this because he had beaten Donzella in a race three times.

"Well do you want the responsibility or not?" Mr. Foster asked.

"Yes...I guess so," Randy answered. He liked Mr. Foster too much to say no to the request.

"Okay then to finish the ancient rite, here's what you've got to do. You've got to turn in a circle three times with your eyes closed. While you're spinning you must say, I am a Negro, with each turn. Spit in the air on the third turn and move out of the way before the spittle hits you. Then you are a bona fide honorary Negro and no one can take that away from you."

Randy stood up. He walked out to a spot on the dirt in front of the Foster homestead. He spun himself around with his head back and his eyes closed.

"I am a Negro. I am a Negro. I am a Negro."

He spit in the air with great emphasis and ran to one side as quickly as he could.

Mr. Foster sat very amused on his wooden step. "Did you feel the spittle?" He asked Randy with deep authority.

"No," Randy said with enthusiasm.

"Then it's done. You, my son, are welcomed into the Negro brotherhood. Be proud of what you are. Don't let names get you down and always respect your race. You are a link between our people. I'm truly proud of you."

Randy was smiling. He could still feel the raised skin on his lower lip from Donzella's bite, but he was bursting from pride that Mr. Foster felt so highly of him.

"I've got to go home now, Mr. Foster. Thank Donzella for me and tell her I'll see her later." Randy said.

Mr. Foster nodded with the bemused smile still etched across his face.

Randy turned and went home through the woods. Mr. Foster watched him go. He figured if everyone was composed of the same stuff as Randy was, the world would be a better place.

Randy had kept his secret for years. Years later Randy came to understand the lesson taught him by the gentle old man. He watched his adopted people suffer many indignities, but he spoke out very little. As he grew older he was more vocal, but in his heart he felt as though he didn't speak forceful enough.

When Mr. Foster died, Randy went to Negro Gospel Church with his sister Karen, his aunt and his uncle. There were not very many white people present. Randy sat with Mrs. Foster, Donzella and the rest of the Foster family. He lost a family member of his own and the emotional pain was great. Two weeks after the formal funeral Mrs. Foster moved away. Randy had not seen her or Donzella since. He missed them all.

Randy leaned his head back against the tree, which helped form his chair. He rarely sat here without a thought of the Fosters. It was a shame someone had vandalized their empty home. These were troubled times but there was little a fifteen-year-old boy could do.

He looked across the creek at the trees and could make out the outline of the Magurk house. He wondered if Mary Jo was at home. He hoped she was not away somewhere visiting some relative or friend for the summer. Hopefully she would be at the pond later in the day.

With this inspiration he pulled himself up from the cold stone chair and brushed off the back of his trousers. One last look at the vista and he turned to walk back through the woods. He wanted to visit with Lee and the gang. With his first step into the woods he encountered an ugly sight that forced him to stop in his tracks.

Chapter 4

Randy was beginning to retreat at the sight of the three wild cats that were feeding on what appeared to be a carcass of something freshly killed. He didn't want to have to defend himself from these crazy-eyed alley cats. Over time, ordinary house cats that area people had discarded for one reason or another took up residence. When no one would adopt the cats, the cats had to fend for themselves. There were many generations of these wild feral cats in the woods.

The cats were as a big a problem to the chicken farmers as the rats that inhabited the surrounding fields. The cats were larger than normal and downright mean. Many people felt that they were rabies carriers as well as vehicles for spreading cat scratch fever. It was said a kitten of one of the wild strays had scratched the Mullen boy and he nearly had to have his arm amputated. It was said that he was in a coma for two days before the doctor realized what had caused his symptoms.

Randy had heard his Aunt Caroline say that she thought most of the story had been exaggerated but Randy steered clear of the cats anyway. Now he was face to face with the cats and the furry balls of death were feasting directly in front of him. He could see the bad intent in their eyes as they munched the red flesh.

This was one time he wished he had brought his gun. Normally, the cats were reclusive and scattered when someone came near them, but these cats held their ground and growled. If he ever felt he could kill something these cats would be at the top of his list.

Randy debated his next move. The cats appeared really aggressive. If he ran, he could at least jump into the creek if they came after him.

He didn't dare try and go around them through the woods; they were on the same path he used to reach his stone chair. He thought he would go back down the creek toward the Foster house and head down the field where the old Gospel Church's charred remains stood. At every move he made, however slight, the cats would emit a sound like a baby shrieking. It was very unnerving. He looked around for some type of big stick. There wasn't anything suitable nearby; not even a decent-sized rock to throw at their evil, fur-matted heads.

Randy turned slightly so he could sprint to the creek. He was envisioning how it would feel to have one of those cats pounce on his back and bite into the exposed skin of his neck. He began to worry himself even more. Keeping his eyes on the orange striped cat that was closest to him he turned a little bit more toward the creek. There was no way he would be able to run down the back to Mr. Foster's house. The creek was his only salvation. Hopefully these cats didn't like to swim.

Randy could see the pupils of the cats eyes widen. The small mouth of the cat opened and let out a horrible cry. The cat lowered its head and raised its rump in a coiled crouch position. Randy could feel the tension and anxiety exuding from the cat.

Randy decided he could not turn his back to this cat. It appeared ready to strike at any moment. Slowly Randy moved his feet backward to begin his retreat. He wished some of the dogs had followed him out here. They would have driven these cats away or tore them apart.

With each little step Randy could see the eyes of the cat grow ever wider. Randy could see the cat begin to tremble and shake its rear end. The cat was ready to pounce on him. It would probably go for his throat and bite his jugular vein. He would bleed out, here in the woods; the cats feasting on his body.

Randy didn't want to wait any longer. He turned and bolted out through the trees. Although he was barely into the woods, he could feel the small branches clutching at his clothing, striking his face with quick whips like bees stinging his face. He could hear the cat snarling and running on the forest debris that lay on the path fallen from the trees above them. He was two or three steps from bank of the creek when he heard a dog barking.

He didn't stop to look. Randy performed a shallow dive into the creek. The cold water took his breath away. He couldn't swim very well with his sneakers on his feet. His pants worked like brakes as he dragged himself through the water. After a couple of strong strokes underwater he broke the surface and turned to observe the commotion on the shore. He was about ten feet from the shoreline. A safe distance from the cat he hoped.

From his vantage point, he could see a medium-sized brown, white and black mutt fighting with the crazed cat. The dog was quick and all business. The snarling, seemingly mad cat didn't have a chance. After trying to claw the dog's eyes, it made a fatal mistake of trying to jump on the dog's back. Once the cat was in the air, it had little real control over the situation. The dog dodged sideways and snatched the cat by the nape of the neck. With a quick twist of his head he snapped the cat's neck leaving it for dead.

Randy moved a little closer to the shore so he wouldn't have to tread water. He was becoming tired. He wondered if the dog was friendly to humans. He had never seen the dog before, but who knew if it was one of the clan. Randy would have to come out of the water sometime.

The dog stood over the cat for a moment, evidently checking to see if it was playing possum. Once it was satisfied, it moved away and turned to sit on the bank directly in front of Randy. He wagged his tail in the sand and uttered soft little whining sounds.

If he was a danger to humans, it wasn't evident to Randy. Without any concern for his safety, Randy ventured closer to the shore and the dog carefully. He spoke to the dog with a soft calming tone. The dog responded by wagging his body back and forth. The dog showed no signs of aggression toward Randy.

Randy slowly emerged from the water and the dog picked itself up and ran over to him. Randy stood stock still for a moment; the dog nuzzled Randy's hand as if he wanted Randy to pet him, which he did. The transformation from cat-killing dog to man's best friend was astonishing. Randy breathed a sigh of relief and could not have been happier or more relieved. He squatted down and hugged the dog around the neck, and then he stood up to go back through the woods. Randy hoped this was another of his Aunt and Uncles dog brood.

Randy stopped before he entered the woods and turned back towards the creek. He felt he should put the dead cat in a shallow grave. If he didn't, it would surely stink to high heaven in a few days, spoiling his fishing spot. Chances were that something from the woods would eat the cat, but he didn't want to take any chances. With a flat piece of driftwood he dug up the soft, very sandy soil and kicked the dead cat in the hole with his very wet shoe. He covered the hole and turned to the dog.

The dog sat and watched. His markings were very distinctive. The black spot across his back covered each side like a small saddle. His brown and white spots were scattered randomly on his fur. Randy sensed the dog had no owner, and decided that if he didn't belong to his Uncle's farm he would name him Pony because he looked like a painted horse from an old western movie.

"C'mon Pony," Randy barked and they headed back into the woods. The dog followed obediently as if he and Randy had been dog and master for a long time.

A few feet into the woods, Randy could see the other cats were gone. A small bit of whatever they were eating remained on the path. Pony went to sniff it, but Randy urged the dog away from it. Randy didn't know what it was, but it wasn't a freshly-killed animal. It looked like something recently butchered, like a piece of beef or pork. He used a stick to pick it up and flung it deep into the trees and brush. Pony looked at him with hungry eyes, but he didn't chase after the meat.

"*Good*", Randy thought, "*I like this dog.*"

The two new companions made good time on their trek back through the woods. Pony ran ahead most of the time sniffing the worn path. Periodically he would look back to keep tabs on Randy.

Randy was wet. His sneakers squished as he walked through the trees. He felt a heavy weight pushing against his back and at first couldn't figure out why it felt so uncomfortable. Then he remembered the Playboy magazine that he had pilfered from Harlan, which he was going to add to the stash at the clubhouse. Now it was ruined.

Damned cats. They messed up his day and his magazine. The thought of the cats caused him to peer around behind him to be sure they were not following him. He hurried to reach the end of the path.

Once out into the open, Randy and Pony cut across the weedy field bypassing his Uncles farmhouse. He didn't feel like answering any unnecessary questions. Uncle Harvey's father was taking a short break leaning on his hoe. His large straw hat was in his hand as he wiped the beads of sweat from his brow. He noticed Randy and waved. Randy waved back. The gesture made him feel good for reasons he didn't even consider.

Bessie, the white German shepherd and a few of the other dogs spied the duo traversing the field. They were on a dead run barking a territorial bark with ferocity.

Pony raised his head to look at Randy and then peered over at the approaching dogs. He seemed to be considering his options.

Pony and Randy stopped in the field near the road. Bessie and her dog posse were on them in no time. Pony stood his ground. He didn't run, but he didn't react in an aggressive manner either. Bessie stood directly in front of Pony and Randy. She was barking in tandem with the other dogs steadily waiting for Pony to flee. The other dogs surrounded Bessie, Randy and Pony on the dirt stage. Bessie barked and looked in Randy's direction as if to say what we should do.

Obviously not a Kearneys' dog Randy thought. "Bessie, sit," he commanded.

Obedience trained, the big white shepherd sat instantly. She stopped barking and waited for Randy to command her. Instead Randy bent and rubbed her head, and then he bent and rubbed Pony's head. He was trying to show the dogs he knew them both. The other dogs sat in a pack and watched barking occasionally.

Randy stood up. There, he thought, that wasn't so hard to do. He took his eyes off Bessie for a moment content he had made peace. Without his eye contact Bessie sprang from her sitting position and ran over to Pony with a huge growl.

"No!" Randy shouted. It was too late. Bessie was on the painted dog in a flash.

Pony didn't fight, but instead rolled over on to his back in a submissive posture. The challenge was over and Bessie, even though a female, she reigned supreme. She was still the master of the farm dogs, the Alpha at least for now. After all Pony was a male and Bessie came into heat twice a year.

"Go home! Go home!" Randy shouted. "Go home!"

Randy had had enough of the dogs today. Slowly they turned around toward the farmhouse and walked without purpose away from him. "Go home!" he barked. One last look and they picked up the pace and ran to the farm. Randy would go to Lee's house without his furry entourage.

Chapter 5

Randy walked at a brisk pace up toward the shady maple tree where his sister was seated talking to her friends. It was quite a distance from the road up to Rhoda's and Carol's house. Randy looked back and forth carefully; his eyes were keenly searching for the sight or sound of Butch.

Butch was the Powell's pet dog that was a mix of boxer and some other exotic breed of dog with a very large head. Randy had no idea what kind of dog that it was, but he did know that he and Butch were not very good friends.

The dog hadn't really liked him since he was a puppy. He would bark incessantly at Randy whenever he visited with Lee and his sisters. As the dog grew older he seemed to tolerate Randy a little more until the incident. An incident that Randy had tried to explain to Lee, but Lee laughed so hard at the story Randy had told that Randy didn't ever tell it again. For six years now Butch had tolerance for Randy and Randy avoided the dog as much as he could. Fortunately for him Butch, lacked road sense and was usually attached to his tether in the back yard. He had almost been hit by cars a few times. It was while Butch was tethered that Randy had witnessed the incident.

He had been nonchalantly walking over to Lee's house and venturing over to the old chicken house on the back of the property that served as the local clubhouse for the boys. As he rounded the corner on the dirt road that led to clubhouse, he heard an odd sound of muffled pleasure cries. Randy slowed down a little and walked with little noise so that he could spy on the weird noise without being seen. He stopped behind the dense lilac bush that was situated on the rounded corner of the road. Back by the barn he could see the tether that held Butch attached to the barn and a telephone pole, this gave Butch a lot of area to run. Placed at one point very near the dirt road, but not close enough for him to actually reach the road.

Randy couldn't believe his eyes. The dog was pleasuring himself, by manipulating his private area in a way that many a young boy did, once they learned that it was possible. The dog wasn't licking himself but actually performing the back and forth motion with his teeth. He groaned as he worked himself faster and Randy slipped a little as he lost his balance while he was squatting behind the bush.

The dog immediately heard the noise and looked into Randy's direction. Randy felt like a voyeur and felt his face flush with embarrassment. Then he thought, "*This is a dog, what am I embarrassed about? Besides the dog was caught not me.* He stood up with a smile on his face and couldn't wait to tell Lee and the boys what he had witnessed.

He walked around the lilac bush and slowly sauntered past Butch. Butch was still lying on the ground staring at Randy. The dog made Randy feel uncomfortable with his stare, so Randy tried to ignore him. As he reach the place in the road in front of Butch the dog took a flying leap and tried to get at Randy. Startled, Randy ran like a track athlete to the clubhouse. He could still hear the snarling, growling and vicious barking resounding from the dog. The near attack shook him up and when he told Lee why he was nervous Lee only laughed. They never spoke of the incident again. Randy figured because Lee was embarrassed for his dog. Randy never had a good relationship with the dog again.

In fact, Randy had once gone to Lee's house to play and he forgot to ask Lee if Butch was tied to his rope run. By the time Randy realized Butch was free, Butch had darted from under the house and Lee was not outside to command the dog- it was far too late. Randy had been halfway up the Powell's lawn when the snarling, big brown well-muscled canine came at a full gallop after him. Randy turned and ran the moment he spied the dog.

Running as fast as he could, Randy calculated he would be across the road before the dog would reach him. He could hear the dog barking, and the scuffing of his paws as Butch ran through the grass in his effort to catch him. Randy was at the edge of the grass about to cross over the macadam roadway when he caught sight of a fast approaching car.

He would have to be run over by the car or bitten to pieces by his nemesis Butch. It was a split second choice, but Randy was no fool. He would suffer the dog bite.

Just as Butch reached Randy snarling and barking with saliva and drool running from his gargantuan mouth, Randy turned to face him. Randy shouted as loud as he could with his hands high in the air like a monster from a movie. The shout was a guttural primal scream. To Randy's astonishment Butch stopped his pursuit dead in his tracks. He peered at Randy with a quizzical look, his head cocked to the side. Then he turned and trotted back up to the house and lay down under the big maple tree.

Randy stood motionless for a second. He had watched the dog retreat back up to the house in a slow confused amble. The dog had been defeated that particular day. Randy looked around to see if anyone had seen this hugely embarrassing scene. He didn't see anyone. At that point he took his rubbery knees and vibrating body back to his aunt's house. He would play with Lee another time.

"Hi, Randy," cooed Carol. "Lee's back at the clubhouse. You want me to walk back there with you?"

"No thank you, Carol." He replied. The last comment stung a little bit. He felt that Carol thought he was afraid of Butch- meaning he was cowardly.

"Are you going to the pond later?" she persisted. "We're going."

"Maybe, Carol. I don't know yet," he said pausing in front of the three girls.

"Why are you all wet?" his sister asked. "It looks like you've already been in the pond .You should swim in your suit ya' know."

The three girls laughed. Randy blushed a deep red hue and a disgusted smirk crossed his face. He could feel the weight of the Playboy magazine grow heavier. He was beginning to feel very uncomfortable. He would tell Karen what had happened later. Right now he wanted to be away from the three of them.

Randy didn't answer Karen immediately. He scanned the backyard and saw Butch glaring back in his direction. To Randy's relief the dog was chained to his rope run.

"I had a small accident. I'll tell you about it later."

"Tell me now."

"I'll tell you later. I've got to go."

He turned to walk away.

"What's that under your shirt?" Karen asked teasingly.

"Where?" Carol inquired.

The older girls ignored the younger girls' question and Randy picked up the pace. He wanted to be free of the questioning.

"Where? What's under his shirt? C'mon tell meee!" Carol pleaded.

The two girls laughed. Carol sulked for a moment. Randy moved forward out of hearing range. He felt a little better as he put distance between himself and the eyes of the prying girls.

He had to walk by Butch, but he knew from years of practice how far away from the rope run he had to distance himself. Butch stayed by his doghouse. Randy could have sworn the dog was laughing at his wet clothes. It was only a short distance to the abandoned two story chicken house from the dog run.

Randy was trying to be as nonchalant as he could be. He stared straight ahead. He kicked at the sandy soil with the toes of his wet Converse sneakers. He passed Butch without incident. He was nervous but feeling better now that he was by the maniac, self-flagellating dog. He felt butterflies in his stomach. He hated that damned dog. He wished it would run away or something.

Feeling a little relief, Randy relaxed and blew out a sigh of air.

"Woof! Woof! Woof!" Butch barked.

Randy could hear the chain run down the heavy rope it was tethered on, like the finger of a guitar player driving down a guitar string. The clip that was on the end of the chain clanged as it hit the pole holding the rope; Randy without looking back bolted forward almost leaving his skin a few steps back. Glancing back while on the move Randy wanted to see if the dog was loose. He wasn't, but he was barking ferociously, straining at his collar with all his strength.

"Damn it!" Randy said aloud. He tried to calm himself as he made the turn to the stairs, which would lead him up to the clubhouse. "I hate that dog!" He said to himself. He turned his head and spit in the dog's direction.

The dog stared with his mouth open, tongue hanging out, like he was having a good chuckle at Randy's expense.

Randy took the steps two at a time. When he reached the landing at the top, he didn't pause before he threw the creaking old weather-beaten door open. He startled the boys inside, causing one to drop his cigarette in a panic.

"Jesus, Randy. I just lit that up, Lee bitched at him. "What a d."

"I see you're happy to see me. You shouldn't smoke those cancer sticks anyway. You're going to stunt your growth."

"Very funny, dog boy." Vern offered.

Randy looked over and saw Vernon Truit sitting on a rusty bucket resting his back against the wall. Vernon was an ornery cuss and he had little nice to say to anyone. Truth was that he was very kind, but had a grumpy demeanor. He was the nephew of Pup, a good reason Randy thought to account for Vern's attitude. Despite his caustic mouth, Randy liked him. He was nice to have around in a sticky situation, because even though he was a nice kid, he would fight at the drop of a hat.

"Dog boy?" Randy repeated with mock indignation. "You're one to talk about dog boys with an uncle named Pup."

"As a matter a fact, we were just discussing your Aunt's and Uncle's dog farm. It looks like they have more dogs than chickens." Vern pushed with a wry smile.

"Not we, you, Vern." Lee protested with a laugh.

"Whatever. Uncle Pup said people around here are pretty tired of all those dogs running around. You can't even drive down the road by their house without slowing down with those puppies always lying down on the road."

"Was he sober or awake, because I know he wasn't sober if he was awake," Lee said.

"Go ahead make fun, but the ole boy has his pulse on the mood in the area. Hell…I think he's play acting most of the time. He wants people to think he's drunk, so then they'd tell him more stuff about what's going on around here. He's nosy as an ole hen."

"Well…he's not acting today. He rode up here from home with us. He's about done with his Mason jar," Randy said.

"Uh oh, Aunt Arleen's going to be pissed. Uncle Pup is supposed to be dry today. She's got some company coming over tonight.

I think there's going to be some fireworks. Providing Uncle Pup shows up."

All three boys laughed.

"Ya' know, Randy, we do hear people talking bad about them dogs. What are your Aunt and Uncle going to do about the puppies that lie in the middle of the road?" Lee asked.

"Don't know. Didn't ask. It's out of my hands…but this isn't," he answered pulling out the semi-soaked *Playboy* magazine from his damp pants.

Lee standing the closest to Randy snatched it from Randy's hands. "Hey it's all wet. What have you been doing with this? Why are you all wet?"

Randy explained to Lee and Vernon what had happened in the woods. Everyone admitted that it was a strange way for the cats to act. The two boys didn't know who owned the multi-colored dog. They decided that later they would try and hunt down the other cats. It would be fun hunting this late in the summer.

While Randy had been telling this tale with the usual teenage embellishment, Lee and Vernon had been leaving through the new addition to the clubhouse library. The two boys were so close in appearance that they could have been mistaken for brothers. Sandy hair with brown eyes and similar builds, but Vern was much more muscular. He lifted weights nearly every day. The three boys had been good friends for many years.

"Hey, this centerfold looks like one of the Magurk girls," Lee stated.

"Sure does," Vern agreed. "Randy, look at this."

Randy moved over to look at the picture. He was curious, but hoped they were not going to say it resembled Mary Jo Magurk.

"That looks just like Leigh Ann," Randy said with relief filled honesty.

"Man, I wish that was her," Lee said dreamily. "What I could do with that babe."

"That makes two of us," Vern concurred. "But she's three years older than we are. She'd never give us a second thought."

"True. I kinda like Mary Jo anyway. I was thinking about asking her out someday."

Lee's statement threw Randy into a small panic. Lee was speaking about his girl. He had to make it known he was after Mary Jo Magurk without seeming too interested.

"I wouldn't mind slobbering over her either," Vern said lustily. "Jesus those sisters are good looking."

Randy remained quiet for the time being.

In fact all the boys were quiet. Lee flipped through the pages of the magazine as the other boys leered at the photos from behind him. Carnal thoughts running rampart through their collective brains.

The door to the clubhouse swung open, just as Lee lit another cigarette. Instinctively he tossed it to the wooden plank floor and stomped it out. The three boys stared at the door. Picker walked through it.

"Jesus, Picker! You scared the crap out of me. I gotta get a lock for that door. Either that or we need a secret knock or something. Cigarettes don't grow on trees you know." Lee was pissed.

"Hello, gents. Good news. The pond is full of people and the water is bobbing with Magurks and their mammaries."

This could have been the actual Magurk sisters or it could have been girls in general. The boys used the term *Magurks* to signify girls in general because of their idolization of them.

"Hey, Randy, when did you get in?" Picker asked.

"Today…the pond is full huh? Well let's get going. I feel like swimming."

The boys were careful to place the magazines underneath the wooden box against the wall. Lee spread his cigarette butts around so that they wouldn't look freshly smoked in case his father visited the clubhouse. They were very careful smoking was a big no-no for Lee's father. If they were caught there would be hell to pay.

Once they were secure with how the place appeared they ran out to change into their shorts or swimming trunks. They would meet out in front of Lee's house on their bicycles before they went to the pond.

Chapter 6

Randy had changed into his cut off blue jeans; told his aunt where he was off to and had retrieved the old faded blue balloon tire bicycle from the shed. He waved to his uncle, who stood by the chicken house cleaning the soles of his shoes. As his Uncle Harvey waved back, Randy hopped onto the bicycle and rode around to the front of the house.

Picker was sitting on his bicycle near the Dogville sign out in front of the Kearney's farm. He was whistling a tuneless song. Randy saw that Picker was wearing a bathing suit, which appeared a size too small. He was sure to take a ribbing about it, but the truth was that Picker really didn't care. Teasing didn't ever seem to bother him; so no one ever bothered because it took the fun out of the deed.

Picker had been born Raymond Fenwick. He had five older sisters and when he was born his father exclaimed, "That's a picker," referring to a term used for fruit or melons which had turned ripe. The name had stuck and everyone in the area had called him Picker. Of course there were people who misunderstood the meaning of the tow headed, knobby kneed boy's name, but again this didn't bother Picker, he would just shrug his bony shoulders and ignore the comments.

Fact was, Randy had noticed recently, girls had a soft spot for the free spirited boy. His sister Karen had noted how cute and nice Picker was. He made the girls laugh with his off the wall humor. Randy had known him a long time and couldn't see the attraction. Randy was feeling peculiar about his position amongst his friends when it came to girls.

He felt a little insecure about how he was perceived here in Colmboro as well as his hometown Delburg. He felt the girls were friendly enough to him, but he needed a boost of confidence to ask a girl to a movie or out to anything that would appear to be a date. He heard through the grapevine some girls liked him, but he never pursued the opportunities. He knew he would take the step sometime. He just didn't know if he was skilled enough to carry the weight of a date.

He didn't know when to begin to kiss, hold hands or progress beyond these points. What if he was too forward, what if he was clumsy, what if he was a bad kisser, what if he offended his date; he didn't want to be laughed at by his peers. Of course he and his friends had talked a thousand times about what they would do with a girl given the chance. Truth was that they only knew the things they wanted to do by reading, watching movies or television and by listening to older boys talk of their experiences. There was little true experience among Randy's friends. He felt that might change this summer.

"Nice suit, Picker. Is that the bottom of one of your sister's bikinis?"

"Not quite. My sisters have moved on a long time ago ya' know."

"Just kidding. I don't think two years is a long time by the way. Tracy still up at the University of Delaware?"

"Long time in dog years isn't it?" Picker grinned at the barb delivered to Randy. "Yes she's still a Fighting Blue Hen which suits her personality. That girl is a scrapper. We argued all the time, but I miss her."

Randy was thinking about the dog comment. He didn't know if Picker was tossing him a jibe or not. He was getting a little sensitive about the subject.

"That's the first time I've ever heard you say you missed any of your sisters."

"The house is kinda lonely with only me and my parents. The girls are a mess but we had some great times together."

"Like the time they told you they wanted to play hide-and-seek in the house and hung you up by your shirt on a coat hook inside of a closet for a half of an hour."

"Yeah well Mom finally heard me hollering and I got pleasure out of their punishment. My neck still hurts from my near strangulation. Besides you have to admit that's a funny story."

"I think it's hilarious."

They sat on their bicycles in silence for a moment, and then Picker began to speak, "Randy, I want to ask you something and I trust you as a friend to keep it a secret. I need some advice on something."

"Shoot."

"I'm supposed to go to the Walker's tonight and I'm supposed to meet a girl there."

Randy thought a minute and then said, "Yeah, so what's the big deal about meeting a girl at the movies. What's playing anyway?" Randy was trying to be nonchalant. Two things were bothering him, one, Picker had a date and two, Randy hoped it wasn't Mary Jo Magurk.

"I don't know. Two Westerns, I think. Anyway, I'm supposed to meet an older girl and I want to ask you something."

Randy interjected, "I see... an older girl, huh? Well... I don't see what the harm is. In fact, it's probably good if she's older, she can drive you around until you get your license. Hell, I think it's great. This is kind of surprising to me. I didn't know you were going out on dates yet. What's her name?"

Picker hesitated. "Well I'm not sure I'm ready to give out her name yet. Besides that's not what I wanted to ask you."

"Oh...what then?"

"Where can I get a rubber?"

Whoa! Randy was feeling a little uncomfortable. Picker was going to have sex or at least he was planning on having it. Who was this girl? And had Picker been out with her enough to be hitting a home run. *Christ,* Randy thought, *I'm the biggest loser in the world. I'd better start thinking about how I can get enough nerve to ask out a girl.*

Randy answered with a professorial type attitude, "Good question. I don't have one, maybe the drugstore."

"Can't, my Aunt Gladys works there."

Randy went fishing. 'Where'd you get the last one?"

"I haven't gotten one yet."

"You did it without a rubber?" Randy was shocked.

"No."

"Tonight's the night?"

"I don't know. But I want to be prepared." Picker was speaking so casually about this that Randy was feeling quite insecure. He hadn't given any thought to his friends having girlfriends or even his friends going on a single date before he did. How had Picker achieved this feat? Why hadn't he been able to summon the courage before Picker?

Randy decided to dig for further answers. "Have you gone out with her before tonight?"

"Not formally…we sort of meet out by the creek."

Before Randy could ask more questions, Lee rode down the lane from his house and joined them at the sign.

"Nice suit, Picker. What are you guys talking about?"

"Party balloons," Picker said without missing a beat.

"Party balloons?" asked Lee with a screwed up expression on his face.

"Yeah, party balloons. We'll discuss it later." Picker said.

Lee looked perplexed. He was quiet as Vern rode up to greet them.

"Nice suit, Picker," Vern said mockingly.

"Thanks, Vernon. Nice of you to notice."

Vern blushed slightly. He had embarrassed himself.

Changing the subject, Lee said, "Hey, let's go up to Mary Lamb's before we go to the pond. I need some smokes."

Lee felt the cigarettes enhanced his image. The only problem with getting the cigarettes was that everyone knew how Lee's father felt about smoking cigarettes, so Lee had trouble buying them. Vern knew it would be up to him to buy them, he knew the drill and it really didn't bother him.

Mary Lamb's Country Store was about two miles from the Mill Pond. The boys would have to ride directly by the swimming hole to reach the store. Mary Lamb's had been the local store for many years and most people still shopped there for their incidental items, but went into town for their weekly shopping at the A & P Supermarket.

Mary and her husband, Bud, worked long hours and appreciated the support they received from the community. They knew everyone by first name and carried a store charge account for a great deal of their customers, scratched onto a spiral notebook. They didn't sell alcohol spirits of any kind, but they were known for having the freshest, most tender beef in the two county area. Sure it cost a little more to buy the beef at the Country Store, but it was well worth it once it was placed on the dinner table. Mary also stocked the finest cheddar cheese anyone had ever tasted and a little taste test was supplied to anyone who stopped by the chopping block where the wheel of cheese sat so prominently.

The cheese came in round wheels packed five wheels to a barrel. Mary and Bud would take a wheel out and place it on the chopping block table to let it warm up to room temperature. On the occasion they had sold the last wheel of cheese before the next shipment arrived, the Lamb's had to turn away slightly irritated cheese lovers with a promise of a little extra cheese in the next order the customer purchased. The cheese was Mary Lamb's Country Store trademark and brought in people from all around the county for its delectable taste.

The boys peddled their bicycles hard racing past one another, always trying to be at the head of the pack. It took a great deal of stamina to lead the group a good while.

Before they rounded the turn, they came to the burnt Black Gospel Church and Caleb "Scar Nose" Fulton's ramshackle trailer. The charred church ruin was set back from the road about two hundred yards from Caleb Fulton's trailer.

The church had been on that piece of property at least a decade before Caleb Fulton moved to his lot with his trailer. However, that didn't stop him from complaining to the white residents in the area that the loud raucous singing and preaching on Sunday mornings emanating from the church was more than annoying to him. He had spoken to Reverend Spikes on numerous occasions threatening to call the authorities. Reverend Spikes spoke civilly to Caleb and quoted verses of the Bible stating he wanted no trouble, but worshipping the Lord was his priority and that the church was in existence long before Caleb had moved to the area.

Fact was, Caleb Fulton never complained about the Wednesday night service. He was usually out and about the town moving from bar to bar acquainting himself with the goings on of the area- which translated into learning the gossip spread by idle, inebriated self-important pillars of the community. Caleb served as a mouthpiece and facilitator for these people who hid behind a cloak of invisible community respect so as not to give the impression of being involved in anything which may sully their family names. Sunday mornings were another matter- after his Saturday night carousing - he needed to provide time for his body to purge the remnants of the demon alcohol spirits he had imbibed the previous evening.

The old church was a gathering site for the elders, leaders and activists of the black community. It served as a place of sanctuary, education, and a community meeting center and symbol of new cohesiveness within the black community. The burnt ruins served as a tactic, a warning to the community as a whole that change of any kind was likely not to be tolerated.

When it rained, the pungent odor of burned wood timbers could still be smelled from the church ruins. It had been a year and a half since it had mysteriously erupted into flames one Monday evening. Randy had been at home and saddened by the news of its destruction.

Randy loved to sit outside of the church and listen to the Reverend Spikes' stormy sermons about the evils of sin. The Reverend Spikes would bring the elderly Negro congregation to a feverish pitch with his biting well-directed words. The word Amen shouted from the flock permeated and punctuated his raucous staccato delivery. He touched on many subjects and the chorus of agreeing utterances filled the air. Sometimes the veiled references in the sermon addressing the civil rights of people added electricity to the feeling of the night.

Randy loved it when the choir began its soulful singing. Once the singing began, the walls of the church vibrated with spirited enthusiasm. He had had the opportunity to sit inside the church only on two occasions.

He had accompanied Mr. and Mrs. Foster to a service and was enthralled with the feeling he experienced sitting within the walls of the sanctuary. Mostly he had sat outside of the church when he had the time, because even with his honorary acceptance into the race by Mr. Foster, he still felt like an outsider and intruder. These were troubled times and a white boy inside the church, as symbolic as it appeared, was too much for some of the folks in the congregation.

Randy didn't want to place the Fosters or Reverend Spikes in the middle a controversy. It had been quite a while since he had stepped inside of the church, before it had burned. His second and last visit had been when he had attended the funeral of his good friend, Mr. Foster. The controversy of the Freedom Riders had taken care of that. He couldn't understand how a group of people so dedicated to peaceful means, like the Freedom Riders, could incite such hatred among the denizens of this rural community.

The Freedom Riders had only suggested that they would be riding through the town on their journey to shine the light on racial inequality, but the divisions along the racial lines caused quite a stir in the whole county. The people were split on the opinion of the ride, but the side against the ride was more vocal and intimidating. They felt that the Civil Rights group was nothing more than a crowd of vandals setting out to cause riots and destruction wherever they appeared. Randy wondered how a group trying to do so much good was painted as a mob of ne'er-do-wells by so many upstanding people.

Everyone blamed Martin Luther King Jr. for a great deal of the goings on in the Negro community. They couldn't fathom as to why the black community felt that they had it so bad. Randy was on the other side of the fence. He could see for himself how people had to live on the other side of his own town- across the railroad tracks- in a community called Frog Town.

The houses for the most part were badly in need of painting and repair; some didn't even have indoor plumbing. That was not to say that the whites on this side of town were much better off financially. The fact was that many of the white people lived under the same conditions. Of course, not all of the houses were downtrodden and clapboard in Frog Town. But for the most part, the community was segregated and considered second class. The whites that lived on this side of the railroad tracks held themselves up to be superior to their neighbors despite their living conditions. Economically and socially, things were the same with the exception of the color of their skins.

The high and mighty across the tracks looked down their noses at both groups.

Randy thought he understood the reason so many people in the Black community were angry. He knew it was more than just poverty style living conditions. He knew it had more to do with the very way in which people were treated. Respect is a treatment everyone deserves. People didn't want to be considered second class or inferior. It wasn't enough to be treated in a mannerly way - that's not real respect. Respect is the acknowledgement that one person is equal to the other and should be given the same opportunities and chances based on ability and not appearance or perceived God given traits.

He thought of how the children in his town had to go to the one-room schoolhouse. All grades were packed into the school and the children were expected to learn in an underfunded, cramped school building with inferior educational materials. The last year had been different when the school board had implemented the racial desegregation ordered by the state. It had been a highly tense period the first month or so, but after the huge social change, things settled down. Not everyone was accepting of his or her new social conditions and some tension remained in the school. Parents of the children didn't exactly help the situation by being hostile and bigoted at home.

As a part of the effort to gain civil rights, the Black community had a more defiant side to equal the White community in the opposition of the changing of existing norms. The Freedom riders had passed word they would be making a ride through the town of Delton to bring attention to inequality in the area. They believed they would shine the light on rural, Southern communities, which supported segregation.

Not knowing when this ride would exactly take place, the local merchants attempted to protect their stores and closed early every night for a month. They had heard rumors that during such rides, there were riots and many cases of vandalism. They were fearful that their properties would be targeted. There was also a rumor that the National Guard would be mobilized. Everything was blown out of proportion by the insidious rumors.

Then one Sunday night, while people were sleeping, a group of vandals, no one knew if they were black or white, rode through Delton and broke three storefront windows downtown. Graffiti was painted on walls but was illegible; the Freedom riders were assigned the blame.

The Freedom Rider spokesperson denied that they were even in the area during that time, but the projected guilt stuck. The White community was terribly upset and agitated, the Black community felt betrayed and framed.

The very next night, the Black Gospel church in Colmboro was torched. Even though Colmboro was so close to Delton, it seemed odd to people why this church was chosen as revenge. Caleb Fulton was questioned and detained as a suspect. However he was also the second cousin of the local police captain. He was released because of the lack of evidence against him. People in Delton had said that for some time they believed Caleb had burned down the church in hushed tones. Some of the people said it was just revenge, others sick to their stomachs over such blatant disregard. Caleb Fulton was mum on the subject and so far as anyone knew; no one else had been picked up for questioning. Randy felt certain it had to be Caleb, but with no proof, he never openly blamed Caleb "Scarnose" Fulton. Besides, the people in Colmboro would only defend him, if the subject were broached. They might bicker amongst within, but they usually protected their own.

Caleb Fulton was well liked in Colmboro, even with his overt prejudices against blacks. He had helped many a farmer in their times of need. They were not willing to turn their backs on him. He was proud of his community and took great pains to keep the area clean and clear of riff raff. The medium-height, redhead's drinking was tolerated. He was a no-trouble boozer and fit in well with many of the local residents.

Caleb had not bothered to clean up the burned remains of the church. He felt if he did, it might encourage the rebuilding of the church, which he didn't want to happen. There really was no fear of rebuilding anyway; the Reverend Spikes had moved his congregation closer to their homes in the Black community of Sunlight Heights, where they felt more comfortable.

Randy glanced over at the ruins of the church and slowed his pace. He thought of Mr. and Mrs. Foster and said a silent prayer. He missed them and he missed the church.

Chapter 7

The four boys rounded the turn of the road and could see a group of people swimming in the water. Someone was atop the rigged up diving platform, which projected out over the pond from the walls of the dam.

The diving platform was a little dangerous because if you stumbled backwards and fell, you would fall onto the smooth rocks behind the dam wall. That would result in severe injuries, but as far as anyone knew, no one had ever fallen the wrong way off the diving board. Caleb Fulton had erected the platform for the local resident's enjoyment. He carefully maintained it every year.

When the older children in the neighborhood were around they would not allow the smaller children to climb the four-foot ladder that led to the platform. It was an unwritten law of the pond that you had to be of a certain age and skill to jump from the makeshift diving platform.

Randy scoured the pond moving his eyes right to left across the pond in an effort to find Mary Jo Magurk. There were about ten people in the pond with Delroy Jones climbing the ladder of the platform. Delroy was a seasoned diver. Delroy had shown Randy a new technique which Randy used, but Randy was nowhere near the proficient diver Delroy was. Delroy snapped from the platform with little effort and cut through the surface of the water so sharply that he barely produced a ripple. A sudden splash popped up where he entered and Randy nodded his head in silent approval.

Randy didn't see Mary Jo. He could see her sisters who waved in the general direction of the boys. Randy spied Picker lagging behind the rest of the crew tossing his hand in the air quickly and then pulling his hand down just as quick. Randy was impressed. He figured Picker had landed one of the Magurk sisters.

Randy could see that the Leigh Ann Magurk was staring intently at Picker and he was returning the gaze. If it were true that Picker and Leigh Ann were an item, then Picker would be the envy of the rest of the boys in the area. Leigh Ann was the middle Magurk sister and the most attractive of all the girls. She had blond hair and beautiful brown eyes. She was the coveted prize to many of the boys in the Colmboro and Delton area. She had turned sixteen about eight months ago. The pairing puzzled Randy immensely, *how in the world could Picker interest Leigh Ann.*

Randy knew that they lived near one another and that their families were very close friends, but for an older girl the likes of Leigh Ann to be interested in a younger boy, especially one as quirky as Picker baffled Randy. Perhaps Leigh Ann saw Picker in a different type of spectrum; perhaps her view of the light Picker emanated was colored through a peculiar type of prism.

The boys stopped their bicycles on the bridge that spanned the creek on the south side of the dam. They looked over the side of the dam and could see the top of Caleb Fulton's head. He was moving the big granite rocks searching for snakes to kill. He had a beer sitting on a rock within reach. The boys knew he had more beer tied up in the water somewhere keeping it cool. They had found his remnants on occasion and had drunk the beer at their clubhouse.

Even though Caleb found a snake to kill on occasion, Randy and the boys felt Caleb came here to ogle the girls in their two piece bathing suits. They didn't fault him, they figured if they were his age they would probably do the same thing.

Delroy stood on the platform again and looked around as he waited for one of the younger children to clear the area in front of the platform. He saw Randy and the gang and waved.

He cupped his hands around his mouth and said, "Hey, Randy. Hey, guys. Are you coming in?"

"After we go to Mary Lamb's," Lee yelled back. He didn't want the cigarettes to be forgotten. Telling everyone at the pond that they were going to Mary Lamb's Country store however was a mistake. A cacophony of voices erupted from the water in the demand for something from the store.

"Bring me some licorice!"

"…Popsicle…cherry!"

"…A coke!"

"Bring me some chips!"

Lee smiled and waved. "Okay, okay, we'll be back soon with all the goodies."

The four boys laughed. Chances were slim anyone would receive anything at all from the store.

Before the boys remounted their bicycles, they saw the other Magurk sisters coming down the road heading for the pond. They could see someone else was with Mary Jo and Leigh Ann, but didn't recognize the face of the girl.

"Let's wait a minute," Randy said.

"Yeah, I'd like to see how well those bathing suits fit," Vern said.

Lee smiled and said, "You're a dog, Vern."

"Bark, bark, bark," Vern sounded, imitating a Hanna Barbara dog and the boys laughed. They all began to bark themselves.

"Good lord, that Mary Jo sure looks good," Randy said a little capriciously.

"Hold on boy, they got laws in this state," Lee added.

"Then let's run for office and change them," Randy said.

"Let's hurry up to Mary Lamb's so we can get back."

"Hold on cigarette breath. Jesus, Lee…what an addict," chided Vern. His attention fixed onto the new girl coming down the road.

"I just want to get back so I can go swimming is all."

"Alright…we'll go as soon as we say hello. Don't be so rude to something so lovely."

The three girls were within hearing distance, so the boys were more guarded in their comments. Mary Jo, Leigh Ann and the stranger walked up to the boys.

"Hello guys. Hi Randy, when did you get here?" Mary Jo asked acknowledging everyone but only looking at Randy.

"Today. Karen's with me."

"Good. Hi guys. I'm glad Karen's here. I've got a lot to tell her. Is she coming to the pond?" Leigh Ann asked.

"She'll be down in a little while. She's visiting with Rhoda."

"By the way-this is our cousin Corrine. She's from New York. She'll be here most of the summer."

"Hi, Corrine, my name is Randy…this is Lee, Vern and Picker."

"Picker?" Corrine asked with a puzzled sneer on her face.

"Well his real name is Earl, but everyone calls him Picker for whatever reason you choose. We hear his dad nicknamed him that because he was a keeper, but we think he had trouble keeping his fingers out of his nose," Lee said before Picker had a chance to respond. The boys laughed. The girls smiled.

"I understand you have a problem keeping your hand out of your pants, Lee. At least that's what your mom told my mom," Picker retorted.

Everyone laughed. "It makes me happy," Lee played along.

"Well it seems I heard a lot about you, Picker. You've got quite a reputation," Corrine stated bluntly. The people from Colmboro weren't quite that forward.

Picker blushed and said, "Well whatever the reputation is...I hope it's a good one."

"Oh...it's always nice to be known as a good kisser."

The three boys looked at Picker with surprise and admiration. This was quite a revelation. Picker knew the intense questioning that was to follow when the boys were on the way to Mary Lamb's Country store.

"Thank you." Picker quietly said and it came out with a slight crack in his voice.

Mary Jo walked over to Randy and stood directly in front of him. It made him feel quite nervous. He was about to say it was time to go to the store so he could be out of the uncomfortable situation he so desperately want to be in, but Mary Jo placed her hand on his as he gripped the rubber handle of the bicycle handlebar. He was self-conscious and his knees actually began to tremble.

"Randy, it's really nice to see you. Are you going to Walker's tonight?" Mary Jo asked a little coyly.

"Sure...I-I-I think so."

"Good maybe we can sit together."

"Okay," Randy said and Mary Jo removed her hand from Randy's hand and gave him a short, sweet smile.

Randy was sure someone had sucked all of the moisture from his mouth. It was so dry he could have drunk half of the pond to quench his thirst. His dream of being with Mary Jo Magurk seemed to be coming true and it came out of nowhere. Things sure do change in hurry when you're a teenager.

Lee and Vern were just as stunned by the turn of events. Picker and Randy were being sought after by girls and they wanted to be a part of it. Later they planned on grilling these two Casanovas to find out just what the hell they were missing. Lee figured it had something to with the party balloons, but he couldn't figure out the connection.

"Well, we'll see you when you come back from the store," Mary Jo said. "We'll be at the pond."

"Okay," Randy said. He was quite anxious to be on the move. He had a date with the girl of his dreams and he was scared to death. He didn't know how he was supposed to act. He didn't know whom to ask. He needed his Dad.

As the girls turned to walk down the little path that led the trail by the bridge, the boys watched the wiggle of their bottoms as they walked away. "Boys...you've got some splainin' to do," Lee said with an exaggerated Ricky Ricardo accent.

The ride to Mary Lamb's store was filled with questions and innuendo. Vern and Lee peppered Randy and Picker with interrogatives one after the other. Randy had no idea how to answer most of the questions, because he was at a loss as much as the two inquisitors -- Picker was effusive, answering with ambiguous and incomplete responses.

Finally they arrived at the store and the interrogation ended. Lee had other things on his mind he wanted his cigarettes.

"Vern...I want Marlboros in the box. Don't forget *in* the box. I don't want the soft pack."

"Okay give me some money."

"Right, I forgot."

Lee pulled money from his pocket and handed it to Vern. Vern took his wallet from his pocket to place the money inside of it, so as to appear normal when he purchased the smokes. Picker was watching the transaction when he saw the round ring indentation on Vern's wallet.

"Hey. What's that ring from?" Picker inquired.

"It's my lucky charm," Vern said.

"Lucky charm?"

"Yeah, if I ever get to use it, I sure will be lucky."

The boys laughed.

"Party balloon?" Lee asked rhetorically.

"Party balloon," Randy answered needlessly.

"Vern, I need to talk to you my friend. Perhaps we could work out a deal," Picker said.

"I'm all ears, Picker. But let me take care of little nicotine boy first."

The boys pulled the screen door open and walked into the store. The fragrant aroma of the store would make anyone's stomach growl. It was a delicious smell. The four boys walked directly to the cheese round and sampled a piece. The trip was worthwhile for the other three boys for a taste of the cheddar cheese.

"What can I do for you boys?" Mr. Lamb asked. He was standing near the pickle barrel rubbing his hands on his slightly soiled white bib apron.

"Uncle Pup asked me to pick him up some cigarettes," Vern said with a little too much conviction.

"Really?" Mr. Lamb inquired with a slight look of bewilderment on his face. This tensed up the group-especially Lee.

"Yes he needs a pack of Marlboros in the box," Vern said in a more relaxed manner.

"That's his brand. But he was here early this morning picking up some beef cuts for a party your Aunt's having. I thought I sold him cigarettes then."

"I don't know. Maybe he lost them. All I know is that he needs a pack."

"Okay, here you go. Be sure he gets 'em."

"Thank you, Mr. Lamb, I will."

The transaction was complete. The boys acted as nonchalant as they could and exited the store. They were on their bicycles and down the road before they spoke.

"Great. This is just great. He's going to tell Pup he sold you those cigarettes. I'm a goner," Lee said.

"Lee, you're one paranoid mother. I'll just tell Uncle Pup he asked me to get the cigarettes, when he's three-quarters through his brandy. He probably couldn't remember if he wanted to."

"Okay. Okay. Toss me them stogies." Lee was still a little unsure, but he wanted the cigarettes.

"For something that's so disgusting, it seems to me you go through a lot of trouble for those cigarettes," Randy said.

"I don't know. I enjoy them. Hold on a sec' while I light one up."

The boys stopped their bicycles while Lee opened the pack of Marlboros and lit up a cigarette. He took in a deep draw and blew out a smoke ring. He had recently learned to blow smoke rings and was constantly demonstrating his skill.

It was funny how the other boys had not picked up the habit. A great deal of the parents everywhere smoked cigarettes, but the foul taste and lightheadedness had never appealed to Randy, Picker or Vern. The fact was that all of their parents smoked. Lee's parents were the only ones who didn't smoke and Lee's dad was a crusader against smoking. Ruins lives he said. His mother had died of cancer when he was a young child.

Lee had signaled he was ready and the boys were about to renew their trek back to the pond, when the sound of a souped-up racing engine caught their ears. They looked in the direction of the noise and could see the grill of a metal flake blue GTO. They decided to wait on the side of the road until the car had passed by them.

Unfortunately the car did pass by, but halted its forward motion and reversed back to where the boys had stopped for Lee to light up his cigarette. There was very little breeze and the sun was pushing the heat down upon them. Randy moved his bike to the dirt because the macadam was too hot for his bare feet. He was apprehensive about the young men in the car.

He could see Sam Hammet in the shotgun seat. Arrington Debussy was driving. Everyone knew Arrington's car - it was the envy of the town. In the back of the car sat Kenny Moft and Bob Spitzer - two of the town's bad asses.

Sam Hammet was the eldest. He turned twenty last winter. The other three were about the same age and at least three or four years older than the three young men on their bicycles.

It's a peculiar thing the way nature works. All eight males knew one another and had grown up together in the same area. They had all been associated in and around Delton and Colmboro at different venues and activities. Be it at school, the pond, boy scouts, church or just plain hanging out, but for some reason, there was always seemed to be a conflict of personalities, which didn't allow everyone to be compatible. In some cases it is a one-on-one incompatibility, in other cases it is all against one.

In Sam Hammet's case, it was usually his disdain and lack of respect for others that caused his problems with other people. He fashioned himself a dominant personality and often worked his bullying tactics on the younger, easier manipulated members of the human race. Sam's attitude reflected his home life. His dad worked constantly and was away from home many days of the year driving his semi-truck across the states. When he was home, he dominated everyone with mental and far too often physical abuse. While Sam's father didn't overindulge in alcohol, it was a different matter for his mom. Unhappy in her marriage and divorce frowned upon; she stayed to keep house, but not a home. The bottles of vodka hidden around the house proved to be easy access for Sam and his siblings. Little respect in the family nucleus proved to transcend into Sam's flawed personality.

Arrington, Kenny and Bob were somewhat more apathetic to their reputations. They were basically boys who did what they felt like doing - consequences be damned. They didn't go out of their way to provoke trouble to prove how macho they were. There was no doubt, however; they weren't to be crossed if it could be helped. The boys had been in trouble with the law on an occasion or two and weren't particularly afraid of the police.

The three of them were playing out the summer. Within the next six months they would possibly be drafted into the military, if they didn't enlist first. It was a subject everyone talked about. Vietnam was a destination they spoke boldly of going to outwardly, but inwardly there was another thought process altogether. Sam Hammet had been drafted. His four F status only damaged his psyche more, because his peers teased him by stating he was afraid to go to Vietnam and had failed the physical on purpose.

Randy, Vern and Picker had little trouble with the occupants of the car for the most part. There were times in which some muscle had been applied to them but nothing out of the ordinary. Lee on the other hand was at the other end of the scale.

Sam Hammet was always picking on Lee. From the first time he was able to venture out and about the neighborhood, Lee was a target for Sam. To exacerbate the situation, at one time Sam had a crush on Lee's sister, Rhoda, and she had spurned him. Sam took this denial out on Lee.

All four boys wished that they had stayed at the store a moment longer or hadn't stopped to watch Lee fire up a cigarette. They felt they may have missed the carload of ne'er do wells on its journey of sure mischief.

Sam Hammet carried a belly a bit bigger than most males his age, mostly due to his massive consumption of beer. He felt his image was enhanced whenever he held a beer can in his hand. Beads of sweat formed on his forehead just below his dark brown crew cut hair. He leaned his head back on the seatback and said to Lee, "Hey, boy, give me those cigarettes."

Even though he was no match for Sam Hammet, Lee felt fairly brave sitting on his bicycle. He retorted with disdain. "I don't think so."

"How about if I get out of this car and take 'em?"

Lee remained silent not picking up Sam's challenge.

"I don't think he heard you, Sam," Bob Spitzer said egging Sam on.

"Sam, why don't you buy your own?" Vern asked.

"I'm not talking to you, Vern. Go take care of that drunk uncle of yours, you little nursemaid."

"Up yours, Sam!"

"Careful boy. You don't want none of this." Sam was trying to sound threatening.

"Aw go on, Vern, take some of it," Picker joined the conversation with a glint in his eye. He disliked everything Sam Hammet represented.

"Quiet, Picker," Randy whispered.

"Hey, Picker, what's the deal with that big mouth of yours? Trouble's coming your way to if you want it," Sam said turning his attention to Picker. "And what's the deal with that bathing suit you're sporting. Your sisters throw it away. Although I do think it shows off those skinny little bird legs of yours quite nicely."

"Bird legs?" Picker stated in mock indignation.

"Yeah…bird legs."

"Hmmm, Sam, I always thought you were an ornithologist. Now we can all be sure. You've just confirmed it for the world to hear," Picker said. He had a slight infuriating smirk on his face.

Sam glared at Picker. Before he could respond, Randy piped in, "No, Picker, I believe he's always been a philatelist."

The boys on the bicycles were now having a good time at Sam Hammet's expense. They had a feeling Sam wasn't going to cause too much trouble, because so far all he had been doing was talking big.

'No, I think he's a numismatist," Lee added.

Sam was extremely embarrassed, as his friends in the car laughed at the remarks by the boys and even repeated them to Sam. He became deeply angered. He was especially angry with Lee. He tossed his half-empty beer can at Lee, who ducked with ease.

"Missed, fat boy."

That was enough for Sam. It appeared that the boys had underestimated how far to go with kidding with Sam. He threw open the door and tried to jump out of the car and grab Lee at the same time. His mind worked quicker than his body. His beer belly and alcohol dulled brain did not work in unison and as he exited the car he stumbled badly and just missed falling to the ground. He caught the top of the car door with his hand and just barely managed to hold himself up.

Lee was off his bicycle and had run out into the cornfield directly behind him. The corn was about three feet high, so Sam could still see Lee. He cursed Lee profusely.

'I'll kick all your asses, you sons' of bitches!"

Picker and Vern had positioned themselves to haul ass into the field if necessary. Vern was itching to fight, but knew they had little chance against Sam and the three rogues in the car. Randy stayed on his bicycle waiting to see how the scenario played out. He felt he was far enough away from Sam to be able to avoid him.

Sam's three cohorts remained in the car. They were yelling encouragement to Sam.

"Beat his ass, Sam!"

"Show 'em who's boss, Sam!"

"Come here, Lee. Fight it out like a man you little pussy. I don't know who has the bigger pussy you or that ugly sister of yours."

"You're a sour grape eatin' asshole, fat boy," Lee yelled.

"I'm going to kill you, Lee. If you don't come here…I'm going to beat Picker's ass. How do you feel about that?" Vern was actually closer to Sam, but Sam was a little wary of Vern. Vern was quite volatile and had a look of anticipation on his face. He seemed to be waiting for Sam to call him out by name.

Lee responded to Sam's taunt, "I think Picker's ass needs a beating."

"Thanks a lot, Lee, but I don't want no fat boy touching my ass."

Sam was getting redder and redder. These boys were making him look like a fool in front of his cohorts. The boys in the car were razzing Sam unmercifully. He lunged at Picker, who along with Vern had dropped their bicycles. Sam was so angry that both boys headed out into the cornfield to join Lee. Randy was too far out of Sam's reach and stayed where he was for the moment. He would wait to see if he had to escape to the green field of corn with his pals.

"I'll tell you what, Lee… if you give me them smokes… I'll leave you and the boys alone." Sam was trying to think of a way to save face. He hoped Lee would take the offer.

"Can't do it, fat boy. Get your own."

"How 'bout if I take your bicycle, tough guy?"

"Don't touch my bike, I mean it. I'm warning you, Sam." Lee was getting pissed himself.

Sam laughed and moved over to Lee's prone bicycle. As he bent down to pick up the bicycle, a clod of dirt came whizzing through the air and hit Sam Hammet square on the head, causing a puff of dust to appear around Sam's head. He staggered backwards and the boys could see a gray mark on his forehead where the dirt clod had struck him. Everyone laughed with the exception of Sam Hammet.

"He warned you, Sam." The guys in the car were laughing hysterically.

"That's it." Sam began to stomp the spokes out of Lee's bicycle wheels. He jammed his foot down two times extremely hard bending the spokes in the front wheel.

"Hey cut it out, fat boy," Lee exclaimed.

"Why don't you leave us alone, Sam," Randy yelled. "Pick on someone your own age and size or are you too scared to, you four effer."

"Yeah four effer," the boys in the field chimed in.

Randy peered out into the field and saw Lee running up to the road with Vern and Picker. He guessed it was time to stand up to this bully, but he feared it was going to be a whipping he would not enjoy. He dismounted his bicycle to prepare for the fight.

Sam had moved toward Randy as he was hopping off his bicycle and grabbed Randy by the shirt and lifted him off the ground. The only good thing about the situation was that at least Sam was alone. The other guys had stayed in the car for the time being, drinking and shouting encouragement to Sam.

"Your mouth is a little bit too big for my taste, dog boy. You should've run away like your sissy little friends."

"Man is your breath bad. Don't you know it's a little too early to be drinking beer?" Randy figured he was going to be pounded, so why not say what he felt. "Why don't you try and fight someone your own age… or are you afraid you can't beat up anyone who can't drive yet?"

Sam pulled Randy tighter to his face and blew his breath into Randy's face. Then he threw him down to the ground. Vern, Lee and Picker were about to reach Sam and Randy, when the doors of the car had clicked open and the three occupants removed themselves from the vehicle.

Sam bent down with a clenched fist he held ready to pound Randy in the face. As Randy was pushing himself up from the ground, Sam Hammet swung his meaty fist at Randy's head with a roundabout haymaker. Unfortunately for Sam, he had mistimed the swing a little too early. Randy had anticipated the swing and held himself low enough to avoid the impact of Sam's fist. The momentum of Sam's swing turned him into a giant corpulent windmill, rotating him in an awkward comical circle. Everyone was laughing again and Sam was steaming like a superheated teapot.

He managed to grab Randy again from behind and held him tightly, pinning Randy's arms at his sides. Randy was cursing Sam to let him go. The onlookers were shouting encouragement to their respective combatants. Sam squeezed Randy so hard, Randy felt as though he was going to puke.

"What are you going to say now big mouth?" Sam was so mad he was shouting through clenched teeth. He closed his grasp on Randy even tighter.

Randy couldn't breathe at all with Sam squeezing the breath from his lungs, so he offered little in response other than a grunt.

"You haven't forgotten his cousin is Dennis Wilts, have you, fat boy?" Picker shouted from about an arm's length away. He wanted to join the fray, but he knew as well as the other boys, that if they did touch Sam at this point, it would have turned into a free for all and they wouldn't be on the winning end. "I would suspect Dennis wouldn't like anyone beating up on his cousin. Especially someone so much older."

The words spoken by Picker rang a definite bell with Sam Hammet and his crew. Dennis Wilts was about the meanest, baddest and most unforgiving young man in the county, let alone the two towns in the area. He had fought his way through life and as skilled at street fighting as anyone was at professional fighting. It was common knowledge that Dennis had little mercy for anyone who had the audacity to pick on his family members or friends.

Sam had felt that fury once before when he had punched Dennis' little brother Ricky. Fact was, Sam's parents had had Dennis arrested for the beating Dennis gave Sam for the indiscretion. The charges were later dropped and Dennis didn't retaliate for the arrest, but warned Sam not to cross the line again. It appeared that it might be too late for Sam had forgotten that Randy was Dennis' cousin.

Sam waited a face saving second or too as he contemplated his possible predicament and then dropped Randy to the ground. Dust from the packed earth billowed around him. Randy gathered himself and his breath. It felt good to out of Sam's grasp and to fill his lungs with fresh air.

"I don't need my cousin to fight my fights," he said. His hands were balled into fists, but he made no effort to strike or attack Sam.

The interjection of Dennis Wilts into the fracas put a damper on the fun for the antagonists from the car. "C'mon Sam…let's get going. Let's leave these panty wastes here to play with themselves," Bob Spitzer said. He winked at Randy as if the whole incident had been a big joke.

"You little ones ought to watch who you get smart with. If it had been someone other than us you might've really have gotten your asses beat,' Sam said with a fake forced chuckle.

"Nice try, fat boy," Lee said. "I hope Randy tells his cousin. Then we'll see your fat bully ass put in its place. What a "D" you are."

Sam glared at Lee. He kept his mouth quiet. He wanted to let the incident die. He was pretty pissed at Randy and Lee and he wanted to make them pay for his embarrassment, but he didn't know how quite yet. It would have to be pretty subtle where Randy was concerned. Lee would be a much easier target.

The four young men piled back into the car. Sam Hammet threw another empty beer can out of the window in Lee's direction. Each of the four occupants of the car opened a new beer and Arrington Debussy fired up the car. He held the brake and stomped the gas, spilling rocks and dirt everywhere. They took off in a flash as he released the brake, squealing their tires on the hot asphalt as the rubber tires struck the road. Blue smoke lingered in the air. The boys could smell the stench of the burned rubber from the tires.

The car fishtailed until the tires achieved the proper traction and contact on the blacktop. The squealing tires had made a hell of a noise and it appeared Arrington may lose control for a moment, but he straighten it out before the car went off onto the soft shoulder of the other side of the road.

The stray dog Randy had seen earlier down by the creek was standing in the road a few yards down from the spot where the boys stood with their bicycles. Randy saw the dog and a surge of panic grabbed him, as it appeared the GTO would run over the dog. It seemed like Arrington and his crew was aiming to intentionally kill the dog. The stray dog stood wide-eyed like a deer staring into headlights as the careening car closed the distance towards it.

Randy could see Sam Hammet raise his hand in a one-finger salute off his beer can. The dog would have no chance to escape the beer-drinking morons.

"No! LOOK OUT!" Randy shouted. He waited and hoped for the brake lights to light up on the rear of the GTO. No such luck. The demented knuckleheads in the car were determined to kill the friendly little dog that had saved Randy from the crazed cats.

Or so they thought. Just as the car was about to smash the dog with the right front tire, the dog with what seemed to be a great deal of calm, leapt sideways away from the car onto the shoulder of the road, out of harm's way. He turned his head to follow the path of the car as if he wanted to be sure it would not return to try to end his life again. Confident that the car was gone, he trotted down to Randy, who bent to hug and pet the marvelous little wonder dog he had named Pony.

Chapter 8

Randy was down on one knee petting the multicolored dog, while the other three boys stood around in a semi-circle. They all had one eye on the dog and the other eye watching the blue GTO's red rear taillights drift down the road through the wavy heat vapor emanating from the asphalt road.

"Whose dog is this?" Randy asked

"Don't know," Picker answered first.

"Me neither," Lee said. Vern shrugged. The dog's owner was a mystery. Someone may have just dropped the dog off, because they no longer wanted to care for it.

"Seems like a nice dog," Picker stated.

"He saved me from that mad cat earlier down by the fishing place…so you guys ain't never seen him before, huh?"

"Nope. Not until today," Picker said. The other two boys nodded in agreement. "You should just as well take him to Carrie's house and add him to the collection. One more is not going to hurt anything."

"I guess you're right. He's already met Bessie. They sort of got along."

"Well, I think we should find Dennis and have him beat that fat ass Sam Hammet to a pulp. Dick head bully. What a "D"."

"As much as I would like to have his butt kicked, I don't think I should involve Dennis, Lee. He gets himself into enough trouble without me helping. I'm sure Aunt Sherry wouldn't appreciate me getting Dennis in jail again."

"Dammit…someone's got to show that fat, boy bully he should pick on someone his own age and size!"

"That's what makes him a bully," Vern interjected.

"Yeah, he'll get his own someday and I hope I'm around to see it," Lee said disgustedly. "And if I'm there, I'm going to kick him when he's down."

The boys turned to retrieve their bicycles. Pony stood peering at them, waiting to join the boys on their journey back to the pond.

His tongue was hanging out and he panted heavily suffering from the hot summer sun.

Lee paused to light up a cigarette before he sat on his bicycle seat. Sam Hammet had bent the rear wheel of his bicycle. Lee looked back at the wheel and rolled forward to see if the bicycle was rideable. The tire rubbed the brace that held the wheel's axle. It produced a very audible squeaking noise with each revolution. The bicycle wobbled as Lee pedaled forward, but it held up and he felt as though he could ride it back to the pond and then to his house.

"What an asshole…have you guys ever seen a bigger jerk than that fat ass Hammet? Because my sister thinks he's a creep, that elephant turd has picked on me forever. Man 'o' man."

"Well if it's any consolation, that dirt chunk you hit him with was pretty damn funny," Randy said with a chuckle. Then all the boys laughed at the image of the dirt mark left on Sam's head.

"Too bad I didn't knock him out."

"That would have been even funnier," Picker laughed.

"Christ, he nearly made me pass out when he was squeezing me so hard. Maybe I should go to Dennis and have him kick his ass. Nah! Aunt Sherry would kill me. Sam Hammet will get his one own day and with his attitude I don't think it's a long time coming." Randy nodded his head after speaking as if to confirm it to himself.

The boys bantered on their way back to the pond. They moved slowly because Lee's bicycle rolled like a shopping cart with a defective wheel. He had tried to straighten it out, but the spokes were too far bent and he was afraid bending them back all the way just may break them altogether.

As they approached the well-populated swimming hole, the boys swung their bicycles across the road and stacked them by a huge weeping willow tree down on the bank. Randy and his friends could see the beautiful, well-formed figure of a girl standing atop the diving platform. Randy was awestruck with the bikini-clad vision of his love. He was so enthralled he didn't hear the lewd comments his associates were muttering under their breaths about the girl.

He watched her leap into the air from the platform, execute a perfect jack-knife dive and cleanly break the surface of the water with very little splash. People in and around the pond were hooting and hollering about how well Mary Jo Magurk had dove into the water.

"C'mon, let's get over there. I've got to see this up close. Where in the hell did that body come from and why has she been hiding it." Vern thought out loud. His comments energized the boys and they ran over the bridge, which led down to the swimming area.

Randy stopped to pull a sand spur from his heel. When he stopped Pony stopped with him, but his friends continued on down to the bank. They stripped off their shirts; all but Picker who didn't have one on and they dove into the water from the grassy shore.

The water was tinted brown from the tannic acid and cold. The heated air and their slow ride from the store on the hot asphalt had warmed their bodies. The splash into the water took away their breaths and made them gasp. The boys squawked about how cold the water was on their bodies. They swam around, ducked their heads under water and tried to locate a warm eddy to tread water in until they became acclimated to the temperature of the pond.

Randy stood on the grassy shore. "Is it cold?" he asked with a laugh. He had an eye on Mary Jo as he edged closer to the water line.

"Not at all you little sissy, city boy. C'mon in," Vern said.

The sissy comment embarrassed Randy. He didn't want Mary Jo to know he had faults. But he didn't want to overreact to the comment either, and look like a jerk.

"Sissy? Sissy? Why I could out swim and out dive you any day, Vern," Randy shouted in retort.

"You're on. In fact I'll dive first to show you how it's done," Vern shouted back.

Randy knew Vern was a good diver. It was up to him to do his best and to not look foolish. Mary Jo swam up to where Randy was standing and treaded water in front of him. She smiled a coquettish smile. She had heard his dare to Vern along with the rest of the kids in and around the pond. Randy looked down at her and returned the smile a bit weakly. He had numerous witty comments running through his mind that he wished he could say to her to demonstrate his coolness.

Unfortunately Randy blurted out, "Is the water wet?" He had meant to say "*Was the water cold?*" He was unaware of what he had really said.

Mary Jo looked at him with puzzlement, "What do you mean, *is it wet?*"

"What do *you* mean? I asked was the water cold?" Randy could see the same pursed lips and furrowed brow mirrored on Mary Jo's face. "Oh, never mind!" He was embarrassed. His knees were like Jell-O and he felt as though if he didn't get into the water he would fall down on the spot.

Taking control of the situation, Mary Jo swam up to Randy and said, "I know you can beat Vern diving, Randy. I've seen you dive. You're the best diver at the pond." With that said Mary Jo pushed herself out of the water and rolled her body over into a shallow dive under the water and swam away from him.

"Thanks," Randy croaked weakly. His ego hugely boosted as he watched her bikini-clad bottom and then her feet disappear under the water with his smiling eyes. The cool water was a pleasant contrast to the warm flush he felt on his body.

"Yo, Randy, better pay attention over here. That young filly ain't going to help you beat this dive."

Randy turned to the voice and saw Vern atop the diving platform. He could see Scarnose peering up at Vern. Scarnose was probably coaching Vern on how he should structure his dive. Randy would receive the same treatment, but he wished Scarnose would just stay in the rocks hunting snakes on the other side of the dam wall. Randy used to like that man until the church had burned down, now he could barely tolerate his presence.

Randy ducked his head under the water to refresh himself; treading water he wiped his hair from his eyes. The group of people in the pond aging from young children to early adulthood had formed a semi-circle out about twenty feet from the diving platform waiting for the diving competition to begin.

"Well, let's get that belly flop over with, Vern. Give the people your best dive, because I'm coming over there to show everyone how it's done. I hope you don't embarrass easily."

"Can't scare me, city boy. I've been diving since I swam from my momma's womb. Fact is, my dad tells me I almost dove from the doctor's hands when he whacked me on the ass to make me cry."

"I think the doctor dropped you on your head and your daddy didn't tell you, Vern," Lee interjected. Everyone was laughing and shouting from the pond.

"Very funny, you cigarette smoking, black lunged weenie boy. When I'm finished teaching that city boy a diving lesson, I'm going to show you how it feels to be dunked underwater until you feel like a fish."

"You can't swim any better than you can dive," Lee laughed. "C'mon Randy, show this braggadocio how a real man dives."

The crowd turned on Vern in a mocking chant. "Randy! Randy! Randy! Randy!"

Vern held up his hand to try and silence the crowd. They cheered even louder for Randy. "Randy! Randy! Randy!"

Vern stood on the end of the rust colored metal platform. He eyed the moving water below. The crowd noise died down as they watched Vern concentrate on his dive. The water cascading over the top of the milldam was the only sound in the area. Vern stretched his hands into the air with ease and grace. It seemed as though he used a springboard from the height he garnered on his leap. He arched his back, threw his arms out wide with his fingers spread. When he reached the apex of his ascent, his legs drew together with his feet and toes pointed backward. The swan dive was a sight to behold. Vern's muscular athletic body was a picture or true grace and perfect form as he headed down toward the water. The entry was perfect and the crowd in and around the pond responded with great enthusiasm. Vern had pumped the adrenaline from his dive into the psyche of the gathered children in the water.

Randy knew his work was cut out for him. He made the short swim up to the metal rungs, which served as a ladder to the platform. The water being pulled over the top of the dam provided an easy trip as the current aided his journey. When Vern had surfaced from the water, he pointed at Randy and Randy could see the supreme look of confidence on Vern's face. Randy smiled back at Vern and winked at him, nodded and said nothing. That dive had been a beauty.

As Randy ascended the ladder, he could hear all kinds of chatter coming from the pond.

"Great dive, Vern!"

"Top that, Randy."

"Come on, Randy. You can do it!"

"Randy!"

"Randy!" The chant began to swell.

"Vern!" Others began to counter. "Vern!"

Randy stood atop the platform. He could see Mary Jo's cousin Corrine had swam up to Vern and was speaking to him. She was very close to him as he treaded water. Even from that distance, Randy could see that Vern was blushing.

Caleb Fulton had moved over to the base of the ladder where it was sunk into the rocks by the milldam. He held on tightly as the water tugged at him, trying to pull him over the dam. "Do the jack knife I taught you, Randy," Caleb said. He had placed his snake-hunting stick down and was watching the competition of his two prized diving pupils.

Randy had mixed emotions about this man. Caleb "Scarnose" Fulton had taught the boys many great outdoor skills. He really looked out for the community to keep it safe and clean. But Randy felt deep down in his heart that Scarnose had burnt down the Negro Gospel Church and Randy didn't believe he could ever forgive the man.

"You coach Vern to that swan?"

"It's his best dive, like the jack knife is yours. You've got a lovely little girl waiting for you to sparkle...don't disappoint her. Concentrate on what you're doing and make me proud."

"I'll do it for myself. I don't need to make you proud,' Randy said harshly.

Caleb's face remained stoic. "Well...don't let me distract you. I'm only trying to help."

Randy felt a pang of regret. He knew he had hurt Caleb's feelings and he was angry with himself for feeling sorry for this man, but he couldn't help it. "I'll do it like you taught me, but if I mess up... maybe it's because of your teaching methods," Randy said lessening his hard tone.

Caleb nodded and smiled.

A cacophony mixture of voices and sounds emanated from the pond's surface. Randy moved to the end of the platform and did his best Olympic dive greeting. He stood with his toes on the end of the platform, feet and legs together, arched his back with his arms raised high above his head. The crowd quieted down as he prepared himself for the dive. He glanced around the pond in search of Mary Jo, but decided not to make eye contact with her. He was too nervous already. If he met eyes with her it may have increased his anxiety. He really wanted to impress her with his skill at diving.

Randy closed his eyes to concentrate. He carried through the whole dive pictured in his mind the way he was taught by Caleb Fulton. Randy took a deep breath, exhaled the air and opened his eyes. He was mentally steeled to perform his best jack knife dive.

Randy raised and lowered his arms, while pushing himself off the diving platform with a fluid knee bending motion. He sprang into the air, reached his apex, seemingly holding the position in the air effortlessly before he bent over double to touch his toes with his fingertips. He opened up on the way down, throwing his legs high in the air vertical to the water's surface. His body was a straight line as he broke the plane of the water, like an aquatic bird diving deftly, effortlessly to capture a fish for that day feeding.

Randy could hear the cheers from the people at the pond as he made his way to the surface of the water. He emerged from the water to see everyone clapping, hooting and cheering his performance. Mary Jo Magurk was beaming with pride as she swam over to where he was watching the group. Randy was elated, but tried to remain calm, keeping an aloof, and no big deal attitude about him. He returned the point of the finger to Vern, who was motioning with his eyes over to Corrine. Randy fully understood the feeling of excitement as Mary Jo tread water next to him. The dives really took a second place for excitement when compared to the jolt of pleasure the girls were providing by their presence. Being teenage boys was a marvelous wonderment on this fine warm summer day.

"Great dive, Randy...I'm glad you chose the jack knife. That's my favorite dive to do as well. I'm glad you did it for me."

Randy was baffled for a moment. What the hell he thought, I'll take a little credit for some serendipity. "Well I saw you doing one when I rode up, so I figured I would do one too," he said somewhat unsure. But Mary Jo seemed not to notice his small white lie demeanor.

"I'm going to dive again. You want to swim over with me?" Mary Jo queried with a sparkle in her eyes.

"Sure," Randy replied. "Let's do it." He was swimming on cloud nine.

By the time the duo reached the platform ladder, a line had formed and everyone was jostling for a position in line for his or her turn to take a dive. Everyone was chatting, splashing and cavorting in the water. Randy looked out at Caleb Fulton who feigned to be searching for snakes in the rocks. Caleb stopped and picked up his beer can to refresh himself. He glanced in Randy's direction, but Randy averted his gaze. Randy was grateful to Caleb; however, he couldn't forgive the man for the past. Caleb placed his can down on the rock he had removed it from and continued his snake finding search.

The pond was full for about two hours, and then it started to thin out, as people left to go home little by little. The Magurk girls had left with their cousin. Mary Jo was going to meet Randy at the movies. Vern had secured a date with Corrine. Picker was secretive about his plans and Lee seemed to be the odd man out.

Karen stood on the bridge across the creek above the milldam overlooking the pond. She was going back to Aunt Carrie's house and was walking back with Ronda and her sister. "Randy, you going back with us?" she asked.

"No, I'll go back with the boys."

"Well don't be too long. We'll have to get Aunt Carrie going early if were going into town tonight. You know she won't let us ride with anyone else. I don't want to be really late."

"Okay…just a bit more and I'll be at home. Get dinner started, woman."

"Aunt Carrie wants to barbecue. So you're the designated burger boy. If you're lucky I'll start the coals providing Uncle Harvey hasn't started them already. Let's not be late, pud puller…sweet Mary Jo may end up sitting with someone else at the movies."

Randy was embarrassed by his sister's openly discussing his date with Mary Jo. Karen wasn't one to feel inhibited by other people. She spoke her mind and she wasn't afraid to back up her thoughts if the need arose to do so.

"Beat it, Sis. I didn't forget you have a hot little number waiting for you as well."

As the girls laughed and turned away, the blue GTO came up the road and pulled up beside Karen, Lee's sisters, Rhoda and Carol. The girls continued to walk and the car rolled gently beside them. Randy could see his sister stop and place her hands on her hips. He could tell from her body language that she was becoming agitated. Randy couldn't hear the conversation from here he was in the water. He could see Caleb 'Scarnose' Fulton climb up on the rocks toward the road beside the bridge.

The car stopped on the road. Randy and the boys swam to shore and raced up the bank to the other end of the bridge. With no towels they wiped the water from their faces and pushed their hair back to stop the water from dripping down into their eyes.

"…better watch that foul mouth of yours," Randy heard his sister bark. The boys in the car were laughing.

Sam Hammet opened his door and got out of the car. With his beer in his hand he rested his upper torso on the top of the car. "Aw, come on, Karen, you know I didn't mean nothing by it. I just think maybe me and you could be buddies. You know, friends are friends, pals are pals, but buddies sleep together."

The boys in the car laughed again at Sam's crude humor. Randy could see Sam, Bob, Arrington and Kenny hadn't been too far from their beer. He was surprised Sam could stand up the way he sounded and staggered. Randy was awful glad his sister and friends hadn't been caught walking alone by these testosterone-laden drunk young men. He could see the way they ogled the girl's bodies that they had an obtuse view of just what they wanted to do to the girls. The look of wild dogs who had cornered prey and were about to savage it for their pleasure.

"Why don't you boys move along and sober up somewhere before you get yourselves into some trouble."

Caleb Fulton stood on the side of the road. He had his snake chasing stick in his hand. His voice had come across firm and loud. The authority it carried placed a damper on the attitude of the GTO's occupants. The momentum swung to the girls and the boys who stood on the side of the road.

"Caleb, we're only having a little fun…who made you our father? You're only my cousin and second cousin at that. I don't think that gives you bossin' rights out here in public," Sam challenged.

Caleb sighed and glared at Sam, who shrank from the glare. Caleb then said to Bob, "Bob, you and Arrington know better than to let that fat loud mouth do your talking. Tell him to get in the car and then you boys go on home and sober up a bit. Arrington, I'll call you later." With that, Caleb swung his stick up over onto his shoulder. He looked Arrington straight in the eyes and Arrington nodded an almost imperceptible nod.

"Sammy, get in the car," Bob said with no room for argument. Knowing that there was no need to bicker Sam looked around at everyone. This was the second time today he had been humbled.

He moved his head around and glared at everyone, his gaze stopping at Randy.

"This is your fault, Dog Boy. Your time is coming," Sam said cryptically.

"Screw off, Fat Boy," Lee retorted.

"Quiet, Lee," Caleb scolded.

Sam feint a move toward Lee, who stood his ground. He was a good twenty feet from Sam on the other side of the car. He could easily elude Sam if he had to. Sam reentered the car. The GTO roared down the road, spinning its tires in quite a powerful flashy show. Randy wondered what the devil Sam was talking about with his comment. He brushed it off to a drunk and tried not to let bother him.

"What a D," Randy said.

"Yeah, what a D," Vern and Lee added.

"More like a Jackass," Karen said. "Thanks, Caleb."

"No problem. You guys want a ride home in my pick up?"

Everyone agreed to take the ride. The picked up their bicycles and placed them in the truck bed of the white rusty Chevy. Karen, Rhoda and Carol sat in the cab waiting for Caleb.

As the boys were climbing into the bed of the truck, Randy noticed Pony lying down on the bank. The dog was watching Randy intently, his tail wagging ferociously.

"Hey, Caleb. You know who owns that dog?" Randy asked.

"Nope...but I saw him over at the Foster house the other day"

The hairs stood out on Randy's arm with Caleb mentioning the Foster name. "What were you doing over there? Randy asked.

"Not that it's any of your business, but I was fishing at the creek. You know that old shack isn't far from my trailer." Caleb said somewhat defensively.

That was true. Randy still didn't like the idea, but there was no way he could stop Caleb from being in the area.

After a pause in the conversation, Randy asked, "Do you mind if the dog rides with us?"

"Don't tell me you're going to get Harvey to keep that mutt?"

"Why not?"

"Damn boy - people are pissed enough with all those dogs they have now. Those freaking puppies lie in the road now and cars are dodging them all day. That furry posse that surrounds the house is starting to become a menace in some people's eyes. People think they're up to no good at night...killing chickens and small animals."

"That's my Uncle's and Aunt's business not yours."

Caleb nodded a knowing nod and peered down at the dog. He pursed his lips and thought over the situation. "Hell then...go and keep the mutt. Seems to me you should speak to Harvey about thinning out that dog herd instead of adding to it though."

Randy ignored Caleb's comment. He motioned to Pony with a wave of his hand. "Come on, Pony."

The dog was elated. He jumped up and raced over to the truck. He leapt from the ground up and over the open tailgate of the truck. Randy rubbed the dog's head and the dog lay in Randy's lap. Caleb started the truck and took his passengers home.

Chapter 9

"I want you two to wait outside of the theater for Harvey to come and get you. Don't ride home with anyone else."

"Aunt Caroline, how many times do we have to hear that same warning? We always wait-no matter how long it takes for Uncle Harvey to come and get us," Karen replied.

"What's that supposed to mean? I come just as soon as you call me," Harvey said.

Everyone laughed but Harvey. "Well, you come as soon as Aunt Carrie wakes you two or three times."

"Alright, alright…that's enough. It's not easy getting up at 4:30 every morning, trying to stay awake until those movies end."

"That's why you should let us find a ride home. We could ride home with the Magurks, which would make my pud-pounding brother happy."

"Caroline, tell her about that language of hers, would you?" Harvey said piously.

Giggling, Carrie said, "She heard you. Karen, behave yourself."

"What'd I say?" Karen asked feigning ignorance.

Randy grabbed his sister's leg just behind the kneecap and squeezed, sending her into a tickled convulsion. "Say uncle."

"Uncle…uncle…uncle!"

"Not good enough. Say you're sorry about calling me names."

"No way," Karen shouted. She was laughing and squirming, but she couldn't break her brother's grasp.

The backseat of the car was boiling with laughter, shouts and screams. Carrie was laughing so hard; she was about to wet her pants.

"Cut it out you kids…I'm trying to drive."

"All she has to do is to say she's sorry, Uncle."

"I can't stand it…he's killing me. HELP! HELP!" Karen was pretending to cry between fits of laughter.

"Randy, stop…you're going to make me pee my pants," Carrie implored her nephew.

"Randy, if your Aunt wets that seat…you'll clean it up," Harvey said sternly.

"What will be, will be. Say it…say you're sorry you little tart."

"Okay, okay. I'm sorry," Karen said capitulating.

"Good…I win. I'm the king." Randy crowed.

"I'm sorry. I'm sorry you're a pud-pulling brother."

"That did it," Randy said. He tried to attack again, but this time his sister was ready. She fended off his repeated attempts to grab her lower thigh. Randy gave up and Karen moved closer to the door away from him.

Randy rested his head back while he watched Karen through almost closed eyes. He was waiting for a chance to catch her off guard, but she wasn't to be fooled after so many years of tussling with her brother.

"I guess I'm lucky your boyfriend Pup's not here. If he hadn't left so suddenly, he would have probably beat my ass for touching you."

"Very funny. Perhaps I should have a talk with Leigh Ann and fill her in on things you would like to do to her younger sister."

"Enough o'sister of mine. You fight dirty."

"Whatever it takes to win."

"Aunt Carrie, why do you let Pup hang around with you guys? That man is nothing but a drunk?" Randy inquired.

"He's not always been that way. He was a nice young man when we were your age. Pup's had a hard life."

"Hard life? The man's rich. His daddy was rich. He's never wanted for anything his whole life…except maybe to be away from that old stuck-up witch of a wife of his," Randy said.

"Randy, be nice. Arleen's a good woman, by golly," Harvey interjected.

"Good for nothing but interfering," Karen whispered, causing Randy to laugh.

Caroline continued, "He may be rich, but his family treated him badly as a child. His dad was real strict and didn't spare the rod. When Pup was old enough to take over the farm, his dad put it into a trust so no one could sell it and keep the money. Pup's sister, Joleen, hasn't forgiven her parents to this day. Fact is, I don't believe

Rick Milone

she let her parents see their grandson Vern more than a few times before they passed away.

"If the farm is sold, the money goes to charity. But if it does well, Pup and his sister split the profits, even though they both have trust funds. Arleen controls the money made from the farm, so Pup lives off his monthly trust stipend."

"Good thing…otherwise he would drink up all the money," Karen spat.

"Nah…he's got an endless supply. He makes his own peach brandy in that old shed down by the quarry," Randy said.

"Stay away from the quarry boy…it's dangerous," Harvey said. He looked at Randy through the rearview mirror to emphasize the point.

Randy ignored his Uncle's comment and broke eye contact with him after a slight look down. He couldn't stay away from the quarry; it was too much fun. Sometimes the boys would meet there and sample some of Pup's homemade brew. It was strong and tasted foul, but the boys sipped a bit on occasion anyway.

Picker was at his absolute funniest when he had a few drinks of the stuff. The only problem was the notorious headache a few hours after. That alone limited the boys to their forays to the shed and its contents.

Changing the subject from the quarry, Randy asked, "Is Pup really going to cook those steaks for his guests like he said?"

"I doubt it. Arleen hired a barbecue chef to do it. Far as I know, Pup couldn't cook a lick. Besides the way he was feeling when he left, I doubt Arleen would let him near an open fire. He might burn the farm down."

"He probably left because he needed to refill his Mason jar," Karen said.

"No doubt…Karen…no doubt."

"I think he left because he knew his comment about adding Pony to the pack was mean…Aunt Carrie you really told him something," Randy said boldly. He knew Caroline and Harvey wouldn't say as much, but they were upset that Pup had suggested they eliminate some of their dog menagerie.

86

The car fell silent. Karen reached over and nudged Randy. When he looked over, Karen gave him a face, meaning he should drop the subject. She knew the two of them were upset over the fact that Arleen had not invited them to dinner. The Kearney's were starting to feel ostracized by their immediate neighbors, but they wouldn't bow to the pressure of thinning out the family of dogs.

Randy made a face back at Karen, but held his tongue.

Harvey pulled the car into the Tastee-Freeze parking lot and the two kids opened the doors and jumped out to take the walk up to the movie house. Harvey and Caroline would have an ice cream sundae, return home and wait for their niece and nephew to call them for the ride home.

"You have enough money?" Aunt Carrie asked from the rolled down window.

"Yes, ma'am," they replied together.

"Jinx you owe me a coke. Stop. One, two, three," Karen blurted.

"Stop!" Randy shouted as fast as he could.

"You owe me three cokes," His sister said.

"As long as I owe you I won't cheat you out of them," he replied.

"Why Randy, I didn't think you were such a quick-witted guy."

"Let's go, Fat Bottom, we've got a long walk." Randy turned to the car and said, "We'll call when the movies over."

"Wait, what about my hug and kiss?" their Aunt asked.

"Aw, Aunt Caroline. Here in public?" Randy asked with a sense of dread.

Karen stooped to kiss her aunt and gave her a slight hug through the window. With a big smile, she stepped back and motioned to Randy that it was his turn. Caroline held out her arms and wiggled her fingers for Randy to come closer. Playfully grimacing Randy walked over to the car to accommodate his Aunt. Randy looked both ways in dramatic fashion to see if anyone was watching. Seeing no one he knew, Randy pretended to wipe imaginary sweat from his brow causing his sister and aunt to laugh. He bent over and kissed his aunt.

"Okay, Harve, it's your turn," Randy stated with a resolve.

"Go on get out of here you, scamp you," Harvey said slightly embarrassed. "Caroline, I'm telling you that boy ain't right, by golly." He laughed his stilted laugh.

"Bye. We'll call." With that said, Karen and Randy began to walk up the hill to the drawbridge, which spanned the Downing River.

The sidewalk was wide enough for the two of them to walk side-by-side up the somewhat steep hill. The pavement was in a mild state of disrepair, cracked here and there with sprouts of grass popping up through breaks in the concrete as well as through the expansion cracks placed purposely in the sidewalk to prevent it from buckling in the summer heat. The twilight air was cooling down from the hot temperature the summer sun had heated it to. A slight breeze blew over the siblings as they leaned forward trudging up the hill toward the bridge.

The first thirty feet or so there was little conversation as they saved their breath for the climb. Cars whizzed past them, honking occasionally as friends and acquaintances recognized the pair during their short trek. Karen could hear the hum of the rubber tires change tone as they bit into the steel mesh grate, which served as the base of the drawbridge just ahead of them.

She dreaded the walk across the bridge. She hated the feeling of falling through the bridge down into the water.

Even though she knew how to swim, she couldn't escape her paranoia of the bridge. She hated all bridges. She was so happy when the county had changed the bridge, which led to Brooksville from a one-lane suspension bridge to a stationary two-lane hill style span over the creek. Randy had had more fun with her over her fear of the bridge. He had scared the daylights out of her many a time on the one lane wooden bridge from hell.

Rustic was how he described the old creaky swaying bridge, Terrifying was how his sister felt.

Stepping from the concrete sidewalk onto the steel mesh grate, Karen held onto the steel green wall, which separated the cars from the pedestrians. She had tried it both ways, walking on the inside by the metal wall and by walking on the outside closer to the bridges edge, which was also protected by a thin wall of riveted steel- inside was better, she hated the view over the side of the bridge. Karen wanted to keep Randy talking about something, so that he wouldn't tease her, but she knew it would not be an easy task. He lived to tease her.

"Do you think I'm pretty?" Karen asked maintaining her focused view of the sidewalk some twenty feet or so at the end of the bridge. Karen knew her brother hated these types of questions. She knew he would want to tease her but he wouldn't want to hurt her feelings either.

Randy peered at his sister. Her shoulder brown highlighted hair was ruffling slightly by the breeze. She had an olive complexion and big soft brown eyes. She wasn't skinny, but she wasn't fat. Her ample bosom made her appear a bit shorter than she was in reality. He knew she was attractive and she didn't lack for suitors. He didn't feel his sister felt insecure about herself- at least not at this moment. Occasionally in the past she had felt a little less secure about her looks, this time he figured correctly wasn't one of those times. He calculated that she had an ulterior motive.

"As a matter of fact, I think you're beautiful. Hold it a minute… no wait. I want to see your beauty with the river in the background." Randy said as he tried to grab his sister's hand to stop her.

Karen pulled away from him. She continued to walk knowing he had found her out. She would kill him on the other side of the bridge.

"Sis…sis, come here," He said not holding back his glee at scaring her.

"Stop it, fool!" Karen had begun to titter a little herself.

Randy grabbed at her once more, but Karen avoided his touch just as he reached out. They were about five feet from the edge of the walk. Thinking he had judged his attempt at a grab perfectly, Randy didn't compensate for an inaccurate move. He lost his balance and did a complete somersault on the metal floor grate. There was a decided loud rip of material.

Randy sat on the grate. Both he and Karen were laughing hysterically. Karen was holding her side because she was laughing so hard. Randy looked down at his pants while he was bent over with laughter and saw his white Fruit of the Loom underwear showing through a hole in his pants at the crotch.

He stuck his finger in the hole, looked up at his sister with a dumb founded look on his face, which made her laugh so hard she buckled in side stitched pain.

"What am I going to do now?" Randy cried out in between laughs.

"Don't worry I've got a safety pin. Just don't stimulate Mr. Johnson and get pricked."

The unintentional pun threw them both into convulsive fits of laughter once more.

Karen stood on the concrete sidewalk and said, "C'mon you waif. You're always in a predicament."

"Help me up."

"No chance I'm coming back on that bridge. If you want me to help you, get up and come with me."

"Alright, alright. But I owe you big time."

"It's your fault for trying to scare me, Mister."

"I ever tell you how really ugly you are?"

"Too late, Dog Boy, too late."

"Dog Boy." Randy's tone was solemn. "Et Tu, Sis? If I'm Dog Boy, you must be Dog Girl…after all; they're you're Aunt and Uncle too."

"True…they're my Aunt and Uncle, but everyone associates you with the canine brood, my dear brother. Now get up and let's go over to the Flying A station so that we can fix your pants and I can have some fun before it's too late."

Karen and Randy crossed the two-lane road over to Mike Wilson's Flying A service station. After talking to Mr. Wilson for a few minutes, they asked him if they could use his bathroom, so that Karen could pin her brother's pants together.

Karen worked quickly and had the pants pinned together in no time. Randy surveyed her work and determined that no one could tell he had ripped his pants at the seam. She cautioned Randy about the pin opening up again, just to place some doubt in his mind.

Randy could feel the pin's outline occasionally as he walked during his forward stride with his left leg, but soon he began to pay no attention to the inconvenience.

A few feet up the walk toward the movie house, their cousin Dennis come whizzing up in his car and stopped to talk to them. "Hey cousins, what are you guys up to?"

"Going to the movies," Randy replied.

"The dance I think," Karen answered.

Randy hadn't considered the dance, besides he didn't know how to dance. However, a small panic entered his mind, what if Mary Jo would rather go to the dance at the youth center. He pursed his lips and nodded his head to himself-he hoped not for embarrassment's sake.

"C'mon, I'll ride you around town a bit if you want."

"Okay," Karen agreed.

"Not now...I'm going to meet Lee at the pool hall," Randy stated.

"Suit yourself, cuz. See ya later."

Karen opened the door and sat down. Dennis punched the gas as the passenger side door latched shut. The car sped away, leaving Randy to walk the next few blocks alone.

Chapter 10

Randy could see the red-painted sidewalk which protruded from the Movie Theater. It was faded and chipped and worn away in spots from the foot traffic that went in and out of the doors. An overhang, which supported the marquis, provided a shadow across the walk deepening the red color, but couldn't hide the fact that the paint needed attention.

Randy walked under the marquis and into the shadow and peered top his left. He could see Miler standing in front of two sets of heavy green-tinted doors. Miler was looking dapper in his well-worn tuxedo; his immaculately shined shoes stood out against the backdrop of the rubberized imitation carpet, which lead to the movie house. Miler had worked for Mr. Walker as head usher for over twenty years.

Randy nodded to Miler who returned the greeting. Miler's first name was a puzzle to most people and a source of entertainment to the patrons of the theater. Randy knew Mr. Walker had to know the name, but he couldn't convince the rotund jovial little man to tell him what Miler's first name was.

Miler was a gaunt, gray-haired man, with coke bottle-bottom glasses. He rarely said anything and was always at work, cleaning, sweeping, polishing or ushering patrons in and out the doors. Miler policed the line for the telephone; used to call parents once the movies were over, with rigid authority. He was a slight man who had the respect of all the customers who visited Walker's movie house.

There had been the consistent rumors that Miler had been declared legally dead two times and had woken up on the undertaker's table both times before he was to be embalmed. Randy didn't know if Miler's appearance attributed to those rumors or was the cause of them. Whatever the reason, folks watched Miler with a careful eye thinking perhaps of his supernatural longevity.

Once past the movie house building there was a gravel covered alley way, which led behind the movie theater and the pool hall- the next building on the street. Underage smokers, secret drinkers and general riff raff usually held court behind the pool hall. Randy had been back there numerous times, but felt out of place. Lee frequented the spot because of his nicotine habit.

The sloping alleyway led to the branch. The branch was a stand of trees about three hundred feet long and about fifty to seventy feet wide, depending where one entered the small wood. A small creek wound its way through the middle of the branch nourishing the foliage as it found its way to the river. A beaten down pathway provided a shortcut to the other side of town. Many people without motorized transportation took the shortcut, especially younger people - albeit it meant going through Nosy Rosy Davies back yard. She objected but was too timid to face the trespassers. The police were called constantly by Nosy Rosy, but no one was charged with trespassing, instead they were warned time and time again if they were caught. Nosy Rosy would then get her revenge by spreading gossip around town.

Randy had crossed through the branch many a time, cautiously steering clear of Nosy Rosy, but was reported quite often to his grandmother who had lived near the branch until she had moved into a trailer park on the other side of town.

Randy stood at the entrance of the gravel-covered alley; he could hear a group of voices having a myriad of conversations down the narrow lane behind the buildings. He wondered if Lee was back there smoking with the rest of the crowd. He decided he would look to see that if Lee was in the pool hall first and if Lee wasn't there then he would venture down the alley to search for him.

As he stepped toward the pool hall entrance, Randy saw Bucky Fistkey come around the corner of the building leading from the alley. Bucky tossed his cigarette butt down to the street and smashed out its glowing end. Bucky looked up and spied Randy by the door. Ordinarily Randy would have made a courteous nod and moved on, but he wanted to know if Lee was back behind the building, so he waited for Bucky to greet him on the sidewalk.

Bucky seemed a bit startled and obviously happy that Randy appeared to be waiting for him to catch up. The too-skinny Bucky hurried, as he didn't want to keep Randy waiting too long and have a chance to walk off. Randy could see that Bucky's wiry hair needed its usual combing, his dark sunken eyes were wide open and his very white buck teeth gleaming as he smiled in anticipation of spending a few moments with his old buddy. He and Randy had been very good friends until about two years ago.

Bucky had lived next door to Randy's grandmother when she had lived down by the branch and they were inseparable when Randy came to visit with his grandmother when they were allowed to go into town. They went to the movies together at Walkers during the summer, when Walkers held matinees during the week to keep kids off the streets and out of mischief. It was at the movie house that decided the fate of their friendship.

The Walker Movie House was a racially-segregated building. The white patronage was seated downstairs and the black patronage was seated up in the balcony. From time to time there would be a mishap of some sort, causing tension between the two groups. It was said prior to the incident, which caused the strain in the friendship between Randy and Bucky, someone from the balcony had spit a lugee and it had landed on Preston Wood's head. Preston stood up and had yelled about the lugee thus causing everyone to shout threats from the balcony to the lower floor and back.

The lugee incident escalated to such a point that the police were called to Walker's to quiet the crowd down. Mr. Walker took the stage at the front of the theater and stood in front of the big green worn velvet curtain and gave an impassioned speech about how everyone should be considerate of one another. He declared he would have no more problems and that everyone connected with such behavior would be banished from his theater forever. He closed the theater for a week, but when it reopened the tension still remained. Randy was disappointed about the closure, because he truly loved the movies.

One week later, Randy and Bucky were sitting in the center of the theater as the first movie concluded and intermission began.

"I'm going to get something to eat," Bucky said.

"Alright, I'll go with you," Randy volunteered.

They left the dark movie area and entered through the doors to the concession space which caused their eyes to narrow into a squint as the bright daylight shone through the big glass doors at the front of the theater. The clack of their shoes sounded like golf cleats as they walked across the plastic Walker vanity mat, which was inscribed with the Walker Movie House logo and the words Concession Stand in large white letters, on their way to the counter to buy their goodies.

"Can I help you?" asked Mr. Walker's 17-year-old blonde-haired niece, Cindy. She directed her gaze at Randy.

"Ahem." Bucky cleared his throat to draw her attention. "I'll have a box of Red Hots."

Cindy bent to retrieve the hard cinnamon button size candy red pellets. The boys tried to glance down her blouse, but she held it close to her chest with her other hand. When she stood up, the boys looked away so as not to embarrass themselves, but Cindy caught Randy looking.

"Anything else?"

"I'll have a Pepsi." Randy felt obligated to get something.

"Nickel for the Red Hots and ten cents for the Pepsi," Cindy stated.

The boys reached into their pockets to bring out their money to pay for their treats. "By the way, Randy," cooed Cindy. "Come and see me when you're a year or two older."

Cindy was only two years older than Randy, but when you're fifteen and the girl is seventeen, in teen years that seems like a decade in experience and development and makes the older woman quite intimidating.

Randy as red as the candy in Bucky's hand managed a frog-throated reply, "Okay."

This caused Bucky to laugh. In return he received a soft punch from Randy, who was making fast tracks away from the concession counter.

"I've got to take a whiz," Bucky said.

"Me too…let's go before the movie starts."

The restrooms were upstairs behind the balcony. The boys climbed the skid resistant stairs two at a time, holding the guide rail as the staircase rounded its way to the second level. A red velvet rope served as a divider separating the way to the restrooms and the entrance to the balcony seats.

People were milling about headed to their respective seats in anticipation of the second movies beginning. There was little mingling of races. The whites stood together as they headed towards the staircase and the blacks walked in-groups back to the three step entrance which led to the balcony seats. This wasn't really that out of the ordinary, but a feeling of tension was in the air over the incident of three weeks prior.

Randy and Bucky pushed their way through the crowds of people that were headed down the stairs. Nodding here and there to people they knew, speaking a word or two to people who addressed them by name.

The boys made their way into the outdated but ornate bathroom. They stood at the urinals and began to take care of their business. Bucky waited until the bathroom was clear before he broached the subject he knew might upset Randy.

Miler was tidying up. He picked up a few errantly tossed paper towels and then was the last person other than the two boys to leave the bathroom.

Finally alone, Bucky said, "You know…I'm still mad about that spittin' from that balcony a few weeks back. I think some of that spit hit me…besides old man Walker had no right telling Preston he couldn't come back for a month. It's not fair…no jig was banned."

Randy was silent thinking how to answer back to Bucky. He knew how Bucky and his dad felt about black people and it was not very favorable, which Randy couldn't understand. After all Bucky's family lived right next door to the Dexter household. They were the friendliest family on the street where Randy's grandmother lived and all twelve inhabitants were black.

Mr. Dexter had helped out the Bucky Fistkey family many a time when things were rough for the family when Bucky's dad was out of work or down on his luck- mostly due to his proclivity to the demon alcohol. They cared for Mrs. Fistkey when her husband was away on his drinking binges. Go figure. Randy would never understand people.

"Look, Bucky, first of all you were sitting next to me and we weren't anywhere near where Preston was sitting. Personally, I don't believe anyone spit on Preston anyway…he's always inventing stuff. He thinks he's funny, but most people think he's a lying asshole."

"Aw…you're always picking on Preston because he's my friend. I think you're jealous. Besides, why are you always sticking up for them jigs? Seems to me you like them better than you do white people."

Randy finished relieving himself and stepped away over to the sink to wash his hands. He decided not to answer Bucky. He didn't feel like arguing the point and he knew he would never change Bucky's mind.

"C'mon the movies going to start. Let's go." Randy stood by the door holding it open. Bucky didn't bother washing his hands. He brushed past Randy and left the bathroom.

The upstairs lobby lights dimmed and the boys could see the movie flickering through the open door of the balcony entrance.

"What's playing?" Bucky asked rhetorically as he hurried to the opening to catch a glimpse of the movie title.

He stood close to the doorway and watched for a moment. Randy caught up with him as Bucky poured some of the Red Hot candies into his hand. Randy remembered he had left his Pepsi on the counter in the bathroom.

"I'll be right back. I've got to get my soda. Wait here for me."

"Okay," Bucky replied.

Randy left to retrieve his Pepsi. After he picked up his drink and was reentering the faded ornate upstairs lobby, he heard someone cry out in anguish. It sounded like a groan of an elderly woman.

He saw Bucky running for the stairs as quick as he could move. Randy looked over at the step up to the balcony seats and saw Mrs. Brown sitting on the worn red and gold colored carpet holding her eye. She was more sprawled than sitting and she had Red Hot candies scattered all about her.

Bucky was going around the corner, headed toward the stairs, but lost his balance and grabbed at the chrome pole holding the velvet rope serving as the divider. He kept his balance, but the pole being unsecured to the floor gave way and created a big metallic banging sound. The noise caught Randy's attention as well as the attention of a small crowd of baffled black people who were exiting the balcony to learn what the commotion was all about.

They could see Mrs. Brown on the floor holding her eye surrounded by the red colored candy. She was moaning softly and pointing at Randy.

"He threw that candy at me and struck me in my eye," she wailed.

Randy was stunned. The crowd was murmuring epithets about white people. Randy could hear unflattering comments being spoken among the ever growing crowd.

"You sure it was him?" Someone in the crowd asked.

"Yep…I'm positive," Mrs. Brown stated assuredly.

"Wa…wa…wait, Mrs. Brown. It's me Randy. You've known me since I was little. I'd never hurt you."

"That's true-I've known you and your grandma for a long time, but I've seen you running with that Bucky Fistkey boy a long time and everybody knows he hates us black folks.

"All I know is that I was getting my granddaughter a box of JuJubees and you throwed candies and hit me in my eye…it hurts mighty bad."

"Look, Mrs. Brown, I'm sorry someone did this to you, but it wasn't me. I was I the bathroom. I left my Pepsi in there and went to get back to get it. When I heard you cry out is when I walked over. Look…I don't even have any candy." Randy held out his hands, one was empty and the other was holding onto his Pepsi. He had an imploring look on his face.

"Nobody else up here, Randy," Sam Elzie said. He was a friend of Randy's but he needed to know who was causing trouble, if it wasn't Randy.

"It was Bucky Fistkey." A voice from the back of the crowd attracted everyone's attention. The slow staccato of the words could have come from only one person and that person was Miler.

He stood with napkins and cups in his hands. "I was retrieving supplies from the closet and saw the boy standing by the doorway. After I reached in to get the napkins I heard Mrs. Brown moan, when I looked out to see the problem, I saw Bucky headed for the stairs. He had a box of candy in his hand…that's when Randy came out of the bathroom and went over to Mrs. Brown."

Miler had spoken. No one had reason to doubt his version of the event. Mrs. Brown was unharmed with the exception of the bruise on her derriere. Bucky Fistkey was banned from the theater not forever, but for the remainder of the summer. Randy though innocent was guilty in some people's eyes by association and his reputation was tarnished.

The incident coated Randy with a belief by some that he was a racist like his friend. They couldn't believe he was totally innocent.

Randy lost his respect for Bucky as a friend not only because of the inane act of trying to incite trouble in the theater, but because Bucky left Randy there to be the fall guy. Bucky had tried to tell Randy he didn't know that Randy would be blamed for the mischief and that was why he hadn't stayed to clear his friend.

Randy didn't argue a great deal about this with Bucky. He merely removed Bucky from his life. Like a Mafioso who kills people that betray them, Randy in effect figuratively killed off his old friend. Bucky was still literally alive and breathing but he was dead in Randy's life. From that point on anything that Bucky tried to do to rekindle their friendship with Randy was rebuffed. Randy wouldn't forgive or forget the transgression.

Randy was cordial to the smiling Bucky. He was always pleasant when they encountered one another, but he tried to avoid Bucky whenever he could avoid him. Randy never encouraged conversation. He always made an excuse to break away. However, now he needed some information from the buck-toothed bigot.

"Hey, Randy, what going on? I didn't know you were in town. Fact is, since your grandmother moved, I didn't know what the heck you've been up to lately." Bucky was rambling. He was excited to see his old friend and wanted to keep the conversation alive.

He wanted things to be the way they used to be between Randy and himself. He truly couldn't understand why Randy was being so distant. Randy had never explained anything to him; he had just stopped talking and calling him when he was in town.

"Hey, Bucky. Is Lee back there?" Randy ignored Bucky's question and statement.

"Didn't see him. But I'll go and look if you want me to."

Before Randy could reply, the door of the pool hall swung open and out walked Lee.

"Hey, Randy." Lee stopped and pulled a cigarette from his flip top box. He motioned with his head toward the back of the alley. He ignored Bucky altogether.

"Naw, I'm going inside. Seen Vern?" Randy asked.

"Not yet. He should be here soon. I talked to him before I came into town. He's excited about his date; I imagine he's still primping himself up. He was saying something about sliding his penis into Venus."

The boys laughed. Bucky laughed a little too hard.

"Want to shoot some pool, Randy?" Bucky asked.

Randy ignored him for a pregnant pause and then said, "Don't have time, Bucky. I'm going to the meet some people. I'm just going in to see what's going on and to say hi to Sticky Bun."

"I'll go with you."

Randy and Lee looked at one another and Lee winked at Randy. "You two go and have some fun. I need to smoke a stogie. See you inside, Randy."

"Fine...see you in a bit," Randy replied with sarcasm dripping in the words. He didn't want to be stuck with Bucky.

Lee walked down the alley to smoke his cigarette. As he walked down the path, Randy and Bucky turned to enter the pool hall when someone called Randy's name. The boys turned to see whom it was shouting at them.

It was Donzella and she was with a very large black man. They came strolling up the alleyway. Randy stood and waited. Bucky was torn. He wanted to be around his old friend, but didn't want to have a conversation with any Negroes.

"See ya inside, Randy," Bucky said with resignation in his voice.

"Yeah…see ya inside." Randy felt relief. He was rid of Bucky. He was also happy to see Donzella. It had been a long time.

"Randy, Randy, Randy." Donzella was genuinely happy to see him and it showed in her body language. She hugged him tightly and kissed him on his cheek.

"No biting," Randy kidded. He hugged her tightly as she hugged him.

"Damn boy, you sure are getting good looking. I may just keep you for myself."

Randy blushed and reached out his hand to the massive male friend accompanying Donzella.

"Randy…"

"Yeah I know…soon as Donzella spotted you, she started filling my head full of Randy stories."

He took Randy's hand and went through a series of claspings that involved most parts of Randy's hand, ending up with a bump on top. Randy tried to follow the motions but was soon lost in the chronology of the soul shake. He tried to follow with a bump of his own, but waved at air making him feel a little foolish. Randy tried to act as if he was stretching his hand but he fooled no one.

"Barry…leave my brother alone," Donzella laughed. "Introduce yourself fool."

"Barry Marshall. Nice to meet any friend of Donzella."

"Oh he's more than a friend. We're related. My Uncle made Randy a member of our race." Donzella had told Barry the story earlier.

"He tasted the blood did he? Well welcome to the enlightened side of life my brother. Any brother of Donzella and her Uncle is a brother of mine."

To Randy's astonishment, the over six foot tall, brown giant of a man with a budding Afro, picked him up and bear hugged him.

Donzella laughed a riotous laugh. Barry set Randy down and joined in the laughter. Randy still a little shocked laughed as well.

They chatted a few more minutes, catching up on old times. Donzella telling Randy she had moved back into town and was living with her mother's sister - Aunt Chloe. She had been back about a week. Barry was from Tailsboro and she had met him while she had lived there after her Uncle and Aunt had passed away. Barry had relatives in town and had come to town with her to visit with them. Barry's aunt lived not too far from where Randy's grandmother had lived down through the branch on Cooper Street.

Randy had asked about Donzella's brother Zachary and found out that he had decided to stay in Tailsboro. He didn't want to come back to Colmboro because of the memories. Randy asked Donzella to give Zachary his best. He told her that Karen was in town with Dennis and would probably turn up soon.

"Karen is going to the dance, I suppose," Randy stated. "You guys going?"

"Where?" Barry asked.

"To the dance fool!" Donzella said laughing.

"Oh yeah. Don't know…it's up to Donzella."

"Maybe…I really don't feel like going to the movies. But I don't know if I want to put up with the white black thing at the dance."

Randy didn't know how he should respond. "I see," He said noncommittally.

"You going to the dance?" Donzella asked.

"No, I'm going to the movies."

"You love them movies…you going with a girl?" Donzella asked innocently.

Randy was taken aback. He didn't know how to respond. He was embarrassed for reasons unknown to him because he had a date. "Yeah…yeah I guess so."

Donzella read Randy's eyes and body motion sensing his embarrassment. She liked him and cared for him, so she decided not to tease him.

"What's her name?"

"Mary Jo Magurk."

"Mary Jo Magurk…that skinny thing?" Donzella said condescendingly. Donzella now felt a little jealous. She couldn't control her slight outburst. Mary Jo posed a threat. Donzella knew Randy had always liked Mary Jo.

Randy was a bit startled.

"Leave him alone, Donnie," Barry said. "You've got me. Picking on a man's date. That's not nice."

"I didn't mean nothing. Just it's…the last time I saw her she was a little thing and a little homely…that's all."

Barry laughed. "Well it's nice you're looking out for your blood brother's welfare, but I doubt he would want to hear how you rate his dates."

Randy more composed, adopted a tender attitude. Barry's comments had helped. He moved over to Donzella and placed his arm around Donzella's slender waist. He drew her close and looked into her eyes. This was new ground for him but he felt comfortable around Donzella.

He could feel her round full breast against his chest. Donzella had put on a pretend pout look with her lips pushed out. Her large brown eyes cast downwardly.

"It's okay…you'll always be in my heart. You've got Barry. Besides incest isn't always best, you know."

"We're not that kind of brother and sister. So take care and watch those wicked white women. You call me if you need me."

Randy hugged and she hugged back. They all laughed as Barry pulled Donzella away.

"C'mon, woman. I see I've got to keep you away from this brother. He's got some kind of animal magnetism." Barry said with mock indignation.

Donzella went freely and placed her arm around Barry. The threesome didn't see Sam Hammet walk up behind them, standing by the pool hall door, listening to their conversation.

"Pretty cozy there ain't you," Sam bellowed, holding his hand on the worn and dented doorknob of the pool hall.

The trio turned to face the voice. All smiles vanished. Barry didn't know Sam Hammet as well as Randy and Donzella but he knew he didn't like the tone in the voice.

"What's that supposed to mean, Hammet?" Donzella asked acerbically.

"Nothing…don't see too much salt and pepper around here that's all. Should have known, Dog Boy, here would have been involved."

"Up yours, Sam. Go crawl into a hole somewhere…oh, I'm sorry with a gut like that you couldn't fit into a hole- it would have to be a quarry," Randy said pointing at Sam's belly. "And stop calling me Dog Boy."

"Dog Boy? What's that mean?" Donzella asked with a puzzled look on her face.

"It means I'm going to whip him like a dog…that's what that means, smart ass. I should've whipped your butt earlier today."

Barry lost his warm demeanor he had had when the three of them were talking amongst themselves. His current façade was one of aloofness a menacing way. His eyes burned with heat seeking intensity. He could feel his blood pulse through his veins, the blood roaring in his ears. The anxious push was attacking his nervous system preparing him for his assault on the transgressor. He didn't know how long he could hold back before he slipped over the edge of reason and pummeled Sam Hammet to the gummed stained sidewalk.

Donzella could feel the muscles in Barry's arm turn to steel under her hand. She could feel him start to move into Sam's direction. She pulled back slightly signaling for Barry not to go yet. Randy was standing in a ready position beside Barry. He was closest to Sam and felt inclined to punch the overweight moron even if he took a beating for it.

Sam, taking note of Barry's size and present attitude, decided this was someone he may not want any part of. He could see the intense fire in Barry's eyes. He could sense the overwhelming feeling that Barry wanted to do him a good deal of bodily harm. He needed a way to save face, a way to alleviate the situation, without having to fight the large black man. Truth was he had nothing against black people, he simply felt like harassing Randy. Unfortunately he had little sense when it came to ragging people beyond a civil line. Randy was pissing him off, causing him nothing but trouble. He would catch up with Randy later and extract his revenge.

Randy's knees quivered with anticipation. His adrenaline was surging through his entire body. He knew Barry was standing beside him in case this obese moron standing at the pool hall door was getting the better of him. He didn't know for sure, but even if Barry didn't assist him, Randy felt as though a battle with Sam Hammet was about to take place.

"Hey, Randy!" A distinct voice called.

The four people embroiled in the immediate confrontation ignored the call.

"Hey, Randy!" The call was closer and persistent. Randy recognized the voice as Vern's voice. Sam Hammet held the same recognition and was even more eager to extinguish this deteriorating situation. Events were not in his favor.

"Randy, do you hear me?" Vern asked impatiently. He was nearly to the group.

Randy answered his friend tersely, slightly turning toward Vern, but keeping his eyes on Sam. "Yes, I hear you."

"Good…I thought you were going deaf for a minute. Either that or I was speaking and the words weren't really coming out of my mouth. I need to talk to you. Have you seen Picker? I gave him something today and I want it back. I--," Vern stopped talking.

He had joined the group and because he was now paying attention to the other people talking to Randy, he felt the tension. He also observed Sam Hammet with disgust. "What's going on?" He asked.

"Sam's mouth has been running over time," Donzella said. Sam was quiet. His eyes were darting around peering at each of his adversaries. He held tightly to the doorknob of the pool hall. It was his only escape.

"Hi, Donzella, long time no see. You come back to see Hammet?" Vern asked mockingly of Sam.

Donzella laughed. The tension of the group relaxed, but Randy and Barry still wanted to thrash Sam Hammet.

"No…I could see fat, bigoted assholes just about anywhere. Sam's the reason I haven't been back in town recently," Donzella said.

A police cruiser rolled up slowly about this time eyeballing the group of young people in front of the pool hall. Sam and Barry both spotted the cruiser. Sam relieved and Barry apprehensive. The two policemen looked the group over with curiosity, but didn't stop the car. Sam took the opportunity to flee the situation. He opened the door to the pool hall and stood half way in and half way out of the doorway straddling the threshold.

Staring directly at Randy, he spat out his words, "Yours is coming, Dog Boy. You better betcha' its coming."

Barry gave a feint with his body in a menacing manner in Sam's direction and Sam Hammet darted in quickly. Everyone snickered at the buffoon. He really was a horse's ass.

"Don't worry about him, Randy," Donzella said.

"I'm not worried. He's a jerk."

"If you need help, let me know," Barry volunteered. "Let's go, Donnie. I feel like an ice cream cone."

"Thanks, Barry. It was nice to meet you, but I'll handle, Fatso. I've got my best buddy Vern here."

Barry ran Randy through the soul shake once again and Randy was just as lost in the pattern, as he was the first time it was attempted. Vern watched with a puzzled look on his face. He just saluted and waved good bye.

"See you later, Donzella," Randy said giving her a peck on the cheek.

"Okay my bother…I mean brother. I'll be around, so come and see me." That said, she and Barry turned and began to walk down to the Tastee-Freeze.

Randy filled Vern in on the events leading up to his arrival and the boys went into Sticky Bun's pool hall.

Chapter II

Sticky Bun sat high above the patrons of his pool hall. He had an elevated platform built of solid concrete, which rose to height of four feet above the floor level.

He watched all four of his pool tables from his vantage point seated comfortably in his red winged high back chair. Behind his head was sign listing the prices of the different kinds of pool games. It cost twenty-five cents for a game of eight ball, ten cents for a game of nine-ball and straight pool was fifty cents an hour.

Sticky Bun was a throwback to the fifties, he had a ducktail haircut - sufficiently greased, Levi blue jeans rolled up at the ankles and he wore a white tee-shirt that held a pack of Camels tucked neatly under one sleeve. He was clean-shaven, sported side burns and didn't miss any of the happenings within his pool hall. He kept strict order and had two broken pool cues at his side to help enforce his no trouble rule.

Randy and Vern had good assurance that there would be no trouble from Hammet here in the pool hall. Sticky Bun's pool cue enforcers and reputation for using them made sure that trouble was taken care outside of his establishment. Sticky Bun loved his pool hall and he took great care of its contents as for the patrons they had to take care of themselves.

Dotted around the pool hall, hanging on the battleship gray walls, were many signs, hand painted by Sticky Bun. One sign declaring in bright red letters "Please Pay After Each Game," another in green lettering stating "No Gambling," a "Break It and You Bought It" in the same green paint and in bright orange paint a sign blaring out the biggest taboo in the establishment, "Absolutely No Fighting, Arguing or Spitting on The Floor".

There was one other written rule, which all the regulars were cognizant of in Sticky Bun's Pool Hall Emporium. The No Smoking rule. Sticky Bun was the only person who was allowed to smoke in the pool hall. Everyone else had to go outside down the alley and around the back to smoke. No flame, fire or burning embers were allowed near or in the vicinity of the green felt covered tables of enjoyment. If someone new entered the pool hall with a lit cigarette or lit one as they entered, the voice high on the perch quickly explained the rule and took no gruff from anyone who rebelled or argued. It was Sticky Bun's way or no way.

Friday night was a busy night at Sticky Bun's. Not only were the regular pool players and gadflies inhabiting the place, the elderly who's who trickled through the front and sauntered to the back room to play a game of high stakes poker. The poker game was held here at Sticky Bun's on Friday night and moved down to the Flying A service station on Saturday nights. It was illegal but accepted and had been going on for years. Fact was that most of the respectable men in the town participated. Town policy, business deals and gossip mongering was all accomplished at these sessions. Agitators of all type attended the poker games, which was exclusively for males only. This was the only gambling allowed at Sticky Bun's and no one questioned Sticky Bun about the contradiction.

Randy and Vern moved over to the side wall where the heavy wooden benches and bar stool style chairs were arranged. The pool cue racks were on this wall, which proved to be the second best vantage point in the pool hall. From there they could see which table was closest to concluding a game, if they desired to play. Most games were called by stating next and by placing a coin on the table to serve as a marker for a place in line. Occasionally a game of straight pool would break out between two of the best players and the table nearest the chairs was almost always chosen for the game so as to showcase the talents of the participants.

Randy sat while Vern stood surveying the busy tables. Sam Hammet caught Randy's eye with a menacing glare and a head bob as if to say you'll get yours. Randy didn't back down and returned the glare. Vern stared at Hammet as well, then he decided that glaring wasn't enough and complimented the glare with a one-finger salute.

Sticky Bun's voice carried over the conversations and the sound of clacking pool balls. "Vern, I don't think that finger would feel very good stuck up your ass. I'll remind you of the sign on the wall. If you feel like causing trouble, take it outside."

Vern sat heavily onto the wooden bench and peered down at the concrete floor wounded like a small child. There were titters in the room as everyone's attention turned to Vern, but no outright laughing. No one wanted a rebuke from the lord of the manor who was sitting stately on his throne.

Randy still stared at Hammet, who had a self-satisfied smirk of menace and enjoyment affixed to his chubby visage - a smirk which lasted only for a few seconds.

The smirk vanished quite quickly as Dennis, Randy's cousin, entered the pool hall. He came in the door with his usual flair, like a bull in a china shop manner.

His large frame filled the door as he surveyed the pool hall. With a quick glance,

he spotted Sam Hammet and burned acknowledging holes into Sam's psyche. Sam tried to avert the black, close-set eyes, but couldn't pull his attention away from Dennis. Sam had an ominous feeling that Dennis Wilts had something he needed to tell him and quite frankly Sam would rather not know what that something was.

Dennis rubbed his close-cropped black hair and advanced into the pool hall. He walked over to Sticky Bun, who had reached behind the chair and retrieved Dennis' custom-made pool cue. He handed it to Dennis, who was still eyeballing Sam Hammet.

Patrons inside murmured their hellos to Dennis in respectful a manner without really approaching him. He nodded an occasional acknowledgement and continued his advance toward the pool table where Sam Hammet stood with Arrington Debussy. The crowd could feel the tension contained in Dennis' aura.

Dennis paused a moment, standing beside his cousin, Randy and Randy's friend Vern. "Hold this for a moment?" He asked of Randy more as an imperative than a question, handing off the pool cue case.

Randy took the case and turned it around so that Dennis could open the catches on the case. Dennis took out the two pieces of tapered rounded wood and screwed together his pool cue. It was a beautiful piece of work, all black from end to end with lightning bolts in a metallic blue decorating the handle. *D. Wilts* was burned under the lacquered upper portion in the same blue hue. Dennis was an excellent pool player and would take on any challenger in any style of game.

He closed the case and refastened the latches before he spoke to Randy again. His deep baritone menacing voice carried above the muted din in the pool hall. "Hey Monkey, your sis tells me that you have had quite an eventful day today." He was speaking to Randy, but his eyes gazed upon Sam Hammet.

"It's been up and down. I suspect that it's going to get quite a bit better soon. I'm going to the movies."

Dennis nodded, glanced briefly away from Sam peered at Randy to gauge his cousin and then returned the heavy gaze toward Sam. "Anybody give you any trouble today?"

Randy replied as casually as he could, "Nothing that I can't take care of."

"Tell him about…" Vern was starting to say. He didn't finish the sentence because Randy's elbow tapped him in the ribs.

"Tell me what, Monkey?" Dennis went to the table where Sam Hammet was racking up the pool balls.

"Nothing, I'll take care of it.'

"Okay…but you let me know if you need me to straighten out some of the chubbier bullies for you." Dennis was now standing beside a nervous, shifty-eyed Sam Hammet.

"Dennis, there will be no trouble in here. You remember last time. Remember I vouched for you so that Haney wouldn't put you in jail." Sticky Bun's voice stilled the crowd, but had not quite soothed Sam's nerves.

"I paid for the broken stuff, Stick."

"Never-the-less, I don't want any trouble. This time I swear I'll let them lock you up. Don't think our friendship will save you every time. No one else fights and comes back. If you push me, I'll ban you forever." Sticky Bun was resolute in his speech.

"Relax, Stick. I'm just going to play pool. You know I like this table best. I'm going to wait my turn and play the winner of the match."

Keith Brake had rights to the next game and stood at the other end of the table waiting to break the balls to begin the game. He didn't like the tension, so he decided to give up his turn. "Here, Dennis, you play. I was leaving anyway."

Dennis moved to the other end away from the waiting Sam Hammet. "Thanks, Keith. I'm kind of in a hurry anyway. But I would like the opportunity to beat - and I mean beat - Sam here. Sam, you ready?"

Sam licked his dry lips and nodded. He didn't speak for the fear that his parched throat would cause his fear-filled voice to crack, embarrassing him in front of his peers.

Dennis lined up the white cue ball and addressed it with his custom-built cue stick. Eyeing the freshly-racked solid and striped balls, he drew a good bead on his target. He pulled back the pool cue a few times to get some momentum going and unleashed a powerful stroke causing the white ball to explode the tightly packed balls to all corners of the table. He pocketed both a solid and striped ball.

Dennis rose up his eyes and cemented them on Sam, who dared not to return the gaze.

"Made one of each. Look the table over, Sam, and tell me which set you would like. Big ones or little ones."

Sam glanced at the table and saw that the stripes were arranged the best for an opportunity to run the table. He wanted to be away from Dennis as soon as possible so he decided to give his adversary the advantage. Albeit with Dennis' skill level, he knew he had little chance of winning anyway.

Clearing his throat Sam meekly replied, "Little ones."

"Figures...little ones...same as in your pants, huh, Fat Boy?" Dennis winked at Arrington and smiled a humorless smile.

Sam didn't reply. Arrington was beginning to get edgy as well. He didn't like the way this conversation was going.

Dennis chalked his stick with a quick squeak of the blue cubed chalk. He began to put a quick end to the game. He sank the other six balls required before Sam even had a shot. The eight ball was a sitting duck and Dennis paused to look his shot over. He hadn't spoken a word while he was playing, sinking ball after ball with a confident ease.

"Looks like game, Sam, my boy. Unfortunately I've got somewhere to go or I'd give you a rematch.

"But before I go, I'd like to tell you a little story. Seems like someone's been giving my cousin a bit of trouble today. When my cousin is given trouble, truth is that troubles me. Now…seems to me I've warned this individual before that I don't think bothering my relatives is a good idea." Dennis paused and stared a menacing stare into Sam's eyes, wrinkled his nose briefly and continued, "If you see anyone pestering my kin, I'd like you to tell them to cease and desist. Can you do that for me, Sam?"

"Now…don't get me wrong. I'm not asking you to fight my battles for my family or me…but if I find out it has happened again - police or no police - I may not be responsible for the thrashing this particular fat boy may get. So will you do that for me, Sam?"

"No problem." Sam forced the answer, trying to keep the quiver from his voice.

Dennis sank the eight ball and finished off the game. He walked over to a lock- kneed Sam Hammet and slapped him hard on the back, so hard that Sam dropped his pool cue. The noise from the slap and pool cue hitting the ground caused anyone not paying attention to the scenario, to suddenly stare intently.

Dennis stood smiling, "Thanks, Sam. You're a peach.'

Sticky Bun watching closely said to Dennis, "Dennis, keep it cool."

"On my way, Stick. On my way out."

With that said Denis walked over to Randy and put away his pool cue and latched up the case. He took the case, winked at Randy and rubbed his head. He walked over to Sticky Bun and handed him the case with the pool cue inside Sticky Bun took it while he eyed his friend cautiously and placed it behind his seat.

"See you later, Randy," said Dennis as he glared one last time at Sam Hammet and went out the door.

Sam and Arrington had a whispered, heated discussion. If it was about Dennis, they definitely didn't want to be overheard. After a few minutes, Sam placed his cue stick up on the rack and gathered something off the bench behind the table. Sam and Arrington gave the appearance that they were leaving and sauntered toward the front door.

Sam made no acknowledgement of Randy as he passed him. He tried to act as if he wasn't bothered in the least by the way Dennis had treated him, but he could hear the snickers as he went through the patrons of the pool hall.

Randy stared at him still a bit angered but feeling a little less so. He didn't keep anger as a rule. He was the forgiving type, but not the forgetting type. Vern smiled at Sam, but Sam wouldn't make eye contact with anyone.

As the duo reached the door, it swung open stopping Sam and Arrington in their tracks. Sam drew in an audible breath, concerned that Dennis was coming back for him, when in walked Caleb Fulton. Caleb had come for the poker game and looked as though he had had a few beers already inside of him. He stopped looked Sam in the eye and then whispered something to him. Sam nodded and then exited through the door. Caleb went through the room and went to the back room where the card game would begin soon. He didn't play, but liked to watch and to contribute to the gossip.

It was approaching seven o'clock and Vern and Randy decided to go outside and wait in front of the movie house for their dates. It had been quite a day so far.

Chapter 12

Lee was coming out of the alleyway and rounding the corner of the red brick building as the two boys exited the pool hall. Sam Hammet and Arrington Debussy were nowhere in sight. Randy felt a little relief because they weren't around and relaxed. He was tired of confrontation and the tense atmosphere.

"You guys leaving already?" Lee asked.

"The girls are supposed to meet us outside of Walker's," Vern answered, nodding toward the movie house.

"You going to the movies or the dance?"

"I'm going to the movies, my dancing skills aren't quite up to par," Vern answered.

"Mine either - besides, I know Mary Jo likes to go to the movies. We've talked about it from time to time," Randy said.

"What if they want to go to the dance instead?" Lee was smiling a mischievous smile.

"Lee, don't be a troublemaker. I'll just say we're going to the movies...that's that...enough said." Vern was defiantly adamant about not going to the dance. "Right, Randy...we go to the movies?"

Randy didn't say anything, but nodded in agreement.

Lee was examining Vern's face a little too closely for Vern's comfort level.

"What are you looking at? I got a zit or something?"

"No zit, but I was wondering when you grew a moustache?"

Vern stood still and tried to act nonchalant. Randy picked up on the examination of Vern's face.

"Hey...it does look like you grew a moustache...not a big one... but I definitely see a line of hair over your lip. Quite a straight line too," Randy said with amusement.

"You guys are nuts...I've had this for a long time...you're just noticing it now, that's all."

Lee reached to touch Vern's upper lip. Vern swatted his hand away. "Don't touch, Homo."

Vern used his thumb and forefinger to smooth his pencil thin moustache. He puffed his chest and boasted to his two friends, "When you boys are mature enough maybe you can grow hair on your faces as well."

"When I do, I'll want it to match my hair growing on my head. Why is your moustache brown and your hair blonde?" Lee asked quizzically.

Vern was stunned momentarily sporting a brief puzzled look on his face. He wanted to change the subject, but was caught with little room to wiggle. While he pondered Lee's question, searching for a good answer, he continued to smooth his moustache with his thumb and finger

"I've got a better question," Randy stated. "How come your moustache is smearing down the side of your mouth and the hair coming off on your finger and thumb?"

"What?" Vern said with a panic. He looked at his hand and could see the brown smears on his thumb and finger. "Oh no...I've got to go to the bathroom. The girls will be here any minute."

Randy and Lee were hysterically laughing at their friend. Vern was panicked, but laughing as well.

"Shut up, you guys."

"What is that mascara?"

"No...shoe polish," Vern said softly.

"Shoe polish," Randy and Lee said together. This made them howl ever more.

"You'd better go wash your face, Kiwi, or Corrine's going to think you ate a turd," Lee said

Randy and Lee laughed until their sides hurt. Vern was embarrassed but was laughing along with them because it was so infectious. Then Vern turned from them and went inside the pool hall to visit the bathroom to wash his face.

Lee and Randy engaged in small talk once they had calmed down, but still on occasion snickering when they thought about Vern. They stood on the sidewalk waiting for the girls to arrive at their rendezvous. Lee told Randy he had seen Sam Hammet and Arrington Debussy leave the pool hall in quite a hurry. Sam had shouted something at him, but Lee was unsure exactly what he had shouted.

Lee expressed his disappointment to Randy that he was the only one without a date. He couldn't figure out how Picker had managed to have a date, let alone one with one of the Magurk sisters. Randy was at a loss to explain Picker himself. He was a strange but likeable guy. Sometime he was around all the time and other times the boys wouldn't see him for weeks at a time.

Picker lived down the road from Randy's aunt and uncle three houses away, a half a mile or so down near the quarry. Even though his house was a half a mile away, Picker's parents' property stretched to the creek and jutted out to the creek's bend, so that Randy could see the tree house Picker had built. If Randy stood out on the bank by his stone chair and peered down the big brown ribbon of water, he had a perfect view of the tree house.

Picker had turned the tree house into quite a little place. It was almost an apartment. He had a comfy chair; a small table, portable radio, Styrofoam ice chest and his most prized possession, a telescope. He had everything with the exception of electricity. Randy figured Picker would have had that as well, but Picker didn't want the electric light to spoil his view of the woods.

Picker loved the woods as much as Randy did. Fact was, Picker and Randy were probably close friends because of their shared appreciation of the wooded land. The other boys liked Picker, but the bond was closest with Randy. The duo had had many long conversations about a great many ideas and subjects sitting on the bank of the creek, at Randy's stone chair or inside of Picker's tree house.

Picker knew the woods exceedingly well and roamed them on a constant basis quite exclusively alone. Picker was very protective of the woods and its inhabitants. He wasn't a hunter and didn't even carry a gun pretending to be one. He didn't like the wild cats, because he felt that they preyed on the young spring-hatched birds. He had vented his passion about the cats on more than one occasion to Randy about how he would like to rid the woods of these animals. The question was *"How would he accomplish the feat?"* Picker was too emotional about extinguishing the life of any animal - even the loathsome predator cats.

He had explained to Randy that he was all for the natural selection of things and that nature was the survival of the fittest, but the cats were not native in his opinion to the woods. Still he hated the farmers' effort to eradicate the cats. He expressed his desire to have them trapped, domesticated, and to relive their lives as house cats and not baby bird- killing varmints.

Thus, this was Randy's friend, Picker. An unusual soul, he didn't quite fit in the norm, but was apparently happier where he stood in society. A boy who expressed his thoughts on consciousness as reality being a fragile sheet of etched glass that once it was broken or distorted it caused death or demise. Randy wasn't quite sure what Picker meant, but accepted the view. Picker's uniqueness didn't seem to bother most folks; it just caused an enigmatic stare, tilt of the head or roll of the eyes. Randy liked and enjoyed his friend; he liked him for the self-satisfying confidence that made Picker-Picker.

Of course Picker's association and close friendship with the Magurk sisters was an added plus as far as Randy was concerned. As a matter of a fact, at this point, Picker seemed to be doing all right for himself with his relationship blooming with Leigh Ann.

The creek bend situated Picker's tree house just across the shore from the Magurk's boat dock, which was on the far end of the property away from Randy's aunt and uncle's property line. During the summer, the girls spent a great deal of time out on the dock. Picker in his tree house or walking in the woods allowed the friendship to grow and blossom into a close association. The Magurk girls and Picker's sisters were good friends as well even though there was a slight disparity in their ages. Picker's sisters were now away at college.

Randy was assuring Lee his chance with girls was imminent. After all Vern's first true date had happened just that morning. He was trying to encourage a reluctant Lee to accompany them to the movie, but the effort wasn't one of great enthusiasm. Randy preferred to be semi-alone with Mary Jo. Even though Vern and

Rick Milone

Corrine would be with them, he was sure the other couple would be preoccupied with one another. The other couple would serve to help Randy in a boost of confidence.

Not wanting to be the fifth wheel, Lee was trying to read Randy's true intentions with open-ended questions when Vern reappeared from the pool hall. Simultaneously, the Magurk girls arrived and parked their car in front of them.

The boys could hear the laughter spilling from the car, because Leigh Ann had stopped the car so abruptly causing everyone inside to careen forward. Leigh Ann drove with Picker seated beside her. Mary Jo and Corrine were seated in the back seat - both girls were brushing their hair in a hurried fashion.

"I've got to talk to Picker a minute," Vern said. He walked over to the passenger side of the car. Randy stood with Lee on the sidewalk watching Mary Jo intently brushing her hair. He was nervous and couldn't think of anything to say.

The car was a two-door vehicle. Leigh Ann and Picker exited the car and Picker reached in and leaned up the seat so that Mary Jo and Corrine could get out of the car. As the girls hopped from the car, Mary Jo peered over the car and smiled as she threw a little wave of her hand at Randy. Randy returned the smile happily, but nervously. He seemed partially paralyzed with angst, his mind was blank, and he had no idea of what to say to Mary Jo.

Vern pulled Picker aside and held a short but animated conversation with him. It looked to Randy as if Picker did most of the talking and at the end Vern shook his head, smirked a half smile. Vern walked away with a puzzled expression on his face. Randy was sure Vern was asking for his condom back, because Vern has presumed some big ideas and wanted to be prepared for his date with Corrine.

Vern rounded the car and stood beside Randy and Lee. Picker and Leigh Ann reentered the car, while Corrine and Mary Jo adjusted their purses. The girls were about to step up on the sidewalk to greet Randy and Vern, when Leigh Ann summoned them over to the car for last-minute instructions. Randy took the opportunity to quiz Vern on his request for his balloon-style protection.

118

"Well, did you get it back?"

"Get what back?"

"Your protection…just in case you have a big moment here on your first date with a girl you don't even know", Lee interjected.

"Look smart ass, things happen and I like to be prepared."

Randy was amused and smiled. "Nothing wrong with that, Vern. Maybe if Lee ever had a date he could sympathize better."

"Very funny, pin dick, but I've got just as much chance of getting a piece of tail as you guys do and I don't even have a date like you have so nicely pointed out." Lee was stung by Randy's barb.

Vern laughed at Lee and said, "Anyway, I didn't get it back. Picker's a strange bird, man. I asked him for it and he goes into some strange explanation that he says comes from some guy named D. H Lawson…"

"D. H. Lawrence." Randy corrected.

"Whoever…anyway something about Lady Jane had found her John Powell and the Gentry had been served again. I took that as a no that he didn't have it and he said that was correct."

"Who's Lady Jane?" Lee asked.

"Got me", Vern said. "I've given up on trying to figure out that boy. I think living with all those sisters has mangled the boy's brain."

"Sure hasn't hurt his sex appeal", a bemused Randy offered.

The three boys standing on the pale gray sidewalk peered in the car at Picker with admiration. He sat next to Leigh Ann seemingly without an ounce of trepidation what so ever. Picker looked at home and quite self-assured, a self-assurance that both Randy and Vern longed for at this particular moment.

Chapter 13

The two girls and three boys stood on the sidewalk together and watched Leigh Anne drive abruptly away from the curb. Randy's sister Karen had walked up just before Leigh Ann had driven away and joined the crew in the car. The five-some on the pavement waved as the raucous noise emanating from the interior of the car faded into the overpowering noise from the racing engine and slightly loose muffler of the aging vehicle.

Once the girls had joined the boys, Lee was set to take his leave. He didn't feel comfortable watching the paired up couples doing a mating dance of becoming familiar with one another. He had decided that he would skip the movie and go to the dance, where he could at least ogle girls even if he couldn't have one. Besides there was a pinball room adjacent to the dance floor area and he could entertain himself with the blinking lights, pinging of the bells and scantily clad ladies painted on the glass of the machines.

Lee cleared his throat to draw everyone's attention, so that he could say his good-byes. Randy and Vern took the opportunity as a brief respite from their one-on-one chats with their respective dates. Conversation was difficult to continue when one was so exposed to the outside world in a somewhat uncomfortable situation. The hope was a more intimate environment would enable them to be less nervous. Vern and Randy didn't know they felt this way consciously, but on a subconscious level, they couldn't wait to be off the street and seated in the dark nurturing milieu of the movie theater.

"I think I'll skip the movie," Lee stated. "I'm going to the dance and take my chances that some half -blind girl will ask me to dance or something."

"Okay, we'll catch up with you after the movie," Randy said.

"I don't want to go to the movie either," Corrine interjected. "I want to dance."

Vern looked at Randy, Randy looked at Mary Jo and Lee smirked trying to hold back his laughter.

Mary Jo began to speak and Randy had a feeling she was going to come to his rescue. She loved movies as much as he did. She would change Corrine's mind and they would go to the movies.

"Yeah…it would be different," Mary Jo added. "In fact, it's kind of exciting. I feel like dancing."

Randy blinked his eyes involuntarily. Vern was appearing like a doofus with his mouth hanging open. Lee was amused beyond his belief.

Finally Randy spoke after an awkward pause. "Great…I'd love to go dancing."

"Me too," Vern added in a voice with a slight crack in its tone. Then he deepened his voice and repeated it again. "I mean me too."

"Great…let's go in and get comfortable," Corrine said.

The two girls moved ahead of the boys with Lee bringing up the rear. Mary Jo opened the door and Corrine moved past her as Randy held the door. Randy shooed Mary Jo in behind Corrine. Vern stopped to look Randy in the eyes with a grimace on his face. Randy shrugged as if to say, what could I do? Lee followed close behind Vern. He was terribly amused at his macho, domineering, *they'll do what we tell them*, friends.

"Boy when you two put your feet down, the entire world shudders. If you guys were any more forceful, I may have had to call a cop."

"Shut up Lee…what a D…remember we still have dates," Vern retorted.

"True, true my friend. You wound me with your words. But at least I don't have to dance if I don't want to…can you say the same?"

Vern was silent. He was panicked about dancing in public. Oh well he thought, you have to learn sometime and now was a good a time as any.

The youth center was really a converted storefront. Overtime it had been a haberdashery, a Five and Dime store and most recently a Western Auto store before its conversion two years ago into its present incarnation of a place to entertain the youth of the area.

There was a great deal of debate around town as to where to place the youth center. Most of the town fathers wanted it placed in the downtown area to help bring in foot traffic for the local businesses. The mothers of the town were not too keen on exposing their children to the seedier side of things - like the pool hall. But when the Western Auto moved to a bigger facility down the hill by the Tastee Freeze, it opened up the current building, which could be leased for a nominal rent.

The town fathers argued that the movie house theater was two doors away from the pool hall and it didn't seem to adversely affect the youth of the town. The women acquiesced, but managed to extract the concession of an eleven o'clock shut down of the youth center on the weekends and a ten o'clock shut down on week days. The mothers wanted their children home at a decent hour.

Partitioned into three separate rooms, the forward room housed the ticket table at the door. The table was used to collect a small admission that was charged on dance nights to help offset the cost of the live band. Nights with no live entertainment had free admission. In the same room was the concession bar and closet which held the game implements such as; the ping pong paddles and balls, knock hockey equipment, record player, etc. The brightly-lit room gave way to a second slightly smaller room, which housed two rows of pinball machines. The dimly-lit room had an eerie effect on the patrons inside. The few incandescent bulbs that were placed haphazardly in the ceiling were of low wattage and combined with the colorful lights of the pinball machines cast ominous shadows across the faces of the people playing the machines.

The pinging of the steel balls striking the bumpers, the ringing bells and shouts of encouragement pervaded the smaller room. There was just enough room to squeeze through people, mostly males, playing the machines. Navigating through the room one had to be careful to watch for flying hands, legs and considerable body language that was used in an effort to keep the round steel ball in play.

Upon exiting the electronic game room - set off to the right - were the rest rooms in a small alcove off the main part of the building. The rest rooms were much more spacious inside than they appeared in relationship to the wood-paneled alcove, which held their male/

female entrance doors. No one was allowed to smoke inside of the rest rooms and occasionally a chaperone would saunter by and peruse the rooms for smokers. Most smokers were too quick for the chaperones and would adamantly deny smoking a cigarette.

Because this was such a nuisance, nearly all the smokers joined the crowd behind the pool hall. The boy's room was used as a gambling room for three boys who pitched quarters closest to the wall in an effort to gain additional coins for their pinball habits. A practiced experience almost exclusively held on nights without a dance happening. There was too much foot traffic on a dance night, which frustrated the coin pitchers.

The main room of the building was quite large. The folded game tables were pushed up against the wall, which held up the back of the building. Albeit there were many tables queued up along the wall, the space in the room was ample. Around the perimeter of the room was an eight-inch wide shelf four feet from the floor. The shelf held drinks, purses and whatnots.

Small wooden empty wire spools used by the local telephone company dotted the room and were used as stools and tables for sitting. A number of plastic chairs were scattered about as well. The walls were decorated by student artists and resembled some sort of abstract painting with little meaning to anyone with the exception of the artists themselves.

In the far corner of the room, next to the game tables, a raised platform held the band's equipment of amplifiers, a drum set, speakers and microphones. The portable dance floor had to be set up each week in front of the band platform. The dance floor was dismantled each week for fear the game tables would damage it. A new floor would exhaust the limited funds of the Youth Center treasury.

Encountering the ticket table, Lee stood behind the couples and watched as both Randy and Vern paid for their dates to enter the dancehall. Mary Jo tried to pay for herself, but Randy wouldn't have it. He pushed her money aside and Mary Jo reluctantly returned her money to her purse.

Vern on the other hand didn't have to worry about struggling with Corrine. She stood back and thanked Vern as he paid for her ticket. Vern wouldn't have let her pay, but he felt peculiar about the situation in relative comparison to Randy and Mary Jo. He sloughed it off but it nagged at him just the same. He didn't like her presumptive attitude.

Lee paid his admission and walked over to the refreshment counter and cashed some one dollar bills in exchange for quarters so he could play the pin ball machines.

"Let's go in and pick a spot and then come back for a drink," Randy said.

Everyone concurred. As they were paying, a line had formed behind them as people were streaming into the building. Grabbing a good spot would be difficult later. It was nice to have a spot with a good view of the room, one not too much in the traffic pathway and far enough away from the band, so that you could carry on a conversation.

"See ya later," Lee said. He surveyed the room and spied his favorite pin ball machine. It was being worked over by Tommy Green. Lee walked to the nearest machine and dropped a quarter in the slot. He heard the familiar thud of his plays register on the machine.

"Okay…we'll see ya inside. Might be a blind girl needs someone to dance with…so don't be long," Vern said needling his friend.

Everyone laughed and Corrine nudged Vern in the side.

"Vern, you're so funny…but looks aren't everything," Lee retorted.

"Gee…so original, Lee. I think I'll quit before you cut me to ribbons with that wit of yours."

"What a d, Corrine, if you need to rest your feet after buffoon boy stomps all over them, come and get me. I'll show you how to play pin ball."

Vern glared at Lee. His temper was starting to rise. Randy walked forward without comment and everyone except Lee followed him. The tension passed and Vern pointed at Lee as if to say watch out. Lee returned the pointed finger and smiled a winning smirk.

Going through the door, Corrine glanced back at Lee, which in turn unnerved him. His expression transformed from confidence to befuddlement.

The group chose a corner directly in line with the doorway. This allowed a vantage point enabling them to observe who entered the room and a vista of the entire room. The band could be heard clearly and were tuning up and testing their equipment as the two couples nested in the corner.

With everything set, Randy said, "Mary Jo, would you like a soda?"

"Sure, I'll have a Tab."

"Anything else?"

She shook her head. "No thank you."

"Corrine?" Vern inquired.

"I'll have a Tab as well."

The two boys waded through the incoming flux of people to retrieve the sodas. As they walked past Lee, Vern bumped the pin ball machine causing it to tilt Lee's game.

"Asshole."

"Thanks, Lee, you say the nicest things."

"Cut it out you guys. Christ, what a bunch of babies," Randy scolded.

"Him not me," Lee sulked.

Vern wrinkled his nose and continued walking through the crowd saying hello to people as he passed them. There wasn't much room to maneuver going against the grain of moving bodies.

Randy felt a tug on his belt and turned to meet Elizabeth Fellur. She smiled brightly at him. "Hi, Randy." She held his gaze - her eyes dancing with anticipation.

"Hi, Lizzy, how are you doing?"

"Great…are you leaving already?"

"Nope, I just got here. I'm going for some sodas."

"I didn't know you came to the dances. Do you think we could dance later?"

'Well…well…I'm here with someone, so I…I don't know. We'll see."

Lizzy frowned slightly and then beamed that winning smile. Still holding eye contact with her sparkling blue eyes, she said, "Okay, I'll catch you later."

Randy nodded and turned to fetch the drinks for Mary Jo and him. He had butterflies in his stomach again, but they felt good. Girls were scary creatures, but he was enjoying the fright.

The boys had returned with the drinks, the band had begun to play and the room was filling up rapidly. Evidently, The Rogues were one of the best bands in the county, because people had come from as far away as Delmona, which was thirty miles to the northeast. The Rogues played top forty hits and the dance floor overflowed to the point where couples were dancing on the carpet that surrounded the dance floor.

Initially, both Randy and Vern were reluctant to take the girls out to the dance area, but after watching some of the other boys' dance, they figured they would appear no worse and tried their luck. Randy had actually enjoyed himself and danced through most of the second half of the songs through the band's first set of songs.

The band broke for a rest and Mary Jo and Corrine excused themselves to use the ladies' room. Lee joined Vern and Randy to learn how things were progressing.

"How are the Astaire brothers doing?" Lee asked sardonically.

"Swimming well, old chap," Randy answered in an affected but terrible English accent. "How's your pin ball lady accepting you? Or should I ask has she rejected you too."

"Et Tu, Randy?" Lee said with a mock surprise hurt emphasis in his voice. "I could see it from Vern here; he's got feelings for no one, but you my friend. I'm hurt…I…I think I'm going to throw up, my stomach is in knots."

"The only knot you've got is in your head - you knot head," Vern said with a laugh.

"Okay, okay…enough about me. I've fully recovered. The TLC you guys show me would make anyone feel better. Tell me about the babes. Did you touch anything?"

"We don't kiss and tell. Find one of your own," Vern said.

"Aha - you're still virgins - good. I'm going to be pissed if you guys get nook before I do." Lee crossed his arms and sniffed the air with indignation.

"Who said anything about not being virgins except you? I never said I was a virgin." Vern sneered to Lee.

"You don't have to say it, Vern. First of all the calluses on your right hand could stop a bullet and most non-virgins, I dare say, would have better sense than to put shoe polish on their upper lip to impress the girl on his first date. I think I can still see it by the way." Lee moved his face over to Vern and pointed at Vern's lip with his finger.

Involuntarily Vern moved his hand up to his lip and looked to Randy for confirmation. Randy squinted his eyes and scrutinized Vern's upper lip and opened his eyes and shrugged, causing a little panic in Vern.

"We're kidding, Vern, would you relax. Mr. Jealous-Lee is trying to bring us down to his level. His only dreams tonight will be one of how a real girl must feel, while you and I will know how their soft warm bodies, touching our hot feverish skins feels pressing up against our passion-filled straining manhoods."

"You'd better stop reading those pervert novels, boy...you're going to go blind. Probably whacking that thing raw."

"Look who's talking. I hear you beat your stick so much one night that the friction caused your underwear to catch fire."

That produced laughter from all three boys. Vern laughed so hard he caused people to turn around and stare at him.

Lee nudged Randy as the three boys peered over the crowd. 'Looks like Lizzy Fellur headed your way, Casanova, and she's got Connie Wolfgang trailing with her. Keep her talking long enough for me to impress one of them. You've already got a girl for the night."

"I'll keep'em talking as long as I can. I'm sure it'd be daybreak before you thought of something to impress them with."

"No respect...just watch me. Those babes on the pin ball machine have got me riled up...inhibition is gone. I'm ready, my brother."

Randy looked at Vern who just smiled and shook his head.

"Hi, Randy. Where's your date?" asked Lizzy coyly.

Randy smiled at Lizzy. She had her head bent slightly down and was peering at him in a seductive way. She held a piece of brown yarn in her hands and was doing a cat's cradle.

"She's in the ladies' room. What are you playing with?"

"It's yarn, but I could think of something better to play with.'

"Lizzy!" Connie exclaimed. "You have no shame."

"Fine by me," interjected Lee with quite a bit of enthusiasm.

Lizzy ignored them both. She continued to hold Randy's eyes with her sparkling ice-blue eyes. Randy was entranced, he couldn't look away. He leaned back against the wall and he could feel the shelf attached to the wall push back against his butt. The space between Randy and Lizzy was razor thin and Randy couldn't back up any further. With every inch he moved Lizzy took up the slack and strayed ever closer.

"Let me do a little trick on you, Randy. Hold out your hands… no put them together…that's right, clasp them together."

Lizzy then worked the yarn over his fingers. She bumped her breasts against his hands with no effort to move them away from his touch. "Now put your hands through the center…that's right-all the way through."

"Uh, Lizzy, that trick's only about three hundred years old," Vern said.

"Not like I do it." She was talking to Vern but gazing at Randy.

Randy stood perfectly still. Lizzy was so close Randy could feel her breath gently roll across his face as she spoke. He could smell the rose water perfume she was wearing. His insides were vibrating like a washing machine in its spin cycle.

He knew the trick-she would release the string and his hands would be caught, she would redirect the string back over her fingers and *voila!* His hands would be freed. He decided to humor her because he liked the attention.

Lizzy released the yarn from her fingers and Randy's hands were captured in the loop. Lizzy took the yarn and wrapped it around and around Randy's clasped hands. She was correct. This was a new twist to the old children's game.

"Let's see how you're going to release his hands now," Lee said a bit puzzled.

"Release them…oh, I'm not going to release them." Lizzy smiled. She pulled Randy's hands tight up against her breasts and smiled even broader. Randy loved the soft feel of her bosom, but was beginning to feel extremely nervous with this close encounter.

Mary Jo would be returning at any moment. He didn't think Mary Jo would be too happy with him holding his hands against another girl's breasts. But Lizzy was overpowering his senses. He had envisioned touching females' body parts for a long time and now that he was accomplishing it, he felt a little uncomfortable especially in such a public venue.

"Bend your head down…close your eyes…whisper the magic word and your hands will be released," cooed Lizzy.

"I don't know the magic word," Randy said.

"What's your Momma always making you say?"

Randy smiled and said, "Please."

"That's right…now bend your head down…a little further-good. Now close your eyes and whisper the magic word."

With his head bent, eyes closed Randy whispered the magic word. As soon as he said the magic word, Lizzy reached up and kissed him hard on the mouth, she pushed her tongue past his lips, causing him to draw back, open mouthed and surprised.

"Gotta go, Randy. I'll talk to you later. C'mon, Connie, let's get a drink. By the way, Randy, you can keep the yarn. I'll come by and get it one day."

Randy shrugged. He smiled at Lizzy with an outward appearance of confidence. Inside he was a quivering like Jell-O.

Lizzy and Connie turned to go when Lee said, "Hey, Lizzy… Connie, I'll buy you a Coke."

Lizzy ignored him, but Connie turned, took his hand and said, "Sure, Lee, I'd like that very much."

"You would?" Lee's surprise was more than obvious.

"Smooth, Lee. Go buy the lady a Coke," Vern mocked.

"Let's go ladies, drinks on big Lee…emphasis on big."

Connie laughed Vern and Randy snickered and Lizzy continued on without looking back. This caused a bewilderment to set in on Randy. He couldn't figure out girls.

This morning he was sitting in his room fantasizing about how it would feel to be actually romantic with a girl. His only experience to this point was a paperback nympho and as exciting as she was time after time, she didn't hold a candle to the thrill he had just encountered at the hands and lips of Lizzy Fellur.

Chapter 14

Randy and Vern discussed Lizzy and her yarn in very excitable, elaborate and decadent terms. Vern remarked to Randy that he had turned into a chick magnet since this morning. Randy modestly said the girls must have lost their senses or mistaken him for someone else. Not that it mattered to him- he would revel in the mistaken identity as long as it lasted.

Mary Jo and Corrine returned as the bands break ended. They were carrying more sodas and muttering how long it took to use the ladies room. Randy was feeling pangs of guilt overwhelming him.

His excitement about Lizzy minutes ago was evolving into an emotional dilemma. He considered the thought of telling Mary Jo, but changed his mind-rationalizing that he might tell her later, if it was necessary. He couldn't look Vern's way. Whenever he did Vern appeared to be the Cheshire Cat with a very knowing grin.

The couples danced the first song and the Lizzy incident was pushed to the back of Randy's mind. The band played a few faster paced numbers and spoke to the crowd about how they were going to slow the music down. Now was the time to get that special someone, hold them close and slowly rock to the music.

Randy grabbed Mary Jo's delicate hand and pulled her towards their seats. She resisted and held her ground. Randy turned to look at her and Mary Jo pulled his hand back toward her.

Randy didn't want to slow dance for a number of reasons. Most importantly, because he didn't know how to slow dance. Secondly, he was afraid he would show himself to be a fool by appearing awkward, stumbling and stepping on her feet. He didn't want to tell Mary Jo, so he attempted once again to subtlety pull her toward the seats. Mary Jo held her ground, crooked her finger in a motioning movement for Randy to come closer to her.

The music was a slow ballad. The effect was strikingly emotional to Randy. As he gazed at Mary Jo with her long brown-colored hair, soft brown eyes, tempting pink-pursed lips with her even white teeth, he became mesmerized with the effect of the moment.

She swayed side to side slightly with the beat of the music. Her long legs exposed by her short skirt were finely proportioned and well toned. The short-sleeved sweater accented her breasts - appealing to the teenage wont of Randy's libido. The sexy kittenish projection was overpowering to Randy.

He felt so lucky to be with her and felt proud that he would catch other members of his sex casting side-glances at his date and hopefully his new girl friend. He decided he would learn to slow dance on the dance floor at that moment. He truly didn't have a choice. His rational mind had no control over the rising inner voice that was urging him to take the soft, curvaceous, intelligent creature into his arms. He gently wrapped his arms around her body and began to sway with the soft beat of the music-almost in time with Mary Jo.

Randy held Mary Jo as she melted into the contours of his body. Her *Windsong* perfume fragrance subtly found its way to his nose, entrancing him evermore. He felt anxious and comfortably at home embracing the girl he had wanted to hold for so long.

The song ended far too quickly for Randy. He didn't want to let go of the warm soft vivacious body that was holding him as snuggly as he held her. On the last beat of the song, he could feel Mary Jo release him slightly. She raised her head up with her eyes closed and Randy knew instinctively that she wanted him to kiss her. This would be his first formal kiss. He remembered how many times he had practiced on his arm. He knew his arm intimately and it appreciated his skill at kissing, but his arm hardly had any experience to judge him by other kissers - perhaps Mary Jo was more experienced.

Randy knew that the moment would evaporate if he didn't act now. He lowered his head quickly turning it to the right then the left and then to the right again to position his head to its best angle. Mary Jo waited patiently with her eyes still closed. The other dancers were beginning to leave the dance floor and the crowd on the hard wood floor was thinning fast. Finally, Randy placed his lips on Mary Jo's lips. Mary Jo pulled back and gazed at his sweetly.

She whispered, "Randy, relax your lips and this will be much more comfortable."

Randy blushed. He had been so nervous that his lips were as tight as ropes. He followed Mary Jo's direction and relaxed his lips and kissed her once again. This time the sensitivity was multiplied a hundred times. He felt the electricity pulse through his body. He also felt a stirring below the belt line, which was going to give way to a huge embarrassment in any second. He held tightly anyway and then released Mary Jo, so that he could catch his breath.

They walked back to their seats. Randy had his arm encircling Mary Jo's waist, pulling her up against his hip. Walking in unison, they resembled contestants at a three-legged race.

Corrine and Vern were situated in the corner oblivious to the crowd, kissing and mauling one another. Corrine was up against Vern, who was pushed tight up against the wall. Randy cleared his throat, so that they would know that he was back with Mary Jo, but Vern waved him off as if to say don't bother me now boy.

Randy reached over and picked up his half-filled cup of soda and offered it to Mary Jo. She took the cup and swallowed a mouth full. Randy regained the cup and finished off the liquid with two big gulps. Randy set the cup down on the wooden flange that hung on the wall, and he watched as Mary Jo unwrapped a couple of pieces of *Juicy Fruit* gum. She placed one in her mouth and held the other piece up to Randy's mouth. He opened up his mouth and she gently pushed it inside. The two never broke eye contact.

With their gum suitably softened, they began to kiss again. This time, a slight more passionately. Mary Jo pressed her body to Randy and he countered the pressure. She held his head with her hand placed behind his neck with a light sensuous touch. Randy held Mary Jo by the waist and wondered if he should move his hands to more forbidden places.

Randy wasn't into the kiss long before he felt himself start to become aroused. He didn't want to offend Mary Jo, but he wanted desperately to push his body strongly to her soft body. He was certain Mary Jo knew he was establishing an erection. Fact was he could feel it touch her causing him to try and avoid any pelvic touching. He tried to situate his lower body, so that his thigh would receive the brunt of Mary Jo's lower body. She swung herself to the side releasing Randy from his predicament.

Randy was in heaven. He pressed his lips with a little more force to Mary Jo's mouth and then experienced another sensation that almost made him shudder. Mary Jo darted her tongue into his mouth, checked out the interior for a brief moment. Without thinking, acting on impulse, Randy's tongue followed hers like a dog in heat. The inside of her mouth tasted like *Juicy Fruit* and was warm and inviting as anything he had ever experienced. His arm kissing had never been like this. He wanted more and moved in after it.

He became emboldened and began to venture to hitherto verboten places on Mary Jo. At first he moved with caution slowly inching his hand from her waist until it covered her firm round buttock. When he encountered no resistance he allowed himself a moment to savor the feel of the soft firm round pliable derriere. He softly caressed it over and over with an occasional gentle squeeze. The more he touched her there, the more he pressed himself against her. Mary Jo responded in kind.

Randy was having the time of his life. The band was playing a fast paced tune, but he was oblivious to the beat of the music, the crowd around them and the ever-present chaperones. He felt somewhat disembodied from everything. He was deeply involved in experiencing the sensations and pleasures of intimacy with a girl, yet even as he pressed his lips to May Jo's lips, tongues parrying back and forth, bodies striking sensitive erogenous zones - he was still cognizant of the mental process of gauging his moves and determining his next assault on his willing target.

His hand left her buttock and roamed to the upper torso. Randy slowed the ascent so as not to scare his prey. He was past her waist and just below her armpit when the edge of his hand found the round curvature of her breast. He could feel her bra through her sweater. The soft-weighing feel of her breast rested on the space on his hand between his thumb and index finger. Electricity and overpowering desire to hold her breast fully in his hand shot through him. He held back the urge and moved slowly with calculated grace.

He thought he detected a slight pull back from Mary Jo. He was trying to determine if had proceeded too far or was she relaxing so that he could have an easier access to his target. He pressed his mouth to hers with more fervor and Mary Jo responded again. He took that as a cue to forward the advance and placed his hand directly on her breast by sliding it up and over rather than picking it up and placing it there.

Mary Jo stopped kissing him and pulled away. She didn't cause much separation staying ever so close to Randy. Randy was surprised and peered at her with a puzzled look on his visage. He still had his hand on her breast. She gently touched his hand and pushed it back down to her hip. Randy smiled a sheepish smile. He didn't know what to do. He felt he had offended Mary Jo and thought that she just might slap him.

She smiled back and moved to kiss Randy again. He returned the kiss, but became considerably more apprehensive about his next move.

As fate would have it, Randy next approach was short-circuited by a feel of thin steel pressing against his Johnson. He wondered if Mary Jo's zipper was poking him, but quickly discounted that because she was wearing a skirt. What could she have under that skirt that would feel like an elliptical wire? He wished he could reach his hand down his pants and adjust his privates. The wiry thing was making him uncomfortable. He couldn't determine if it was affecting Mary Jo. The evidence pointed to no; she continued her pressure upon his hips.

Randy tried to ignore it. He slid his hand back from Mary Jo's hip to the more familiar ground of her rounded buttock with just a little apprehension. He suffered no rebuff, encouraging him to caress gently.

Then the bee stung Randy at the base of his penis- right between his hanging package and tower of blood-filled love.

"Ouch!" Randy pulled away with a little difficulty because he couldn't straighten up his body without causing himself more pain. He stared at a bewildered Mary Jo with a look of *why did you do that to me* and *what the hell was it that you did* look.

"What's the matter?" She asked anxiously. "Did I break it?"

"I can't straighten up. I've got a pain down there." Randy tried to pull his pants away from his private area. When he did, he remembered the safety pin Karen had used to plug the hole in his pants.

Evidently it had opened up and was now skewering his most prized possession. He painfully pondered how his quickly shrinking manhood must look. Probably a little like a cocktail wienie on a toothpick.

"Everything alright here?" A chaperone asked.

Great, Randy thought. *How am I going to explain this?*

"Everything's fine," Randy said still bent over.

Mary Jo not knowing exactly what the problem was began to laugh at the sight of Randy. Vern and Corrine were just as puzzled and Mary Jo's laughter became infectious. Soon everyone but Randy was laughing.

The chaperone stood with his hands on his hips. "I've been watching you kids for a while. This is a dance not lover's lane…so please cool the making out for later. I can't allow it here…okay?"

"No problem," Randy moaned.

His three companions laughed along with the chaperone, who laughed only because the other three did. Randy grimaced with his face scarlet red. The chaperone walked away to splash a metaphoric bucket of water on other hormone-filled couples.

While his companions peered at Randy with their puzzled faces, he sucked up his embarrassment, turned to the wall and reached his hand inside of his pants. With his hand down in his underwear, he gently pushed his underwear and pants away from his privates. The relief was immediate. He was able to stand up once again.

When he turned around, the girls feigned to be perusing the crowd on the dance floor. Vern was observing his friend with a cautious concerned look. He mouthed the words, *are you alright?* to Randy. Randy nodded and headed to the bathroom to examine the damage.

"Randy?' Mary Jo asked

"Be right back," came the reply. Mary Jo could only see the back of his head as he walked with stiff caution to the bathroom.

Randy could hear the snickers from behind. He laughed to himself. He could never tell anyone what had just really occurred.

Randy returned in short order. He had removed the safety pin from his pants and had inspected the small pinprick in his skin. A great pun was in order but he kept it to himself. The damage was minimal, a small hole not too deep at all and very little blood. He decided to throw away the underwear when he arrived at home, because he didn't want to explain the circumstances to his aunt at laundry time. He didn't care if anyone saw the hole in his pants, better the hole in his pants than to risk the stabbing with that dysfunctional safety pin again.

On his return, Vern and the two girls were laughing heartily. They toned down the laughter as Randy joined them. Randy had a feeling they were amusing themselves at his expense and his face flushed with more annoyance and embarrassment than anger.

Recognizing Randy's slight pique by his facial expression, Mary Jo took his hand in hers and said, "Vern was just telling us about Bob Warren. He says that Bob tries to be cool by placing six aspirins at the bottom of his Pepsi and then acts goofy like he was high or something. But that everyone knows but Bob that Bob comes by his goofiness naturally."

"Yeah, Randy, remember when you and me were riding our bikes over to the store a couple of years ago when Bob, Tim Wilson and Bob's brother Ray were speeding up on us in old man Warren's pick up."

'Sure do," Randy said trying to move past his awkward moment. "Bob and Tim were in the back of the pickup waving at us like damned fools."

"Right…Bob was standing on a watermelon, both arms above his head, waving like a wounded bird. Shoot…Ray must have had his dad's Ford Ranger going about forty-five miles an hour coming down the road almost right at us. Ray ain't too bright himself. Randy and me moved over on the shoulder of the road until we were almost on the grass."

"Then a small wind must have picked up and swooped Bob right off the Crimson Sweet melon and right out of the bed of the pickup. He did a double flip in the air…didn't he, Randy? I swear to God. Didn't he, Randy?"

The girls looked at Randy, who nodded his head in agreement.

"Well, he hit the asphalt, bounced at least twice, got up… screamed and went over and laid down in the front yard of Jerry Roth. Mrs. Roth must have been looking out of her window and she came out screaming too. Ray saw Bob fly out of the pickup bed in his mirror…stopped the truck and backed up to the Roth's yard.

"Ray hopped out of the truck and ran over to his brother…who was moaning, writhing and rolling in pain with Mrs. Roth trying to comfort him. Ray looked down at his brother and said *"Son of a bitch, Bob, the old man's gonna be pissed for a week. How the hell did you fall out of the truck?"*

"Well, Mr. Roth had called an ambulance and they took Bob to the hospital, but he only suffered some scrapes and a broken arm. He was lucky the fall wasn't worse. Who knows what that crazy dad of theirs did to them? All I know is that Ray hasn't driven that truck since, and Bob has been trying to improve his image ever since."

"I don't think aspirin in your Coke will do it," Corrine volunteered.

"Pepsi," corrected Vern.

"Whatever," replied Corrine. "C'mon, Vern, Let's go for a walk… the chaperone isn't outside."

"Love to stay and chat, but I gotta go," Vern said to Randy. Corrine then led him through the crowd by the hand.

A slight pause appeared between Mary Jo and Randy as Corrine and Vern exited the dance. Finally, Mary Jo said, "Are you okay? I didn't break anything did I?"

Randy laughed nervously. "No. I'm fine. Just a little cramp or something."

"Good. Do you want to dance or take a walk?"

Randy wanted to walk but not sure if everything was perfect in his private area, he said, "Let's dance."

"Great," she said. 'I love this song."

Chapter 15

The remainder of the dance continued without incident. Randy didn't see Vern again until the bright fluorescent lights flickered to life bathing the room full of gyrating teen-agers and young men and women in artificial daylight. The band had played their last chord, beat their last drum thump and had thanked everyone for coming to the dance.

Squinting from the bright light, the crowd filtered its way through the pinball room to the out of doors. Vern and Corrine joined Randy, Mary Jo, and Lee, who was escorting Connie Wolfgang

Randy could see a bewildered, expressive look in Vern's face. Corrine was seemingly aloof to Vern and flirting more with himself and Lee. Randy would ask Vern what the deal was later.

For the amount of people exiting the dance, it was a remarkably short period of time before the crowd diminished - leaving only a few people standing on the sidewalk in the moderately warm night air. The movie had let out fifteen minutes before the dance ended, and Mr. Miler stood sweeping the walk in front on the glass doors.

Leigh Ann had driven up with Picker, but without Randy's sister, Karen. Leigh Ann told Randy that Karen would be along in about ten minutes and had requested that he call his Uncle Harvey, so that he could come and pick them up. Vern, Corrine and Mary Jo would go home in the Magurk car. Lee decided to wait and go home with Randy's uncle. He wanted to spend a few more minutes with Connie.

Mary Jo and Randy embraced and kissed before she entered the car to a car full of oohs and ahs from the inhabitants. Randy was very embarrassed but it seemed to have little effect on Mary Jo. With another quick peck on his lips, she turned, winked at him and pushed her way into the carload of giggling teenagers. Picker saluted at Randy and turned his attention to the radio. He increased the volume as the car raced away leaving behind a puff of blue white smoke emitting from the tailpipe.

Randy had promised to call Mary Jo in the morning. They thought perhaps that they would go swimming or see one another sometime during the day tomorrow. Randy was ecstatic about the relationship with her and except for the safety pin incident, his evening had been a true success. He would avenge the safety pin incident with his sister somehow. He knew it wasn't her fault but he wanted revenge never the less.

Lee and Connie stood intimately close whispering to one another in a completely engrossed conversation - occasionally kissing each other lightly on the lips. Randy felt uncomfortable standing on the sidewalk with them. He tried not to watch, but some urge compelled him to glance frequently at the couple. He wondered if he and Mary Jo appeared as awkward to people around them as Lee and Connie appeared to him.

Sometimes Lee seemed out of position for a kiss of longer duration, his hands unsettled as where to be suitably placed. Connie appeared more in control and at ease with the situation. She compensated for Lee as much as she could. Not to say she was unhappy or frustrated with Lee, because she was cooing, giggling and sometimes very deep in a lover's clutch.

Finally, Connie's mother arrived to pick up her daughter. Lee became stiff as a board the moment the station wagon drove up to the curb. Connie's little brother and sister had their faces pressed against the side window holding Lee in a watchful contempt. Connie's mom paid little attention to her daughter's amorous adventure. She smiled and waited for Connie to join her in the car. Connie tried to kiss Lee good bye but only managed to kiss his mannequin stiff lips.

Lee croaked out a good bye in a barely audible voice and waved a weak adieu with his hand.

After they drove away, Lee let out a very loud holler, "Yahoo!" He walked out into the road and watched the tail lights disappear. "Randy, my friend, I'm in love."

"Glad to see a girl likes you. I was worried about old man Thomas' sheep."

"Very funny young man, but you can't take the glow off this happy face. You're looking at a man who has entered the game and advanced to at last first base. That girl's enamored with me and sure to spread the word on my sexual magnetism."

"What if Connie talks to Ron Waller about your sexual magnetism?" Randy queried.

Lee frowned. Ron Waller was Connie's boyfriend. At least he was until tonight. They had been a couple for a very long time. Ron was about three years older than Connie, and Connie was a year older than Lee. Ron Waller was a tall muscular football player who played defensive end and had a reputation for being very jealous - albeit he was a gentle giant by nature. He did however beat the tar out of Stanley Toner for insulting Connie one time.

"What's Ron Waller got to do with anything? They broke up."

"She say that?"

"No…but why would she be with me if she didn't break up with him?" Lee asked skeptically. "Why are you raining on my parade?"

"I'm not. I'm just looking out for your welfare."

'Well I'm not scared. Didn't you ever hear of David beating Goliath, a blind pig finding an acorn, or Samson boning Delilah?"

"What the hell does that mean?"

"I don't really know. I'll cross the river by the way of the bridge… oops, now I'm out of clichés. You just leave my baby alone and tend to that vixen of your own. Ha, now I'm a poet. Soon you'll have to scrape the women off of me.

"I'm going for a smoke. Call me when your Uncle Harvey arrives."

Randy nodded and watched Lee pull his cigarettes from his pocket on his way around the corner down the alleyway.

Mr. Miler was still sweeping the sidewalk nonchalantly as if he was oblivious to the last few people standing in front of the youth center. Randy was about to ask Miler if he could use the telephone in the ticket office when he heard someone behind him clear his throat.

"How ya doing, Randy?"

Randy turned and stood face to face with a well-oiled Caleb Fulton. Caleb was so close to Randy, he could see the gin blossoms that spread across Caleb's bulbous scarred nose. The alcohol pushed its odor through the elder man's pores. Randy snapped back and involuntarily and rubbed his nose to chase away the stale smell.

"Hey, Caleb, poker game finished?"

"Naw...I'm bored with the gossip. Gonna go on home. Got something to do tomorrow. You need a ride home?" Caleb struggled with his thoughts. He paused a second or two between sentences.

"No thanks, Uncle Harvey's coming to get me...but I appreciate the offer," Randy lied. He wanted the drunken man to leave so that he could place the call to his uncle. Randy was also aware that Miler had stopped sweeping because he couldn't hear the brush of the broom across the sidewalk. He hoped Miler hadn't gone inside and locked the doors, but he didn't want to turn away from Caleb.

There was a slight pause in the conversation.

"What's your uncle gonna do about them dogs? How's he keeping them in food? Must be costing him a fortune." Caleb asked with his head bobbing counter to his slight side-to-side sway. His questions came one after the other out of the blue.

"Ask my uncle. Maybe people should concern themselves about their own business, Caleb," Randy said. His blood was starting to simmer. "He don't ask you about your drinking does he?"

"Don't smart ass me, boy. You should have some respect for people who have been good to you." Caleb was stung by Randy's comment.

"Caleb, things will never be the same between you and me. You taught me how to dive and I appreciate it, but you know things go deeper. It's not your business is all I'm saying...so lay off my Uncle and his dogs." Randy had enough today and wasn't going to back down.

Caleb sneered at Randy. His thoughts were vague and swimming in a sea of alcohol. He reached around to his back pocket and pulled out a half-pint bottle of whiskey. He opened the bottle and took a long swig.

Randy stood shifting his weight from side to side. He was anxious for Caleb to vacate the premises. He took a quick glance back to the area where he thought Miler may still be standing in spite of his determination not to do so. Miler was still there leaning on his broom perusing the slow passing cars. Randy took some comfort in this and refocused his attention on Caleb "Scar Nose" Fulton.

Putting away his half-pint, Caleb said in a slow, slurred speech, "You're still blaming me for something I didn't do, aren't you? I swear...but I'm not...I can't change that situation of yours...so be it."

Caleb bowed a comical bow. "See ya later, Sport. You need to think about things in the right kind of manner."

With that said, he turned without waiting for a reply from Randy who glared at Caleb Fulton. Randy hadn't offered a reply anyway. Caleb Fulton disgusted him immensely.

"No movie tonight, Randy? You missed a good one. *Beau Geste*." The clipped sentences came from behind Randy accompanied by the sweeping sound of a straw broom across an already clean pavement.

Randy turned, pigeon holing Scar Nose Fulton's idiocy in the back of his mind. He said, "No, Mr. Miler, I went to the dance tonight. Do you think I could use the telephone to call my uncle?"

"Door's open. Mr. Walker's going to close the booth shortly, so don't take long." Miler pulled the door for Randy.

"Okay...thanks, Mr. Miler, I appreciate it."

Randy went inside and felt the warmth and comfort of the lobby. The air was redolent with the aroma of fresh-popped popcorn. He had been coming here for so many years that it seemed like he was expected, like he felt when he entered his aunt's or grandmother's home. He veered to the left and entered the cramped ticket booth. The telephone sat next to the three buttons on the ticket machine. Randy was always tempted to push one of the buttons to see the ticket spring to life. When he was younger, he envisioned working inside the booth with the power to send ordinary people on an hour and half adventure for a mere sixty-five cents.

Randy had completed the call and passed the bespectacled caretaker holding the broom as Miler entered the theater as Randy was leaving. He thanked Miler again as he went by and stood on the walk waiting for his sister, uncle and Lee.

Lost in is thoughts about Mary Jo, he didn't hear Bucky come around the corner up from the alley. Randy was smiling to himself, feeling happy and content with most of the evening. He was critical of himself for being so stiff in his moves. He didn't know how Mary Jo could be so confident in the way that she kissed. He wondered if it was easier for girls to be amorous than boys were. She was only fifteen like him and as far as he knew she really hadn't been on other dates. Perhaps she wasn't as confident as she appeared; perhaps he was imagining the situation. No. No. She definitely was more in control. Well he would improve and felt he had improved a great deal this evening.

Then he thought of his first kiss and how she instructed him to soften his lips. *Dammit, I must have seemed like a bumpkin,* he thought. His good mood soured a bit. What the devil must she be thinking of him? Would she discuss his kissing with other girls? *Oh crap, what about when I placed my hand on her breast?* She'd tell the other girls I'm a pervert. He nearly sent himself into a panic.

Calm down. Calm down. He told himself. Remember you're supposed to call her tomorrow, she asked you to call tomorrow. Well, he would have to wait until tomorrow, which was an eternity away.

"Randy…Randy…" Bucky was repeating.

"What!" Randy said with a jolt. Bucky had jolted him from his thoughts.

'You'd better come down here to the smoke spot. I think Lee's in a bit of trouble with Hammet…looks like there's going to be a fight."

Randy stared at Bucky. He couldn't tell if the buck-toothed, skinny weasel was happy about the situation or concerned. No doubt happy if he knew Bucky.

Chapter 16

Randy stood for a split second, trying to determine Bucky's motive for informing him of Lee's plight. He decided whatever the reason he had to go and help Lee. He felt nervous as his adrenaline surged through his veins.

He knew it was only Lee and himself and he didn't know if he could count on Bucky. Past history hadn't been kind to Bucky's reputation. He was more likely to stand at a distance or take leave of the area when it came to have been a part of the circumstances.

Randy hoped Arrington and his mates weren't behind the pool hall consorting with Hammet. Hammet would be a handful on his own, if he had help; Randy and Lee were in for a whipping. His cousin Dennis was nowhere near, as far as Randy knew.

He began to walk rapidly as Bucky was filling his ear with a rapid-fire explanation of how the altercation came to fruition.

"Sam was talking about bicycles and a dirt chunk hitting him in the head and how he was going to beat Lee's ass, your ass, Vern's ass and Picker's too. He said he didn't care if Dennis Wilts killed him. He said it'd be worth it to make you black and blue.

"Lee told Hammet that he had never looked as good as he did with all those dirt bombs bouncing on his head. That's when I came to get you."

Randy said nothing. He walked steadily down the alleyway hearing the crunch of pebble-sized rocks under his feet, mixed with the drone of Bucky's excited speech pattern. As he neared the corner of the building loud voices added to the din.

Randy rounded the corner with Bucky right on his heels like a puppy. Bucky almost ran into Randy as Randy stopped to view the scene. Bucky averted Randy and stood next to him. He was watching Randy more than the scene in front of them.

There were three people standing with their backs against the brick building, two sitting on the stoop to the back door of the pool hall and Basil Watts standing on the path, which led to the branch and its shortcut to the other side of town.

Randy didn't recognize a few of the spectators, but he knew Basil, the Truitts - Jim and Skylar - who were leaning on the wall, and he knew Todd Sturgiss, the state wrestling champ, one of the boys sitting on the stoop. No one seemed to want to help Lee who was being held in a headlock by Sam Hammet.

Most of the onlookers were older than Lee and Randy and knew Sam better, but Randy would have thought someone would have broken up the fight. He didn't expect everyone to come to Lee's immediate aid, because Lee did have a sarcastic way about him, but Sam Hammet wasn't the most beloved citizen of the area. Todd Sturgiss was the most puzzling, because Sam Hammet surely didn't intimidate him. He could stomp the dickens out of the fat bully with relative ease if he had the desire.

Todd had dated Lee's sister Rhoda for a while last summer, so Randy thought that Todd and Lee had a good relationship. Unless of course the breakup with Rhoda wasn't a clean one and Todd was pissed. Perhaps he was waiting to help after Sam placed a good scare into Lee, until Randy noticed Todd pick up a beer bottle resting on the step between his legs and spill the contents down his shirt. He wavered and peered down at the mess and didn't bother to clean it off. Todd was too drunk to tend to himself. He was in no condition to help Lee even if he had a mind to come to his aid.

"Well…well, Lee, look who's coming to join the public beating… the Dog Boy of Colmboro. Welcome, Dog Boy, I'll be with you in short order…this twiddle won't take long at all…right you smart mouth little shit." Sam Hammet squeezed Lee's head and neck a little harder. "How's that feel?"

Lee grunted with pain but managed to say, "Back off, Randy. I've got little dick right where I want him. Only if he tries to give me a French kiss…oomph…"

Sam punched Lee in the stomach. "That hurt, smart mouth?" he said giggling shrilly.

"Leave him alone, fat ass. You're such an asshole. You get that courage out of a beer can?" Randy asked angrily. He was edging closer to the entangled duo, his eyes in square contact with Sam Hammet's eyes.

"*Fat ass*…aw you hurt my feelings, Dog Boy, and look, you hurt piss heads' feelings too." Sam punched Lee in the stomach again. 'Don't go nowhere, Dog Boy or should I say woof, woof, woof, woof, bark, bark, bark, so that you can understand me better."

Lee looking silly bent over with his head in the crook of Sam's arm held tight retorted, "Run, Randy, Fatso is calling his girlfriends!"

The crowd chuckled and Lee took another blow to his stomach.

"That did it you tub of shit." Lee was angry and hurting from the last blow. He reached around Sam and squeezed Sam's scrotum with a great deal of force.

Sam roared with pain and released his hold on Lee. Lee let go of Sam's privates and attempted to scamper away. He was a bit lightheaded because he raised his head so fast and he stumbled on the loose gravel on the worn-out black-topped surface.

Sam held his privates with his right hand and reached out to grab Lee with his left hand. Lee didn't see Sam's arm coming and turned his head to see why the crowd was yelling to him to be careful. Sam's outstretched hand was inches from Lee's face, and with a force, Sam's reaching arm hit Lee's turned face. A loud slap was heard as Lee's eye made contact with Sam's fleshy hand.

Lee fell backward holding his hand to his eye.

Sam Hammet was still in pain from Lee's underhanded tactic, but the pain was waning. He laughed at Lee and felt a surge of bloodlust enter his psyche. He moved to pummel Lee until Lee cried out for his mommy. *Let's see how Rhoda feels about that, Sam thought.*

He didn't have a chance to strike Lee again. Sam Hammet had forgotten about Randy with his attention on Lee and his private pain. Randy had run up beside Sam ignoring Lee for a moment. He threw a punch that snapped Sam Hammet's head slightly to the left. It hurt Randy's fist more than it did Sam's rock-hard head, Randy reckoned.

Randy backed up. He jumped into his best pugilistic stance awaiting the fat bully's return fire. Sam kicked a futile kick at Lee before he turned to face Randy. Lee ducked and rolled clear. He rubbed his eye, stood up and prepared himself to jump onto Sam's back.

When Sam had fully turned to face Randy, Sam smiled a smile Randy didn't like to see. The smile held a great deal of contempt. Randy knew this time he wouldn't be let off the hook lightly. Sam knew Dennis would beat his ass later, but evidently beating Randy's ass now was going to be worth the thrashing that was to surely come.

Randy held his ground, fists up and legs apart. Sam raised his fists and Randy was nervous but prepared. There was no conversation except for the cheering of the bloodthirsty crew of ne'er-do-wells and drunks watching the fist of cuffs.

Sam charged Randy, his fist flying. Randy prepared to meet the challenge, which came much faster than he had anticipated. As Sam was charging, Lee had run up behind him and jumped onto Sam Hammet's back. The momentum caused the three, would-be fighters to tumble to the ground - the worst case scenario for the younger boys. Sam was too large on the ground, and he was sitting on Randy holding him down. With his meaty arm he was trying to pull Lee off his back so that he could pound Randy's face.

Randy was having trouble breathing with Sam on his chest. Lee didn't fair very well either. Sam had pulled him so hard that Lee had fallen off and struck his head on the hard blacktop and was momentarily dazed.

"I'm going to enjoy this," sneered Sam as he glared down at Randy.

Randy while finding it hard to breath with the crushing weight of Sam Hammet sitting on his chest tried to spit at Sam anyway. Randy was concerned that Sam would beat his face pretty good, but he was helpless to prevent it. He was pinned under Sam with his arms useless at his sides. He hoped that Lee would be able to help, and he wondered where his so-called friend Bucky was with trouble happening so lightning fast.

Randy closed his eyes in preparation to receive the heavy-fisted blows from his antagonizer. The he felt the weighty burden rise off his chest, and he heard Sam Hammet squeal a high-pitched wail of pain. Randy opened his eyes expecting to see Lee doing something dreadful to Sam Hammet, but it wasn't his friend Lee helping at all.

Barry Marshall had Sam by the hair and was jerking the two hundred-pound plus man literally off Randy and the ground with an easy-muscled effort. Barry's face was burning with intensity. Randy could see the surrounding crew of onlookers racing to the alleyway and out of harm's way.

"Let go of my hair you asshole! Ouch! Ouch!" Sam was hollering like a little kid in voice so high that it was laughable.

"Okay." A short reply was heard from Barry as he tossed Sam just to the right of Randy and Lee.

Sam Hammet had gone from the hunter to the prey. Everyone who had been watching Sam beat up on two young teens had exited with the exception of Todd Sturgiss. He appeared to have passed out on the steps and no one waited around to revive him so that he could leave as well.

Barry towered over Sam as Sam stayed on the ground rubbing his head, hoping he had suffered the worst Barry was going to administer. He resembled a cowering dog vanquished by a superior rival.

Lee and Randy were on their feet glaring down at the rotund blob, whom no longer appeared menacing but sheepish instead. It was incredibly quiet as Barry hovered with his dominant presence holding back his aggression momentarily. Lee felt the need to keep his thoughts to himself absorbing Barry's command of the situation.

"L-l-l-look, Barry, I…" Sam stuttered holding his arms up toward the large man then sweeping them over to Randy and Lee to stand up

Barry remained quiet, but interrupted Sam by placing a finger to his lips and shaking his head. He motioned for Sam to stand up. With a great deal of apprehension Sam Hammet raised himself to his feet and stood like a schoolboy caught by his teacher acting naughtily. He kicked softly at the ground peering down at his shoes.

"Randy, my man, take your buddy here and move on up to the front of the pool hall. I've got some words that need to be said to our mutual friend, and it's best that I say them in private."

There was no argument from Randy or Lee. Randy felt a little sorry for Sam and almost spoke to Barry about mercy. But Sam had earned what he was about to receive and sometimes it takes a hard lesson to learn proper behavior.

As they turned to walk away, Lee muttered under his breath to Randy, "I hope he busts him up good, the fat shit."

"He just may do that, Lee. That is if Barry doesn't mind getting shit and piss on his hands. I think Sam's messed up big this time."

The boys rounded the corner of the building and without turning back to see if anything was happening, they heard the pounding of footsteps as if someone was running and someone was chasing them. The chase didn't last long and the boys heard a muffled cry accompanied by one or two open-handed slaps. Evidently Barry didn't want to leave too many bruises. Lee felt some satisfaction and Randy had mixed feelings knowing Sam Hammet had taken his stupid beating for reasons only that Sam knew the answers.

Karen was waiting in front of the movie theater talking to Donzella when the two boys arrived. Randy could see Harvey driving up the hill toward them to pick them up for the ride home.

"Where's Barry?" Donzella asked.

"Chasing varmints," Lee answered.

"What?" Karen and Donzella asked simultaneously.

"Nothing, he's talking to Sam Hammet," Randy said with a gentle nod toward Mr. Miler who was standing behind the glass doors most likely listening to their conversation.

Lee glanced over in the direction of Randy's nod and smiled.

Harvey pulled up and stopped the car. He said hello to Donzella through the open window and waited for the kids to enter the car. Barry rounded the corner appearing perfectly normal.

"Ready, Donnie?" he asked.

"Guess so...everything alright?"

"Is now..."

"Thanks, Barry," Randy said.

"No problem, my brother...like I said...if you're a good enough to be Donnie's blood...you're a friend of mine."

"What's going on?" Karen asked. "Lee, what happened to you?"

"I'll tell you on the ride home, sis," Randy said.

With that said, they kissed Donzella goodbye waved to Barry once more, and entered the car for the ride back to the farm.

Randy could see Bucky standing down on the corner under the street sign mixing with some of the other spectators dragging on a cigarette. He nodded at Randy displaying a sheepish look on his visage. Randy gazed through him and ignored the boy like he was invisible.

Randy didn't see the old beat-up pickup truck parked in the Silco parking lot. Inside Caleb Fulton surveyed the conclusion of the night's events. He drank from a Mason jar holding whiskey, gently tapping on the steering wheel, pondering thoughts that were wondering through his mind. He reached over with his right hand holding the Mason jar and nudged the obviously inebriated man sitting on the passenger side of the truck. Pup raised his head from his chest and peered at the offering somewhat confused. Not needing another drop of the magic water, he took the jar anyway and slurped down a swallow leaving whiskey trails down the sides of his chin. He returned the jar to the driver and rested his head on his chest in a drunken slumber.

Caleb put away the Mason jar by placing it between his legs. He started the truck and drove out of the parking lot. He went at least three or four blocks before he remembered to turn on his headlights. He knew it was time to go home. He would let Pup sleep off his inebriation in the truck. He wondered if Pup's wife missed him after Pup had vacated the big-time barbecue. Probably not, she hadn't wanted him there anyway. Caleb was thankful Pup had been around today. He could use him for companionship and other sordid things.

Chapter 17

While Sam Hammet nursed his wounds, both physical and mental, and Harvey drove the car towards his farmhouse, the night air was cooling down. The heat was escaping from the earth and radiating up into the atmosphere. The clear sky sparkled with brilliant white dots somewhat irregular in shape. Off in the distance just above the horizon, a low stratus of light blinked a layer of incandescent glow. The heat lightning was a marvel of summertime indicating a thunderstorm for someone somewhere.

With the air cooling and the black-topped macadam still warm, slowly releasing its heat, the six-month-old puppies gradually found their way onto the surface for its dangerous comfort. The puppies had a habit for a while now of laying on the road and most drivers in the area knew they might be sleeping on the road. The drivers would take care when driving by the Kearny's farm to avoid the little furry dogs.

As the puppies aged, experience taught them lessons vastly needed for survival. They knew they should move from the road as cars and trucks ventured upon them. But as with children of any species, judgment was sometimes lacking. Just that afternoon, Harvey had to shoo the three miniature canines to his grassy front yard when he had approached his farm after fetching Karen and Randy.

The comfort from the warm country road provided a dangerous enticement for the three sleepy siblings. They were often too slow to move even when they had decided they should. Their keen sense of hearing notified them a vehicle of some type was approaching. They could hear the rubber tires grabbing at polished stones in the black topped surface. They could hear the purring hum of the motor as it moved ever closer. They could see the headlights of the car as it bored down upon them.

Three little heads rose from the road from the warm in unison. The familiar sound of the Ford LTD set the puppy's tails to wagging.

But as the car approached, the warmth of the road coupled with the comfort of the played-out puppies proved to be a strong attraction to the young dogs and they were powerless to resist. It was like sleeping in soft bed snuggled under the covers on a dark rainy morning as the alarm clock sounded the knell for another day of work.

The car slowed on the approach but was moving a little too quickly to pull to a complete stop. The pups had positioned themselves in a new spot on the road partially hidden in a small dip in the roadway obscuring the view of Harvey as he motored toward the farm. He hit the brakes hard squealing the tires, while Karen had let out a shriek, which produced an expletive from the normally sedate Harvey.

The heavy car strained at the brake pedal with little distance to complete the stop. Serendipity played a hand with the car pulling to the right and the young pups managing to stand up and scamper to the left of the car. The wheel of the driver's side nearly finished the life of the first born, clipping his tail, causing him to yelp and hop like a scared rabbit to the shoulder of the road. By the grace of God the trio of puppies remained intact, but for an inch or two the trio would be a duo.

Harvey guided the car to a stop and jumped out of the door in a motion so fast, Randy sat in disbelief. He didn't know his slow-moving uncle had such quick reflexes. He saw him as an elderly man whose youth had passed him by even though his uncle was only thirty-six years old.

Harvey surveyed the doe-eyed dogs. They looked scared but wagged their tails furiously with the attention from the alpha male. Harvey's voice boomed, "GET THE HELL IN THE BACK YARD. GO ON! GO ON! DAMN YOUR HIDES!"

The puppies turned and scampered away happy to be away from the shouting and agitated farmer.

Harvey reentered the quiet car. Only the smooth-running engine could be heard inside. Karen had turned off the radio. All heads turned to Harvey as he pulled the door closed carefully without slamming it. He seemed to have regained his composure instantly. He depressed the brake pedal and moved the gearshift into the drive position and ventured the remaining few feet onto the gravel driveway.

The usual posse of dogs greeted the car. Betsy the shepherd was at the head of the pack. The dogs surrounded the car with tails wagging, noising small groans of affection and a great deal of maneuvering for a pet on the head. Randy, Lee and Karen rubbed as many heads as they could, feeling happy for a greeting and knowing that the puppies were still alive.

Harvey and Karen waded their way through the crowd of dogs toward the house. Karen went inside and Harvey sauntered toward his chicken houses for one last look around for the night. He turned his head sideways to peer at the puppies, which were lying down under the cherry tree by the picnic table. All three were resting their heads on their paws with a sorrowful expression on their faces. They moved only their eyes to watch Harvey trying to seem indifferent, but wanting his approval. The large light pole illuminated the back yard and large bugs flew around attracted by the light.

Harvey smiled a very slight smile, his lips barely moving on the corner of his mouth turning up ever so slightly. The puppies were too cute to ignore or to be angry at anymore. He tapped his outer thigh and clucked his tongue. The puppies responded immediately. They sprang to their feet and raced to catch up with the gentle, quiet man. Nipping at his heels, they followed him while he made his final night time check.

Randy and Lee chatted a few moments before Lee crossed the road to go home. They talked about Sam Hammet briefly, but really had set the incident behind them for the time being. They had purposely not spoken of the fight on the ride home because they didn't want to involve Harvey. Karen kept her discretion knowing Randy would fill her in later.

The elation the boys felt-that even Sam Hammet couldn't dampen, was their forays into the world of romance. They were giddy about having to have actually held, kissed, and caressed creatures of the opposite sex. Their usual lewd comments relating to actions they would have taken given the opportunity were muted when discussing their respective dates. Respect and possessiveness was dominant in the conversation when boasting of whom had the prettiest, nicest girl.

Randy entered the house whistling '*That's Amore*' subconsciously while he fantasized about Mary Jo. He guided himself over to the refrigerator surveyed the contents and pulled a piece of ham from its package. He repeated the procedure with a piece of provolone cheese and rolled the two together. He stopped whistling long enough to devour the light snack. He grabbed the glass bottle of milk popped the cardboard stopper and drank down a few gulps before replacing it on the wire metal shelf. His aunt would have a fit watching him, but he knew she was dead asleep by this time in her four- poster bed.

Randy skipped up the stairs as light as a feather softly whistling his tune occasionally singing the chorus when it was appropriate. He passed his sister's room at the top of the stairs and glanced inside the darkened room. He could see Karen's silhouette under the covers.

"Quiet, lover boy, some people are trying to sleep."

Randy laughed. "My happiness kills you don't it?"

"Quite the contrary, my inferior little sibling. I figure it's about time you went out with a girl. My friends were starting to ask me if my brother was sweet on boys or something."

"Your jealous friends should ask the lover boy himself. If they're nice enough perhaps, and I repeat *perhaps*, they may have a chance at experiencing my Casanova- style skills," Randy quipped. He moved into the room and sat down on the edge of his sister's bed.

"I guess you had a pretty good time tonight with Mary Jo," Karen said as she sat up and fluffed the pillows behind her.

"It was great and Mary Jo is great. Where were you all night?"

"I went to the drive-in in Denton. I met Chuck there and we had a nice chat…to tell you the truth…it was kind of nice just to sit and talk without having to fend off an octopus trying to paw my parts."

"You like Chuck, don't you?"

"Yeah he's nice and gentlemanly. However I like Gregory for different reasons. Some I can't explain, but to tell you the truth…he's unpredictable and spontaneous and I find that exciting. Although it's difficult occasionally because for some reason he tries my patience something terrible."

Randy was thinking about how Mary Jo perceived him. Who was he and who did he want to be? He didn't know if a Gregory personality was manufactured or if Gregory was born as crazy as he was. Randy knew one thing - Gregory sure had sex appeal, because lots of girls found him attractive. Perhaps Randy thought they found him desirable and it was a subconscious competition between the girls to see who would be the victor to tame the wild child.

"Was Picker with you?" Randy asked.

"He was in the car with Leigh Ann. Your buddy Picker's quite the kisser I hear."

"Must have practiced on his sisters."

Karen laughed. "Incest is best I hear."

"We will never know. Don't tell anyone I was in your bed tonight or they'll get the wrong idea."

"Don't worry, pud puller, that's the last thing I would want being spread around about me."

"By the way, I owe you big time for that safety pin you fixed me up with…my turn will come, missy."

Randy and Karen talked another fifteen minutes with Karen almost rolling out of bed with laughter as Randy told his sister what had transpired with the safety pin she had used to close the hole in his pants.

He filled her in on Sam Hammet and she steamed about the bloated bully while he told the story. They both agreed Sam had deserved the beating Barry had administered to Sam. They wondered how bad Dennis would beat him if he caught wind of the incident, and chances were pretty good he'd find out with so many spectators observing the ruckus.

Randy walked himself out and over to his room at the top of the stairs. He actually had to step down into the room. Harvey had this part of the house added on after the original structure had been built. Randy had stayed in that room since he was a tot. At first both he and his sister had slept there, but as they grew older, Karen had taken the room to the left at the top of the staircase.

The room had many advantages. It was above the kitchen with a register to help heat the room cut through the floor to the ceiling below. The wonderful aromas of Caroline's cooking filtered up easily through the metal grate warming Randy's heart and making his stomach growl with anticipation; especially on Sunday mornings when his aunt cooked the tomato sauce for that evening's dinner.

The room also gave easy access to the roof of the porch and Randy and Karen liked to sit on the roof watching the unfolding of country life.

If the room had one failing, it was that the door to the attic led out from the room. When the room was built, in order to accommodate the adjacent wall, the stairs to the attic were rerouted with a slight twist and turn, so that the door was placed in the very room Randy slept in on his frequent visits, because of aesthetics.

Randy and his sister had visited the attic innumerable times. It was full of wonderful old junk hat they had examined time after time. Their aunt had collected *Reader Digest* magazines since her marriage to Harvey and there were stacks and stacks of the condensed-storied magazines. There were many other artifacts of his aunt's youth and on occasion he would find an artifact once possessed by his absent father.

Randy had collected all the possessions with his father's touch and had placed them in a chest by the lone window of the attic. He would sit by the window and examine this booty and daydream about how it would be to wear his father's shoes when he was young. Randy's sister Karen wouldn't have anything to do with the memories. She wouldn't even discuss her reasons why with Randy, which was rare, because they usually discussed everything they had experienced in life.

Randy had asked his aunt if he could perhaps take some of the items home with him on many occasions, but she was reluctant and insisted that the items stay there at the farm. He didn't push the subject. He only asked her permission from time to time hoping that she would change her mind.

These were the fun aspects of the attic. The attic was also a scary place especially when it was dark outside. Randy had been up in the attic by himself on a very rare occasion. The place haunted him when he was alone. He felt such an eerie feeling; any noise, creak or squeak of the floorboards set his nerves on edge. When it was windy outside, the wind seemed to blow through the attic causing a slight shrill whistle to sound up in the garret like a ghostly boo, a wooing noise raising and lowering in pitch. When he was younger, he had his uncle investigate the noise before he would be able to go to sleep.

On nights that he had watched a thriller style movie in town at Walker's theater the attic was overwhelmingly intimidating. Sometimes the sneaky wind would roll down the winding stairs of the attic and wobble the door a time or two before falling silent, touching Randy with terror. It tempted him to run and seek help for demons imagined so vividly that they were all too real.

His sister shared his apprehension when she had shared the room with him, but when she had matured and had moved to her present bedroom, she left the feeling behind her. Randy had only in the past few years been mature enough not to let his imagination run away with him. This did not however stop him from resorting to the old time tactic he and his sister had used many times of covering their heads like ostriches when given the heebie jeebies by the almost alive attic.

Tonight was not a night to feel the effects of those demons. Randy lay on his bed under a sheet and he could feel the breeze of the rotating fan blow across his body on regular intervals. The hum of the motor and purr of the fan blades were a comfort to him. It was not entirely warm enough for the fan, but Randy liked it to be cool when he slept and the fan enabled him to snuggle under his sheet as the night faded into morning.

He was in his sleep twilight thinking of Mary Jo and he was content. He could still smell her hair, feel her soft skin and taste her sweet mouth. He remembered her taunt rear end and his embarrassing venture to feel her breast. He would never forget the smell of her Windsong perfume as long as he lived. He reached his hand inside of his underwear and held himself with great comfort. He felt he had taken a major step tonight in his rite into manhood. His path from bicycle riding, prepubescent early teenager into, in his opinion, early manhood was now a path leading into a future of more mature experiences.

Mary Jo his object of his affection was a reality he could now enjoy. He remembered the night in intense detail. He went over each moment step by step suddenly moving into a sense of uncertainty. *Did I do this right or should I have done this at that time…why did I do that…how should I have acted when she did that?*

He reassured himself by thinking everything went just fine with the exception of the safety pin incident. But then the doubts came roaring back. *What if she thought he was a dweeb for sticking himself with the safety pin?* He couldn't wait to see tomorrow to see how she would react to him. Now he felt that the night would never end. He had to know how she felt about him. Perhaps he would ask her if she thought he was weird. No, that would be stupid. Maybe he shouldn't bring that to her attention. Oh hell, he didn't know what to do. He needed to see her soon to get a feel for the situation.

Randy was on the verge of falling into a deep sleep and at the moment he would have traversed over to the subconscious side of time, his uncle began to stomp and scrape at his work boots on the cement block set up by the porch door. It was set there on purpose to help clean the chicken manure from the soles of his heavy steel toed boots. Caroline had insisted that they be as clean as possible before entering the porch. Once on the porch, which was screened in the summer and had storm windows applied in the winter for outdoor sitting, the boots were to be removed and set upon the mat just inside of the door. Harvey knew the routine and followed the procedure perfectly so as not to incite the fiery temper of his Italian wife.

Randy and Karen had sat through many an argument between the couple. Harvey was sitting quietly interjecting an occasional jab to stoke the fire of his quick-to-flare spouse. Caroline even though quick to ire was also quick to laugh and most arguments turned to laughter once both participants had conveyed their points.

Randy hearing his uncle and recognizing the familiar sounds drifted off to his slumber. His uncle made his way to the master bedroom and had begun to undress and prepare himself for bed.

As Karen, Randy and Caroline slept and Harvey was pulling his leg from his trousers, a roaring engine could be heard outside racing down the road. Harvey knew the car was moving fast because of how quick it had been between his first recognition of the sound to how fast the volume increased in intensity. He shook his head at the immaturity of the driver and hoped that whoever was driving the car wasn't drunk.

He didn't anticipate the squealing tires and the yelping of dogs. The noise was extremely loud. It sounded as though the car would be crashing through their front door. He leapt up to pull his trousers back on his body. The noise woke up Caroline from a dead sleep.

"What's going on?" She asked as she sat bolt upright.

'Don't know," Harvey said racing to the front door.

Karen and Randy had met him at the bottom of the stairs. They all hurried outside to find the dreadful sight of the poor little puppies. There was no hope. All three lay still with moon illuminating their inert bodies. A black liquid surrounded their heads and dripped from their muzzles. The three siblings had been scattered around the road and weren't really close to one another. It appeared that whoever was driving the long-gone car had deliberately swerved to kill the puppies intentionally.

Caroline and Karen were in tears. Harvey silently checked the puppies for any sign of life of which there was none. Randy stood misty eyed and surveyed the scene. The other dogs had come and circled the humans and dead puppies hanging their heads in an apparent cognitive gesture. One dog stood back, his colors shone black and gray under the bright white celestial orb above the gathering. He began to howl with sadness and was joined by Bessie and all the other dogs in the sadness, creating an eerie chorus of a death knell.

Death comes to all species and saddens the heart, but the death of babies, of ones so young, creates a much deeper sadness no one cares to experience.

Chapter 18

Randy and his aunt helped Karen back inside of the house. She was bordering on the hysterical, crying and shaking and drawing in rapid, short breaths between heavy sobs. Aunt Caroline had retrieved a paper bag and was having Karen breathe into it to stop the hyperventilation.

Harvey had shooed everyone away and was taking care of the burial by himself. He wanted to be alone and convinced Randy to help his aunt take care of his sister. It really didn't take a great deal of convincing; Randy had no desire to deal with the dead dogs. And while he wasn't too savvy at comforting people who were sad or distressed, it was the lesser of two evils.

Eventually they had settled Karen down to a reasonable emotional level. The three of them retired for the evening going to their respective bedrooms.

Randy could hear muffled sobs emanate from his sister's room on occasion and wondered how long his sister would continue to cry. He knew she was very emotional and she hated to see any creatures hurt or killed. She deplored hunting and wouldn't even let Randy squash bugs, providing they were outside. Inside, the bugs were a different matter, she didn't want them dead, but she was reluctant to have them inside with her. She loved dogs as much as anyone did and Randy knew she was hurt deep down. She would mourn quite a while for the poor puppies. He felt sadness, but realized in a day or so, he would move on emotionally.

He had heard his uncle reenter the house. Randy really didn't know how long it had been since uncle had been out burying the puppies. Time wasn't really relevant now. He heard his uncle go through the ritual of cleaning his boots, placing them by the door and finally locking up the house.

Randy felt sleep coming, and again closed his eyes. His uncle had come in the house and had sat in his wing-backed chair with the lights out. Softly he cried by himself for the despair he felt for his babies. He meditated about twenty minutes and then went to bed. He didn't want his wife to know he had been crying, even though she knew.

Caroline had feigned sleep as he climbed into bed. She had her back to him. Harvey scooted close and wrapped his arms around her rotund body. He held her close and Caroline moaned with comforting feel of his body. They both lay awake for awhile contemplating the events of the past few days. Not knowing each was thinking on the same page, their thoughts were that this incident was no accident. Someone had deliberately killed those puppies.

Randy awoke with the call of the rooster. The sun was barely above the horizon. He lay on his back with his arms behind his head on the soft foam rubber pillow. He stared up at the ornate light fixture above that hung from the ceiling. With his mind somewhat blank, he began to count the square ceiling tiles by row and then by column trying to calculate how many were glued on the ceiling. He attempted this many times, but usually gave up because near the walls, the ceiling tiles weren't square and he was defeated by his attempt to cipher how many there would be if they were reassembled into whole pieces.

His night had been very restless one. He must have slept, but didn't feel like he had at all. It was a sleep on the surface of sleep. He was never able to shut down his mind fully. Yesterday had been an event filled day; beginning with his arrival at the farm. The adventure in the woods, his surprise at the attention of Mary Jo Magurk, the not one but two altercations with Sam Hammet, his fantasy dancing date with Mary Jo and finally the abrupt sadness at the deaths of the young puppies. All too much for his mind to file away in its proper compartments in one short night.

He rolled to the side of the bed and sat up. His feet reached the hardwood floor and it felt a little sticky from the humidity beginning to build in the atmosphere. The gentle fan rotated in his direction and brushed its mechanically produced wind across his face.

Randy stood up and walked over to the chair sitting beside the dresser holding his clothes. He dressed himself and looked in the mirror at his reflection. He fluffed his hair. It would need help to tame a cowlick or two. This he would handle in the bathroom.

He walked down the stairs after taking a peek into Karen's room, noting she was still in bed. He tried to be quiet, but the stairs creaked as he walked down them.

He refreshed himself in the bathroom and headed into the kitchen. He couldn't shake the feeling something wasn't quite right. He sighed heavily and greeted his aunt a good morning.

She was seated at the table drinking coffee. His uncle was surely making his rounds already. A farm and its chores waited for no one. There were things to done, no matter the circumstance of the day.

Randy begged off breakfast explaining to his aunt that he wasn't hungry yet. He would return in an hour or two and grab a bite to eat. He wanted to walk in the woods sit by the bank of the creek and clear his head. Afterward he would come back and help his uncle with some of the work around the farm and then sit down with her to eat some chow.

Usually his aunt wouldn't tolerate this type of thought process. She would have insisted he first sit down and have his breakfast, and then he would have to help his uncle clear up the morning tasks. Only then would he have the time for himself considered. But this morning was an emotional one, sadness producing lethargy, not of laziness but of emotional draining of the soul and spirit. Life was precious here on the farm and the killing that was done was done only for food.

The Kearny's loved their dogs. Last night's tragedy was akin to losing family members - family members who were sadly so young.

Even though Randy said he wasn't hungry, he picked up a glazed donut off the freezer, which had been delivered by the Bond Bread salesman on his visit the previous day. Randy exited the house and was greeted by a few members of the tail wagging pack that populated the farm. He rubbed some heads and talked to the groaning, happy whining canines. They continued bumping his hands for more petting, but Randy walked briskly to the woods. The dogs followed a short distance, then stopped and returned to the farmhouse. It would be feeding time soon and they didn't want to miss their turns at their food bowls.

The trip across the field went quickly. Randy pushed his way through the waist high weeds that was leftover from the winter wheat mixed with some wild oats and tall grass shoots. His uncle would plow this under during the early fall or late summer and plant the winter wheat or hay to sell for extra cash to the area livestock farmers. Randy's gait was too quick on occasion and he caught his toe in the ground once or twice and did a quick recovery before stumbling to the ground. He could feel the long plants grabbing and pulling at his legs.

The sun was warming up fast and the humidity gathered around him causing sweat beads to form on his face because of his exertion. As he neared the woods, he remembered the wild cats and this caused him to slow and pause. He wondered what he should do if he encountered the cats again. He didn't want to go without protection. He hadn't brought his 22-caliber rifle as he had intended and didn't wish to depend on Pony the wonder dog. He didn't even know where the Pony was or if he was even still in the neighborhood.

Randy surveyed the area leading up and into the woods. Morning Glories bloomed peppering the vine like grass with sheets of color - purples, reds and blues. Small saplings sprouted from the ground, and the underbrush though very thin was forging its way out of the woods encroaching onto the soon-to-be-tilled land. He spied one or two heavy sticks he felt might be suitable for use in protecting himself against the cats if necessary. He bent to pick up each stick feeling its heft, smoothness of its bark and its density. He selected the first one over the second and crossed over to the opening in the trees. He skirted along the path, which led down to the creek.

A few yards down the path, Randy saw a pole he felt that would be perfect for his protection. Bent over and broken near its base was a Devil's Walking stick - a plant that had sharp thorns covering its bark. He kicked it over with some difficulty because even though it was broken it held fast to its stump. Once he had it free, he delicately picked it up and knocked enough thorns off one end with his pocket knife so that he could hold it and swing it with both hands.

He felt well protected now. He imagined himself a medieval knight with a spiked sword ready to tear his enemy to smithereens. He was empowered with courage while he held his weapon of destruction. Let the crazed cats attack. Randy wasn't one to cause harm to living animals, but they had attacked him first and he wanted some retribution or at least the need to feel superior to the lower species of life. He daydreamed about swatting the cats to the side causing them to retreat in terror.

Randy began to move forward on the path again swinging his club back and forth at the reaching tree limbs hacking them off with relative ease. It was cool under the temperate canopy of trees. Occasionally a drop of water remaining from the dew's condensation would drop down landing in front of and behind him and sometimes a direct hit on his body. The sunlight dappled the path dancing as a small breeze rustled the trees. The birds sang their morning songs, chirping was heard among the whistling tones of the refreshed birds. He could hear off in the distance the call of a bob white sounding its self-naming moniker.

He was nearing the place on the beaten down dirt path where the cats had been devouring their meal on his last visit. He could feel himself tense up, his eyes darting back and forth searching for any signs of the wild animals. His heart beat a fast beat thumping in his ears as he moved forward. He was apprehensive and confused as to whether or not he really wanted to encounter his day-before nemesis.

A snap of a twig or perhaps a falling branch echoed seemingly close to where Randy was walking. Adding to his on-the-edge state of nervousness, the noise prodded Randy to panic. He suddenly burst into a full running start. He was near enough to the opening instinctively his decision was to reach the clearing for additional space in which to defend himself if it became necessary. After three or four loping strides his coordination became slightly confused because of his thorned stick. The stick struck the ground digging its end into the dirt resulting in Randy releasing his handled end. As he let go, the stick stayed implanted and Randy ran a half step striking the end of the stick, which jabbed painfully into his groin. Randy basically pole vaulted using his lower abdomen through the air. The pain was terribly intense but Randy didn't stop. He hobbled quickly through the trees to the open area beside the creek.

Once he was through he turned to see what was behind him and saw nothing but his imagination. He bent over and laughed at his antic and groaned at the same time. He was happy no one was around to see him. He was too jumpy. He held his abdomen in a bent over position and walked slowly to his stone chair for a well-earned rest.

Randy looked at his chair and sitting in it was the dog Pony. The dog made no effort to move. His tail wasn't wagging and while he didn't appear to be aggressive, Randy was unnerved. Invoking a friendly tone in his voice while clapping his hands Randy said, "Hey, Pony...how you doing boy?"

After hearing Randy's voice the dog barked softly, his tail began to wag and he walked over to Randy with his head bowed-apparently expecting a pet on the head. Randy obliged by rubbing his head and scratching behind the dog's ears. Randy reached into his top pocket for the half of a donut he had saved for his respite by the creek. It came out in crumbling pieces.

Pony eyed the donut with anxious hunger. Randy felt the pressure of the famished dog and tossed him the remaining pieces. He wished that he had more to feed the dog. He would coax the dog up to the farmhouse and feed him something shortly.

The dog eyeballed Randy and his hands and realized that there was no more food. He turned and walked to the creek gingerly. Leaning back on his haunches at the water edge he carefully craned his neck to allow his muzzle to hover near the water's surface. He gently lapped at the brownish water to quench his thirst.

Randy still sore from the inadvertent pole vault held his groin and walked over to his stone chair and sat down. The seat was warm from the dog's body heat and contrasted to the coolness of the rock serving as the back and arms of the chair.

He sat back and watched the gentle flow of the creek. As he stretched out his legs, he began to cool off from his short but arduous trek from the farmhouse to his seat in his Shangri-La. Pony sat by the bank with his nose in the air sniffing at the slight intermittent breeze that was blowing across the open area of the creek and sand that was sandwiched between the woods lining the edges of nature's watery road.

Randy was peering through the trees on the other side of the creek and could see the outline of the Magurk house. He wished that he could see Mary Jo peering in return from her bedroom window. He had such a good time with her. He couldn't wait to see her once again. Perhaps he would see her at the millpond later, if not, surely she would be at the barrel-racing corral tonight. The Glenns sponsored barrel racing and other rodeo events occasionally at the small rodeo grounds that they had built on their land down on the big curve a quarter of a mile from the millpond. Their daughter, Joy, was a proficient rider and used the events to showcase her talents. It was said that she was a world-class rider, but wasn't allowed on the circuit because her dad couldn't bear to have her away from him so often without at least one parent nearby to watch over her.

Intensely independent, Joy agreed not to venture out onto the rodeo circuit, but she insisted that she be able to have an outlet to practice her skills in view of an appreciative audience. Over the years, a number of people had taken up barrel racing as a sport, and the Glenns had erected the grounds to allow an occasional competition. The summer date was a big one and drew riders from around the state.

Joy had been satisfied with the arrangement and truly wouldn't have left to compete anyway because her boyfriend, now fiancé, Rob Romo.

The Romo family owned a great deal of land in the county and Rob's uncle was a State Legislator. There was a small amount of friction between the Glenns and Romos because of a land squabble from years past, but Joy and Rob's relationship bridged the gap on the surface.

Both the Romos and Glenns lived in stately manor homes. The Romo house was set back deep into their surrounding acreage with the tall maples shading the huge brick home. The electronic gate protecting the long oyster shell drive to the entrance was more of a showpiece for the community than a security device, because a well-painted split rail fence, which anyone could step over or crawl underneath with little effort, surrounded the homestead.

The Glenn house was set on the curve between the millpond and rodeo corral. It set up on a hill, which was completely out of character for the topography of the surrounding land. With all the land around it flat as a pancake, the large, white, wood- frame house sat majestically with its tall pillars and expansive veranda on top of the hill. The road leading up to the house was paved and lined with flowering shrubs and towering trees. Down the slope to the creek, which flowed by, was well-manicured grass. The grass was mowed but allowed to retain some length so that a breeze of any sort would ripple across the lea creating a beautiful effect.

The two families had a huge influence in the community of Colmboro, but largely kept to themselves. They attended the church and made appearances at high-profile social events. They were invited to Pup and Arlene's barbecue. Arlene would have been beside herself and would have attained enormous social standing among her peers had they shown up, but both families had sent their regrets at having had previous commitments.

Randy's sister Karen was acquainted with Joy, and they had hung around with the older Magurk sister, Leigh Ann, a few years ago. As time passed and the age difference affected the teen age years of the girls, they hung around with each other a lot less of the time. Joy was three years older and in teenage years, that was as a good as a decade in appearance. Joy was still friendly but with a debutante's remoteness.

Randy's uncle sold winter hay to the Glenns, but did little if no business with the Romos. The Romos had tried to acquire Harvey's land but had been rebuffed many times, much to Stanley Romo's dismay.

Stanley Romo wanted the land that bordered the creek to enhance his land holding portfolio, but he had been stymied for years. The land bordering the creek was held precious by the farmers and had been owned by the families for years. They were not about to relinquish their titles at a reasonable price. The land held more than value, it was a legacy passed from one generation to another.

Randy was half dozing. He was extremely comfortable and dog-tired. The shading of the trees kept him cool enough even as the summer sun was rising rapidly above the tree line. His thoughts were moving from one subject to another, randomly touching areas of pleasure and angst, finally settling on his desire and intimacy for and with Mary Jo.

Pony rose from his prone position on the sandy soil. His ears perked up and he concentrated his gaze up the creek toward the direction of the Foster cabin. He didn't bark. It was more of a low-throated growl - not threatening but enough to catch Randy's attention.

"What's up, boy" Randy asked.

Pony glared at him and returned his focus back up the creek. He sat dead still staring but not barking.

Randy scratched his head and curiosity rolled through his body. He pushed himself up and walked over to the dog and stayed with him.

Randy could see Picker walking slowly toward him. Picker had his hand down and didn't see Randy observing him.

"PICKER!" Randy shouted.

A startled Picker, who was deep in thought, froze in his tracks resembling a mannequin in a walking pose.

Randy laughed.

"You scared me," Picker laughed. "What are you doing out here so early?"

"Trying to be alone. What are you doing out here?"

"Walking the woods. I love it the first thing in the morning. I see that dog is still here. He was here when I walked by earlier… sleeping on your stone throne."

"Yeah I don't know where he came from, but I like him. Besides he kept the chair warm for my butt…sometimes the base takes awhile to warm up. Probably going to give me hemorrhoids or something." Randy bent to rub the dog's head. "I call him Pony."

"Pony? You're calling a dog, Pony?"

"What's wrong with that?" Randy asked.

"I don't know. It just seems odd to name an animal another animal's name."

"Picker, I didn't give it that much thought. But now it's too late. Once you've got a name it can't be changed otherwise you become someone else."

Picker screwed up his face and looked at Randy with the puzzled look on his visage. "What the hell are you talking about?"

Randy moved back to his chair and sat down. "Trivialities my friend…trivialities. What did you find on your walk?"

"Well I'll tell you this - those wild cats must be multiplying pretty fast because I see far too many locations where something has feasted on birds, and it's causing me to seek methods of eradication I would never have considered before."

"How do you know something ate the birds? Maybe they just lost some feathers."

"Randy, I've walked these woods for years. I know the difference between one or two loose feathers from molting birds and piles of feathers containing bird parts."

"Don't tell me…the bird parts gave it away."

Picker scrunched his brow and nodded in Randy's direction. "You're one clever young man, Randy."

Randy laughed. 'What do you mean you're going to do something drastic about the cats? You going to shoot them?"

"Don't know. I'm not usually for harming any animal but they're killing my birds and that's pissing me off."

"Speaking of birds, have a seat and let us discuss the prospects of being brother-in-laws." Randy motioned for Picker to sit down on a log resting beside his chair.

Picker peered at him with an amused grin. He moved over to the log, brushed it off with a sweep of his hand and sat down. "I see the king keeps the throne and allows the peons to sit on an old piece of termite infested wood so as to garner valuable Magurk information."

"Well yes - all I really need is a scepter and an orb to rule conclusively. I do think it would be wise of my subjects to share information regarding the Magurk clan as it would be in their best interest as well."

"I don't know about the orb, but you truly are a sphincter. What do you want to know about the Magurks?" Picker mused. "I really don't know if I would like to have you as a brother-in-law though?"

"Quite insolent you are my subject, but I'll forgive you. Let's move on to a better topic.

"Did you boink Leigh Ann last night? Better yet, how many times have you boinked her?"

Picker played in the sand with a stick. He sat pensively for a moment and then he said, "Strange thing, Randy, all these years we've discussed exactly what we would do to girls, especially the Magurk girls - if we had the chance. But now that I'm seeing Leigh Ann…I feel like it would be demeaning to her to discuss the intimacy that we share.

"Don't get me wrong. I would love to stand on top of the roof and crow like a rooster about it, but it just doesn't seem right."

Randy leaned back in his chair until his head touched the back of the stone chair. He stretched his legs out and bounced his heels lightly in the sand. He said, "I'm not asking you to put it on the eleven o'clock news. I just want to live through your worldly eyes. You know how much I look up to you."

Picker snickered with a slight snort and said, "You're full of it. Besides why would you need to live vicariously through me when you had Mary Jo purring like a kitten at the dance?"

Randy blushed and blossomed with a happy emotion like a peacock fanning out his tail to impress a nearby peahen.

"I want to learn from you. You had Vern's rain gear and were unable to return it."

"I could have lost it you know."

"Then the gentry wouldn't have been served would it?"

Picker sat amused. He tossed the twig he was using to draw in the sand far into the creek. Pony watched as it flew into the water. Pony and Randy then turned their heads to Picker in anticipation of hearing sordid details.

Randy leaned forward rubbed the small of his back and then settled back into his chair crossing his legs at his ankles. Pony rose to his feet and ambled over to Randy and lay at Randy's thigh within reach of his hand. Pony rested his chin on Randy's leg and rolled his eyes up at Randy enticing Randy to rub his head. Randy obliged slowly stroking the furry head of his newfound friend.

A few more minutes of human silence followed, interrupted by singing birds, rustling leaves and an almost audible movement of the water as the creek steadily washed by the trio.

Finally Picker took a deep breath and relaxed a huge I give up sigh. He said, "I'll tell you this and even this is for our ears only. Okay?"

Randy nodded in agreement.

"Ya know I've been around females all my life. I've grown up with three older sisters and known the Magurk girls since I can remember anything at all. My sisters and the Magurk girls dressed me up and used me as a baby and sometimes used me to practice their kissing. I enjoyed the last part the best of course…I'm really comfortable with girls.'

Picker paused a second before carrying on with his dissertation, as was his habit when he was making a point through conversation. He resumed reflectively, "Through the years Leigh Anne and I always had an affinity for one another. Sometimes when no one else was around we played together - even though she is older than I am. She withstood the ribbing from her sisters as well as mine…I'll tell you, this created a giant affection from me as well as a respect for her by not caving to peer pressure.

"Small moments build blocks of emotion caused a caring relationship to form and before we knew it or at least before I knew it, the two of us had bonded pretty strongly. We weren't physically active until recently and kept it to ourselves until the past week, as I'm sure you've noticed.

"But I keep you from the details you really care about." Picker paused again. He bent his head down and appeared pensive. Raising his head he began again. "Let's talk about this in an abstract non-identifying nature." He stopped talking and probed Randy for a reaction.

Aware he should reply in some manner, Randy shuffled in his seat uncomfortably with an awkward movement. He said, "Okay, but I'm really not sure what you mean."

"I mean…I'll tell you how it felt to reach the ultimate intimacy with a person of the opposite sex from a detached view without identifying the person involved so as not to incriminate anyone."

"What are you…a walking thesaurus? Just tell me the freaking story. I'll play along and pretend it's not you know who and believe me I won't tell a soul."

Picker grinned and shook his head. "First of all if you would read something other than girlie magazines perhaps you would build your own lexicon and secondly what makes you think I haven't had the opportunity to share the love-making process with other females?"

Randy thought the second part over more than the first and had his doubts about Picker grabbing his sexual gusto before yesterday, but with Picker one never really knew if they should ever ultimately doubt him. For some reason this conjured up a feeling of inferiority in Randy. He was afraid Picker was well ahead of him in experiencing life.

"I like girlie magazines, thank you…and if I want to grow my vocabulary, I'll go to summer school. So go ahead, Casanova, regale me with your exploits", Randy retorted. "Regale…exploits…pretty good, huh?"

Picker smiled but didn't comment on the fifty-cent words spoken by Randy. He started directly in on his experience of his sexual nature. "I must say reality isn't always on course with one's imagination, at least not with my imagination. I've imagined the way sex would be with a girl…oh, I dunno thousands upon thousands of times before actually experiencing the reality and truthfully the imagined part wasn't even close to the real thing.

"I've laid out the course of things, planned and planned how I would be smooth as silk… no blemishes on my technique. I figured I would impress with how knowledgeable I was. However…once I began the process the wheels on the cart were pretty loose and I felt once or twice they would come completely off the cart leaving me so embarrassed I would have to kill myself or at the least move to a new town.

"I made the assumption and couldn't remove from my head that my partner knew exactly what to do and I had to be perfect to anticipate all the right moves…and I'll tell you it sure did seem like she knew, because as far as I could tell she made no mistakes. But then again, when you're lying next to a completely naked girl, at that moment, I did all I could to please her, to keep her naked and responsive."

Randy sat rapt with attention. He empathized with Picker on the part where he assumed that the girl was not only more experienced, but knew exactly how intimacy worked. The girls must have a book on it or perhaps their mothers coached them. There must be something inherent in their makeup that was embodied to them by nature.

Picker continued while Randy tried to appear casual-not desiring to look over eager for details. "Well I'm not giving a blow-by-blow description of everything that happened. But I'll…"

"Blow-by-blow…is that a pun or event?" interrupted Randy laughing.

Picker snickered. "A figure of speech unfortunately. But, Randy, I'll tell you… that once we began to make out and I started undressing her, I became detached from the goings on. It's hard to explain, but I was physically involved of which there was no doubt. I could feel all the wonderful sensations as my skin touched hers. As I felt and hefted her breasts to feel the weight and kissed her nipples, as I watched her nipples rise and become erect. The wonderful feel of her derriere in my hands as I kneaded her firm cheeks. The wonderful sleekness of her womanhood was more than I could bear. I mean if my Johnson had been any harder, I think I could've poked a hole in an aircraft carrier. Hell the steel sides of the ship wouldn't have had a chance. It would be like stabbing a wet Kleenex with a sharpened screwdriver.

"But it did seem to me as though I was kind of clinical…above the actual events. I thought it would be more of a spiritual experience shared by the two of us. I was more concerned with doing the right thing, making the correct caress, proceeding from the proper step, advancing through the process. Now granted there was quite the conflict going on with my logical self and my emotional self. At the end, the emotional self won the battle. It was short trip but big trip from heavy petting to where we were at that moment.

"I'm telling you…there were more kissing noises, squishing noises as our sweaty bodies were rubbing together everywhere they could possibly touch, heavy breathing with an occasional moan sounding out. And let me tell you that to hear a girl moan like that can be quite stimulating. It makes me shiver with pleasure… really… the moaning alone. Anyway all this action is going on and I'm wrapped up in it when my logical self strikes me…at what my emotional self declares is obviously very bad timing with a thought about pregnancy.

"Well I roll off and fight the package that holds the raincoat and after what seems like a clumsy eternity, I've torn open the package. Then I promptly drop the contents on the floor. More blood is rushing to my face from my embarrassment and you know that the blood has to come from somewhere, but it didn't have to drain from my favorite body part of the moment. Nevertheless, I carried on occasionally glancing at my partner to see if she was losing her mood.

"Everything was fine there and I had retrieved the gentleman's raincoat, but when I tried to slip it over his head, all he would do was bow, dodge and refuse to be covered. More blood rushed to my face and I sorely wanted to hide or get up get dressed and say I'll see you later."

Randy wanted to ask a question but Picker was zoned out recalling events so Randy decided to wait, besides this was good stuff, real stuff not stuff read from a book.

"At that point of ultimate crisis, a soft tender hand reached around and enveloped my Jolly Roger, which instantly caught the figurative wind and rose to flagpole height- stiff and eager. I mean I could feel it grow like a beanstalk. Well I rolled over and forgot about protection and attempted to pierce the warm soft lush waiting…"

"Love muffin," blurted Randy.

"Uh, right," Picker said momentarily stopping his dissertation to peer at Randy. "I might have used a more proper noun, but that one will do.'

"Go on, go on. We'll practice English later," Randy said.

"Okay…well the detachment I was telling you about earlier left me for an instant and I continued to poke with my Jolly Roger by gyrating my hips and it felt good but not quite right when that wonderful darling hand grabbed a hold of him and guided him home.

"Randy, I'm going to tell you, I've never felt anything so wonderfully good as being couple as one. I can't truly describe it. It was comfortable, soft, warm and seemingly endless. All I could envision was being in a pocket full of happiness. It took all the restraint I had. I counted numbers backwards, tried to think of other things, like swimming or running, but I kept coming back to the beautiful soft pleasure surrounding my little man. Truth was I couldn't hold back any longer and it erupted. And then I woke up from my dream, but it sure seemed real."

Randy gaped at Picker with his mouth wide open. Picker smirked back with a twinkle in his eye. Randy was thinking and thinking hard. Did Picker make it up or was he telling the truth?

Randy queried, "You made that up? It was a dream?"

"A good one, huh?" Before Randy could answer Picker stood up, brushed off the seat of his pants and turned toward the Foster cabin. "Come on there is something I want to show you at the Old Man Fosters."

Randy sat back and thought for a moment. Picker was a clever soul, he thought, perhaps it was true or quite possibly not true. Picker sure was descriptive and Randy knew he sure wanted to experience a dream just as good. He stood up and followed Picker back to the cabin.

Chapter 19

Randy and Picker walked along the bank of the creek toward the Foster cabin. The path was almost wide enough for the two of them but not quite. Randy walked slightly in front of Picker who trailed just behind on the beaten dirt path. Pony lagged behind them stopping occasionally to sniff here and there.

Randy filled in Picker on the events of the last evening that he had missed seeing. He told him of how Sam Hammet had been about to rearrange his face and how Sam Hammet had punched Lee and how Donzella's boyfriend Barry had happened by at just the right time.

Picker laughed with glee at the beating he could have imagined that the fat ass Sam Hammet had endured. He also wondered aloud with Randy at how the police would react if Sam had reported the incident. Randy doubted Sam would report the incident for a couple of reasons. For one, he had started the fight and Randy and Lee would attest to the fact and secondly, Sam Hammet would be quite embarrassed if it came out the way Barry had taken him to task.

Randy told Picker about the puppies and it appeared that someone had deliberately swerved to run over all three of the young dogs. They discussed how the day before Arrington Debussy driving his GTO had tried to run over Pony and he thought perhaps that Sam had a hand in killing the dogs. They wondered if he was that much of a monster that he would exact his revenge on poor innocent pups.

Randy really didn't believe it was a GTO, because he thought he would have recognized the souped up engine sound if it had been racing down the road. No, he thought it was someone from the neighborhood. Picker agreed it could be someone nearby, but he couldn't place a finger on anyone that sinister. People around there were farmers and while they were hard on their animals, they had a great respect for them and loved them. Even though there were a few people around who thought the Kearneys had too many dogs, he doubted that they would do anything so extreme. At least to animals, some of the farmers were pretty ornery folks and if you differed too much from the norm they didn't have much room for you. People had much more to fear than the animals did.

The boys had a good chat about their amorous night without going into too much detail. Randy understood Pickers feeling about being a gentleman, so they discussed who liked who and their sudden growth into the world of love and girls especially Randy's emergence. Randy was still into denial, he actually was dancing and kissing and on a date with his dream girl, Mary Jo.

Picker assured him that it was true. He had ridden home with the Magurk sisters and he had heard things usually reserved for girl's ears only. It was one of the few times he was embarrassed to be amongst the girls as the only male. His embarrassment caused by thoughts of how he may have been portrayed by Leigh Ann when he wasn't around and she was talking to the girls. She had patted his leg and had assured him that if she had said anything about him it surely would be positive. At which the other girls giggled and began to call him Don Juan Junior.

When Mary Jo had spoken of Randy, she did so with dreamy accolades. Picker told Randy it was almost sickening listening to Mary Jo talk about his soft sensual eyes, his glistening black hair that any girl would envy and his quiet mature demeanor. Randy feigned embarrassment but urged Picker for more details. Picker obliged and Randy listened with eagerness that was reserved for little children on Christmas Eve.

Eventually the talk came to Vern and Corrine and Picker's not too subtle characterization of Corrine. She was a prima donna, prick teaser and was only stringing Vern along, dangling him like a marionette. Her fun was pulling boys around by the nose, keeping them in check with amorous kisses, a brief caress of a breast and promises of much, much more. Truth was that she had a fiancée back in New York and wanted to remain pure for him. She didn't mind flirting and felt that she was doing Mary Jo a favor by occupying Vern, while Mary Jo was with Randy. The girls felt that the boys would be more comfortable as a double-dating couple, at least in the early stages of the relationships. Corrine was due to leave in a week or so but she felt she had set the stage for Mary Jo and Randy.

Mary Jo had insisted in the car the previous night that she could manage Randy just fine on her own and didn't really need Corrine's help. Corrine had pooh poohed the notion and besides she was having fun with Vern. He was good looking, well-built and not too much of a threat. She would play her little game feeling like she was committing herself to a community service making Vern feel good.

Randy sympathized with his friend Vern, but agreed with Picker that it really wasn't their business. If they told Vern the things that Picker knew he may not believe them and hence they would be the bad guys. Why not let him enjoy himself while he could and let him get what he could while he could. Who knew, perhaps he could break the walls down and score a goal if Corrine had a weak moment. It would serve her right they agreed.

The boys stopped in front of the cabin while Pony ran ahead of them and circled the cabin sniffing and investigating the surrounding grounds as though he knew the boys were there to check out the place. Randy peered at the old Foster homestead and flushed with warm memories.

He envisioned himself being invited inside after an afternoon of cane-pole fishing with Mr. Foster. Mrs. Foster standing in the doorway with her apron pulled around her ample waist, smiling a bemused smile wearing that shock of white hair accenting her chocolate brown round face. Randy would protest slightly saying he should leave, but wanting Mrs. Foster to insist that he come in and have a piece of apple or peach pie - whichever flavor she had sitting by the wood stove. She had always insisted in her soft prodding way while Mr. Foster was more aloof when he spoke to Randy even though his body language was as amiable as could be.

Once inside Randy began to feel at home, the cabin air was redolent with the familiar aromas that careened deep into his senses. The smell of the oil used to fry the freshly caught fish - when Mr. Foster went cane poling he always returned with fish - or the heavenly delicious aroma of a pork loin being slowly roasted in the wood-stoked stove, which would delay the fish fry for the next day.

Randy would partake in the feast to a degree depending upon the time of day. If it were too close to dinner at his aunt's house, he would chow down on a piece of pie or two not refusing Mrs. Foster as she encouraged him to eat the second piece. Mr. Foster would usually sit in his rocking chair by the stove recanting the day's events to his loving wife stopping only as Randy interjected a comment or correcting something Mr. Foster had said if it concerned Randy's fishing technique. Mr. Foster would smile his broad smile as he verbally jabbed at the young boy with gentle barbs, which raised Randy's polite pseudo ire.

Randy felt a chill as he stepped upon the weather worn wooden step which led into the cabin. He waited a moment for the goose bumps to diminish, watching Picker turn the dented brown steel knob of the door and push it ahead into the living room. Picker pivoted and glanced at Randy motioning with his head for Randy to follow him into the cabin. Randy crossed over the threshold and observed the size of the room. The walls had seemed to have grown closer together each time he had come to visit. As many times as he had passed the cabin since the Fosters' deaths on his walks through the woods, he rarely went inside, instead he would peek through the dust covered windows on occasion to refill his reserve senses with nostalgia.

After the time travel sensation part, Randy began to take in the objects in the room. He saw the old rocker sitting in the corner covered in cobwebs but appearing to have been sat in recently. While the cobwebs covered the sides from arm to seat the seat and back of the chair were wiped nearly clean. Beside the chair was an apparently fresh beer can that sat within reaching distance of someone who had occupied the seat. The freshness of the can was easily detectable because of its unfaded color scattered around the floor of the cabin were numerous other cans- beer and soda- which had been littered there long ago and through time.

Vandals had abused the place at various spots but for the most part the cabin wasn't in bad shape for a structure that wasn't taken care of anymore. The occasional drifter would wander by and take up residence for a few days, but were always driven off by Caleb

Fulton - the neighborhood watchman - or by Harvey's father, Chester. Chester may have been elderly but he was cantankerous and sometimes downright mean when provoked even though his gruff exterior shielded a fair, giving heart.

Chester had a white head of hair that he kept in a short crew cut, a large barrel chest, arms the size of small logs and hands at the end of those arms that could crush walnuts as easily as empty egg shells. He exuded the good old boy charm that when you met and spoke with him, you knew he was all business and he was not to be taken lightly. His penetrating pale blue eyes told all there was to know about the man. No one could hold the interrogating gaze too long before looking away dominated by a mere scan of his or her face.

It was Chester who had given the cabin to the Fosters to live in so many years ago. At first Mr. Foster had lived in town and had worked handy man jobs doing this and that trying to survive. He worked most of his life in town and rarely went to the countryside because his only mode of transportation was his God given feet. Chester had needed someone to come and help him repair his barn after a strong winter storm had had blew in with seventy-mile-an-hour winds, damaging the structure's doors. There was plenty of work as a result of the storm all around the county and quite a shortage of available skilled men to help repair the damage.

Mr. Foster, who had recently married his lovely bride, was a man in great demand. He could have his choice of jobs and asked a good price on most but for some reason he felt he should help Chester even though his offering price wasn't as high as some of the other farmers who had bid for Mr. Foster's services. Mr. Foster held many of those asking for his help in a quiet contempt for the way that they usually spoke to the black folk and he wouldn't have worked for them no matter the amount of money they would offer him.

Chester, however, was a man of principles. While he didn't go out of his way to be patronizingly civil to most blacks or people of any color for that matter, he was at least respectful of their rights as equal people. If you walked by him he would nod his head and say "good day" instead of walking by as if you didn't exist. He held doors for women, all women, who exited or entered a door before or after him. His demeanor, while not being overtly nice, was a respectful one with a tinge of gruffness reserved for everyone. He was a fair man who treated people in a manner in which he would like to be treated - basically cordial with room for aloofness so as not to infringe on his time or feelings.

Mr. Foster worked for Chester for a month caring for the barn and other buildings, which needed repairing while Chester and his son Harvey tended the other chores on the farm. After the month was complete, Mr. Foster told Chester he would like to stay around town for a while because after all he hadn't been married long and wanted to spend more time with his wife. Chester realized how much Mr. Foster had helped around the farm and loved the work ethic of the young man who had performed his tasks with a perfection element to all he tackled. He offered Mr. Foster a steady job on the farm and a place to live, the cabin by the creek. Mr. Foster thanked him but he also wanted to carry on working other odd jobs as well and if they could work that out, he would love to continue to work on the Kearny farm. Chester agreed and Mr. Foster brought his wife out to the cabin. The Fosters kept a small garden out by the cabin and lived there for many years.

Chester had let Mr. Foster maintain the cabin and surrounding land. Through time the small patch of land was considered to be the Foster farm even though Chester Kearny still technically owned it. The farm held a special place in Chester' and Randy's hearts. Perhaps it should have been torn down with the death of the Fosters, but Chester didn't have the heart to demolish the memories that the small homestead held by destroying the building. He settled for having time and nature slowly erode away the structure, keeping intact the sensibilities and warm feelings he held for the cabin's former occupants.

Randy moved over to the old rocker, kicking a can or two out of his path. He sat in the chair and rocked back and forth a few times. The squeak of the wood caused Picker to glance back over his shoulder at Randy. He moved toward the sink and stepped on a curved piece of glass round bowed side up the points grabbing at the worn wooden floor. The snap of the glass sounded muted as Picker's shoe broke the glass fragment.

He looked down at the glass and observed that it had came from a jar, which had been broken and most of it having been cleaned up. The bottom of the jar sat by the base of the sink with broken glass piled up on top of it. The jar appeared to be an old mayonnaise jar, but Picker couldn't tell. He casually pushed it out of the way so he wouldn't step on it again.

Picker placed his hands on the wooded sink splash and peered down into the sink basin. Nothing there but a few brown stains, which appeared to be dried blood. He grabbed the pump handle, which supplied the water from the well and gave it a few good pumps. He could hear and feel the suction grab at the stopper and water came trickling down the pump's spout. The third pump brought a gush of water down the spout flowing easily into the sink.

"Looks like the pumps were used pretty often. I didn't even need to prime it." Pickers stopped pumping the water and watched it swirl around in the basin and go down the drain. The dried blood streaks turned dark but didn't wash away. "Looks like somebody's been here and cleaned some fish or something."

"How do you know?" Randy asked as he pushed himself up out of the rocking chair. He made his way over to the sink to stand beside Picker.

Pointing to the dried blood streaks in the sink, Picker said, "Look here…see those streaks…looks like blood doesn't it?"

"Could be, Sherlock, but if that's from the fish they must have been awful bloody or awfully large to leave that much blood"

Randy's response caused Picker to rethink his guess. "Maybe someone was cleaning fish and cut themselves and bled in the sink."

Reaching over to pick up something at the end of the counter, Randy said, "Whatever it was, I think it came from this paper." He stretched out brown butcher paper with dried brown streaks and spots covering one side of it.

"Excellent work, Watson. I guess we've got squatters around here. I wonder if Mr. Kearny chased them off already, because I haven't seen anyone around here on my walks. Although I've been slipping a little lately, I haven't been as consistent as I have been in the past. I've had other things on my mind." Picker smiled at Randy like the cat that had swallowed the proverbial canary.

Randy rolled his eyes and said, "Yes, I guess you have been busy. I'm just not sure if it's fact or fantasy at this point. But if someone was staying here it looks like they're gone now." He crumpled the paper and tossed it into the sink. Peering out the window he said, "Look"

From the window the boys could see Corrine, Leigh Ann and Mary Jo floating by in an aluminum canoe. Mary Jo was rowing, first on the right side with the wooden oar and then moving to the left side. She was seated at the back and used the oar as a rudder to steer the canoe on a straight course in the middle of the creek. They were moving with the current and her strokes were smooth and without much effort. Leigh Ann was seated in the center and Corrine sat in the bottom of the canoe up front with her hands grasping the sides of the canoe like she might fall out at any time.

Picker bolted from the run down cabin and ran toward the bank waving his arms shouting at the girls to draw their attention. Randy followed behind a step slower but just as eager. The girls turned their heads to the commotion and Mary Jo steered the canoe to the left, turning it with ease. She began to stroke hard to turn the momentum of the metal vessel in the direction of the boys. Randy could tell she was experienced because of how adroitly she completed the turn. It was effortless.

Randy stared at Mary Jo pushing the oar through the water, her firm muscles tense as she stroked from side to side. Her brown hair pulled back into a ponytail showed her pretty face that was beaming like the ingénue that she was. He watched like a voyeur as her breasts moved with her motion in her skimpy bikini top. He felt a flash of irritation knowing she wore the two piece swimsuit and other males would leer at her well-toned body. He raised his eyes back to her face. Randy felt warm all over as his eyes met hers and he became nervous as her bright smile locked onto his heart.

Mary Jo deftly guided the canoe to the shore sculling it up and onto a sandy portion of the bank. Randy reached out and grabbed the end of the aluminum-hulled craft. Corrine had put forth her hand thinking that Randy had reached for her. She pulled back her arm and fluffed her hair trying to act as if she had intended to straighten it all along. Randy was embarrassed and flushed crimson red. The other two girls giggled as Picker helped Corrine out of the canoe.

"What's so funny?" Corrine asked as innocently as she could.

After Picker had deposited Corrine, he helped out Leigh Ann who answered her cousin. "Oh nothing, my self-centered little cousin. Your hair looks perfect."

"Hmm…who lives here?" Corrine asked as she gestured to the Foster cabin changing the subject.

"No one… anymore anyway." The reply came from Randy and was more tersely spoken than he had wanted. Corrine was getting under his skin. He disliked her attitude and the way she was treating his friend Vern.

"I see,' she said slowly. "Would it be okay if we looked inside?"

"Don't ask me. I don't own it.' Again Randy was gruff. Mary Jo touched his arm and he flushed with embarrassment again.

Picker broke the tension. "C'mon I'll show you around and tell you about the wonderful people who used to live here."

He took Leigh Ann, who obviously knew the former inhabitants and their story by his left hand and Corrine by his right hand and led them up to the porch. Corrine turned her head around and stuck out her tongue at Randy. She made him smile despite himself.

Corrine's raven hair shone blue black under the summer sun framing her angelic face and cool as ice green eyes. Her dainty facial features belied the conniving vixen Randy felt her to be. He had to admit her slender body - well shaped and proportioned could have seduced and entranced any strong-willed male. She knew how to talk to boys, place a hand at the right time at the right spot. A puppeteer who could pull the heart strings with the ease of a Greek goddess. She certainly had vexed his friend Vern. She had cast a spell with her wily feminine skills, which had clouded Vern's thinking.

Randy's eyes lingered on Corrine's bikini-clad body as she walked to the cabin with Picker and Leigh Ann. He thought about her last action toward him. Just by sticking out her tongue and contorting her face slightly, she had actually warmed him up inside, breaking down his well thought out animosity for her and her careless disregard for his friend. How could this be? Her gesture wasn't overtly a flirtatious one, but somehow he felt it was sending him a message somehow. He smiled and soaked in the view of her swinging bottom and tanned legs. Maybe Vern wasn't so crazy after all- perhaps Corrine was a witch of some sort and most certainly not one he had ever read about in any novel.

Randy snapped back to reality when he heard Mary Jo say, "She leaves tomorrow. She's flying back to New York. Her parents are cutting their vacation short."

Randy turned toward Mary Jo. He was a little flustered at being caught surveying Corrine. He heard a tone in Mary Jo's voice that showed a little displeasure at his actions, but not an angry tone - a tone which sent a message telling him he had upset her in some way.

Randy changed the subject and said, "How long have you been canoeing?"

She smiled a coy smile. She knew he had grasped her inflection and she carried on the conversation much to Randy's relief. "About three months ago. Dad bought the canoe for the family and once I learned how to maneuver it, I've grown to really love it. It's great exercise and it helps keep me in shape. I usually row down to Bernice's place turn around, go to Picker's tree house and then back to our dock. Takes me…oh I don't know…about an hour and a half.

"I love the peaceful solitude, hearing the birds sing, the insects chirp and buzz. I even like the sound of the oar as I dip and pull it through the water. I've often envied you as you sat in that stone chair of yours holding that cane fishing pole seemingly to contemplate life. In fact I've rowed up to that spot and sat in your chair on an occasion or two so that I can absorb your perspective of things. And actually it's quite different from our dock…a little refreshing."

Randy was taken aback slightly. "You mean you've watched me sitting in that chair without me knowing that you were watching me? That makes me feel kinda creepy. I hope I didn't do anything embarrassing, like pick my nose or something."

Mary Jo laughed. "No I didn't see anything, which would cause you embarrassment." She smiled wryly and hopped out of the canoe. Her smile wasn't that reassuring to Randy.

There was a pause in the conversation. Randy was thinking about some of the things he had done in that chair. Nothing he could think of was too totally humiliating. Except for one time he did remember concerning an incident with Vern.

They had been down to the quarry drinking beer and had walked back to the creek to skip some stones or perhaps fish for awhile. Once they had arrived at the stone chair they sat and talked about solving the problems of the day. One thing led to another and they began a little bragging contest and Vern declared he had to relieve himself. He told Randy that he could probably send a stream of urine clean across the creek to the other side. Randy declared he could out piss Vern any day.

The two of them stood on the bank right at the water's edge and proceeded to try and project their discharges out into the creek with all the force that they could muster. While not going out more than three feet or so Randy declared himself the winner because he had a much higher arc on his stream than Vern did. Vern taking umbrage to Randy's declaration had laughingly shouted that Randy was full of crap and that he would show Randy how he would strike a bird that was flying overhead.

Unfortunately, as he looked up, Vern lost his equilibrium and staggered backward, trying to right himself he over compensated by shifting his weight forward. That caused him to fall face first into the creek, still holding his weapon when he stood up, drenched by the tannic water of the creek, Vern deadpanned that he had just shot the eye out of a fish with a mighty burst of piss.

The two of them had laughed long and hard for quite a while before going home. Randy hoped Mary Jo hadn't witnessed that scene, even though it would probably be more embarrassing to Vern than to himself. He thought that perhaps it would be best to drop the whole subject and to concentrate on his present relationship with Mary Jo.

The two of them sat on the sand and talked about the night before and the fun they had had at the dance. The conversation was awkward at first but they warmed up to each other with considerable ease. The intimacy was really the only new addition to their relationship, because of the many chats that they had had in their platonic past.

Mary Jo was horrified at the killing of the puppies. She had told Randy the news had spread quickly and that she had learned of the dreadful deed shortly after breakfast. It seems Vern's Uncle Pup had dropped by to discuss his wife's barbecue with Mary Jo's dad and had related the news to the family. Randy listened to Mary Jo's version of the macabre details. He corrected minor details, but added little more to the story.

They spoke of Sam Hammet and Mary Jo seemed somewhat titillated by the fight, especially knowing Sam had been taught a lesson about being a bully. Randy felt his pride rise as he told of his part in the fight. He embellished the tale, adding small enhancements to his and Lee's involvement in the scuffle, nothing too outrageous, but small things to bring out the courage of the two protagonists. Mary Jo asked Randy if he was going to attend the rodeo that evening and he informed her that he would be there. She told him she would be there as well and that she would meet him at the concession stand. She might be a little late because of a late afternoon appointment she would have to accompany her mom on. She didn't volunteer where she was going and Randy didn't ask where the appointment was going to be.

He sat looking at her, fighting internally with himself. He wanted to hold her, hug her and caress her. He at least wanted to kiss her to taste her tender mouth but he couldn't summon the courage for fear he would insult her in some way. The last thing he wanted to do was to draw her ire by doing something inappropriate. He wondered how he would know when the time would be right for such close casual contact. Would there be a signal? Would it be a natural reaction?

Mary Jo sat beside him gazing across the water; the wind blowing against her face caused her to squint slightly. Randy could see the soft stray brown curls of her hair, which were renegades from her pulled back pony tail blowing across her forehead. He decided he couldn't wait any longer and trouble be damned, he was going to try and give her a kiss.

He moved closer and touched her cheek gently with his hand. Mary Jo turned to face him; her head turned upward, eyes closed in anticipation of his kiss. How the hell did she know his intention? It had to be some kind of intuition or womanly witchcraft. Whatever it was it was exciting enough for Randy.

He bent his head and their lips touched. It sent a jolt of emotion through the adolescent couple. Randy felt a stirring he wished that he wouldn't have at that particular moment at this spot in broad daylight. There was no place to hide and nothing to hide it with. Their tongues fenced like epees, raising their passion up a notch.

"Jesus…everywhere I go there are young people in love." Corrine had come out of the Foster cabin and was standing behind the couple sitting on the freshwater beach. She startled Randy and Mary Jo causing them to collapse on one another in a nervous giggling heap. "I feel like a spare tire, useful but not needed at the moment."

Randy and Mary Jo righted themselves and stood up to face Corrine. Mary Jo picked up her oar and leaned on it. She bent over slightly because the oar was shorter in length than she was causing her breast to be the focus of Randy's attention. He tried to look away but the top of her breast swells attracted him like a magnet to iron. Mary Jo became self-conscious and stood up which in turned flushed Randy's face red with the knowledge he had been caught ogling her breasts.

Awkwardly Randy shuffled his feet and tried desperately to think of something witty to say. Instead he said to Corrine, "Well you're certainly not a flat spare tire." His voice cracked as he said it and his red face turned crimson as he realized his unintended reference.

Mary Jo smiled a slight smirk. Corrine cupped her breasts barely covered by her bikini top and peered down at them dramatically.

Looking up with eyes while keeping her head down, she glowered seductively at Randy. "Thanks for the compliment, Randy, but I'm not sure you should be commenting on other girls body parts in front of your girlfriend."

"I-I didn't mean that, I meant...oh never mind," he tried unsuccessfully to explain. He stopped speaking in the hope to fade away somehow. That damn Corrine sure did rile him up.

The girls giggled and Mary Jo moved over to Randy and took his hand in hers.

She whispered into his ear. "I know what you meant. Too bad she came outside so fast. I'll see you tonight." Then she pecked him on the lips and left him as she picked up her oar and stepped into the canoe.

Randy nodded and stood stock still with a perplexed look on his face.

"Randy, have you talked to Vern today?" Corrine cooed.

Randy squint his eyes and gnawed at his lower lip. Should he say something to her about screwing around his friend or should he let things play out? He opted for the latter. He figured if he caused a problem, Vern would be angry with him and Corrine would be long gone.

He wrinkled his nose and said, "Not yet today. Maybe a little later."

"Is he going to the western thing tonight?"

"Rodeo," Mary Jo said.

"Whatever...rodeo. Is he going to go tonight?"

"I couldn't tell you, Corrine. His parents are kind of weird. Sometimes he has a lot of chores to do." Randy said. He didn't want to encourage her. Fact was he kind of wanted to deflate her.

"Well I hope he does go. If you hear from him, could you have him call me at the Magurk's house? Tonight's my last night. I have to go home tomorrow.

"To tell you the truth, I was kind of rough with him last night. I find myself liking him more than I want to like him. After all I've got a boyfriend back home. I don't know why I'm telling you this... God, I'm so embarrassed...Mary Jo shouldn't we be going home for lunch now?"

"Yes we should, Corrine," Mary Jo said. Then she shouted for Leigh Ann to hurry along.

Randy was mulling over Corrine's admission about Vern when Picker and Leigh Ann walked off the stoop from the cabin. Picker stopped beside Randy and Leigh Ann stepped into the canoe to join Mary Jo. Picker's hair was tousled and Leigh Ann's bathing suit was slightly askew.

Corrine smiled at Leigh Ann and said, "Leigh Ann, did you find that puppy inside? He has the cutest little nose."

Leigh Ann had a confused look on her face and peered down in the direction of Corrine's gaze. Her bra top was lifted exposing her nipple. She swung around quickly and adjusted her bathing suit top. Corrine laughed heartily while the other members of the party laughed a muffled laugh not wanting to embarrass Leigh Ann more than she was already. She waved with her face turned to the creek.

Picker walked over to the canoe and pushed it out on to the water three quarters of the way. He held the bow and turned to Corrine. He motioned with his head toward the direction of the canoe, indicating to her that she should enter the canoe.

Bewitched, Randy could not help himself. He held her arm and steadied her as she climbed clumsily over the side of the canoe. Corrine's weight shifted backward forcing Randy to place his hand on her bottom to steady her. With one leg in and one leg out of the aluminum craft she would have toppled into the creek without his help.

"Nice grab, Randy, my boy," Picker said.

Randy didn't respond, but he glanced at Mary Jo who turned her head as she caught his glance. He couldn't tell if she was ticked off or trying to maneuver the canoe.

Corrine plopped down on the bottom of the canoe. The weight of the three girls held the canoe to the sandy bottom of the creek.

"Randy, give me a hand pushing the girls off," Picker said.

"Okay." Randy bent to help and their combined strength moved the canoe across the two feet of beach scraping noisily on a rock lodged underneath.

Just as the canoe broke free of the earth to bob slightly on the creek's surface, Picker passed gas with a blurt, like air escaping from a freshly blown-up balloon.

A few seconds passed and then everyone laughed breaking the short standstill moment.

Picker pulled himself to a regal posture and said, "As the winds blows free the pressure is off me."

Randy shook his head and shrugged his shoulders as if to say "what are you going to do with him?" The girls continued to giggle as Mary Jo piloted the canoe toward her family's home. Leigh Ann had picked up the other oar to help Mary Jo scull the canoe against the slow moving current. Ordinarily Mary Jo could manage the gentle nature's force single handily, but with the weight of three people extra strength was needed to row the floating craft to the pier.

Randy kept his eyes on Mary Jo as she turned the canoe deftly maneuvering the oar, while she guided her sister's effort with verbal instructions. He wanted to catch her eye to see his feeling of insecurity was warranted. He felt his helping Corrine into the canoe had resulted in Mary Jo becoming angry with him.

Finally, once she had succeeded in pointing the watercraft in the proper direction, she turned her pretty head to glance at Randy. His face lit up with a puppy-dog grin and his eyes were expectant awaiting her recognition. She waved at him with short flap of her fingers and smiled. Randy returned the wave and felt like leaping in the air and kicking his heels together with delight but he restrained himself. He kept the butterflies in his belly in check. He couldn't wait until the rodeo that night.

Picker tugged at Randy's arm and said, "Come on, I've got to return home. I've a few chores to attend to on the farm. The quicker I start them the quicker I'll finish them."

"Yeah me too. I promised my uncle I'd help him repair a couple of windows on the big chicken house. It's so hot we need to keep the windows open. A few of them have torn screens, which let your cats get in too easily," Randy replied.

"Not my cats," Picker said with conviction. "I'll think of a way to rid this area of those pests yet."

"Maybe you could use some of that gas you used to propel the canoe out onto the water," Randy jibed.

"Randy, my friend…that's special gas I used on this particular occasion. I don't use it on every occasion."

"I don't know what constitutes a special occasion to you, but I'm betting you have lots of them. Because as long as I've known you, slipping warm, ugly-flavored air into any event has been a forte of yours for a very long time."

"I am a special person. Not everyone has such a gift," Picker said pompously.

"At least not people willing to share so much anyway," Randy kidded.

Chapter 20

Randy and Picker walked back to the stone chair on a leisurely pace. The day was heating up pretty well by now and there was the beginning of storm clouds on the horizon. A small wind was picking up rustling the leaves on the trees in small bursts, shimmering the green shiny shingles. The leaves seemed to turn themselves backside up anticipating the wet natural nourishment promised from above.

The boys watched the gentle rhythmic rowing of the Magurk sisters as they gradually approached the dock for their landing. They could barely see Corrine's head as she sat on the bottom of the canoe, but they could clearly see her gripping fingers holding on the side of the canoe. Corrine was a good swimmer so it was a kind of a mystery as to why she was apprehensive sitting in the canoe.

Randy and Picker discussed the girls, Corrine's involvement with Vern and the possibility someone had been inhabiting the Foster cabin.

The rodeo tonight was an event they had both looked forward to attending. Not only did it provide a venue to be with the girls, but it was also a chance to show off their prizes, especially for Randy. Picker was more secure in himself, but having Leigh Ann with him produced a swelling of pride within himself as well.

Randy related to Picker his conversation with Corrine concerning Vern explaining that he felt that perhaps Corrine was sincere. Picker remained skeptical and caused Randy to doubt Corrine's sincerity without much prodding. They would be able to see later at the corral if she was sincere or not.

Picker took his leave of Randy and sauntered down toward his tree house with the intent on heading along his well traveled route to his home. He walked nonchalantly casually observing his surroundings and the subtle changes to the environment were noted, cataloged mentally and saved for future comparisons. Picker was a true environmentalist and a lover of nature.

Randy decided he wanted to wait a few moments alone to digest the last day's events. He was quite happy to be by himself and preferred it on many occasions. His elation with the promising relationship with Mary Jo helped dull the pain of the past negative events. He would gradually lose his remorse over the dead puppies and life would move on to other events.

Albeit it was growing ever warmer, his seat under the tree was cool enough with its shaded position. The breeze blew softly across his body with a warm rolling caress almost inducing sleep. He looked up at the forming dark storm clouds and hoped that if it would rain that it would be a brief storm, which wouldn't hinder the rodeo planned for that evening.

Sitting in his chair reminded Randy of the places he felt that provided him of such comfort. His love of the dark quiet movie theater was unsurpassed by any other venue. Sitting with a box of popcorn engrossed in a story being splashed across the large white screen filled his heart with joy. He knew where every dent, pockmark and stain was located on the screen at Walker's movie house. His special joy was a movie almost unattended, because this provided little chance of irritating chatter or other nonsense.

A place that rivaled the movie house and induced a feeling of protective sanctuary was the library. He could sit in the library leafing through magazines, reference books or powering his way through a mystery book for hours on end. He liked the feel of the knowledge sitting on the shelves surrounding him, daring him to take a chance on absorbing something new.

He wasn't exactly a scholar, but he enjoyed learning things in an off-handed arbitrary way. While he produced above average grades with an occasional C in a subject or two, he learned in a trivia manner and could speak intelligently on many subjects.

The library provided a source for intellectual gathering and held his interest for both the opportunities to garner knowledge as well as a quiet place to mend categorize and organize his thoughts. If he were truly troubled by something, he would head to the library to collect and sort out his thoughts.

Randy pondered the question of his being a loner. He often sifted through reasons he felt that he was or wasn't a loner, but he reasoned that even though he enjoyed his time by himself and sometimes turned down invitations to specific events to avoid chatty crowds, he really did enjoy being around his friends and enjoying new experiences. He did however like to do it on his own terms. His minor obsession with determining whether or not he was a loner stemmed from the fact he didn't wish to become a hermit.

He had read a book about a hermit once and the pathetic old man had seemed so unhappy even though he had chosen the life for himself. The old man had tried to grow closer to his family in his later years but was emotionally unable to complete the transition and had tragically killed himself.

The story weighed heavily on Randy's mind and he didn't want such a fate for his own life. He knew fate was fate and destiny was predetermined but he hoped to be able to tweak the direction of destiny if it were at all possible.

Perhaps small things could have an effect on the trail of life. He thought of his own cousin Scott, the younger brother of Dennis. Scott and Randy were very close in age but also as emotionally close they could have been brothers. They spent a great deal of time together until two years ago when seemingly small events affected the destiny of his beloved cousin.

The dreadful event began on a rainy Friday evening with Scott waiting for a ride to the dance at the youth center. He had turned fifteen two days earlier and was scheduled to meet Sue Rosewell at the dance to celebrate her birthday, which fell on that particular Friday.

Sue and Scott had known one another since third grade. They had been good friends and celebrate their birthdays together for many years. They had begun to date and their relationship changed from good friends to one of boyfriend/girlfriend.

During the school year, Randy didn't visit his cousin unless it was a long weekend or he was terribly bored at home. The weekend of Scott's death was one where Randy had decided to stay at home, even though it was Scott's birthday weekend. Harlan had relatives visiting and Randy's mom convinced him that it would be rude to leave while Harlan's folks were there. Randy promised his cousin that they would celebrate his birthday on the following weekend.

Scott had convinced his mom that since he was fifteen that he should be able to ride with his friends who were old enough to drive. Reluctantly she had agreed because it was against her better judgment, but with Scott's constant badgering he had worn down her resolve and patience. Besides Dennis wasn't home to take him to the dance and her car was in desperate need of windshield wipers. She didn't feel safe driving in the rain with inadequate equipment.

Scott had left with his friend Keith Marshall and Keith's older brother Bryan. Bryan was driving, which eased Scott's mother's angst because he was seventeen and had been driving for almost two years. She watched as Scott and Keith jostled for the shotgun seat in the drizzling rain. Scott managed to sneak in the front passenger side door and slam his hand down on the button door lock, exiling Keith to the backseat.

As the car sped off, Randy's Aunt could see the boys laughing and clowning around inside of the car. She was happy her son was enjoying life but her intuition gnawed at her for unexplained reasons and she felt a sense of foreboding. She discounted the thoughts to an over reactive sense of parental over protection.

The night was a good one for Scott and he called his mother letting her know he was stopping at the Tastee-Freeze for a late snack and he would be home around midnight. She bickered with him about the time and they compromised on the time and they agreed upon eleven thirty for his deadline.

At midnight he wasn't home and she sat by the telephone in her easy chair facing the door. Dennis had come in early and was upstairs in his bed. He told his mom that he had seen his brother at the dance and later at the Tastee-Freeze briefly and offered him a ride home. Scott had declined the offer saying that Bryan and Keith were going his way and he would ride with them after he finished his cheeseburger and shake.

Just after one in the morning the call came waking Randy's aunt from an unintended slumber in her chair giving her a start, which caused her to bark a cry of surprise involuntarily. With a craggy voice she answered the telephone and began to wail and sob in an uncontrollable shudder.

Dennis ran down the stairs to find why his mother was so hysterical. Scott had been killed in a freak accident. He had been sitting in the passenger side seat next to Bryan on the short journey home. The rain had stopped and the boys had the windows down, allowing the cool breeze to blow over them, when a dog or a deer or some kind of animal had crossed the road in front of them. No one could say for sure what kind of animal it was, because Keith was slumped in the back not looking and Bryan couldn't adequately describe the animal and Scott was dead.

The car had veered off the road and Bryan had difficulty controlling the car. They hit a large dip in the ground and Scott's door popped open. Bryan began to brake the car to help him regain control, as Scott draped his arm out of the window to pull the door and to hold it shut until the car stopped. As they were almost stopped Scott was partially out of the car with his head shoulder and arm outside of the window. He was looking at Bryan telling him to slow down nervously laughing at the predicament, when a road sign clipped his head killing him instantly.

Randy clicked off the things that could have altered the eventuality, the things that may have modified the course of destiny, things that may or may not have prevented the loss of his beloved cousin. All the what ifs, which couldn't be changed now in retrospect. What if Randy had visited and insisted on going to movies instead of the dance? What if Scott's mom's car had been in working order? What if Scott had been sitting in the backseat instead of the front seat? What if it had still been raining and the windows had been rolled up? What if Scott had ridden home with his brother? What if Scott's father hadn't divorced Scott's mother and had been around to maintain the car?

Too many probabilities with the chance of one changing the entire sequence of destined events.

Randy shook the memory from his head focusing back onto Mary Jo. He pushed himself up from his stone chair, brushed the back of his pants off and stretched. He wanted to go and help his uncle with the chores as he had promised to do. He would need a nap because of his light sleep from the night before.

He didn't see Pony anywhere nearby. He dismissed the dog as a loner perhaps and followed the trail through the woods to his uncle's farm watching the bushes for any sudden movements. He gained courage as he grew closer to the open field and felt a sudden flush of satisfaction for reasons unknown to him.

- 0 -

Randy sat on the front step of his aunt's house staring out into space in the general direction of Lee's house. The twilight of the evening was beginning to descend upon the countryside and there was a moist smell of rain in the air. Dark clouds hovered nearby.

The clouds were black and ominous in the dwindling sunlight. The threat of rain had hung around all day like the sword of Damocles causing Randy anxiety concerning the possibility of the postponement of the barrel racing rodeo.

He had called Lee twenty minutes earlier and was waiting for him to come outside so that they could walk down to the corral together. An occasional car would roar by beeping their horns in recognition after spying Randy sitting on the stoop.

Earlier in the day after Randy had returned from the creek and his chance meeting with Mary Jo, he had sought out his uncle to help him with repairing the windows in the chicken house. His uncle had completed the task and had asked Randy to clean a few of the water troughs, which Randy finished in a little over an hour. His uncle was still solemn but seemed to be perking up a bit as the late morning turned into the afternoon.

Randy went to the house for something to eat mid-afternoon and his sister fixed him a ham and cheese sandwich that Randy devoured in five ravenous bites. His Aunt Caroline and Karen spoke of vengeance for the puppies' demise. Randy listened but didn't say anything. His thoughts were, who would they take their revenge out on, they didn't know who the culprit was or even if it was an accident.

Although it sure didn't appear to be an accident, still strange things have happened. Perhaps someone would come forward in the next couple of days after suffering from the remorse and guilt to put an end to the eerie atmosphere surrounding the farm.

Randy settled down in the living room trying to watch television, but the reception was poor even with Uncle Harvey's new outside aerial. If the picture wasn't filled with electronic snow, the vertical wouldn't hold and the picture rolled up and over constantly frustrating Randy so much that he just shut it off. He leafed through a Reader's Digest that his aunt so diligently subscribed to pass the time.

Eventually his eyes betrayed him as he sank into the comfortable armchair with his feet propped up on the soft round hassock. He fell asleep for two hours oblivious to his surroundings. Usually a light sleeper Randy would awaken at the slightest noise out of the ordinary, but he was so tired from the sleepless night before that he slept soundly with an occasional snore his sister had imitated to him when he finally woke up.

Once rested, he called Vern and spoke with him on a number of things including the prospect of Vern attending the rodeo that evening and how Corrine was asking about him earlier at the Foster cabin. Vern's mood elevated to an excitable level once Randy filled him in on Corrine's revelation concerning him. He had been a monotone answering machine until he thought of seeing Corrine and knowing that she wanted to see him once again.

Randy felt a guilt reflex thinking he was actually leading his friend into an emotional quagmire of which there was no way to extricate Vern. Vern had fallen hard for the northern vixen and Randy was helpless to open Vern's eyes to the she-devil Randy thought she was. The good thing about the situation at least according to Randy's perspective was that Corrine was leaving soon and Vern would be able to move on to other prospects.

Randy wondered if he appeared to be as smitten with Mary Jo as his friends appeared to be with their prospective mates. Only Picker seemed to be in control, which didn't surprise Randy one iota.

Not long after Randy spoke with Vern, Pup came by to visit carrying his Mason jar half full of peach brandy. Randy tried to figure out where Pup kept his stash of brandy and why the jar was always half full, even though Pup was in a continual state of semi-inebriation. Pup was ranting about the dead puppies, the neighborhood view that the Kearny's dog allotment, and about the barbecue at his house the night before he hadn't really attended.

He rambled on and on moving from one subject to another occasionally asking Randy's aunt for affirmation on a just spoken statement with an, "Ain't that right, Carrie." Or a "You know that's true, Caroline." And she would reply with a nod or shake of her head, which meant little to Pup as he blabbered on continually not really meaning to secure Caroline's blessing. It was his way of checking to see if she was paying attention.

He would populate his conversation or more aptly his soliloquy with his patented poor attempts at humor. He would laugh dramatically with his husky alcohol-soaked vocal cords stopping only when the phlegm caught in his throat, caused by his continual chain smoking, prompted him to catch a coughing fit.

Randy had stayed away from Pup's incessant chatter by sitting in the living room and his sister joined him once she had tired of Pup's routine and constant leers at her body. He made her feel dirty. Eventually they retired to their rooms to begin preparations for their night out. With only one bathroom and four people to shower, they would have to begin the rotation early.

Pup never left and joined everyone for dinner, discussing everyone's business in the neighborhood enhancing any stories he could with his warped view of life. After dinner Randy's uncle politely asked Pup to wait in the enclosed porch while everyone finished getting ready for the evening.

Pup agreed with a politeness reserved for drunks - while seemingly genuine - the politeness was really a self-serving method of keeping in the good graces of their present hosts.

Randy had readied himself first and after he had called Lee, he had positioned himself outside on the stoop to wait for his friend's arrival. Karen had come out a few minutes earlier and had been picked up by Chuck.

Randy had asked her why she wasn't taking Pup with her and she had responded with a look of death and a sharp punch aimed at her brother's arm.

After she had driven away with Chuck, Randy waited impatiently for Lee. He knew Lee's father was probably giving Lee a lecture concerning life or was having him perform last-minute chores of some kind. Lee's dad was strict and Lee followed the routine for the sake of his teenage freedom. Randy figured Lee's dad's strictness was the reason Lee smoked cigarettes. It was a sort of clandestine rebellion - a rebellion really not secret enough to hide forever from Lee's dad. But if Lee eventually wanted the confrontation there was little anyone could do about it.

Randy was lost in thought staring at a whirling dervish as it twirled leaves and sand round and round like a little tornado near the corner of the house when Lee shouted from across the road. He had already started the trek up the road and was waving his arm at Randy to come along.

Randy picked himself up and trotted to catch up with his friend.

Chapter 21

Randy stood beside Lee, both boys with their backs against the white washed plywood concession stand. People ambled up to the window and ducked under the swung out shutter to order sodas, hot dogs, hamburgers, popcorn or other all American fare on a continual basis.

The food smelled good to Randy and he considered buying a hamburger, but he thought he would wait for Mary Jo to return to see if she desired anything as well. She had walked to the parking lot to speak to her sister Leigh Ann concerning a ride home. Leigh Ann was leaving for a while with Picker, Corrine and Vern on the pretense of showing Corrine, Vern's aunt and uncle's collection of Hummels.

It seemed that Corrine was a collector as well and Vern's aunt had three curio cabinets full of the ceramic German statuettes. The hand-painted marvels were beautifully done with many of them being collected just after World War II. The statuettes had been rendered from drawings beginning in 1931 by a nun, Sister Maria Innocentia Hummel or M.I. Hummel. They had been declared works of art by the US Government in 1952.

Regardless of the reason stated, the teenagers knew the real reason the couples desired to get away from the crowded corral. They had exploring to do and it really was a one-on-one kind of discovery technique that was to be used. Randy wished he was going with them but didn't ask to go when Mary Jo seemed content to stay at the barrel racing.

There were smells of horses, hay and the result from horses after they had eaten the hay. People milling about socializing and people who sat on the sturdy bleachers observing the contest. Randy knew the farmers would be discussing crop yields, animal breeding, how much they would be receiving per pound for their livestock and poultry, as well as, how the weather would be affecting everything previously mentioned. The women would catch up on social concerns, family in far-off places who had moved on for various reasons and pass the word on about who had been ill, allegedly unfaithful or imbibing the devil's spirits too often.

He wasn't listening to Lee's off-color remarks or caustic comments concerning anyone who walked by their position by the concession stand because he was lost in a day dream. Lee stood with his sprained arm in a sling a result of his altercation the previous night with the locally infamous Sam Hammet. Lee's eye was black underneath from running into Sam's fist. He wore his wounds with pride like he had received a Purple Heart medal. It brought him attention and Lee loved attention. He jibed Randy about not having any visible wounds in which Randy could garner sympathy from the girls. Lee told Randy that he would have to keep all the tender loving care for himself. Besides Randy had Mary Jo and he wasn't sure if Connie would be attending the rodeo tonight.

Lee had spoken to Connie, but she was noncommittal about coming to view the barrel racing. She told Lee that she would try to attend because Lizzy Fulton was racing and Lizzy was her best friend. However, she had planned a tentative date with Ron Peterson, her current beau. She had told Lee that she would try and break her date so that she could be with him, but she didn't know if Ron would let her break the date without causing a scene. He was very possessive. Lee was hoping for the best. He didn't want to have a confrontation with Ron, who was slightly crazy, well-muscled and not particularly fond of Lee. But Lee wanted to see Connie to continue his budding relationship - a relationship that gave him status and hope for a future in the world of girls, promised experiences that he would cherish forever.

Lee continued to whisper asides to Randy whenever anyone caught his eye he felt worthy of commenting on but Randy was staring out into space. His mind was a thousand miles away.

The loud speaker was blaring with country music filling the interlude between events. Without warning an electronic squeal pierced the air causing a collective shudder and groan among the patrons recoiling from the irritating noise.

The PA announcer excused the noise with a casual so what attitude of a young man that he was and announced the next event and first rider.

"Our first rider in the hair pin barrel racing finals is Lizzy Fulton. She has the best time so far tonight or 18.45 seconds and will compete against Joy Glenn and Debra Hughes for the Glenn Barrel Racing Trophy. Let's give a big hand for …"

That was all of the announcement Randy caught. Lee had poked him in the ribs to draw his attention.

"You day dreaming about Lizzy?" Lee kidded.

"Lizzy who?" Randy replied quizzically.

"Yeah right…you probably have that yarn wrapped around your little soldier right now. A man of many women you are…yes sir, a man of many women."

"Well it could be one less if Mary Jo hears you. I had nothing to do with what happened last night. You pay attention to yourself and leave my love life alone. If you're lucky I'll call the police when Ron Peterson starts beating your ass for stealing his girlfriend. And don't count on me calling the police too fast because you deserve a good beating for being a home wrecker."

"Randy, my boy…you hurt me. Connie's the jezebel; I'm just her play toy…a willing play toy, but a play toy none-the-less."

"Always the victim. It's no wonder you're always in trouble."

Lee turned from Randy and looked to his left at the sound of people approaching and said, "A victim of circumstance my poor goody two shoed friend." He paused, let out a sigh and continued, "Speaking of trouble here comes Pa-toot and his mentally-abridged brothers."

Randy snickered, "Trouble for you not me. He likes me. Maybe it pays to be a goody two shoes. Piute is just another member of the Lee is an asshole fan club."

"Funny…very funny."

Both boys acted nonchalant putting on their cool facades as Piute Dickerson and his brothers approached them. It was obvious that Randy and Lee was the object of the Dickerson brother's attention from their purposeful walk and stare in their direction. Lee flipped a cigarette in his mouth and lit it with his Zippo lighter. He cupped it down at his side to try and keep it hidden from view of the spies who may inform his dad. But he needed its relaxing effects to deal with Piute and his abnormal brothers.

Piute Dickerson, whose real name was Phillip, was built like a brick building with a bowling-ball head. His close-cropped red hair was smooth across his nearly perfect round head, which appeared to sit on his upper torso without a neck. His freckles covered his entire exposed skin giving off an appearance of a dappled tan with white dots splattered at various spaces. His log-size arms stuck out of his body as if they weren't able to relax at his sides because they had joints, which didn't allow them to fall down close to his body.

But with an appearance, which was attention grabbing as a piece of coal lying in a snow drift, it was nothing compared to his eyes. His eyes and that of his brother's were a stunningly clear grey. They reminded Randy of a movie he once saw called *The Village of the Damned.* They seemed to penetrate your soul as you looked into them. And as much as Piute's other physical attributes reflected an appearance of a mentally challenged man, the eyes radiated a sense of complete knowing holding an ability to break down falsely-erected barriers.

Piute was a unique boy growing into a man. His brothers on the other hand were less than mentally capable of living life in an ordinary constructive way. It was rumored that Piute's family pattern was abnormal; conventional wisdom believed by most in the community was that the Dickersons had interbred too often. Piute's family appearance was considered a direct result of this unfounded accusation. People perpetuated this thinking by claiming that Piute's father had visited North Georgia and met and married his half-sister, who had been sired by Piute's grandfather on another trip when Piute's father was a boy of two years old.

Piute's clan claimed that the Dickersons were really second cousins, which didn't help eliminate the rumors in any way. Regardless, the Dickersons didn't really bother anyone in the community and kept to themselves and their farm most of the time. The farm was large and took a great deal of work, which prevented the boys from getting a well founded education.

Piute was the oldest and missed a great deal of school each year. He had been bussed to Randy's school during his fifth grade year to attend remedial classes and ended up in Randy's classroom for two years. The classroom was split with Miss Magee handling the regular students and the students that needed additional help. Miss Magee was a remedial specialist and handled cases from all around the county. The students were mixed so as not be stigmatized. Piute was two years older than Randy, but took a liking to him for reasons Piute explained to Randy, but the actual events weren't remembered by Randy.

Piute claimed that Randy had been the only pupil nice to him the first day of his arrival by showing him where the room, his locker and the bathroom were located. Piute also claimed that Randy sat with him at lunch when no one else would venture near him. Piute was an intimidating figure whose appearance didn't belie his demeanor on most occasions. He was cantankerous, moody and not one to take gruff from any antagonist.

One final link obscure as it seemed was a defining link that the boys actually felt was the glue which cemented their friendship and that was the hatred of mayonnaise. Randy had never cared for the slimy feel of the white, detestable concoction on his tongue, let alone the abhorrent taste of the food desecrating ointment. Piute on the other hand had a story to turn off multitudes of existing users of the egg-white death.

Piute had been sitting at the dining room table with his parents enjoying lunch one midday afternoon after a long morning of chores. He was nine years old and his brothers Mike and Stanley were sitting beside one another across from his mom and dad. The boys were eating peanut butter and jelly sandwiches, while their parents had tuna fish on toast.

The boys were horsing around letting off some steam from the pressure of their work filled morning and their mom chastised them for not minding their manners. Ordinarily the boys would have been well behaved in front of their father, because he tolerated little disobedience. He was a strict disciplinarian and quick with a slap, the belt, a switch or fist, which ever was handy and warranted the offense. In a rare display of frivolity, he had provoked the boys to laugh by making funny faces at their mother as she had placed his sandwich in front of him. Unaware of his playful prank, she paid him no mind and when she would turn her head away, he would contort his face again sending the boys into hysterics. Finally with a quick turn of her head she caught her husband sticking his tongue out with chewed food on it. Her dumbfounded look caused even greater laughter.

Piute was laughing so hard he was gasping for air, when the look on his mom's face caused his dad to guffaw sending a mouthful of chewed tuna fish and mayonnaise directly into his oldest son's mouth. Piute swallowed the chewed morsel and gagged immediately. Not from choking, but from the thought of previously-chewed food entering is body. He wailed and ran around the room as if he had been shot. Everyone laughed except for Piute. He was disgusted. He couldn't wash the taste of mayonnaise from his mouth. The very mention of the word today sends shivers down his spine.

No boys ever picked on Randy while Piute had been in school with him. Finally Piute was sent back to his local school, but the friendship continued with boys seeing one another occasionally because the Dickerson's lived near Randy's aunt and uncle. They lived on the other side of the road down from the pond up the road from the Glenn's house.

Piute's brothers were a different story altogether. Randy could recall a time he was bored and had ventured down to the quarry in an effort to seek out his friends but was unable to find them. The quarry appeared to be empty at first but Randy soon heard a dinking noise of metal like someone banging on the side of a can with a hard object, followed by a grunting sound and deep long laughter echoing across the huge man made hole. It was coming from the other side of the boarded up overseer's shack up on the far side of the quarry. He couldn't ride his bicycle over so he cautiously sauntered over to take a peek.

Randy stuck his head around the corner and saw Piute and his brother Mike bouncing empty cans off their other brother, Stanley's head. Stanley was holding his hands out as if he was trying to catch or deflect the cans, but was never successful. He would grunt each time a can struck his crew cut head, but he didn't try and run away.

Stanley couldn't shout for his brothers to stop throwing the cans at him, because he was born without the ability to speak. He was uneducated and followed his brothers everywhere emulating their every move and mannerism. Randy felt sorry for Stanley even though Stanley seemed to be a happy go lucky kid that hardly ever was in a depressed mood. He stood up for himself on the rare occasion his brothers weren't there to defend him. His brothers were the only people allowed to harass Stanley because the boys wouldn't tolerate anyone making fun of their brother. Piute was not one to use words as a deterrent. He struck first and fast not caring if he was justified or not - his impression was the correct impression.

Mike, while just as volatile as Piute, seemed more like a cur. He would stay back in the shadows and strike more from behind without warning. He wasn't quite as stocky as Piute and Stanley and when he stood with the two of them he actually looked slender. He carried more hair on the top of his head with a generous supply of bangs that hung down over his hungry gray eyes. All the boys had those eyes, except instead of penetrating and omnipotent like Piute's eyes, Mike's were like a scared cornered animal. He had a terrible habit of laughing like a hyena at everything that Piute said or did, whether or not if it was funny or serious. This bothered Piute and sometimes his ire rose quickly and Piute would slap or punch Mike causing Stanley to laugh with glee. Mike was powerless to take revenge on Stanley as long as Piute was around.

Randy watched the spectacle of cans bouncing off Stanley's head for a moment or two before revealing himself to the brothers. A can was tossed not real hard, but not too softly, end over end through Stanley' out reached hands, bonking with a hollow metallic sound of his slightly-ducked head. While Stanley gave appearance of trying to avoid the cans, Randy could see that it wasn't a true effort on Stanley's part. Randy knew that Stanley was much more agile than he was showing at this point. With each boink of the can, Mike would laugh his hyena laugh, looking over at Piute for his continued approval. Piute who was also participating with the can toss didn't laugh out loud but he had a happy smirk on his face that Randy knew to reflect Piute's happy state of mind.

Once the boys had thrown their last can near their feet, Piute noticed Randy by seeing Stanley gaze over the shoulders of his brothers at something behind them. Piute signaled for Randy to come and join them with a wave of his hand. Randy obliged him.

Randy felt a little embarrassed to have caught the boys abusing their brother. He sauntered over to them trying to think of something to say which would expedite his exit. But before he could think of something to say, he could see that Stanley had gathered the cans in his arms and had dropped them at his brothers feet. He assumed his positioned and beckoned for Piute and Mike to recommence the tossing of the cans.

Piute offered Randy a can, who quickly deferred the offer hoping not to insult the whole Dickerson clan. Fortunately Piute shrugged as if it was okay, Mike laughed his annoying laugh while he kept his eye on his brother Piute. Stanley pleaded in his grunting way for the boys to start the cans bouncing off his head. Randy had stayed for what he felt was an appropriate amount of time and took his leave. He kept a memory of the event with him forever. It was one he was unlikely to forget.

Piute stood before Randy and Lee with his brothers side by side, one step behind him. Randy could tell Piute had something to say to him because Piute stared him in the face with those intense gray eyes causing Randy to block out the current surroundings and focus on the eldest Dickerson son.

"Hey, Randy, I need to talk to you," Piute bellowed with his deep baritone voice.

"Yeah, Randy, we need to talk to you," echoed Mike bobbing his head and giving a short snicker afterward which was his habit.

Piute glanced at his brother sharply causing Mike to flinch slightly and to take a step away from Piute.

"Hi, Piute…boys," Randy said. He nodded at the boys. "What do you need?"

"What's up, Piute?" Lee interjected acting as casual a he could. Piute's glance was all Lee needed to see that he wasn't going to be involved in the conversation. Lee puffed his cigarette and sank back into the background once again. He smirked but didn't use any hostile body language that might set off Piute.

"I heard from my cousin Darlene before I came down here to the rodeo and she told me something about your cousin, Dennis," Piute said. Darlene was his cousin who worked as a dispatcher at the police department on a part time basis.

"She says that Dennis was going to whip the tar out of Sam Hammet and Arrington Debussy for picking on you and that there Powell boy."

Randy stifled a laugh not wanting to look in Lee's direction. Piute was talking about Lee as if he wasn't there and Randy knew that Lee had that hound-dog look on his face right now. Randy bit his cheek and concentrated on the seriousness of his cousin's action.

"She says old man Renfro was going to arrest Dennis when he caught up with him, even though he hadn't whooped either boy yet." Piute stopped talking.

Randy took the cue. "How does anyone know that Dennis is looking for Hammet?"

"He's been passing the word, asking people if they had seen Hammet around. But I don't know what's going to happen. Seems like Hammet got spooked and went to the police station...says he got beat up by a negro last night while he was minding his own business - some boy who was hanging out with Mr. Foster's niece, Donazella."

"Donzella," Randy corrected.

Piute looked at Randy and nodded while he absorbed the correction.

"Yeah that's right, Donzella. Anyway, he says he doesn't want to fight Dennis, so that's why he went to the police. He wants the police to find the boy that whooped him last night and he wants Dennis arrested so that he won't get whooped by Dennis tonight I guess."

Randy was thinking this through. It was odd he hadn't heard from or had seen Dennis tonight. Dennis always made an appearance at events. Randy hoped that he wasn't in jail, his aunt would be pissed.

"Everyone knows that Hammet started the fight with me and Lee and that Barry just helped us out. There were a lot of people in the back of Walker's last night," Randy said.

"Yeah, Darlene says that the police know about your frackus. But they say that don't give that black boy no reason to be beating up on Hammet. So they are looking for him anyway."

Randy didn't correct Piute's pronunciation of fracas. If Piute wanted to say frackus, that was fine with him. Randy hoped that Barry had left town and he knew Barry probably had gone because staying in town after beating up a local wasn't exactly the most intelligent thing to do-especially if you were black and you were fighting with a white man.

"Thanks for the information, Piute, I appreciate it. I hope that Dennis didn't do anything foolish," Randy said.

"Yeah, we got more," Mike said hurriedly with a truncated laugh.

Piute paused looked at the ground but didn't acknowledge his brother. It seemed to Randy that Piute was losing patience with his human echo of a brother.

Mike on the other hand didn't seem to catch on to Piute's body language. He felt Piute's silence was a signal to help the conversation. He moved closer to Piute which wasn't a good strategic move. Randy watched Stanley who was standing aside peering at his brothers with a knowing grin on his face.

"Darlene says that while Sam Hammet was sitting there telling Old man Renfro about his ass whooping..." Piute was saying.

"Yeah his ass whooping," interrupted his cackling brother.

Suddenly without warning of any kind, Piute flashed a movement with his hand and as quick as lightning struck his brother Mike dead on between the eyes. Fortunately for Mike the hammer hard hand of Piute was opened and not closed into a fist. The blow took Mike off his feet and onto his backside, squeezing the breath from his lungs. He sat blinking, trying to pull oxygen from the air around him into his lungs without much success. Finally he was able to suck the life nourishing gas in with a huge effort. He looked up at his brother with an injured animal stare, grinned and laughed his stupid laugh. Piute barely bothered to acknowledge him and kept his concentration on Randy.

Randy was biting his lip trying not to laugh. Lee wasn't so subtle and was guffawing like a donkey. Stanley was pointing at Mike and grunting an I-told-you-so, you-got-in-trouble gesture.

Mike picked himself up without any help from his brothers. They neither offered nor did he expect to be offered help. Mike dusted the back of his breeches off and stood back out of Piute's reach. He continued to laugh intermittently but never took his sideways gaze away from his older brother.

Piute continued to speak to Randy as if nothing had just occurred and then all of the boys settled down with an occasional titter of laughter emitted from Lee.

"So as Sam Hammet was talking about Donazella's...I mean Donzella's friend whooping up on him...says the Negro hit him from behind when he weren't looking by the way; all of a sudden Hammet starts to get all quivery and shaky when Deputy Renfro asks him about the fight.

"Darlene says Deputy Renfro tells Sam to calm down and not to be scared but to just to tell the truth in that way Renfro talks...you know like you done something wrong and he knows it."

Randy nodded. He knew exactly what Piute meant. Deputy Renfro never met an innocent man.

"Now Darlene is sitting two desks over listening to the whole thing; she says that as Sam's talking he's watching Renfro playing with a can of spray paint. He's just rolling it round and round in his hands, like he's keeping himself busy while he's talking to Hammet.

"But Hammet thinks Renfro is suggesting that he knows something about the paint can. So Hammet starts to cry and confesses out of the blue that he was the one along with Debussy who done painted the shops with Freedom Rider stuff. And not only did they do it, but it was Caleb Fulton that put them up to and paid them twenty dollars and a case of beer."

Randy stood stunned for a moment. His eyes scanned the grounds and they stopped on the grand stand area near the broadcast booth. He could see Caleb Fulton talking to Mr. Romo. Caleb didn't seem to be worried about anything. He seemed to be his usual cool self holding his beer can loosely at his side.

"If it's true how come they don't pick Caleb Fulton up?" Randy asked Piute while he still watched Caleb.

"Don't know for sure, but I just spoke to Darlene a few minutes before I came over here to the horse show." Piute seemed to be finishing up his conversation with Randy. He waved his hand for his brothers to follow him like a cavalry officer motioning his troops to form ranks and to move on down the trail. "Maybe they ain't had time to send someone over to get him."

Randy thought differently. He figured being related to the police chief had everything to do with it.

Scar nose Fulton filled Randy's heart with contempt so vile that Randy had trouble rectifying it with his natural ability to let things be what they were to be. If it was true that he had placed Hammet and Debussy up to the painting of the inflammatory graffiti, Randy was doubly convinced that it was Caleb Fulton who had burned down the church. Caleb had so often assured Randy that he had no connection to the burning, but now Randy felt as though he knew the truth.

Randy stood steaming, not that he was so incensed that Sam Hammet and Arrington Debussy had written the graffiti and maybe not because Caleb Fulton had contracted them to do it. He was pissed because Caleb Fulton would probably get away with promoting his agenda without impunity, He was too well connected. Even here in Colmboro people would condemn things on the surface, but with an underlying opinion and behind closed doors they supported Caleb Fulton's causes. People were so hypocritical, it turned Randy's stomach.

Perhaps Piute was correct. Maybe the police just haven't had time to come and arrest Scar Nose yet. Maybe they didn't know where to find him. But if they had sent someone over to his trailer surely they would have come to the corral. After all, it wasn't that far from Caleb's place. And if Piute had come from his home as he had said, it wouldn't have been that long ago. Piute and his brothers lived on the other side of the Glenn estate down on the creek by the old lighthouse and vineyard.

Randy began to calm down somewhat. He decided to wait a little while to see if Caleb would be arrested and if he wasn't he would call the police station and tell them where Caleb Fulton was located. At least that was what Randy was thinking. He didn't know if he could rat out the bigot or not. He hoped he wouldn't have to do it, but he wanted Caleb to pay for his crime. Jesus, how he hated Caleb Fulton.

Randy had been wrapped up in his own thoughts, staring at Caleb Fulton, observing him from afar, when finally he came back to consciousness hearing Lee calling his name.

"Randy! Randy!" Lee shouted.

Randy was about to turn to Lee, about to take his eyes off of the man he detested, when Caleb Fulton had turned to walk away from Mr. Romo and he caught Randy's eye. Caleb nodded in acknowledgement, a cordial how-do you-do nod. In a reflex move Randy nodded back and immediately kicked himself in the ass for the act. He tried to turn away in a contempt type fashion, but it was too late. Caleb had his attention drawn away and was listening attentively to someone that Randy couldn't identify clearly. Caleb looked around the venue as if he was searching for something or someone. He shook the hand of the other person and disappeared behind the grandstand.

Randy had a sinking nervous dreadful feeling pass through his stomach. He wanted to take back the nod he had tossed Caleb Fulton's way, but it was too late. He wanted to punish Caleb emotionally as well as physically. He wanted to take something from Caleb that Caleb dearly loved. He wanted to cause him to lose stature in the close knit community. One thing Randy realized was that he had already emotionally pummeled Caleb by being so aloof for the past few years because of the church burning down. They had been so close, Randy, Caleb, Vern, Picker and to some extent Lee, but with Randy's lead all the boys shunned Caleb to some extent- thus causing the next generation of Colmboro youth to deal with social issues on a different plane.

As Randy began to eat away at himself over Caleb Fulton, Lee was trying to pull him back. Randy was gnawing his lower lip, stewing inside, eyes to the ground in concentration when Lee nudged him not so gently and pointed toward two girls making a beeline to them.

"Where the hell are you at, boy? Look who's headed over our way, your girlfriend, Lizzie Fulton, and my girl Connie. I want you to put old Piute and the Dickerson ding dong brothers out of your mind. The law will get Uncle Scar Nose and take care of him. Sam Hammet's already getting his and Dennis is doing just fine I'm sure. If he didn't beat up Sam or Arrington then he's out drinking beer somewhere…probably with Blue Dog over at Clarke's Bar.

"Now while you were in a trance, I'm guessing you didn't hear the PA guy announce that Lizzie has beaten Joy Glenn for the first time in the barrel race. As far as I know, that's the first time anyone has beaten Joy in one of these local yokel rodeo events. I don't know for sure but maybe Joy's getting old. But I do know that Lizzie won and she's coming this way with my girl. So be nice and don't scare Lizzie off because she might take Connie with her." Lee stopped talking and looked from right to left. "By the way, where is Mary Jo?"

Lee had said all this to Randy without taking a breath, because the two girls were approaching them quickly. The girls were giggling and huge smiles on their faces. People were offering small gestures of congratulations to Lizzie for her winning time. While they were careful not to be showy with their praise, so as not to show up Joy Glenn, most spectators were warm and genuine with their accolades.

Lizzy was walking with purpose; she had her bright blue eyes set dead on Randy. He could see the confidant victorious sparkle reflect off of them as she looked directly at him. It was as if she was gliding toward him, no bump in her step, closing the distance quickly and smoothly. Perhaps, he thought, she was headed for a Coke to celebrate her victory; after all he was standing in front of the concession stand. How vain he was to think she was heading his way. He thought of the yarn on the dresser at his aunt's house. He meant to toss it away but captured a thrill when he held it in his hands and he delayed disposing of it.

Lizzy was a pretty girl. Her shoulder-length blonde hair was pulled back in a pony tail that sat low on her head to accommodate her cowgirl hat. Her smile was infectious and moved across her face with a gentle ease. She had a dangerous appeal to her. She was a daredevil kind of girl who took risks for thrills and wouldn't shun any dare if she felt the task was possible.

The outfit she had on accentuated her curves with her tight riding pants nothing more than washed out Levi blue jeans that adhered to her body in a sexy way. She wore a cowgirl's shirt with fringe that traversed her bosom. The fringe moved back and forth as her breasts swayed with her every movement.

As she closed the distance, Randy forgot all about Scar Nose and began to feel that excited-type nervousness in his stomach, which was more thrill than dread. His butterflies were swarming as fast as they could swarm, trying to bust free of his stomach. For a moment he thought that he would wet his pants with excitement when the image of Mary Jo crossed his mind. He didn't want to upset her by appearing to have an interest in Lizzy Fulton, but the sparks of electricity he was feeling was going to prove hard not to disassociate himself from that hellcat, Lizzy.

As chance would have it, Randy didn't have an opportunity to play his cool aloof act. Lizzy walked up to him. Her eyes locked on Randy's eyes melting his resolve. She wrapped her arms around his neck, pushed her body tight up against his and kissed him squared on the mouth. She backed up and kissed him lightly on the mouth again.

With their lips millimeters apart and her solid tight body still pressed against him she whispered in a soft sexy way, "Call me and call me soon."

Lizzy released him, gave him a slight nudge away from her with her hands at his shoulders and stared into his eyes for a second or two. Randy was spellbound peering into her blue eyes as if she was casting a silent incantation by moving them back and forth slightly coquettishly as lovers would do before kissing. Suddenly she turned on the heels of her cowgirl boots and walked back toward the contestant area swaying her hips suggestively as she went.

Randy stood and stared. He watched her as she made her way through the small thin crowd dust was kicking up from her feet. He was on fire and a little embarrassed.

"Damn if you aren't turning into a stud, boy," Lee stated.

"Humph," Randy replied.

He looked back at Lee who had turned his attention back to Connie. Connie was ordering a Coke and Lee took over the task. The two of them were small talking. Randy could over hear Lee embellishing about his wounds like a Texan amplifying tall tales to impress the ladies.

Randy snickered to himself listening to Lee boast and surveyed the crowd for Mary Jo. He didn't have to look far. She was standing about twenty feet from him with her hands on her hips. The look on her face told Randy all he needed to know. Mary Jo had witnessed Lizzy Fellur planting a big one on his face.

When their eyes met, Randy could see the fierceness emanating from Mary Jo's eyes. She stood there defiantly. It seemed to Randy that if he moved to her that she would bolt and run like a cat that was in a standoff with another cat once the first move was made. From the appearance that she gave, he couldn't tell if she would be the aggressor or not. Perhaps she was so mad that she might whack him across the face. He could see her color rise second by second.

Finally he reacted to the situation. He splayed his hands and arms out in a "what-did-I-do" manner accompanied with an imploring questioning look. His sympathy approach caused a reaction he didn't expect. Mary Jo's defiant face turned to a disgusted sad visage. She shook her pretty head from side to side slowly as if wounded emotionally by someone she thought that she could trust.

This roller coaster ride that Randy had been on for the last fifteen minutes was definitely on the downside of the fun meter. From meeting Mary Jo tonight, Caleb "Scar Nose" Fulton to Lizzy Fellur back to Mary Jo, he had had so many ups and downs that he thought he would lose it. He had to salvage this situation. He really hadn't done anything wrong. He didn't encourage Lizzy in any way. He hoped that Lee would attest to it but he never knew what that crazy man might say. He was innocent but appeared very guilty. How many times in his life was he the victim of circumstance? So many that he couldn't count.

With a heavy sigh and a pursed lip grimace, Randy started toward Mary Jo to explain the situation to her. He would use all the charm he could and if need be, he would use Lee and hopefully Connie as back up to his story. Unfortunately as soon as he had taken a step in her direction, Mary Jo turned and moved quickly in the direction of the grandstand. Randy could see Mr. Magurk standing at the base of the grandstand speaking to the man that Randy had seen with Caleb Fulton a few minutes earlier. It was Mr. Romo, Randy could tell from the clothes that Mr. Romo was wearing; the white shirt and brown vest were the same as Randy had seen the man wearing earlier.

Mary Jo was making tracks as fast as she could away from Randy. The crowd which seemed so thin earlier now took upon a thickness that's seemed to slow Randy down like he was trudging through an obstacle course. He repeated, "Excuse me" so many time that it lost its meaning and enunciation. It was coming out sounding like "Scoos may". The grounds weren't that large and shouldn't have taken Randy too much time to overtake Mary Jo, but he felt like he was running through a forest of people trees all moving in different directions never allowing him to pick up a head of steam.

Randy watched as Mary Jo reached her dad. He could see the concern on her dad's face as he peered down at his distraught daughter. Mr. Romo looked upon the father daughter tandem and could be visibly seen excusing himself from the two of them. He quickly shook hands with Mr. Magurk and slid away from them. Mr. Magurk hugged his daughter to comfort her for brief second or two before Mary Jo pulled away and stomped her foot in anger explaining something to her dad.

Randy gulped and assumed that she was filling her dad in on the events which caused her emotional distress. He continued to advance toward them but not without a large case of apprehension. Mr. Magurk was a huge man and known around the area for his temper and possessiveness of his daughters. But Randy knew he was innocent and wanted an opportunity to explain the situation. He would take his chances armed with the truth.

Ten feet away from the duo, Randy slowed down; his resolve was waning as he neared them. He could see Mr. Magurk's eyes settle on him as he approached and

Mary Jo turned around to face him. She said something to her father, who briefly glared at Randy taking his eyes from his daughter. Randy noticed a subtle knowing nod of Mr. Magurk's head in his direction before Mr. Magurk took his leave to sit on the bleachers of the grandstand very close to his daughter. Mary Jo stood with her hands on her hips, her face wearing a defiant, aggravated expression. She stood her ground with confidence as Randy advanced the final few feet to stand in front of her.

"Mary Jo," he began, "I'm sorry but you need to let me explain what happened. I didn't know she was going to kiss me. I didn't…"

"You didn't stop her," she interrupted without mercy.

True he thought. When you're right you're right was Randy's motto but he was damned if he was going to give up so easily. He had liked Mary Jo for so long and he finally had his chance to be with her and now one kiss from Lizzy Fellur threatened to blow up the whole opportunity. How stupid could he be? Why didn't he stop Lizzy? He decided that he was a weak man when it came to women but he had to salvage this relationship and he set about doing it.

"Mary Jo, please just listen to me and I'll explain the situation. Lee will back me up and Connie will too. When I'm done and you're still mad…and I don't blame you if you are…let me make it up to you somehow. I swear it won't happen again. I'm stupid sometimes I know, but I'm innocent."

Randy shut up waiting for her to reply. He felt a little embarrassed not from kissing Lizzy Fellur but from the way he was talking to Mary Jo. He was groveling and he felt spineless and actually didn't have much control over it. The words just rolled out of his mouth, his brain pondering their meaning only after they had been said. He had dated the girl for a date and a half and he was already whipped.

Finally Mary Jo said, "Okay, explain. I'm all ears."

"Cute one's too if I may say so," Randy tried to add a little humor to diffuse the situation.

Holding back a smile Mary Jo said, "I'm waiting for an explanation and please make it a good one."

Chapter 22

The night's festivities were over and there was a sense of hurriedness in the air to complete the shutdown of the corral. A slight drizzle covered everything and everybody that remained to help close up the concession stand, PA booth and bathroom facilities. The remaining few people felt the anticipation of a down pour which had threatened to happen at any moment and they wanted to be in their cars and trucks high and dry on their way to their respective homes.

All the horses had been trailered first with everyone pitching in to help one another. The barrels and cones from the inner corral had been stowed in the storage area beneath the PA booth and most of the litter had been picked up and placed in the waste cans that were scattered in and around the grounds. Mr. Glenn had recruited some of his farm hands to help with the clean up, because experience had taught him that most people wouldn't move three feet out of their way to dispose of trash properly. He was glad to pay his hands a little money to help keep the area clean.

Randy had stayed to help because for one of the few times in his life, albeit he was distraught, instead of being alone to think he wanted to be near people to take his mind off his predicament. He was in a wait-and-see situation with Mary Jo and his friends had suddenly developed lives that took them currently in different directions. With no one to bounce things off of, he decided to keep his idle mind busy working physically at the corral.

Mary Jo had informed Randy that she would take his explanation under consideration and would call him tomorrow. She wasn't feeling well and she went home with her parents. She assured him that she would call tomorrow after Randy had given her a hound-dog pitiful hurt look. She had explained that she and Lizzy Fellur had had similar rival situations in the past.

Lizzy had muscled in on her friendship with Doris Raines when they were in elementary school and had managed to tell Doris enough lies to poison Mary Jo's relationship with Doris. Throughout their lives, they had managed to steer clear of one another the majority of the time, but when the occasion came to needle one another, neither girl wanted to pass up the opportunity. Mary Jo admitted that she hadn't always been passive in the minor rivalry, but she insisted that she only retaliated when she felt it was warranted.

Randy didn't ask for examples. He didn't want to belabor the discussion concerning Lizzy Fellur. It did set him to wondering if Lizzy was being nice to him only to aggravate Mary Jo. If so, he didn't like being a pawn but his ego wouldn't let him believe Lizzy's attention was only to piss off Mary Jo. He felt that he merited some attention, he wasn't that ugly. At least he hoped that he wasn't that ugly. His confidence swayed from strong to weak and he tried to put the thoughts completely out of his head.

He would wait for Mary Jo to call and he would do his best not to fall under that horse riding vixen's charm. It wouldn't be easy to ignore Lizzy, but if he wanted to be with Mary Jo he would have to give his best effort to ward her off.

When Mary Jo had left she gave him a quick peck on the lips and an acquaintance type hug. Both of which left him with wanting more. He was encouraged that he had at least received a kiss at all. If she was overly angry, she wouldn't have even touched him so his hopes were high but unfortunately they were on hold until the next sunrise.

Randy sat on the fence's top rail with his feet resting on the center rail observing the last of the cleanup effort. His aunt and uncle had departed earlier with Pup, because his uncle wanted to get back to the farm and raise the windows in the chicken houses before the expected rain came. They had offered him a ride, but he declined saying that he would hitch a ride with someone after he had helped clear the grounds.

Now as he scoured the area for a ride, he didn't see anyone who would be headed towards his aunt and uncle's farm. He didn't want to inconvenience anyone, so he leveraged himself off the fence with his arms, plopping down onto the soft dirt and began to walk the half of a mile walk back to the farm. He thought that if walked fast enough he could beat the rain and even if he didn't make it, the rain wouldn't hurt one bit. It might even take his mind off the events of the day. The last two days were filled with enough adventure, excitement and revelation to last him a life time.

Too bad that Lee had been caught smoking a cigarette by his dad, because he could have walked home with him. Lee was unaware that his father was even going to attend the rodeo. It was unusual for Mr. Powell to be out that late in the evening. He had to rise early in the morning in order to get to work- for delivering bread was an early morning chore and shop keepers wanted the bread ready when they opened their stores. Mr. Powell was usually home by noon or one in the afternoon and his day was done, but his nights were short and he went to bed early including nights in which he didn't go to work on the following day. It was just bad luck for Lee that his dad wanted to step out a little to enjoy himself without telling his son.

Lee had been acting his cool-fool-self, entertaining Connie and Randy with his fabricated stories of the neighborhood, when his dad appeared out of nowhere. Lee was in the middle of a story about Pup, acting like a drunk, when he stopped in the middle of the story to take a drag on his cigarette to emphasize a point of the story. As he drew in the smoke, it curled from the end of the cigarette and brushed against Lee's eye causing him to squint as he exhaled the smoke from his lungs. Once the smoke was exhaled, Lee's eyes grew to twice their normal size and he flicked away the cigarette as fast as a frog would flick his tongue to capture a fly. He was quick with the action, but the deed had been done. His dad had spotted him smoking and had strolled into the circle of Randy, Connie and Lee with an, *I got you attitude.*

Mr. Powell was much calmer about the situation than Randy would have ever thought he would be. Perhaps Lee's physical condition played a part in it because he sure looked pitiful with his black eye and sprained arm, not to mention the wounded look that rested on his face. Mr. Powell motioned with his finger in a crooked come here gesture and Lee had not hesitated for one moment. The two of them stood away from Connie and Randy and they had a quiet quick conversation with Mr. Powell doing most of the speaking.

Randy and Connie had moved closer together for support as they watched the father and son chat, both were a little apprehensive, hoping for the best for Lee. They didn't say anything to each other, but they could feel the support each held for their friend in their body language.

Lee and his dad stopped speaking. Lee then peered at his shoe tops for a moment or two gathering himself for his exit from the night's festivities. He strode over to his friends, his dad holding his place waiting patiently for his son. Lee approached Randy and Connie, his back to his father with a wry smile on his face. He mouthed the word 'oops' and smiled even broader.

He explained to them that he was obligated to leave and may not see them for the next few days. While he didn't think he was in for a physical beating at this time, he knew his privilege of being a free teenager was about to be severely limited. He kissed Connie and gave her a one-armed hug and promised to call her. She smiled and gave him a feeble disappointed finger-wave good-bye. He bowed and then threw a last kiss her way by way of his out stretched hand. He nodded to Randy and then hustled behind his father gesturing animatedly obviously trying to talk his way out of the situation. It wasn't long before they had left the area and Randy could see Mr. Powell's pickup truck leave the parking area.

Connie didn't hang around long once Lee had exited the grounds. Randy was glad Connie didn't stay to discuss Lee's predicament for fear that it might attract Connie's friend Lizzy Fellur, thus placing him in more hot water with Mary Jo. Randy knew there was a plethora of eyes watching him and he didn't want anyone reporting back to Mary Jo that he had been fooling around with Lizzy while she was out of sight.

He stood with his back to the wall of the concession stand, pondering the barrel race when Vern stopped by to chat with him.

Vern had an air of ebullient joy about him - he was smiling, giddy and gregarious. He talked so much that Randy didn't have an opportunity to hardly work a word into the conversation. Vern was acting differently from his usual demeanor. He was more like Randy in that he was usually reserved in conversation and small talk was not something that he took in unless forced by the situation.

Vern indicated that he had something that he wanted to share with Randy but now wasn't the appropriate time to do it. His eyes danced mischievously and couldn't keep still. Finally he wandered off and went to the bathroom telling Randy to wait for him by the concession stand until Picker, Leigh Ann and Corrine showed up. Randy asked where they were and why Corrine wasn't with him now. Vern explained that Mr. Magurk had stopped them but that he had excused himself to use the rest room.

Randy's heart had sunk at the mention of Mr. Magurk but he didn't say anything to Vern about the situation. He didn't want Vern to know, but was okay with Picker and Lee knowing. Vern wasn't the most sympathetic person and tended to tell things which should have been held in confidence.

Once Vern had ambled off toward the bathroom, the trio of Leigh Ann, Corrine and Picker came from the opposite direction, startling Randy as he was in deep thought as he watched Vern make his way to the wooden bathroom with the half moon cut out of the door. He hadn't seen them coming and certainly didn't expect them so soon.

Noticing that he startled Randy, Picker remarked, "Pretty jumpy for a guy standing out in the open surrounded by people."

"I guess I was day dreaming a bit", Randy said quietly. He felt self-conscious feeling Leigh Ann's probing eyes upon him. At least he thought they were probing him for signs of the cad he assumed her father or sister had informed her that he was.

"Why is Mary Jo going home with Dad?" she asked Randy.

He thought for a moment. Did she know why? Was she testing his honesty? Christ sake, why did everyone have to know his business?

"We had a little misunderstanding and she wanted time to think," he said. He hoped that this would suffice.

After an awkward pause of a moment or two, Leigh Ann nodded her head while watching Randy with focused eyes and she simply said, "Oh, I see."

Randy didn't think to be true, but he also didn't volunteer any more information.

"I'm thirsty. Let's get a drink," Corrine said.

"Okay." Leigh Ann agreed and the girls moved over to the concession stand window to purchase a drink. Turning her head over her shoulder, Leigh Ann asked Picker if he wanted a drink and he shook his head no.

Picker was alone and apart from Randy. He said, "Bad night, huh?"

"Could have been better," Randy replied. "That damn Lizzy Fellur's going to be the death of me yet."

"There are worse ways to go, my man," Picker said with a small air of comfort.

"Yeah but I like Mary Jo and Lizzy's gumming up the works. Don't worry, I'll work it out." Randy kicked at the dirt and changed the subject. "What's up with Vern? He's walking on air?"

"Don't know for sure, but I think Corrine has moved our muscle-bound friend over from boyhood's thinking of chasing the brass ring to that of one who has caught the ring and tried it on."

"Corrine gave it up?" Randy inquired doubtfully. He assumed that was what the hell Picker was referring to.

"Can't say for sure… I wasn't in the room with them. But knowing what I know about Corrine and a little idiosyncrasy that she has, I'm supposing that she did."

"What idiosyncrasy?"

"Well the way she tells it that once she does the deed, she hankers for a cigarette and a Pepsi. She doesn't usually smoke, but she had one on the way here. And all the way during the ride over she proclaimed how thirsty that she was. Let's see if she comes back with a Pepsi."

Randy smiled. His curiosity was piqued and it wasn't but thirty seconds before he quenched the curiosity. Corrine came back holding a clear bottle with a cola colored liquid in it displaying the Pepsi logo very prominently. He smiled a little broader and glanced at Picker who smirked in return.

After a short conversation, Randy learned that Vern would be accompanying Corrine to the airport the following day with Mr.

Magurk and Leigh Ann. Picker had declined the invitation to tag along mainly because he wasn't enamored with a two hour drive to the airport. This time of year the drive across the bay was so congested with western shore tourists trying to reach the Atlantic beaches that the drive seemed interminable. Vern however was in love and knowing that he wouldn't see Corrine for a very long time, if ever, and he wanted to be with her as long as he could.

Randy had stood by the concession stand a short while after his friends had left. He had declined a ride thinking that he would be able to grab one from someone at closing time.

Now he was starting the trek home. The lights of the corral grounds illuminated the way for him a good deal of the way. There was no moon because of the cloudy sky above and he made his way through the misty rain with a brisk walk. He could see the various pole lights from the homes he would have to pass on his short journey to his aunt's house. He contemplated on how he would be received if for some reason he ran into trouble on his walk by certain members of the community. It was getting late and most people were probably preparing for bed. He knew that there was some discussion during the night concerning the dogs at his uncle's farm and the community was split over the issue.

He didn't think that anyone would be discourteous to him and everyone would certainly help him if he needed help. But sometimes even people who were courteous could still project a cold resistance of doing what was expected of them. He wasn't sure what he was worrying about, but he had a feeling of anticipated doom and he couldn't shake it. Perhaps he was tired. The events of the last two nights had been draining not to mention the lack of sleep from the prior night. He was emotionally drained. Plus he had to pass by Scar Nose's trailer on his way home. He had already decided that he would run as fast as he could by the trailer. He didn't want to see Caleb, who sometimes sat in an old wooden rocking chair on his front porch drinking beer. Randy hoped that the man was in police custody and sitting in jail.

Chapter 23

A halo of artificial light glowed from the pole lights of the back yards, which served as street lights spaced widely and irregularly at the farmhouses lined up and down the road. Just past Randy's Uncle Harvey's childhood home the lights from the corral were extinguished. With only the soft glow of the property lights sporadically placed behind the farmhouses, usually closest to the barn or chicken houses, Randy was surrounded by a misty foreboding darkness. He had traveled about one hundred yards and he had a good half a mile to go. He longed for his bicycle or a ride now that he was enveloped in the darkness, but wishing wouldn't produce reality, so he trudged on toward home. He was thinking that it was just his luck that the lights at the corral were turned off so soon. He had thought that he would be half way home past Caleb Fulton's house before the lights were shut off.

Another few yards down the middle of the road, the mist began to change to a drizzle. It felt good on Randy's face because his pace was fast-not quite a run-but a brisk hardy walk. He could feel the heat escaping from the road as the earth cooled releasing up around him in a humid vapor causing his body to heat up even more. He could feel the road beneath his feet slope right and left as he walked the crown of the black top. While he was riding in a car or on his bicycle he hadn't realized how crowned the road was in order to let the rain run off so that puddles wouldn't accumulate in the center of the road. He felt safe in the center of the road and it was much smoother than the shoulder.

He rounded the bend in the road, which would bring Randy past a small stand of trees. He could see Caleb Fulton's rusted mobile home. A light shone through the window dimly, silhouetting two high back wooden slat chairs that sat underneath Caleb's metal awning overhang. Randy couldn't really observe anyone in either of the chairs from this distance on the road. It was too shadowy and the drizzle splashing him on the face hindered his sight line. He knew that it was entirely possible that Caleb was sitting back watching his world with a can of beer in his hand.

Randy looked for Caleb's signature pickup truck but he didn't see it anywhere. He felt that this was a good sign but he knew Caleb could have parked it around the back by the old wooden garage that Caleb kept so diligently locked.

A few more yards and Randy decided that he would begin to accelerate his pace. He could feel the adrenaline begin to pump through his veins. He was actually shaking a bit, his eyes wide concentrating on the wooden chairs, watching for any kind of movement, feeling the sting of the rain drops on his eyes, which caused him to blink the blur away.

Involuntarily Randy began to run. His subconscious mind placed into gear the survival reflex. He didn't know if at any time he feared Caleb Fulton or just didn't want to talk to him. Whatever the reason he was now into a full-fledged race to be past Caleb Fulton's abode before he could be stopped. He decided that even if Caleb was there and called to him, he would ignore Caleb and keep on his path.

He pulled even with the chairs and Randy concentrated as hard as he could on the road ahead. He could see the lot where the old church had stood; the black timbered ashes jutting up carelessly in the air resembling a woodpile in disarray. Beyond that he could see a soft light glowing out of Miss Manly's cabin window. The cabin set back far from the road almost hidden by the pine trees surrounding it. Randy knew that after Miss Manly's cabin that only an open field stood between himself and his Aunt Caroline's house and then he would be home free.

He didn't want to look over at the chairs. He fought with his curiosity and apprehension not to take a glance. By running past the trailer, he managed to control himself and he didn't look. The rain began to change from a drizzle to much larger drops. A big drop landed atop of Randy's head and the accompanying breeze moved through a wind chime that hung from Caleb's awning. The drop and the chiming noise caused Randy to run even quicker.

Once he past the trailer and his mind had time to evaluate the last two sensations, he pulled up and began to walk. His breath came in gasps and he could feel the burn of the oxygen cross his windpipe falling into his lungs. He was winded but he was exhilarated. He was close to home and he was past the demon's house. His walk slowed to a crawl and the rain came down more heavily. Randy turned his heat filled face to the heavens. He was thankful for the rain and the being above - then he heard the clacking footfalls behind him.

Randy was winded from the sprint past Scar Nose's mobile home. He could feel the hair on the back of his neck rise as goose bumps of apprehension scattered across his body. He walked quickly as his oxygen-depleted lungs could carry his leaden legs. He didn't know what was following him, but he could distinctly hear something clacking claws on the road behind him. He tried to slow his breathing so that he could hear the sound better. The clacking noise was definitely on all fours and it was keeping its distance between them at the same interval.

Randy stopped walking altogether and half turned to the sound behind him. When he stopped the clacking noise stopped with him. He began to think it was possibly his imagination, perhaps it was the rain falling on the road, dirt and plants, playing tricks on his ears as he walked ahead on the road. Then he thought he hadn't heard the noise before he was past Caleb's place and the small wood adjacent to Caleb's trailer. He peered in the darkness and falling rain but he didn't see anything in the road.

When he was about to turn back around, he caught a luminescent reflection of eyes ever so brief in the middle of the road about 150 feet or so behind him. He turned to see how far he was away from his uncle's house. He figured he would have to run another one hundred yards before he could call to Bessie and the other dogs to come to him. The pack at his aunt's house would surely drive off the animal behind him.

One good thing about whatever was behind him was that it didn't seem to be aggressive - at least yet. He began to think that perhaps it was hunting him, waiting for the right moment to jump on his back and rip out his throat. He remembered a story he had heard about a wolverine that supposedly lived in the woods by the creek.

He knew that wolverines had two speeds fast and stop. He also knew that wolverines were supposed to live in the northern states, but he had heard that someone had brought one back from Alaska and that it had lived here in the woods. There was a story that it came around the farms sometimes and killed cows. It didn't always eat the cow, but when it was full it would bury the cow and spray it with his musk odor to find it again later. Word was that it had chased Mr. Lilau around his barn and nearly jumped on his back before his dogs frightened it away. Everyone said it could kill with its sharp claws and teeth in a matter of seconds. He also knew that Mr. Lilau was known to have a few drinks in the evening, but that knowledge did little to allay his fears at this time.

The rain began to drive harder, splashing large drops on and around Randy. He felt that he had regained enough breath to try and sprint close enough to his aunt and uncle's farmhouse to bellow a call to the dogs. He was happy now that there was a large crowd of dogs at the house. They would certainly overpower the animal stalking him. Let the neighbors bitch about the dogs Randy couldn't have been happier that his uncle had kept all of the canines.

He ran as fast as he was able to run. Randy listened with all his might to see if he could hear anything running behind him. Between gasping for air, his feet striking the pavement and the pouring down of the rain, he couldn't hear anything possibly behind him. His heart beat thumped continually in his ears. His breath wouldn't hold out and he had to slow down before his lungs would burst. He had only covered about fifty yards. The run past Caleb Fulton's place had winded him and he hadn't had enough time to recover before he had to sprint again. He hoped that he had let the pursuing creature behind him.

Randy stood very still with his hands on his hips, mouth open wide pulling in deep breaths for his overworked lungs. His mind was racing for an idea to help relieve the situation. He needed a weapon, but none were available. Perhaps he could take off a shoe and use it as a club, but he'd have to be pretty close to get a good whack at the animal and if he was that close, it was a good bet the wild animal would conquer the tennis shoe wielding prey. He considered screaming for Bessie and the dog cavalry, but figured that they would never hear him in the pouring rain. He had but one option and he felt that he would have to use it. He would use the Butch tactic. He would scream and yell like a madman charging directly at the demon seed that wanted to eat him. It worked once and hopefully it would work again. Never-the-less, Randy was so scared that he thought he might wet his pants. Good thing that it was raining, if he did wet his pants, at least no one would know it when they found his torn and ravaged body.

He readied himself to begin his offensive charge. He stood trying to calm his mind, to capture his breath and to steel his nerves for the assault on his stalking nemesis. He envisioned the wild animal turning in terror and bolting across the open field for the sanctuary of the woods. But that vision lasted only a brief few moments and was replaced by one of the thing behind him ripping his face off with its claws and then settling down and having him for dinner.

He considered running for the house one more time. The rain splashed so hard, that it was like standing in a waterfall. Randy caught a shiver. No he decided he would have to turn and try and scare the animal away.

He acted on an impulse and turned to face his foe with a blood-curdling scream. He waved his arms wildly above his head, unknowingly using a primal urge to project himself larger than he really was. He ran with his eyes half closed hoping that it would protect them in case the animal jumped for his face and throat. About fifty feet into his full-blown Kamikaze attack, Randy stopped abruptly and stared down at the animal, which had lain down on the road in a submissive position. Pony stared up at Randy like Randy was a lunatic. Randy peered down at the dog that he had grown to really like over the past few days and he felt like crap. Here was a dog that had saved his life just yesterday and he had almost scared the life out of him. That's gratitude for you, Randy was sure that was what the dog was thinking.

Chapter 24

Randy felt so bad about terrorizing Pony that he had sat down in the middle of the road with the dog in the pouring rain and he had rubbed the dog's belly. He talked to the dog in a reassuring manner, explaining his actions to the rain-drenched dog. When he felt that he had apologized enough and Pony had gotten to his feet, Randy stood as well and they began the slow trot home. Occasionally Randy would look down at the dog and Pony would look back up at Randy. The dog and his master were formed. Randy was happy that Pony was so forgiving.

About ten yards from the house, still adjacent to the open field beside the house, Pony left Randy's side and bolted out into the wet knee high grass toward the woods. Randy watched him go wondering where the dog was going and wondering what had provoked him to dart through the grass so suddenly. Out near the wood's edge Randy thought that he saw a light flicker. He stood in the road and stared at the spot where he thought that he had seen the glimpse of light. He thought that he would see the light again, but as much as he tried he couldn't spot it again.

It must have been his imagination, because he couldn't see anything. But it sure seemed that he caught a glimpse of yellow light, so it couldn't have been a reflection. It was more like a flashlight beam or a lantern light. Pony hadn't barked, but then again Pony wasn't a barking dog.

Randy was standing a few yards from the house and he began to wonder where the other dogs were and why they weren't barking at the strange light out in the woods. Bessie, Queenie, Blackie and the gang must be over at the old barn staying dry and out of the rain - otherwise they would be producing a huge barking racket. It must be his imagination, because the dogs didn't seemed concerned about anything unusual or concerned about anyone they weren't familiar with.

A startling flash of lightning with its corresponding clap of thunder shoved all other thoughts from Randy's mind. Thank goodness he was nearly in the house and the lightning portion of the storm had waited for him to arrive at home. He hated the lightning and couldn't wait to be inside of the house. His only thought was of how his uncle had told him as a little boy that Harvey's dad had been struck by lightning while tending to the mules.

Randy reached the door of the screened in porch and ducked under the torrent of rain water cascading off the metal roof running over the gutter attached to it. Even though he ducked his head it did little to ward off the water and the heavy splash striking him in the middle of the back caused him to arch his back when the concentrated cool water flooded over him. He stood under the small overhang and turned to peer out into the rain.

The shadows near the house were gothic in appearance; the trees appeared as creatures standing in place hunched over waiting to converge on unsuspecting prey. He could see further down by the chicken houses where the pole light illuminated the dirt road and buildings on a normal evening, muted now by the dense heavy rain. He felt secure now that he was at home and he was actually enjoying the view with the splashing rain in front of him and the sound of it pounding on the metal porch roof. Then the lightning flashed again and it moved him to enter the porch as quickly as he could move.

He shook off the rain and was greeted by Queenie, the only dog allowed in the house, with a wag of her tail. She was curled up on the sofa glider snuggled down into the soft cushion that dressed the sofa. He walked by rubbed her rear and scratched behind her ears. Queenie sat and accepted the affection patiently. She was older and tolerated the petting, but she was not a dog that encouraged human contact.

Randy took off his rain-soaked shoes and went into the house.

He walked through the outer room which led into the kitchen and he could hear his aunt and uncle having a muted intense discussion. He would have thought that all the lights would have been extinguished and appliances unplugged. This was a habit of his uncle during thunderstorms. His uncle didn't want to tempt fate or

Mother Nature by attracting the lightning to manmade electronic gadgets. Uncle Harvey's father early life's experience with lightning had scarred Harvey for eternity.

The discussion must be important or Harvey would be sitting in a chair in the dark in the center of the room demanding that everyone be quiet. He didn't tolerate jocularity when it was storming.

A fact not wasted on Randy and Karen when they were younger they would tease their uncle unmercifully until their laughing aunt would pee her pants and force the two of them to behave themselves.

Randy took a step up from the outer room and entered the fluorescent lit kitchen. His uncle's back was to him as he sat in his customary kitchen table chair. His aunt was sitting directly across from his uncle her face resting in her hands, propped up by her elbows on the table.

Aunt Caroline's eyes took a what-happened-to-you-look while she observed Randy.

Reading her look he said, "It's raining."

His uncle turned around in his chair and peered at Randy, who resembled a drowned rat.

"Better get them clothes off, boy, before you catch a cold.' Harvey said this more matter of a fact in his tone than he did with conviction.

"Okay I don't need a lot of convincing," Randy said.

"How did you get home?' Caroline asked.

"Walked."

"Walked? Why didn't you get a ride?" inquired his aunt. "Wouldn't anyone give you a ride?"

"Didn't ask. When I left it wasn't raining that hard and everyone still there when I was leaving lived the other way...so I decided to walk. I didn't think the rain would come down so heavy. Besides it didn't get really cold until I came into the house. That rain is cooling me down."

Harvey turned back to face his wife and picked up his glass of iced tea. "Sure no one refused you a ride?" He asked with a heavy dose of sarcasm.

"Why would someone refuse to give me a ride?" Randy was puzzled.

"Your uncle's mad because the Glenns questioned the amount of dogs we have. Which wouldn't have been so bad, but Mr. Romo made a sarcastic remark about it too. Harvey got mad and told them to mind their own business. Told'em the dogs didn't bother anyone so what was the big deal.

"Mr. Glenn tried to tell Harvey to calm down but Harvey was too far gone. You know him…once he's got his feelings hurt. Harvey told me that they we needed to go and so we left. We've been debating what we should do because we know a lot of the neighbors think that there are too many dogs here, but we can't bear to part with any of them."

Harvey spoke, "That damn Pup didn't help my mood much."

"What did he say?"

"That old drunk…he said we ought to take them down to the quarry and get rid of a few."

Caroline knew Harvey was mad at Pup for the insensitive remark, but Harvey's real frustration came from the attention that Pup paid to her. Harvey kept his feelings inside for the most part and didn't vent his emotions or speak his thoughts, perhaps when he should really express them. Caroline knew it irked Harvey when Pup was flirting with her, touching her arm or her back when he spoke to her or would always try and sit next to her, but she liked the attention ashamedly. She wished that Harvey was more physical in their relationship. She knew that it was harmless fun on her part and she would never do anything to break her vow of fidelity she had promised her husband.

Pup had tried to fend off the anger that he had instilled in Harvey by explaining away his remark about the quarry. He had tried to say that he meant that Harvey should take the complaining neighbors down to the rock pit and get rid of a few of them. But Harvey was agitated to the point of no return with the frustrations of the evening. He hadn't raised his voice to the oafish drunk, but Pup could feel the tension in Harvey's voice when Harvey joined in the conversation from the point of Pup's vocal faux pas.

Caroline laughed at her husband as was her habit when he became angry, trying to ease her tension, but this only served to intensify Harvey's choler. Pup excused himself feeling very unwelcome and he had headed for the door to venture home. He slowed long enough to see if Harvey or Caroline would offer him a ride down to his farm- an offer which never came.

So he said his good byes and scurried out clinging to his half full Mason jar of homemade brandy.

Caroline related most of the story to Randy omitting the jealousy of Harvey and Randy headed off to his room to change out of his wet clothes. He thought his uncle must have been really riled because the lightning storm had showed no effect on him whatsoever.

He was dead tired from the lack of sleep from the night before and his emotional event filled evening. He couldn't wait to warm up and to climb into his bed.

The rain had cooled the evening down, combining with the natural cooling of the earth during the night time heat transfer and his rotating fan, Randy felt as though it was a cool springtime night, just made for a snuggling-style sleep.

He ditched his wet clothes in the downstairs bathroom and he had scampered up the stairs with a towel draped around his waist. With his wet clothes hung over the tub and shower curtain rod he didn't have anything to wear. He had decided to show restraint and he had not asked his aunt to retrieve anything for him to wear from his room, because he didn't want to aggravate his uncle any more than it was necessary. He didn't call for his sister because he wasn't even sure that she had returned from her night out.

He briefly glimpsed into Karen's bedroom, but the door was partially closed, so he hadn't received a good look inside. There was a dim light on and he surmised that she wasn't home yet and only the night light glowed beside her bed.

The rain hammered down outside with sporadic thunder booming and lightning illuminating the shingled roof outside of his window.

Randy dropped the towel and pulled on his Fruit of the Loom jockey shorts. He stood before a full length mirror that was attached to wheels in a heavy wooden frame making it portable. The mirror had never left the room as far back as Randy could remember. It was built to swivel with fulcrums on each side in the center. The opposite side of the mirror contained a beautiful elaborate wooden carving that Randy used to pretend was the family crest when he pretended to be the valiant knight and his bedroom was the throne room.

He often played by himself when he was younger. His aunt and uncle's farm was a great source of ideas that allowed his imagination to run wild. He often jousted with the trees in the small peach orchard across from the driveway opposite the enclosed porch. The trees rarely gave fruit for reasons not really known to Randy, but the small group of trees proved to be a forest primeval to a young boy with a free-wheeling mind.

If no one was available to play with during the day, which was a frequent occurrence in Colmboro farming area, because farm work didn't wait and his friends often had chores that endured throughout the day. Randy was often on his own. His sister did girl things and Randy would fall into his own world that would come together with his imaginary friends as if he had never left them.

He gravitated to the peach orchard quite often. At one point, two of the trees had intertwined with one another providing a maze of limbs easily climbed by Randy. These two trees became the focal point of his outdoor imagination. When they were in full foliage, he could sit between them on the ground without being detected. He considered this to be his fortress. The low growing gnarly limbs almost resembled a wooden pole puzzle that had been slapped together arbitrarily.

On the outside of the fortress was a limb that sat six inches off the ground. The limb had grown along the ground and up into the adjacent tree wedging itself between a tight fork. Over time the fork had closed over the intruding limb linking the two trees as if they were one. Randy would place his foot on the low slung branch and swing back and forth pretending that he was on a flying carpet surveying his kingdom for the dreaded enemies which needed vanquishing.

Randy peered into the mirror and began to critique his physique. A sinewy and slender pretty well tanned reflection stared back at him. He wished that he had the drive to lift weights to build up some muscle like Vern did. Randy would begin a regimen of working out, but usually after a week or two he would decide that it was too much work and the work took too much of his time away from other things. The rationalization wasn't lost on Randy but he accepted it because it made him happy.

He began to flex his biceps, trying to emulate Charles Atlas from the back of his comic books. With his arms raised and biceps tight he growled at the mirror with a mean look fixed upon his face.

"In love with yourself, Pud Puller?"

Randy glanced in the mirror and saw his sister standing in the doorway. Her hair was dripping wet obviously from being caught outside in the rain. He flushed a deep red and tried to compose himself. Nonchalantly he tried to hide his embarrassment.

"Among the many I fear. I'm surprised everyone isn't in love with this glorious body," Randy said sarcastically. "Why are you peeking at your brother, pervert?"

"Don't flatter yourself, string bean. I just dropped in to tell you that the police were at Caleb Fulton's house with full lights flashing."

"Did they pick him up?"

"I don't know. I don't even know why they would want the old drunk."

Randy explained to his sister what he had heard earlier.

"Well I hope they did catch him… serves the old drunk vigilante right."

"Where have you been? In the shower with your clothes on?" Randy asked.

"You're so funny…so funny," Karen retorted. "If you hadn't noticed, it's raining outside. I went out with Chuck tonight, but Dennis brought me home. I saw him at the Tastee-Freeze and decided that I couldn't stand being with Chuck anymore, so I asked Denny to bring me home."

What did Chuck say?"

"Nothing really…I don't think he really cared. I wasn't much of a date. I miss Gregory so much."

Randy pulled on a pair of shorts and sat on the bed. "So my sissy's in love. Did Dennis say anything about the law being after him?"

"They stopped him but they didn't have anything to hold him on so they let him go with a stern warning about getting into fights… toss me that towel would you?'

Randy tossed her the towel and she began to rub her hair vigorously. "Did you know that Sam Hammet is in jail?"

"Yep I just told you that. Anyway that's where that fat ass belongs." Randy answered.

"That's right you did when you were explaining about Caleb Fulton, and you're right that is where he belongs.

"How did your date with Mary Jo go?"

"Kind of tough…we had a little spat, but I think things will be better tomorrow."

"So goes love my little brother. Well I'm going to turn in and listen to the rain hit the roof and hope that it puts me to sleep. Good night."

"Good night," Randy said. He was glad his sister didn't press him for details on the Mary Jo subject. He didn't really want to talk about it. But he was glad that his sister stopped in to talk to him. He was happy the police were at Caleb Fulton's place and he was happy that Sam Hammet was in jail. The night hadn't been a total loss.

Chapter 25

Randy's eyelids fluttered with exertion as they tried to blink themselves open. It seemed as though glue had been applied to the edges or like a thousand tiny weights were holding down the lashes making it impossible for the lids to pop open in order to see what was disrupting his sleep.

He was so exhausted from receiving a restless sleep from the night before that Randy's limbs were like dead weights. He was so comfortable in the snuggly bed with the fan blowing air across him in a back and forth motion it caused him to sink deeper under the covers into a dreamless peaceful sleep. But his subconscious was tapping the shoulder of his consciousness trying to awaken him to something out of the ordinary.

Finally he rolled open his tired eyes. He lay still and looked up at the ceiling. His eyes rotated to the attic door and an old apprehension gripped him. He hated that door earlier in his youth because he was convinced that there was surely something hiding up in the attic ready to pounce on him while he was asleep.

He had always made sure that the door was locked before he went to bed. Sometimes he had placed a metal souvenir of the Washington Monument that his aunt had brought back from the nations capital on the step which led to the door. He figured that if something or someone came through the door it would have to knock the metal object over causing such a racket that it would awaken him in time to flee or scream for help.

Occasionally the strong wind outside would force pressure in the attic to pull and push the door slightly causing a perceptible rattle and it gave the appearance of something trying to open the door. Randy would lay awake on those nights until he couldn't stand it anymore and sheer exhaustion would overcome him and drive him to sleep. When he would awake in the morning still alive and not ravaged in any way he would feel foolish and cowardly for thinking something was lurking in his aunt's attic.

He kept his feeling to himself. He would investigate the attic during the daylight hours so that he could allay his night time fears, but some nights especially after a horror movie at the theater, he couldn't stop his vivid imagination from taking control of his mind and his thoughts. He welcomed nights that his sister developed the heebie jeebies and wanted to sleep with him. He liked the company and teased his sister about being a scaredy cat.

Randy observed the door and stared hard at the brown dented doorknob. He couldn't see the dent in the darkness, but he knew it was there. Karen had told him when he was nine years old that after they had watched *The Creature from the Black Lagoon* on the Friday night chiller program that a similar creature had lived in the attic and the powerful creature's hand had caused the dent when it had grabbed the doorknob.

This attempt at scaring her younger brother had back fired causing her to become the one who needed company in order to go to sleep.

After she had left him alone in his room with the attic door and its contrived content looming over him, Karen had gone to bed in her bed next door. The wind had picked up outside and a branch from the shady elm tree beside the house began to scratch intermittently on the pane of glass that sounded like a clawed hand rasping on the glass. Karen had spun her tale about the creature so well that she had frightened herself to a near panic.

She was convinced that something was coming through the window to carry her to the creek back behind the woods. She howled a scream that moved her uncle to jump out of his bed with his boxers on his slender body. He raced up the stairs to find out what the devil was wrong with his niece.

Harvey took two steps at a time, miscalculating the last two, because he had only had one more to navigate. He thought that there was an extra step and over reached with his leg and tumbled past a startled Randy who stood in the doorway of his sister's room.

Harvey somersaulted over the landing at the top of the stairs and down the step into Randy's room. He ended up seated on the floor, his legs wide and his back facing the doorway.

By this time Caroline had made her way up the stairs and stood with her hands on her hips. She surveyed the sight. Harvey was on the floor in his underwear, Randy was looking around like a wide-eyed deer baffled by the confusion and Karen was crying in her bed with the covers securely over her head.

She suddenly burst out laughing. She was giggling hard while she pointed at Harvey.

Harvey stood up indignantly. His farmers tan radiant, arms brown, head and neck brown and the rest of the exposed skin as white as a freshly purchased bed sheet.

Caroline laughed so hard that she had wet her pants before she had made her way down to the bathroom. Harvey gathered himself together and gave his niece a short lecture on being overly dramatic and told her to sleep with her brother for the night.

He had to investigate the noise outside of the window before Karen was satisfied that no one or anything was outside trying to come in the house to take her away. Randy rejoiced internally that he had someone to sleep with him in the room and he managed to tease Karen for many days to come over the window scratching incident.

Now he lay awake listening at the wind howl outside. He could hear the rain come down and it still came down heavily, but not as heavily as it had before he had went to sleep. The gusty wind would push the rain hard in heavy splatters on to the window panes. He heard nothing else that was out of the ordinary during the storm. He waited for the lightning and its partner thunder, but no flash or rumble came to his alert senses.

Randy figured that he must have been awakened by a bad dream or something. He couldn't figure out why he was awake- then he heard the howl of a dog. No barking - but a long whooping howl like the song of a coyote.

A silence filled Randy ears even though he could still hear the whipping wind and pattering rain striking surfaces outside. He was honed in on the long howling of the dog. It struck again. A short stuttering burst followed by a long mournful howl.

"Ow! Ow! Ow! Owwooo!"

Randy thought that he recognized the howling and thought that it was Pony. It sounded like the same howl as the night before when the puppies had been run over and lay dead on the blacktop outside in front of the house. A feeling of loss pervaded Randy. The puppies had died needlessly and some demented joy riding jerk had snuffed their lives out for a sadistic thrill.

Why would Pony be howling tonight? Was one of the other dogs lying dead on the road in the rain with the life running out of them with no one stepping up to help them?

Randy had heard old wives tales of howling dogs. It was a bad harbinger. Someone was to die. With the howling so close, it must have meant someone nearby was going to die. Randy hoped that it wasn't someone that he liked, but what could he do about it.

The omens he had heard about before meant nothing to him but superstitious nonsense, until the blackbird had flown down the flue at his aunt's house. He remembered how upset that Caroline had been when she had seen the free-flying bird in the space between the spare bedroom and the hallway.

He and Karen had watched while his aunt from the doorway as the poor disoriented bird had flown back and forth in the room slamming its head into the window panes trying in its effort to free itself of the human-constructed prison.

Caroline was mumbling about the death knell that it represented and insisted that the death would come within forty-eight hours. Her mother had taught her the signs of good luck and bad luck when she was very young and this was one of the worst.

Caroline had convinced her nephew to enter the room to open a window to give the bird an avenue to escape. But when Randy had warily maneuvered over to one of the windows, ducking under the panicked bird with a fright of his own, he found that the window had been nailed shut by his uncle. Randy stood watching the bird for a few moments before deciding what his next course of action would be. He thought for a moment of breaking the window, but discarded the idea as drastic and most certainly unacceptable by his aunt and uncle.

The bird flew directly at Randy and he stood in front of the window, causing him to hit the floor with reckless abandon and causing his sister to double over with laughter. Randy pulled himself up with nervous laughter holding onto the arm of a chair which was covered by a sheet that served as a dust cover.

He stood cursing his sister with mild expletives laughing with her but still warily watching the fluttering blackbird. His aunt chastised him for his language but he shrugged it off. He knew that she wouldn't do anything to him about his saucy mouth if he took care of the bird.

Then the bird exhausted from its effort to escape alit upon a lampshade no more than three feet from Randy. Randy could see the wild expression in its desperate eyes. The bird's beak was open and Randy could see the bird panting like a dog. He could hear his sister yelling to him to grab the bird and he yelled back to her how crazy that she was.

However the thought wasn't a bad one. He slowly lifted the sheet from the chair beside him. No sudden movement because he didn't want to scare his flighty feathered friend. He then used the sheet as a net and tossed it over the large blackbird. The bird fought like crazy to free itself of the cloth binding, but by now it was totally exhausted and finally resigned itself to being immobilized. Randy gathered up the errant traveler and released it outside.

The bird flew away and sat in the cherry tree behind the house as if nothing had happened to it all. Caroline was happy to have the bird out of her house. Randy and Karen recanted the story and laughed long and hard at the exploit. The next day Harvey's Aunt Sally passed away in her sleep. Caroline had a knowing look upon her face and Randy had become a converted believer in his aunt's superstitions.

Pony howled his long melancholy howl once again. Randy lay still staring up at the ceiling, he watched a soft shadowed reflection dance on the darkened façade. The oscillating fan hummed its way across his bed causing him to snuggle deeper still under the covers. Sleep was beginning to overwhelm him even though Pony was still howling. Randy rationalized the reality of the superstitions as being nothing more than ignorance and coincidence. Aunt Sally was old; she wasn't going to last much longer anyway. His sleep pushed aside his fears and his twilight dreams rolled over into pleasant thoughts of Mary Jo and he lost conscious thought of his surroundings as he fell back to sleep.

But his sleep was brief.

"Move over, Pud Puller," his sister said. "I've decided to sleep in here to protect you. You're probably scared with all of that howling stuff going on. Ugly night and downright spooky. I know you hate that attic. Go to sleep now...you're big sister is here."

"Thank God that you've arrived," Randy muttered. "I was almost in tears from fright."

"Sleep, baby brother," Karen said. "There is nothing to fear.'

Randy smiled and went to sleep. Karen snuggled close. She had no doubt about her Aunt Caroline's superstitions. Something bad was surely to happen.

Chapter 26

"No…no…Nooo!" A mournful wail burst through the open heat register in the bedroom floor where Randy slept. His bedroom directly over the kitchen was inundated with a horrible sad cry of his sister.

Randy sat bolt upright in his bed and he looked cautiously at the attic door. It was still closed and he brushed aside his childhood fears. Sunlight filtered through the window shade so he knew that it had stopped raining. No howl of the wind for the storm had passed over them.

At once alert but still a little groggy from his restful sleep, he tried to comprehend the sadness being emoted from his sister. His last recollection was that of Pony howling outside last night and Karen coming into his room to sleep beside him

He hadn't awoken when she had arisen from the bed and had ventured down the stairs.

Something terrible must have happened when he was sleeping and his sister knew exactly what it was that had taken place.

Randy hopped out of bed and pulled on a pair of pants, which were draped over the chair. While he tossed on his t-shirt he could hear his sister sobbing and his aunt trying to console her. He picked up his sneakers and he hurried out of the bedroom and bounded down the stairs lickety split, skipping stairs as he descended them.

He made his way into the kitchen and saw his aunt hugging his sister, stroking her hair consoling her.

"What's going on?" Randy asked. His eyes were wide with anticipation. He sat down on a chair in order to pull on his shoes, while he waited for an answer.

His aunt held Karen close as she sobbed. Caroline's back was to Randy. Karen glanced up with tear filled eyes and wet cheeks, which were flushed red from her crying. Randy could see that she was trying hard to compose herself. He peered at her with emotional pain on his face not knowing what she was going to tell him.

Between sobs and tears streaming down her face she stammered. "Bessie's dead, they're all dead." Then she buried her face back into her aunt's shoulder and cried even louder.

Randy could see her shoulders heave up and down with the force of her crying. Karen's condition caused Randy to feel himself begin to breakdown. His own eyes filled with tears as he fought to control himself. His stomach fluttered and his legs lost some of their rigidity. He knew that if he wanted to stand up that he would have to hold onto the table.

"What do you mean dead?' How?" he asked.

"We don't know how. Your uncle went out this morning to check on the chickens and found them all dead," Caroline said. "Go and find your uncle and help him bury the dogs."

"Okay", Randy whispered. His voice broke, so he cleared his throat and stated, "Okay" again with more steel in his voice.

He needed to be away from his sister before he broke down and sobbed along with her.

Randy walked by his aunt and sister and rubbed his sister's back as he went by in a consoling caress. Karen broke free from her aunt and hugged her brother tightly. She was more under control now and let him go after a brief embrace.

"Don't let Queenie out yet. She's in the porch. I don't want her to die too," Karen said.

"I won't," Randy answered. Trying to lighten the mood he added, "Clean yourself up some. You got boogers hanging on your upper lip."

Karen smiled a weak smile, punched her brother gently and said, "Beat it, Pud Puller. I've got some more crying to do before I wipe anything from my face."

Caroline handed Karen a napkin to cleanse her face and Randy headed out from the kitchen to greet the smell of death awaiting him outside.

As he exited the inner room leading to the porch he could see Queenie sitting patiently by the door that led to the outside world watching something with great interest. She wagged her stumpy tail when she heard Randy approaching, but didn't look back at him; she stared straight ahead with an unwavering interest.

Randy reached down to stroke Queenie's head. He rubbed between her ears and continued his petting down her back. He could feel a slight quiver of her skin beneath her brown and white wiry fur coat. He stood back up and studied her intently and he couldn't see her visibly shaking but there was definitely a trembling taking place within the dog. Perhaps she was tense he thought and she was ready to bolt out through the door when he opened it. He would have to be careful that she didn't get by him when he went outside.

Randy grabbed the door handle - more of a lever really and stepped in front of Queenie to impede her path, blocking her from racing outside. As he opened the door he kept his eye on her to be sure she stayed inside the porch. To his amazement Queenie didn't even move. Not even a nudge to escape the porch. Randy felt odd about it. What was she staring at so intently? Why didn't she want to race outside to where she was staring?

Randy threw caution to the wind and threw the door wide open and stood aside expecting Queenie scurry outside. It didn't happen. She stayed put, glanced her doggy glare, wagged her tail slightly showing her appreciation to Randy's offer and befuddled Randy even more.

Randy began to transverse the yard in the direction of his uncle. Harvey was just visible to the right of the huge black walnut tree located at the far end of the peach orchard behind the laying hens coop, but before the chicken house that held the chickens grown as fryers. This was the traditional burial ground for the farms deceased pets.

The ground was saturated from the heavy downpour which fell so continuously the previous evening. The grass beneath Randy's feet squished with moisture and the earth moved from side to side as the water soak dirt below gave way under his weight. The earth was so wet that it had the consistency of a sponge. Puddles had formed on the gravel filled driveway. It was impossible to walk anywhere in an effort to keep his shoes dry, so Randy trod through the shallowest puddles he could find.

Birds were singing morning songs filling the nice cool morning with cheerful sounds belying the sadness of the farm. Bird's lives had to continue and they had little concern over the death of the four-legged earth walkers.

Randy had popped out of bed so quickly this morning upon hearing his sister's wailing in distress that he hadn't even noticed the time of day. As he walked toward his uncle he observed the sun still hanging low over the horizon. It was still very early. He stifled a yawn and rubbed at an itchy eye. He blinked a few times and wiped the corner of his eyes closest to his nose and brushed away the crusty remnants of sleep.

Randy closed the distance between himself and his uncle at an exaggerated pace. He slowed his trek without really knowing that he was lessening his motion. He walked under the extended canopy of the black walnut tree, the sunshine turned to shade and Randy's mood became dark and gloomy.

Just on the other side of the tree his uncle worked with a determined rhythm, tossing the heavy wet dirt out of a long trench that he had been toiling on evidently for quite a while. The trench was over ten feet long and more a less, three feet wide and nearly four feet deep from Randy's estimation. Sweat poured from his Uncle Harvey's face and a straight-line grimace was etched onto his face. He seemed unaware of Randy's approach.

Randy could hear the shovel's metallic sound slice across and through the dirt. He wondered if the hole was filling up with water from the wet ground. He knew under normal conditions that if you dug too deeply, water would seep into the hole and lay at the bottom. From where he was situated he couldn't see the splash or drops of water emanate from the metal blade of the shovel.

Harvey's nephew stopped altogether just a few yards short of where his uncle worked tirelessly at his task. Lined-up carefully and obviously lovingly were many generations of dogs, which had populated the Kearney farm. Their eyes were closed and their mouths were partially open, their feet out stretched, the dogs looked as though they had lined up for a military slumber. A few of the dogs had begun to bloat with the gases that couldn't escape their dead bodies. Summer flies buzzed about them, their large green bodies hung in the air or alit on the eyes, snouts and mouths of the inanimate dogs.

Randy peered down through increasingly blurry eyes. The sight of the dogs he had known for so long laying not just dead, but all of them dead at one time rocked his emotions. The heartbreak was more than he could bear. At first he began to feel the tears run down his cheeks, his chest began to heave and he suddenly began to sob. He tried to check his emotions, but the more he strained and tried to suppress the feeling, the more he felt that he would explode.

He could see the beautiful white German shepherd, Bessie, lying so serenely. He remembered how playful she was a puppy - biting shoelaces when you walked by her, hanging on with puppy ferocity growling as if she were fighting another dog for the last morsel of meat. She would hide in the deep grass wiggle her backside like a cat gathering rhythm to leap on the other dogs as they trod casually by her.

Bessie became the leader of the pack and had stood majestically when she held her head back high sniffing the air.

Randy could picture Blackie, named for his pitch black fur in his youth, the eldest of the lot and the crankiest as well. Basically toothless with age, bright gray fur covering his muzzle, Blackie took the role of the elder statesman and usually began the barking when someone or something ventured near the territory of the Kearney farm.

Many times Blackie became confused, his eyesight failing and would mount a furious charge at people he hadn't had contact with in a while only to back off when the scent of the perceived intruder had been detected by his wrinkled muzzle. Often Randy would call out before walking up the driveway to head off Blackie's charge before he had to raise his weary bones for the attack. Randy had noted the puzzled faces of the other dogs when Blackie had begun some of his assaults. They seemed to be thinking the old fool is at it again.

Blackie, undaunted would woof a last grumbling bark as if to get in the last word, demanding respect for his old age, letting his companions know he would still protect the farm if it needed protecting.

Now he lay motionless and Randy would only be able to pull the memory of the venerable old dog from the recesses of his mind.

Randy saw the *trio* paw to back, paw to back, paw to back - a quiet slumber so unusual for three of the friskiest dogs of the lot. Born to Queenie almost two years ago, fathered by a dog from one of the surrounding farms, the three dogs were inseparable. Distinguished only by markings of the white spots on different body parts, the brown adolescent dogs amused everybody they encountered with their antics.

Randy's aunt had named them Huey, Dewey and Louie. Huey with white spots dappled on his head, Dewey with two white paws and Louie's tail tip was as white as snow. Caroline had the ability to discern who was who, but Randy could never remember. He always had to ask his aunt to point out each dog and its qualifying name.

Sometimes he thought his aunt changed the names around to confuse him, but when he questioned her she slyly smirked and denied doing it.

Somewhat people shy the three dogs rarely ventured near anyone not living in the Kearney house. They adored Caroline and would swarm her feet whenever they encountered her outside. Creatures of habit they would not leave her alone until she had scratched not only their heads, but their rumps as well. Once Caroline had preformed the ritual task on all three dogs, the trio would race away tumbling and jumping on one another as if they had just won the doggy lottery.

The boys would play every waking moment until they dropped from exhaustion. Randy had once seen them out in the open field which led up to the woods, chasing grasshoppers and butterflies for an entire morning. With seemingly tireless energy, they raced to and fro, snapping and barking at the flying insects. Occasionally they captured a grasshopper with a lucky bite but they never actually neared the elusive carefree butterflies with their white canine teeth.

By noon, Randy had seen that the young dogs had worn themselves out and were asleep underneath the wild cherry tree.

They were curled up on one another, tangled together in such a way that Randy could hardly tell where one dog began and the other dogs left off - a paw here, a tail there. It appeared to be a mythical three-headed dog creature.

The memory brought a smile to Randy's puckered, wrinkled face. The taunt smile lasted only a fleeting second or two. Randy's eyed the line of dead dogs, from one end to the other. He couldn't believe that this had happened. Deep down in his gut he knew that this wasn't something of a natural cause. Someone had done the unthinkable - they had murdered innocent, fun loving pets, which never really bothered anyone.

The community had decided it was time to cull the herd and to enforce their will. No one was above the sanctioning of the people. Randy knew most people would show the right amount of indignation and outrage that such an occurrence could happen in their small close knit community, but someone knew who the culprit was who had done this dastardly deed. Fact was probably more than one person knew who did it. Unless there was a break from the silence - no one would be found out.

Randy had his idea, but he didn't know how the murders were accomplished or how he could prove it. He began to think Caleb Fulton's arrest last night was some sort of ruse. He knew it had to be Scar Nose. No one else would dirty their hands by killing some one's pet dogs. Surely it was the snake killer.

Randy surveyed the dogs one last time - Bessie, Blackie, the trio, Rusty, Duchess, Toby, Sparkle and Lightning. Tears filled his eyes, his chest heaved and his face lost total control. His macho left him and Randy sobbed into his hands. His heart was breaking into little pieces for his furry friends. The anger at the killer clawed at his need for revenge. It consumed his emotions and collided with his sadness.

Randy shouted a four letter word at the top of his lungs and felt his knees wobble.

He didn't hit the ground only because his Uncle Harvey had grabbed him by the shoulders and hugged the boy heartily. Harvey hadn't even hugged Randy before this moment - at least not a time that Randy could remember. They embraced without speaking and in a while Randy calmed himself down.

He released his uncle and stood back peering at his Uncle Harvey through moist blurry eyes.

"You okay, son?"

Randy nodded and wiped his eyes.

Harvey placed his arm around Randy's shoulder and walked him past the dead dogs. Randy slid his eyes quickly down and caught the deathly sight again and he could feel himself become emotional. He stifled the feeling the best that he could, but he knew that he was unable to talk at this point for fear of breaking down once more.

Uncle Harvey sat Randy down on an old stump and absently rubbed Randy's head.

"Terrible thing happened here, boy," Harvey lamented. "But we've got a job to do. We've got to give these pups a good burial. Then we'll find out what the cause for this was and take it from there."

That said, he picked up his shovel to finish out the hole, which would become the sanctuary for the innocent dogs.

An hour later the task was nearing completion. Randy and his uncle had dug deep into the earth, so that the animals from the woods wouldn't be able to unearth the remains of their beloved pets. They had laid the dogs carefully side by side after Harvey had wrapped the dogs in cheesecloth. The dogs had begun to stiffen up from rigor mortis, but the grave was wide and long enough to accommodate even Bessie the large German Shepherd.

Randy thought that they had looked like mummies from an ancient animal world. He actually could disassociate himself emotionally once he didn't have to see the dog's fur and faces. He had steeled himself to help his uncle, but was glad when there was enough dirt to cover the last of the white death shrouds

Randy was resting on his shovel sipping from a glass of iced tea that his sister had brought out of the house. She had carried a plastic pitcher full of sweet tea and two glasses for the grave diggers. She didn't stay long and she didn't utter a word. She couldn't catch anyone's eye for fear of crying. Uncle Harvey had muttered a muted thanks and Randy said nothing. No one had wanted to tempt the tenuous peace that Karen had bestowed upon herself. For some reason, she curtsied slightly and fled to the house. Randy smiled at her action - amused, but the amusement left him as quickly as it had come.

Uncle Harvey was sitting on the stump wiping his brow with his handkerchief that he always had in his pocket. Randy stared over Harvey's head toward the chicken houses and saw Pony sitting in the driveway between the two houses. Pony observed Randy and wagged his tail, but made no effort approach. Randy didn't call him. He wondered why the dog was still alive.

Chapter 27

Uncle Harvey stood up and replaced his sweat filled handkerchief back into his pants pocket. He looked at Randy who was staring past him with a puzzling scowl on his visage.

Uncle Harvey turned to see exactly what it was that was catching Randy's attention and causing such consternation. He saw Pony sitting in the driveway wagging his tail.

"Why do you think he survived?" Randy asked with a slight tinge of bitterness in his voice.

"Right time at the right place, I reckon," his uncle replied. "Whatever those dogs got into seems to be localized. Probably that dog was out in the woods wandering somewhere. He didn't really fit with the clan quite yet."

"Hmmm," Randy muttered. "Perhaps that's true. On my way home last night in the rain I saw some kind of light back by the woods. At least I thought I saw a light...like a lantern or a flashlight kind of flicker...I'm not really sure. Anyway Pony took off out toward the woods. That's what made me look out there when I thought I saw the light. He didn't bark or growl...just ran out into the woods.

"You know what...it was odd last night. It was raining so hard I thought the dogs were in the barn, but I guess they were dead already."

"No, they were in the barn out of the rain," Harvey said. "After Pup left last night I went to check the chickens before I went to bed and Bessie joined me for the walk."

Randy stood with his hands on his hips staring at Pony. Pony stared back with his tail still wagging.

"Pony, come here. Pony, come!" Randy cajoled.

Pony jumped up and ran over to Randy and sat imploringly in front of him. He wanted to be petted, but he waited for Randy to make the first move. When Randy bent to rub the dog's head, Pony almost turned himself inside out with happiness. Randy sat in a squat position and let the dog lick his face. Randy was close to crying.

"What's going on?"

Uncle Harvey and Randy turned to see Pup standing over by the grave. He was peering at the grave site holding a half full jar of what was sure to be his homemade peach Randy. It was no more than ten o'clock in the morning.

"Had a little trouble last night," Harvey replied. He didn't volunteer any information. He waited for Pup to ask.

"Trouble? What kind of trouble?"

"Dog trouble."

"Dog trouble...what they do kill somebody?" Pup chuckled. He thought that he was being funny.

"No, someone killed our dogs, you dumb shit," Randy blurted. His fists were clenched and he wanted to clock Pup a good one on his wizened whisker-stubbled face.

"Now look here, Randy. Ain't no call for that kind of language," Pup said. He squinted at Randy and rolled his eyes over to Harvey as if to wait for Harvey to rebuke his nephew.

Normally Harvey would have chastised him and would have had Randy apologize to his elders. Harvey was a stickler for manners and respecting one's elders was at the top of his list.

The awkward pause drifted in the air. Pup rubbed his whiskered face and looked as though he was dying to draw a drink from his jar. He was uncomfortable and wished that he had gone to see Caroline instead of traveling out to see Harvey and his nephew out by the old black walnut tree.

Finally Harvey said, "Randy, do me a favor and tote them glasses up to the house. I need to jaw with Pup here a few minutes."

"Gladly," Randy snorted. "Smells better up by the house anyway." He picked up the drinking glasses and glanced at Pup as he turned to walk back up to the house.

Randy didn't know why he was particularly agitated with Pup, but he didn't really try and reason it out. Pup was an irritant on any occasion and on this morning his sick, stupid alcoholic jokes turned Randy's stomach.

Randy was a hundred feet away before he heard a conversation between his uncle and Pup begin with a slow, low, stunted, uncomfortable monotone. Randy didn't know exactly what his uncle had in mind to tell Pup, but he hoped that it was severe and so to the point that Pup would turn tail and go hopping through the mud home.

Thinking about Pup traipsing back home caused a grin to break Randy's scowl - more a sinister smirk than a grin. This was a sadistic helping of humor that was out of character for Randy.

As Randy approached the door to the porch, he saw Lee with his arm in a sling standing by his mailbox across the street. Lee was holding the newspaper, which he had taken from the cubby underneath the mailbox. This was where the newspaper was delivered in this rural setting.

Lee was dressed in his Sunday church clothes and was waving for Randy to come over to see him.

Randy opened the door to place the glasses on the table inside for the time being. While he held the door open to set the glasses down, Queenie hopped up from the cushioned glider to greet Randy.

He held the door for her and she walked outside to wait for him.

"He looked down at her and asked, "Feeling better?"

Queenie didn't respond. No tail wag. Just a vacant stare. A stare attributed to someone that had lost someone dear to them - a funeral stare.

Randy looked back down the driveway to see where Pony was. He saw the dog's multicolored rear end as it rounded the other side of the house.

That's a strange dog Randy thought.

'Come on, Queenie. Get some air, girl," Randy coaxed. The thought of his sister imploring him not to let Queenie outside flashed through his mind. Too late for that Queenie was outside and probably had to use the great outdoors before her bladder burst. Besides he would be there if anything happened. If anything was to happen, it would have taken a hold of Pony by now.

Queenie followed Randy across the street, moving lethargically at first. She moved her head from side to side as if to seek something or someone. Randy walked faster and Queenie picked up the pace.

Randy crossed the road, but Queenie stopped at the end of the driveway and watched Randy. She seldom left the property. She sniffed the air and sat still like a statue.

"Why are you dressed up?" Randy asked Lee.

"Why out here in the civilized country we still respect the Lord on Sunday," Lee sermonized. "Unlike you pagans, who worship who knows what - pasta most likely. I've been in that pagan shrine of yours."

Randy had forgotten that it was Sunday. The unusual circumstance of the morning was the only reason that his aunt and uncle had missed the early service. They would no doubt be at church this evening. In fact the whole community would be there this night. There was much to be discussed this evening.

Randy filled Lee in on the events of the morning, including his small spat with Pup. Lee was stunned. He excused himself and went to check on his dog Butch.

Picker showed up on his bicycle before Lee had returned and Randy repeated his story to Picker.

Lee greeted Picker upon his return.

"What's up, Picker?"

"Not much...Butch still breathing?" Picker asked somewhat cavalierly.

Picker's attitude stung Randy, but he held his tongue.

"Yep, he's still breathing," Lee said solemnly respecting Randy's feelings. After a slight pause he said, "What do you think happened to the dogs?"

"We don't really know. Queenie's okay but she was shut in all night. Pony's around here somewhere but he doesn't stay in the yard most of the time. He wanders all around. Besides Pony's only been around for a couple of days he didn't hang with the pack.

"Uncle Harvey said that there weren't any type of marks on the dogs. No punctures, no cuts, so he thinks it may be poison of some kind, but where would it come from and how would they get to it?"

"What about rat or cat poison?" Picker suggested.

"No it's kept locked up pretty good. If it's in a tray in the chicken houses, it's usually in the first room where the dogs can't get at in and the chickens are forced out."

"Maybe some rats ate some and the dogs ate the rats," Lee said.

"I don't know, that sure sounds like a long shot to me," Randy replied. "I think if that was the case this would have happened before this."

"True," Picker said. "What's your uncle going to do about it?"

"I don't know that either. I think he's got to find out what happened first. You guys didn't hear about this at church this morning?"

"Not a word," Lee said.

Picker shook his head with pursed lips and his brow scrunched as if he were thinking hard about his morning conversations.

Thinking of church brought Mary Jo to Randy's mind and he shifted gears from the heavy dead dog conversation. "Was Mary Jo there?"

"Yes, she was sitting with Tim Schyler. A little too close if you ask me…rubbing his arm and all. I thought that she was going to kiss him at one point." Lee looked down at the ground and kicked the dirt.

Randy tried to scan Lee's face to see if Lee was teasing him, but he was so concerned with Lee's statement that he couldn't read Lee's countenance. Randy's eyes widened and his mouth was agape as he turned toward Picker for confirmation. Picker turned his head away and stared down the road.

"Y-y-you're kidding?' Randy asked with a slight stutter.

"Of course, numb nuts…geez you're an emotional wreck. She was there and she wants to meet you tonight by the creek about seven o'clock she's going out rowing that canoe. She'll see you then to *talk*." Lee stared at his friend. The word talk was emphasized with a quotation gesture with his hands and spoken in a high pitched voice.

"I think she's going to row the boat with no top on, but alas I won't be able to hide in the bushes and trees. I've got yard duty for a week or so. Cigarettes are a bad, bad thing. Just ask my dad."

"I'd like to feel sorry for you, but after that little joke I'm almost happy that you've become a prisoner of the Powell penal colony," Randy intoned with mock seriousness.

"Ha! That shows you what you know, Mister piss-off-his-girlfriend. For your information, Dad's allowing me to have someone come over and visit and her name is Connie. You know her don't you, Lizzy Fellur's friend, your other girlfriend."

"Ouch…you sure know how to kick a man when he's down, Lee." Picker was taking up for Randy

"He started it, wishing me a slow boring death sucking up to my dad. It makes me shiver just thinking about it."

"Maybe you shouldn't smoke," Picker said.

"What now I've got two dads," Lee said shaking his head.

Randy laughed. "As crazy as you are, you need two dads - one with you at all times. How in the world did you get your father to allow Connie to come over?"

"I think he felt sorry for me with all of my injuries." Lee feigned weakness. "Besides Connie was at the church service. She came especially to see me. When she approached us I introduced her to Dad. Last night didn't seem to be the best time for an introduction and I suggested that she come by later for a chat.

"Dad gritted his teeth and said that he'd love to see her. She agreed and I stayed away from dad until it was time to leave. By then he had calmed down. When we got in the car to come home, he just looked at me, shook his head and sighed like I was incorrible… what's that word, Picker?"

"Incorrigible."

"Yeah, what Picker said."

"Beautiful," Randy said. "You mentioned Lizzy, was she with Connie?"

"You dog - you want both girls don't you. I don't blame you, the more the merrier. Who started this one guy one girl crap anyway?"

"So you think Connie should date more guys than you?"

"No, I think girls should date one guy but that guys can date as many girls as they want. I'm a double standard kind of guy. Now you guys can deny you feel differently, but then I'd just have to call you liars. Then what happens - we call each other names and get all hostile and everything but you can't fight with me because I'm already broken up and it wouldn't be fair to you two goody two shoes." Lee smirked with a know-it-all smirk peering at Randy and Picker.

Randy shook his head and changed the subject. "Did you hear anything about Scar Nose?"

"Yeah, I was listening to my Dad talk to Mr. Romo about him. The police went over to his place last night but couldn't find him. His door was unlocked and his truck was around back. I'll bet that someone tipped him off that the police were looking for him-probably that Barney Fife cousin of his.

"Anyway, the way Mr. Romo tells it, Caleb's in dire straits. They've linked him to the graffiti that was sprayed downtown-something about inciting a riot. Sam Hammet implicated him and Arrington. They caught Arrington last night. Someone said Sam cried like a baby and confessed to everything." Picker paused and looked at Randy.

Randy was listening intently. "Did they link Caleb to the church fire?"

"Man, you don't ever give up on that, do you? Lee asked.

"One day you'll find out that I'm right."

"Hold on, hold on, I didn't say that I didn't think that Caleb burned it down. I only mean no one's going to link it to him. Too many people wanted that church gone. Face it Randy there's a lot of collusion around here," Lee said explaining himself.

"Collusion- that's a big word, Lee." Picker smiled

"Yeah, well, I've got myself some sophistication. I'm practicing for my honey, who should be here just after twelve thirty. I want to impress her." Lee was holding his nose in the air emulating a snotty high-society-type person.

Picker then brought the conversation to an abrupt standstill with a loud flapping passing of gas. This took an edge off Randy's thoughts of Caleb Fulton and all three boys laughed.

"Now that's sophistication," Picker said and the boys laughed even harder.

"You need to harness that gas, Picker," Lee said with amusement. "It may come in handy one day."

"Or at least the noise," Randy added. "It's quite unique. Man, you are the loudest farter I've ever heard."

"Farter?" Picker laughed. The other boys laughed with him.

Once the boys composed themselves, there was a moment of silence. Randy looked away from Picker and Lee to keep his composure. His eyes focused on Queenie who was moving more and more, exploring the small front yard of the Kearney house by sniffing the ground seemingly an inch at a time. She was onto the scent of something.

A little further down the road in an open filed, Randy could see Pony lying in the grass with his nose to the wind, sniffing leisurely at the air currents. Randy was mesmerized for a moment or two, then he turned his attention back to his friends.

"Was Vern at church today?" Randy asked still staring into space.

Lee turned his head to look back into the direction that Randy was staring, seeing nothing of interest to him he turned back to face Randy and said, "Yes, he was sitting with Corrine. I think he was a little too touchy feely for his aunt. She kept sneaking peeks back at the two of them. She was trying to catch his eye but he was avoiding her. She looked like she had swallowed a lemon by the end of the sermon...face all puckered up, her eyes glaring at Vern."

"What did Vern do after the sermon? Did she go over to him?" Randy was amused by the event.

"He was up and out before she could get around the pew to reach him," Picker interjected. "He had asked his Uncle if he could accompany Corrine and Mr. Magurk on the ride to the airport. Corrine's going back to New York today."

"I'm assuming Pup let him go."

"Yep, they're on their way now. Leigh Ann's with them," Picker said.

"Looks like Vern's entered the man's world," lee said. "I wonder who is left."

Randy was quiet. Picker said, "I think it's still you, Lee."

Lee blushed. "Maybe still you, Picker." Picker smiled a confidant smile with a twinkle in his eyes - his smile so confident that Lee retreated his body language showing acceptance of defeat.

Randy was eager to change the subject before he became the focus of attention said, "Where do you think old Scar Nose is? If he didn't take his truck, he must still be in the neighborhood."

Picker picked up the conversation. "He probably had someone transport him somewhere no doubt. There are other people around here with things to hide. They may be afraid that he'll spill the beans on something they don't want the light to be shown on."

"Here we go again. Everything is a conspiracy. I'm glad that they got that fat assed Hammet in jail. He deserves to stew in jail a while. Although I must admit this arm is getting me a lot of sympathy. Even my Dad feels a little sorry for me. I don't think he would have let Connie come over here without that small amount of pity. He was pretty pissed off about seeing me smoking cigarettes. I'm dying for one right now."

"Lee, you're one crazy man," Randy said. "Tell me what else Mary Jo told you."

Before he could answer Lee's father shouted from the house. "Lee, your girl's on the phone - come on get up here. You're supposed to be restricted to the house."

"Okay," Lee shouted back. Then in a whisper he said, "See you guys. The master calls."

"Later, Lee," Randy said.

Randy continued his attention on Picker, who was still on his bicycle turning the front wheel back and forth with small casual turns. They heard a screen door slam as Lee had entered his house. It was quiet with the exception of the summer insect noises.

Randy broke the silence. "What did Mary Jo say again?"

"She really didn't say much. She said that she wants to meet you at your stone chair this evening when she sculls her canoe."

"Was she happy...sad...indifferent when she talked about me? Come on, Picker, you know these girls - Leigh Ann must have told you something. Give it up, my man. I've had a couple of bad days."

Picker smiled a bemused smile. "Alright, I know that Mary Jo thinks that she overreacted, but still thinks that she was right to be upset with you. After all she did catch you kissing Lizzy Fellur full on the lips."

"She kissed me," Randy interrupted.

"From what I hear you didn't exactly push her away."

With a sigh Randy said, "True, very true, I know I should've, but to tell you the truth it felt good and was pretty exciting. I'm just getting the feel of this girl stuff and I'm finding out that it's a lot of fun, but extremely frustrating."

"Well, I can tell you this," Picker advised, "I'd watch what I was doing if I was you or else Mary Jo may just be choosing someone new to be going out with."

"*Jesus,* Picker, you don't think I don't know that. I'll just stay away from Lizzy. Anyway, first things first. I'll meet her out there this afternoon. She usually goes out there about four o'clock, doesn't she?"

"I'm not sure. She's in town with her mom today. She didn't want to go with Leigh Ann and Corrine to Baltimore, so her mom asked her to run some errands with her. Mary Jo said she'd be out by the creek around six thirty."

"What kind of errands can they be running on a Sunday?"

"I don't know."

Randy gave up. "Okay six thirty it is. I hope she's still not mad at me."

"Not to worry my friend. She's over it and believes that you didn't initiate the Lizzy romance. She's looking for reinforcement, so be sure to tell her that she's the only one for you."

"Yes, oh Master Cupid" Randy bowed as he said it, but he took the advice to heart.

"Well I have to go home. Mom's laying out the Sunday luncheon spread and I'm starving. Do you want to join us?'

Randy considered it. Picker's mom could produce a marvelous lunch. Picker's house was open house on Sundays. His family received many visitors and the smorgasbord of fried chicken, deviled eggs, baked ham, buttermilk biscuits, fresh vegetables and homemade pies had continued to bring the welcomed guests for many years.

"Thanks for the offer, but with what happened here morning I'd better stay at home and support the clan. But thinking of that layout your mother puts out has me starving too."

"Later," Picker said. He then rode his bicycle down the road to his house.

As Picker spun the pedals of his bike across the blacktop road, Randy turned his head towards his uncle house. He looked both ways in case a car was approaching and crossed over the road from Lee's mailbox. He could see Pup and his uncle coming down the driveway. They were chatting or at least Pup was chatting as they slowly sauntered to the house. Neither man took care to avoid the small drying puddles. They sloshed through them as if they didn't even notice that they existed.

Randy could feel the heat from the sun bringing the comfortable warmth to a hot beating energy. He peered up at the pale yellow dot rising higher in the sky. Bright but not appearing overly large, the sun was producing a heat that would be stifling before the end of the day.

Randy caught up with Queenie, who was still exploring the ground with a strong zeal. He could hear the sniffing repeatedly. Randy looked over at where Pony had been lying in the grass and noted that Pony had vacated the area. Queenie had stopped sniffing and the lack of noise grabbed Randy's attention.

When he focused on the venerable old lady dog, he saw that she was about to devour a burgundy piece of meat covered in sand. Randy felt a flush of panic rush through his body.

"DROP IT! QUEENIE DROP IT!" Randy shouted as he rushed over to the dog.

Near panic he grabbed he dog's muzzle and tried to open her mouth. Queenie rolled onto her side with Randy's attack and opened her mouth with ease as Randy used pressure to separate her jaws.

It was too late. Whatever she had found had been consumed. Randy picked up the scared dog and held her close to his chest. He began to run from the front of the house and around the corner to the side porch entrance. He could hear the squish of his shoes in the still wet grass. He could feel the panting nervous dog in his arms, her eyes wide with confusion, his own heart beating with thunderous thumps in his chest. He had to hurry to his uncle to tell him of the events which had transpired.

Randy didn't have to travel very far to find his uncle. Pup and Harvey were at the porch door kicking and scraping mud from their shoes before they entered the porch. When they saw Randy running toward them with panicked eyes they stopped all motions and stared at him and his disoriented passenger.

"Uncle Harvey, Queenie ate something that looked like a piece of meat…" Randy paused to catch his breath. "But she ate it so fast I couldn't really tell what it was. Do you think it's what the other dogs ate?"

"Don't know, Randy," his uncle said with a steady gaze. If he was concerned it was hard to tell. Then he said, "Give her to me. If it's poisoned meat, we'll never get her to the vet in time. We'll have to have her throw it up."

Randy handed the squirming dog to his uncle. Queenie stopped squirming in Harvey's strong arms. Her eyes were still wide with excitement, but knowing enough to keep still when Harvey was in control.

"Got any lard?' Pup asked.

"I'm sure we do," Randy's uncle answered.

"Lard? What do you need that for?" Randy asked.

"We're going to heat it up and pour it down her throat to get her to regurgitate whatever she ate," his uncle told him.

From that point on, the events of the morning became extremely chaotic, noisy and fast moving. Harvey had carried Queenie into the house, while shouting for Caroline, who stood no more than two feet from him in the kitchen, but behind him out of his view. With everyone's nerves reaching the breaking point, Caroline had responded by shouting back at her husband not to shout.

Harvey regained his composure and with clenched teeth explained the situation to his spouse. Caroline fired up the gas burner on the top of the stove and plopped a heavy spoonful of Crisco shortening into a pan which began to melt immediately.

Pup was spelling out the procedure on how to administer the melted lard from a chair at the kitchen table, his ever present Mason jar in front of him still half full of his brandied concoction. If anyone was paying attention to him, it was hard to tell. Whenever there was a needed instruction, Caroline and Randy consulted Harvey who commanded the situation. Pup would repeat Harvey's instructions as if it added authority to them.

Karen who was at her emotional wits end, sat in the living room, her hands clasped in her lap. She was rocking back and forth in an overstuffed chair that featured an ottoman at its base.

Queenie, a dog not really keen on attention, had far more of it than she could have ever wished to have been placed upon her. Harvey held her steady as the grease was first heated to its melting point and beyond until it was cool enough not to scald the dog's throat when it was poured down to her stomach.

After testing the melted grease by touch and determining that it was sufficiently cooled, Harvey held Queenie's jaws open and had Randy pour the warm melted liquid down the dog's throat. Once the first of the lard went down Queenie's throat, she decided that she had had enough of this madness and resisted with passion. The amount of resistance caught Harvey off guard and he lost control of the dog. She bolted for the porch, but Pup, moving much faster than Randy would have suspected, stood in the doorway causing Queenie to change tracks for the living room.

This commotion was accompanied by a large amount of hollering and raised voice cacophony by the kitchen's occupants. Karen added to the din when Queenie bolted past her with Pup and Randy in hot pursuit.

They cornered the dog by the front door and carried the scared, shaking dog back into the kitchen where they administered more of the molten lard.

Not long after the second dose, the dog brought forth the contents of her stomach. Queenie wretched for a solid five minutes, bringing up her breakfast of brown round dog food, seemingly massive quantities of oily Crisco and a piece of meat that appeared as though it had been left out in the elements for most of the day. The kitchen floor was a total vomit-filled disaster.

Queenie stopped retching and hid under the wooded kitchen table. Harvey and Pup debated on whether or not to induce more vomiting or to take the dog to the vet. Harvey decided that the vet was next. He was going to take the regurgitated meat as well to have it tested.

When Pup volunteered to take the suspicious meat and have it analyzed by another source, there was an air of distrust immediately felt by Randy. He could sense the same distrust emanating from his uncle. Pup backed off the statement and then volunteered to accompany Harvey to the veterinarian's office. They gathered the meat, which was placed in a brown paper bag wrapped in Saran wrap, went out the door to Harvey's truck for the trip to the animal doctor.

Harvey had Randy call Dr. Bolor to be sure that he would meet them at his office. After all it was Sunday. Randy made the call gladly to get out of the badly- smelling kitchen. Karen had gone to help her aunt clean up the remaining mess and Randy was happy that he wasn't called to help.

Chapter 28

The rest of the day was a quiet peaceful reflective day. In the house the subdued discussion centered on what had happened to the family of dogs, whose lives had been terminated during the early hours of the morning.

Pup and Harvey had returned from the veterinarians office without Queenie, who the vet had wanted to keep overnight at his house for observation. Dr. Bolor seemed to think that Queenie would be fine, but wanted to have her nearby in case he needed to administer to her.

When the two had entered the house without Queenie, Karen was close to tears, thinking that Queenie had died before Harvey let her know the circumstance. Karen calmed down and retired to her bedroom for an afternoon respite. She slept most of the afternoon away emotionally exhausted.

Pup loitered around the kitchen sipping from his Mason jar most of the afternoon. Occasionally he would empty the vessel and await Caroline's generosity for a refill of Kearney brandy. Caroline kept a bottle on hand for such occasions. It was rarely used by Pup and never used by anyone else. Pup was drinking on a faster pace than his usual simmer to boil imbuement.

Randy attributed Pup's thirst to the excitement of the day, but he also listened attentively for Pup to leak some morsel of information that would attach Pup to the death of the dogs. He was unsuccessful in catching Pup uttering any clues at all. This didn't take away from Randy's suspicions. He felt that Pup was way too eager to take the regurgitated meat that had been dislodged from Queenie to be analyzed.

Harvey was in and out of the house most of the afternoon tending to the chickens. This composed of walking through the chicken houses observing their behavior. He needed to be sure that the chickens didn't become overheated under the hot summer sun. He judged when to open the windows and when to turn on the enormous electric fans. Too much heat would cause the overheated, panting chickens to die in mass quantities, thus lowering the revenues when they were sold.

Harvey did no other work because to Harvey, Sunday was God's day of rest. He had worked hard that morning burying the dogs. That was not work out of necessity, but a task of love for his beloved canine family.

Harvey wouldn't stay outside for more than fifteen minutes at a time. He sat at the table with Pup and listened to his neighbor theorize on the particulars of the morning's events. Harvey would comment on occasion, but was more of an observer and listener than a contributor.

Caroline on the other hand weighed in on Pup's ramblings quite often with skepticism. Pup was prone to alcohol-induced hyperbole and basically impugned everyone in the area omitting himself and the Kearneys. Caroline found fault with Pup's insinuations one at a time pushing Pup to leap to another suspect once he had no adequate retort to her.

Pup's ramblings became annoying to Randy after a time and he found himself day dreaming, tuning Pup out even though he felt that it was necessary to listen for the clues that would incriminate Pup.

Randy did notice that Pup had spent precious small amounts of time discussing the Romos and Glenns. They carried a huge amount of weight in the community and Pup was probably cognizant of the fact that his rumor mongering had a propensity to seep out into the community. The powerful had many ways of making life uncomfortable as Pup had learned in the past. He didn't need his domineering wife more involved in his life than she already was.

Caleb Fulton came up more than once in the scattershot guilt parade that Pup was leading in the Kearney kitchen. From his acerbic comments, Pup seemed to hold no love or respect for a man who had appeared to be one of his favorite drinking buddies. When Caroline pointed out that the law had been around to take Caleb into custody and had not found him the likelihood of Caleb being in the neighborhood was pretty negligible, Pup would back off his accusations with a smirk and nod in agreement.

As the dinner hour approached that Sunday evening, Randy was feeling the pangs of hunger as the air was redolent with the aroma of tomato sauce, which had simmered all day, infiltrated his senses. He would occasionally dip a piece of bread in the bubbling red tomato gravy savoring the beef-flavored concoction being prepared by his Aunt Caroline. The sauce was different from time to time, depending on the meat used to add flavor. Sometimes Italian sausage was added to complement the beef and this was Randy's ideal mix. He didn't care for the occasional seafood additive, but would tolerate it. Tonight, of course, no sausage was added, but there were meatballs and cubes of well cooked beautiful falling apart tomato sauce soaked beef.

Pup feeling that he was intruding on their dinner sheepishly excused himself. He waited a half step as though his mind could be changed, but no one offered him a seat at the table and even Caroline kept her back to him as she said good-bye. Pup had worn out his welcome.

Dinner was subdued and the conversation was muted, centering around church that evening and not at all touching on the events of the day.

"Uncle Harvey, can you pick me up at Mary Jo's house later tonight?" Randy asked. He was going to go over to the Magurk's house in Mary Jo's canoe when he met her out by the creek. Picker had called and had informed him that he would be at the Magurks with Leigh Ann so the four of them could be together tonight.

"You're not going to church this evening?" Caroline asked before Harvey could reply. Her tone indicated that she thought Randy should attend the service.

Randy glanced at his uncle and then back to his aunt. He felt the pressure to attend because of today's events, but he had to make things right with Mary Jo, so he mustered his courage. "No, not tonight. I've got to talk to Mary Jo about something personal."

Randy could sense his sister's eyes transfixed on him. He didn't know if he wanted her to say anything concerning the subject. She was still broken up about the death of the dogs and she might side with their aunt and uncle, which would start to enflame the situation. Everyone was still emotionally raw.

Harvey cleared his throat. 'Okay, Randy, give me a call and I'll swing by to pick you up. Not too late though…it's been a tough day and I'm pretty tired."

Randy felt a feeling of relief, but then his sister spoke something in a whispery voice so low that no one heard what she had uttered. Randy's heart sank for a moment. He thought that he was home free. He waited for her to repeat what she had just said, but didn't ask her to repeat it-his aunt did.

"Say again, Karen, we couldn't hear you."

A little louder Karen said, "Dennis is going to meet me after church to pick me up. I asked him to take me home. I can't stay here - it's too sad." Her voice trailed off and trembled with a soft quiver.

"I can take you home," Harvey said flatly.

"No, no thank you, Uncle Harvey. You stay here and rest after church. I don't mind going with Dennis and he actually volunteered to take me."

"Okay, whatever you want," Harvey replied in a neutral tone of resignation.

Randy's thought was one of relief. He wondered why his sister didn't wait one more day. She was due to go home on Monday anyway. He was going to stay for about two weeks. The dogs dying truly affected his sister much deeper than him and he thought that he was saddened to a point of depression. His only respite now was making up with Mary Jo Magurk.

Randy held his tongue and silence settled upon the table. They finished their meal with only the ticking of the kitchen clock and clicking of forks on their plates breaking the vacuum of silence.

After dinner Harvey went outside for a trip around the chicken houses to check to see things were in proper order. He would spend the time more as a therapeutically quiet time rather than an actual need to secure the chickens. He wanted the confidence that things were copasetic in his world beyond the day's routine divergence. He wanted to be alone in his world and declined Randy's offer of help. He would spend twenty minutes perusing his changes and then came back to the house to shower for the early service at church. By the time he had reentered the house; the dishes would have been cleared, cleaned and placed into the china cupboard. Caroline and Karen would be ready or almost ready for the short trip to church in the Ford LTD.

Randy was content to wait for everyone to leave before he primped himself for his rendezvous with Mary Jo. He was glad no one had asked how he would arrive at Mary Jo's house, because for some unsettling reason, he felt that it was embarrassing for Mary Jo to be canoeing him across the creek. He could envision her rowing, peering into his eyes as she rowed, her fluid body moved with each pull of the oar and this caused to excite him. But he felt that it wasn't manly to be rowed around by a girl. Kind of like Picker being driven around by Leigh Ann; Picker didn't mind, but Randy felt it to be weird in a male-dominated world.

As much as he hated to succumb to peer pressure, he knew kidding which affected his macho, raised the hair on the back of his neck. Picker was different in so many ways and Randy admired him for being so strong mentally.

Randy showered, dressed down while dressing up. He wanted to look nice, but couldn't very well wear his church going clothes to meet someone by the creek; besides Mary Jo would probably be wearing her bathing suit when she rowed her canoe. It didn't dawn on him that she would most likely change her clothes when they arrived back at her house.

Once he was dressed, the self debate became whether or not to rub cologne on his face. The only cologne he saw in the bathroom was his Uncle Harvey's Old Spice. He eyed the bottle for a long time before deciding not to wear his uncle's scent. He would wear the scent of the soap. He hoped that it would stay with him because he had overheard one of his sister's friends once say that a man without cologne smelled like a goat. He didn't want to offend Mary Jo with a malodorous body.

Finally ready, he gazed at himself in the mirror and hoped that Mary Jo would be attracted to the person peering back at him. He sometimes wouldn't look at himself in the mirror to long, because he really didn't like the way he appeared on the outside. He much preferred the way he looked from the mental image he had formed of himself. It was easier for him to look from behind his face, rather than at his face. *What the hell did girls like about his appearance anyway?* Randy's insecurities mounted as the time neared for him to meet with Mary Jo.

He glanced at the clock and saw that the long hand click to the three indicating that it was six fifteen. He had fifteen minutes to reach his stone chair and he decided that it was time to go. He wanted to be there early.

As he passed through the porch door the thought of the wild cats entered his mind. For a moment he considered going back inside for a .22 caliber rifle, but wasn't quite sure what he would do with it when it was time to go to the Magurk house. Besides he didn't know how he would explain the rifle to Mary Jo. He certainly didn't want her to think that he was afraid of a couple of wild cats.

He walked through the field that approached the woods and he searched for a large stick or pole, but he couldn't find anything to use as a weapon. Everything that he observed was too puny or the size of a tree trunk.

He entered the woods and a feeling of apprehension overcame him. He thought that he could push the feeling behind him, but the cats had really spooked him. He thought perhaps that he would run as fast as the narrow path would let him run, but he didn't want to be smelly if his soap scent gave way to his perspiration.

Just as he resolved himself to the fact that he was weaponless and would have to move as quickly as he could without sweating in the warm humid summer air, he saw a small pile of rocks sitting beside a puddle that had formed from the rain that had fallen from the previous night. He stopped and scooped up a handful of the smooth round rocks and judged their weight in his hand.

There were a number of larger ones which he kept and the rest were not much larger that pebbles - stones really about the size of small navy beans. Randy reconsidered throwing them away and then decided to keep them all. He would throw the larger ones first and if he needed to the pebbles, he would toss them five or six together for a better effect- kind of like a machine gun.

He placed them in his pocket and kept his hand in there with the rocks so that he would be at the ready for any kind of trouble that may come to his attention.

He was on full alert as he paced quietly and quickly through the trees. His journey down the path was a little squishy from the soft earth, but it was uneventful for once this week end. He broke into the clearing by the creek and breathed a sigh of relief. He was glad that his uncle would be picking him up at the Magurk's house.

Randy gazed across the creek and could see the canoe tied up protectively to the dock over the sloping bank which led up to the Magurk property. He thought of how nice it would be to have a home so close to the water and not to have to trek through the forest to reach the creek.

The Magurk side of the creek was much more conducive to having homes built on it. The land sloped gradually up and a swollen creek would be of little consequence unless it was at extreme flood levels. Randy's uncle's side was much flatter and contended with high levels of rising water much more often.

In fact Mr. Foster's old house was built up high on its foundation to accommodate the occasional rising creek which happened seemingly every ten years or so. The house had actually flooded inside once that Randy had known about and that was before he was born. Mr. Foster had told him the story once when flash flood warnings had been issued and he was over at the Foster house visiting. Mrs. Foster had gone to her sister's house, Donzella's mother, because she was afraid of the rising water. Mr. Foster had stayed to protect the property and promised his wife that if the water was to rise too high that he would leave for Harvey's or for Harvey's dad's house.

Randy had left Mr. Foster at his home rocking on the porch, watching the steady rain. He worried all night about Mr. Foster, hoping that the rain would let up. In the morning he went with his uncle to check on things and was greeted with a smiling Mr. Foster. The water had come up to the base of the porch's top step and had crested there. Randy was filled with relief at the sight of the smiling gray haired man.

Randy was lost in thought. Mary Jo wasn't in sight, so he reached into his pocket with the smooth stones and pulled out the larger ones and he began to try and skip them across the surface of the slow moving water.

The first couple of stones did little more than dive directly into the drink- then Randy became a little sharper with his tosses. He flat armed the stones in a parallel motion to the ground and watched as they skipped lightly across the water's fluid skin. They brought little splash as they hit the water surface and they jumped airborne a few inches above the tannic-colored creek to the next send off spot. His best toss garnered a five skip run that ended a good thirty feet out into the creek.

He stopped skipping stones and sat on his stone chair. He hadn't looked down at the seat and as a consequence he could feel the water from the small puddle he had sat in. Randy hopped up but it was too late. His clothes had sopped up the moisture. His bottom now wet, Randy resigned himself to the fact that no matter how careful he was trying to be, there would be some sort of embarrassment to contend with whenever he was around Mary Jo.

He sat back feeling the dampness on his pants. He watched carefully for Mary Jo to climb down the bank to her canoe. She was a little late he thought because surely it was six thirty by now.

The creek rolled by. A small breeze picked up and blew the leaves above his head. The sun stilled shined brightly overhead but was definitely on its downward slide to the west.

It was hard for Randy to believe the sequence of events that had happened in the last five days; the fight with Hammet, the puppies dying, the older dogs dying last night, his problems with Mary Jo and Lizzy. He hoped that the next few days were a little more smooth and uneventful.

He wondered about the dogs. Would the meat being tested come back with traces of poison? Would Queenie survive? Would other farm animals suffer the same fate as the dogs? Who was the dastardly culprit? It disgusted Randy to think of some low life still out there who would poison innocent dogs.

Was the light he saw last night somehow connected to the dogs' deaths? Randy had a strong feeling that the light was certainly connected. He wished that he had told his uncle about it last night, and then maybe the dogs would still be alive.

He wanted to link Pup to this deed. What about Caleb Fulton? He also had said that there were too many dogs at the Kearney farm. But he must have been out of the area when the police were searching for him. It couldn't be Sam Hammet, that idiot was at the police station.

An unhappy thought crossed Randy's mind. Picker sure didn't show much remorse this day when they were talking with Lee. Picker had mentioned getting rid of the wild cats in the same way. What if he spread the meat here in the woods for the cats and the dogs had found it and ate it? But how did the piece Queenie ate arrive at the front yard?

Randy shook his head and pushed his negative thoughts concerning Picker from his mind. Picker hated those cats, but he was such a nature lover that surely he wouldn't send them to their deaths in such a cruel way. Still it was curious he didn't seem more sympathetic earlier in the day.

Randy thought about dog heaven. Was there such a place? Must be, what could a dog do that would subjugate him to hell?

His thought of heaven rolled his thoughts to Mr. Foster. Randy smiled involuntarily while thinking of the story Mr. Foster had related to him about heaven.

According to Mr. Foster, who was told the story by a very reliable source, that everyone has a chance to enter heaven when they die. In fact, they all started out with a short distance from the Pearly Gates conversing with Saint Peter.

Mr. Foster had told Randy that this was true because an aunt of his was a *white lighter*. She had died, seen the white light, gone beyond it and had conversed with Saint Peter before it was discovered that it wasn't her turn to leave the earth for the Promised Land. She was revived to live another few years on the blue planet and she had related her experience to her nephew (and anyone else who she could corner for her story).

Randy thought about Mr. Miler and his experiences with near death and wondered if he should ask him if this was how he felt after he awakened. But he thought that perhaps it may insult Mr. Miler, so he pushed that thought aside.

Mr. Foster's aunts story began with Saint Peter greeting you when you pass away with a huge sack a short distance from the Pearly Gates. He then explains to you that you may enter Heaven by walking the distance from the Pearly Gates, but as you walk to enter you must stop to pick up the sins you've committed during you life and place them in the sack. The sins are laid out along the path to the Pearly Gates.

Some people's journeys are longer because they have to stop more often to gather more sins. Some people's journeys are longer because some sins are heavier than others due to their severity. Some people's journeys are faster because they've accepted the teachings of the Lord and this helps to lighten the load. But all people face the sins that they have committed, so that they can see the pain that they have caused. Once in the Pearly Gates, God blesses the soul and accepts them into Heaven.

Sometimes the journey from the start to finish seems as though it may never end.

Randy asked Mr. Foster that if the never-ending journey with a sack of sins was akin to being in Hell. Mr. Foster told him that he didn't know, but that he hoped that he had lead a good enough life to be able to fulfill the journey. Randy hoped that this was so for him as well. He hoped for himself and for Mr. Foster.

Randy's mind moved to his dad. He hadn't heard from him since he was seven years old. His mom wouldn't budge with any information. All that she would say was that his dad hadn't returned home from work one day. As much as Randy pried his mom, she feigned ignorance. Randy couldn't even persuade his aunt, his father's sister to pony up any information. A brick wall had been erected and it surrounded the mystery of his father.

Randy and Karen had discussed the issue on many occasions. Karen was convinced that their father had run away with another woman, after all as she had stated many a time, "Men are pigs!"

Randy wanted to believe that it was something more mysterious and interesting; like that he was an undercover spy working on a long assignment. He continued to have hope, but sometimes his disappointment for his dad came through because Randy felt abandoned. The only father he had now was that buffoon Harlan. Randy felt that his uncle was a better father than Harlan.

Perhaps his father had been killed in his CIA assignment and the CIA wouldn't let Randy's mother tell him until a certain time period had elapsed. National security could be at risk if anyone knew why or how he was killed. Randy hoped the time to reveal the mystery would pass soon. If his father was dead, Randy hoped that he was in heaven. He also hoped that the sack wasn't too full or too heavy.

Movement across the creek caught Randy's eye and brought him out of his daydream state. Mary Jo was standing on the Magurk dock waving at him. He stood and waved back.

Mary Jo was wearing a pair of white, very short shorts. She had on a red bathing suit top and white tennis shoes. Her brown hair was pulled back into a tight pony tail. The pony tail swayed back and forth as she readied the canoe for its journey.

Randy marveled at her dexterity with the canoe. She had it unmoored and away from the dock in no time at all. She had boarded the vessel with virtual ease, no rocking back and forth. She had entered the canoe like a hand entering a glove. They were one and she was in command.

Randy began to feel a nervous tension. He hadn't thought of what he would say to her. He had explained everything about Lizzy that he could think of the previous evening at the horse show.

Picker had told him that he didn't have anything to worry about with Mary Jo, but Randy had a strong sense of foreboding. What if she was going to tell him that they should just be friends? That she really liked him as a platonic friend and not as a boy friend. Randy tried to suppress the thought. He didn't want to panic.

He stood as she neared his side of the shore. Mary Jo had traversed the creek very quickly. He watched as she guided the paddle stroking it deep into the water with Mary Jo alternating the paddle from side to side, occasionally holding the oar in the water near the rear of the canoe to steer it on course.

Her tanned lithe body was in motion like a graceful feline walking nonchalantly but with purpose. Her eyes were intent on the target across the creek. Randy was unsure if she was focused on him or the shoreline. There was no smile on her face, which was stoic. The brown eyes however held and intensity that excited Randy and filled him with anticipation. He was an emotional wreck for he was excited both happily and angst filled.

He began to feel more excited the closer she came to the shore.

Randy walked to the edge of the shoreline and grabbed the front of the canoe as it scraped across the sandy bottom in a smooth motion. His excitement caused his adrenaline to surge through his body enabling him to heave the canoe nearly out of the water.

Mary Jo's expression changed from one of determination to mild surprise as Randy had pulled the canoe out of the water. She stood and stepped from the canoe onto the sandy shore with Randy holding her hand for unneeded balance. He was acting like the gentleman and she accommodated him by letting him take her hand.

Randy was enthralled. He could smell her perfume and it sent his mind to an intense pleasure zone. He soaked in Mary Jo's physical beauty. He actually could see nothing but Mary Jo; around her was a white illuminating fog, which highlighted her tanned pretty face. He was in the presence of his earthbound angel.

As he absorbed the moment, she stepped so close to him that her body touched his body. He could feel her breast press softly against his chest. The bathing suit top, thin in cloth, seemed nonexistent. It felt to Randy as if she was wearing no top at all.

Mary Jo placed her hands behind Randy's head and gently held his head as she pulled his face towards hers. Their lips met and Randy could taste her sweet mouth as they kissed. He was weakened and rubbery with excitement. He was on sensory overload. All the bells and whistles relating to his sexual emotions and tendencies were ringing and blowing with joy. He was now conscious of how close Mary Jo's body was to his. His arousal was monumental and he was thankful that his trousers weren't sporting any kind of safety pin.

Randy returned her kiss with much more comfort than he had the previous evening. He was a quick learner and he let his natural instincts take over the moment. He was concerned about his quite noticeable protrusion straining at his pants and backed away from Mary Jo to release the contact. He was happy that she hadn't exclaimed "*What's that?*" and had run back to her canoe, but he wasn't taking any chances of offending her.

Mary Jo released them from their kiss and their lips produced a smacking sound. They both laughed at the innocuous sound.

She looked sexy and coy.

Randy retreated while he held her hand. He examined her like she was prize to behold. Mary Jo released his hand and adjusted her hair by removing the rubber band that was holding her ponytail in place.

Her hair cascaded around her face and neck and landed on her shoulders. She fluffed it and the sight of her working her hair almost made Randy faint. He wanted to pinch himself to be sure that this moment was real and not a figment of his imagination.

"Can we talk about last night?" Randy whispered. Not because he wanted to whisper, but his vocal chords weren't as pliable as he would have liked them to be.

He cleared his throat and was going to repeat the question again in a much bolder and deep voice. Mary Jo held her finger to his lips to quiet him.

She said, "No, I believe you. Let's forget last night and put it behind us. Just remember...Lizzy Fellur is trouble - trouble especially for you and me."

She didn't say anymore about the subject and Randy didn't have to hear anymore about the Lizzy, Mary Jo, and Randy relationship. He understood exactly what Mary Jo didn't have to say. He hoped that he was as strong in actual situations as his resolve was at that moment.

The two of them moved over to the stone chair. Randy sat down and Mary Jo sat in his lap. They conversed about many subjects, including the many events effecting the past few days- omitting anything to do with Lizzy Fellur.

In between, they cautiously explored their combined sensuality for quite a long time. Randy was experiencing the wondrous activities that up until the present he had only been able to dream or fantasize about - like his first touch of a breast and actual visual contact up close and the warmth of a girl so close and willing to participate with him.

He was cautious with his proceedings and stopped anytime that Mary Jo resisted his advances. She was helpful and responsive to some of his more awkward moments and she helped him feel comfortable when he paused wondering where to proceed next in his ventures.

Light petting, heavy kissing and a good deal of talking was the rule of the day. The two bonded together and moved forward with their intimacy.

Randy was as happy as he could be at that moment in time. He hoped that he was producing the same feeling in Mary Jo as well.

Time slipped by quickly and dusk was beginning to descend upon them. They decided that it was time to go across the creek to Mary Jo's house.

Mary Jo stood up and adjusted her swim suit top moving the cup over her partially exposed breast. Her white breast was quite the contrast to her overall tan. Randy involuntarily smiled. Seeing her exposed nipple reminded him of Corrine and her puppy dog question that she had lobbed at Leigh Ann. He tried to keep his eyes fixated on Mary Jo's eyes as she adjusted the top, but he couldn't help glancing at her bared breast before she could conceal it. She smiled at him and he sheepishly smiled back, feeling as though he had been caught doing something naughty.

Mary Jo turned around without any commentary and walked to the canoe. Randy grateful that the moment had passed stood up and straightened his shorts the best that he could he was still somewhat aroused and he tried to will himself to become flaccid with some success. His junior ego was relaxing but was also ready for battle at a moment's notice of bare flesh or even suggestive words from Mary Jo.

A movement a few yards down on the shore caught Randy's attention and he glanced away from Mary Jo to see the cause of the movement. He saw Picker standing on the sandy shore half the way between the tree line and the shoreline. Picker was smiling a half smile like he had been caught with his hand in the cookie jar.

Mary Jo turned to focus her attention in the direction that Randy was staring. She was slightly startled at seeing Picker standing with his hands in his pockets, smiling at them like a little child. He didn't say anything. He just stood there calmly and smiled the crooked half of a smile with his hands deep in his pockets.

It was eerie.

"Picker," Randy said sharply bringing the three of them out of their trance. "How long have you been staring...I mean standing there?" Randy was indignant. He felt that his privacy had been violated.

"I just came out of the woods. When I stepped out is when you saw me." Picker was firm in his voice. He knew that he needed for Randy to believe him.

Randy was unconvinced. With skepticism in his voice he queried, "Where did you come from...your house?"

Picker's house was on the other side of Randy's stone chair. If Picker had come from his house then he would have had to have gone around Randy and Mary Jo while they were sitting in the stone chair together.

"Randy, I was out doing my walk in the woods before we supposed to rendezvous here. You do remember that we were supposed to meet here don't you?" Picker paused. He had succeeded in pushing the guilt back onto Randy.

Randy nodded in agreement, but his resolve was apparent on his face. He waited for Picker to finish his explanation.

"Good, I'm glad that you remember. Anyway...I was coming down the shore to my path and saw Mary Jo's canoe, but I didn't see you two. Not wanting to surprise anyone or to intrude on your privacy, I circled back and walked my route through the woods in reverse tonight."

"What didn't you want to interrupt?" Randy's tone was accusatory.

Picker didn't take the bait. He remained calm. He thought over his response wanting to extinguish this conversation. He glanced from Randy to Mary Jo and then back to Randy. Both faces showed a certain amount of expectation, Randy's face appearing more expectant than Mary Jo's face.

"Randy, you've been talking to me all day about how you needed to work out things with Mary Jo concerning Lizzy Fellur. I assumed that that is what you have been doing. However, if you have been engaged in something which may be embarrassing I think that I would rather not be thinking about it."

Mary Jo laughed at Picker. He was clever. She knew that Randy was too modest to explain that they had been necking and she also knew that Randy was certainly not eager to talk about Lizzy Fellur. Randy had been checkmated and she felt that Picker had respected their intimacy. She was happy to let the whole thing pass.

Randy was perplexed. He had no clue as to why Mary Jo was laughing because he didn't see the humor in Picker's statement. But Mary Jo was correct in assuming that Randy didn't want to further the Lizzy Fellur discussion.

"Oh, forget it.' Randy laughed a faux laugh. "Let's go over to Mary Jo's house, Leigh Ann is probably waiting for us."

Picker walked closer to the couple as Mary Jo readied the canoe.

"Before we go I want to go back to Mr. Foster's cabin," Picker said.

'Why, it's almost dark?' Randy asked.

"I think I saw a light on," Picker said. "I think maybe Caleb Fulton's there."

The trio had traversed the relatively short distance from the chair to a spot some twenty feet from the cabin. A light was clearly on inside of the cabin and they could see someone moving around inside. Whoever it was they were pacing around in the kitchen holding a shovel cocked on their shoulder like a soldier carrying a rifle.

Randy whispered to the other two so low that they had to lean closer to understand his words. "Let's go up this side by the side window behind the kitchen. That way we can see whoever it is and they shouldn't be able to see us."

Randy looked at Mary Jo and she seemed to show some anxiety on her face. He whispered, "Do you want to wait here for us?"

Without hesitation and with a look of ire on her visage, she shook her head slightly back and forth- the look she gave Randy forced a blink of surprise and generated a snicker from Picker.

Randy frowned and nodded approval and whispered, "Okay, okay…just asking. Come on let's go."

Picker led the way as they circled around the cabin staying twenty feet or so from the building.

When they had reached a line parallel with the side window, they could see the window clearly and it was noticeably darker than the kitchen window. There was a patch of plants, knee high, covering the ground between the trio and the cabin.

Picker forged through the growth of wild plants towards the window. Mary Jo followed and Randy brought up the rear. They were crouching low in the thought that it would render them more difficult to be seen.

Sneaking up to the window proved to be more difficult than the three teens imagined. As they proceeded through the knee high foliage, the plants grabbed at their bare legs with tiny sharp thorns, which scrapped, cut and tripped them. After covering a quarter of the distance to the window Picker stopped and the two co-investigators stopped with him.

Picker signaled with his hand that they should go back out of the brush. He also signaled that they should discuss the situation after they cleared the brush; they stood where they could hear a voice emanating from the cabin. The voice modulated from loud to soft and audible and inaudible.

A minute or two of careful prowling and they were out of the brush and far enough away from the cabin to be comfortable in speaking to one another.

"I forgot about Mr. Foster's blackberry patch," Randy said as he rubbed his legs.

"I'm sure that's Caleb Fulton's voice," Picker said with some excitement. He too was rubbing his legs along with Mary Jo.

"Me, too," Randy agreed.

"What do we do now?" Mary Jo asked.

Everyone was talking in hushed tones.

"I gotta see if it's him. If it is we'll go back to your house and call the police," Picker said. "Everyone agree?"

"Fine with me."

"Me, too," Mary Jo added. "Besides the mosquitoes are beginning to enjoy my blood a little too much."

Both boys nodded.

"Let's go around to the other side take a quick peek and haul ass to the canoe."

"Randy, I couldn't have said it better myself," Picker said. "We'll try the front window in the living room up by the porch."

"Picker, lead the way," Mary Jo directed with a wave of her hand.

Picker stepped forward and promptly popped a small expulsion of natural man made gas.

The other two peered at him with mock distain and held their noses. Everyone had to suppress their laughter.

Randy grabbed Pickers shoulder and moved him to the rear of the line. "I'll lead the way. You kill the creatures that follow us with that uncontrollable weapon of yours."

Again they were snickering while they kept an eye on the cabin in front of them.

Randy led them around the cabin. Going around the back he took a familiar trail which hugged the rear wall tightly. There were no windows on this side of the cabin.

They could hear a voice rising up and down inside of the Foster's dilapidated home. It mixed with the sounds of chirping crickets and croaking bull frogs and other sounds of woods denizens. The buzz of the mosquitoes filled the gallant trio's ears, but they only waved at them, they feared that a slap would alert the occupants of the cabin.

Randy was proud of Mary Jo's courage walking through the weeds. He was nervous, more about the cabin's occupants than the woods filled with creatures. He had forgotten about the wild cats.

They came around the side of the cabin and Randy stepped on a mound of freshly dug earth. He sank in a little and then he hopped out of the dirt as if he had stepped into a fire and snatched his foot out.

Mary Jo let out a little whoop because Randy startled her with his action. She covered her mouth and held her nose to stifle a giggle.

Picker bit his lip to hold back his nervous laugh and Randy held his hand tightly over his own mouth.

After a few moments of collecting themselves, Mary Jo looked at Randy and shrugged, as if to say what happened to you.

He pointed down at the freshly dug earth and motioned for them to skirt around it.

They followed him and were soon just below the window of the living room of the Foster cabin.

Cautiously Randy raised his head to see inside. He had to stand on his tip toes to see because the cabin had been raised so high off of the ground.

Sure enough, Caleb Fulton was inside. He had stopped pacing and he had stopped talking. He was standing over someone sitting slumped over in the rickety chair that had furnished the cabin. It was Pup. His Mason jar sat empty on the worn wooded plank cabin floor.

Caleb stood still with the shovel on his shoulder. He glared at Pup, who was motionless. Pup appeared to have passed out.

Randy slowly receded from the window. He was ready to go.

Mary Jo motioned to Randy that she wanted to see inside. He was hesitant, but he remembered the death glare he had received a few moments earlier. He nodded and she moved over to the window. She wasn't tall enough to see on her tip toes.

Randy cupped his hands and signaled for her to place her foot into the boost so that she could see through the window. Mary Jo nodded her understanding and placed her foot in is cupped hands.

She held the sill with her fingers and Randy gave her the support that she needed.

Slowly she raised her head up and over the sill to peer inside. Randy was praying that they wouldn't produce any noise to alert Caleb. He could smell Mary Jo's sweet perfume and he moved closed to her body.

Caleb barked at Pup like a dog. "WOOF! WOOF!"

A startled Randy twitched and in turn frightened Mary Jo; she shot him a quick glance and motioned with her head for him to lower her. Randy did as she silently requested.

Randy was really ready to vacate the premises now and motioned for them to go retreat back around the cabin. He wanted to retrieve the police and bring them here as quickly as possible.

Picker shook his head no. He pointed at his eyes and then at the window. He wanted to observe the same scene that Randy and Mary Jo had witnessed.

Randy sighed a silent sigh and gave Picker the thumbs up of approval.

Caleb Fulton then began to speak and move around the cabin once again. Caleb's boots echoed on the wooden floor as he scraped and trod on the floor boards.

"Poisoned dogs…how thoughtless someone is. The law is after me because someone's poisoning dogs!" Caleb was blaring.

Picker waited. He wanted Caleb to be stationary when he peeked over the sill through the dirty broken pane of glass.

"Pup…do you hear me?" Caleb demanded.

"Didn't poison no dogs," Pup slurred. He wasn't as loud as Caleb and hesitated between his words, not every word, but between pairings.

"Did I say that you did? Did I say that you did…you drunken old sot."

Pup answered, "Didn't poison no dogs."

Caleb was still moving around the cabin. The teens couldn't see him but they could hear his heavy steps stomp and squeak the floor boards.

Caleb picked up a bottle next to the kerosene lantern that was sitting of the washboard by the sink. He ambled over to Pup and stood with the shovel on his shoulder and the bottle of liquor in his other hand.

"Pick up that glass jar and let me freshen your drink."

'Don't want no more brandy."

Caleb shouted, "PICK UP THAT JAR, PUP!"

The kids could hear Pup whimpering. The clink of glass on glass a little too heavy confirmed that Pup had followed Caleb's directions.

"Drink up, Pup my boy. It's better for you to be numb."

The three witnesses peered at one another with puzzlement. What had Caleb meant by that statement?

"Well, let's see now," Caleb said as the sound of a can losing its carbonation filtered to the eaves dropping ears of the teens. Caleb had forced a can opener into a beer can opening it for himself. "What do we have in this shack? I see butcher paper that steaks were wrapped in from the market…and who had a party recently where a bunch of meat was bought from the market? Why, Pup, I believe that was you. Mr. Cordery will probably remember that pretty well.

"Let's see what else we have here…seems like to me I see a box of strychnine poison used as seasoning for the steaks…steaks that were probably used to poison the Kearny dogs."

Pup gained courage and mumbled, "I didn't poison no dogs."

Caleb swilled from his beer can and burped rudely, "Pup, Pup, Pup, I think you're one drunken liar. It seems to me that everyone in the area knows what you are - a gossiping old drunk who tells people a tale to suit himself, just so that he'll get a refill in that damned Mason jar that he carries around everywhere that he goes."

"I didn't kill them dogs."

Caleb didn't respond. He had stopped pacing as well. He stood and glared at Pup his lips twitched with loathing.

After a few seconds Picker pointed his eyes again while he looked at Randy. Randy shrugged and with a wave of his hand toward the window motioned for Picker to take a peek.

Randy and Mary Jo were ready to leave. Scar Nose Fulton's tirade was making them nervous.

Picker stepped up to the window. Randy was too close and wasn't giving Picker enough room to maneuver, so he shuffled around Picker placing himself closer to the front of the house. He was exposed to anyone coming through the front door out onto the porch.

Mary Jo stayed put placing her closer to the back of the cabin on the right side of Picker.

After everyone had become comfortable with their position, Picker glanced around and was assured that Mary Jo and Randy were at the ready, he placed his hands on the window sill and raised himself up to peek through the bottom pane of cloudy glass.

He saw Caleb Fulton standing in front of Pup, who was still slouched over in the rickety wooden chair. Pup was holding his mason jar close to his chest. His eyes were half open and staring straight at the floor.

Caleb Fulton held the shovel on his shoulder and squatted to place his beer can on the floor. He straightened himself up full, and swung the shovel off his shoulder with both hands.

Pup flinched as if he thought that Caleb was going to strike him with the shovel.

Picker thought that if Caleb hit Pup with the shovel that it would kill him.

Caleb laughed at Pup and feigned a lunge in Pup's direction causing Pup to cover his head with his arms. Pup dropped his Mason jar of inebriant, its contents flowing over his clothes.

Caleb laughed harder.

Randy tugged at Picker's shorts. Picker looked away from the window momentarily to see why Randy was tugging at him.

Randy motioned for them to scoot.

Picker nodded in agreement and took one last peek.

He saw the menace on Caleb's face. It sent shivers down Picker's spine and he shook involuntarily.

He was about to lower himself when Caleb Fulton said in a mocking voice, "Didn't kill them dogs, didn't kill them dogs...well you old drunk, it doesn't really matter what you say does it."

With that Caleb 'Scar Nose' Fulton swung the shovel violently and knocked Pup from the chair. Pup crumpled like aluminum foil squeezed by strong hands. He didn't utter a sound.

Caleb appeared to be mustering up another blow with the shovel to the prone body of Pup. Picker couldn't see Pup as well as he would have liked to see and stood higher up on his tip toes.

Randy tugged at Picker's shorts more urgently. Mary Jo was edging toward the back of the cabin to the trail which had brought them to where they stood.

Picker's straining to see Pup, Caleb raising the shovel for another strike to Pup's body and Randy pulling at Picker's shorts caused Picker to do something he wished he hadn't done.

He expelled a burst of gas that would have made a whoopee cushion proud- a long loud explosion that could have been heard inside of the cabin.

Caleb Fulton's head jerked in the direction of the window. He stopped his assault on Pup and headed over to the front porch to investigate the noise. Caleb Fulton burst through the front door, the screen door coming unhinged at the top and swung backward against the cabin wall. Caleb was standing at the railing of the front porch before Randy had a chance to react.

Randy was preoccupied with Picker. After Picker had alerted Caleb with his bodily explosion, he had lost his fingertip grip on the window sill and had slipped on the rain soaked loose dirt under his feet.

Picker was picking himself up with the help of a very frightened Mary Jo. Picker was scrambling to stand up- feeling the same apprehension as Mary Jo.

Caleb stared Randy directly in the face. Their eyes locked. Randy could feel the animosity transcend the distance between them. Caleb didn't appear at all to be in a friendly mood.

Randy didn't dare to sneak a peek at his compatriots. He could see them peripherally as Picker gained his balance and footing as he stood up with Mary Jo's helping hand.

"Randy?" Caleb inquired, his voice a little too loud and too controlled. Randy sensed that Caleb was straining to be calm while he sized up the situation. Caleb didn't want Randy doing anything rash. "What are you doing here, boy?"

"Go call," Randy said nervously. He kept his gaze fixed on Caleb.

Mary Jo and Picker hesitated. They didn't want to leave Randy. Caleb blinked and a puzzled look shifted to his face.

The moonlight beamed on Randy's face. He knew that Caleb definitely recognized him.

"Go call." The urgency in Randy's voice was clear.

"Gocal…what the hell are you talking about?" Caleb asked. He was inching closer to the low slung railing of the porch.

Randy was too close to the porch and he figured that Caleb was close enough. Randy pictured him vaulting the railing to get closer to where he stood. Randy watched with alarm, but didn't retreat an inch. He waited until he couldn't see Mary Jo and Picker out of the corner of his eye.

Randy quickly weighed his options. He could try and attempt to catch up with his friends to take the canoe across the creek to the Magurk house or perhaps he should head down the creek to someone's house this side of the creek.

If he went after his friends, he risked bringing Scar Nose Fulton with him. If Caleb decided to pursue him, Randy didn't want to endanger Mary Jo, so he ruled out the first scenario.

He knew that he would head down the creek toward the milldam. He tried to think about the residences down the creek and which one was the closest to his present position. There were a number of properties on his side of the creek, but most weren't that accessible from the shore. The woods provided a barrier to Miss Arlene's, the Culvers and to Caleb Fulton's property. In between was the old property where the Gospel church had stood.

The only true option, which sat on the creek, albeit some forty yards up a sloping incline, was Helda Peters' place down by the milldam.

Helda Peters was a widow in her mid-fifties. Her husband, Cliff, had died early in a hunting accident when the young couple were in the fifth year of their marriage. She was twenty three, and he was twenty-five. The Peters came from a wealthy background and Helda was financially set for life. However the death of her husband took a huge toll on her mental state and she became more reclusive and eccentric as the years added to her life.

Her in-laws cared for her monetarily and for reasons known only to Helda, she severed all ties to her immediate blood family. She didn't allow them to visit or call and she returned all letters written to her unopened.

The rumors among the area gossips was that Helda's family had tried to parley Cliff's death into a monetary gain for themselves by trying to force Helda into selling the their creek side property to the Romo family for quite a tidy sum of money; a sum that included a rather large commission for having persuaded Helda to sell the property.

Helda lived an eccentric life from that point forward. She stayed by herself the majority of the time, but managed to help on occasion with local charities and attended church services on Wednesdays and Sundays. She was social to people who addressed her, but practically never initiated a conversation.

Her main objective in life was caring for her property. It was immaculate. The grounds were as nice as any in *Home Beautiful* magazine. She planted, mowed, cultivated and arranged anything in her power. Tasks that required a man's help was usually taken care of by Mr. Foster until his death. Since his demise, she had been using Piute - the pairing both unusual and sense making at the same time.

Helda had no room for Caleb Fulton. The two had been at odds ever since Caleb had loudly rebuked Helda at church in the parking lot for bathing in the creek behind her house, a practice that she had partaken in since the death of Cliff.

No one knew the significance of the bathing ritual and quite honestly no one cared to speculate as to why she bathed where anyone could view her at their whim. The public wrote it off as she being slightly addled by the death of her husband.

Caleb had tried to embarrass her out of her nightly baths, by confronting her before her neighborhood peers, but Helda held her ground. She gave him such a tongue lashing with the vehemence of a mother duck protecting her young, that Caleb, even though drunk, swallowed his machismo and backed down with his tail between his legs.

This was one part of the community that remained as it was. Helda continued to take her baths in the pond. For the most part everyone respected her privacy, with the exception of an occasional ogle by the adolescent boys' wonting for a peek at a naked female body. Caleb Fulton had no influence with Helda and left her alone.

Randy decided that he would head to Helda's because of her disdain for Caleb.

Randy was keeping a close eye on Caleb. Caleb was slowly moving forward, inching ever closer to the handrail, which had decorated the Foster's porch. Randy had determined the proximity that Caleb would have to reach in the relationship to the railing before he would turn to head up the creek to Helda's house. He didn't want to wait too long before he turned to go.

Randy assumed that Mary Jo and Picker were well on their way to the canoe. At least he hoped so. Caleb's next step forward was going to be Randy's cue.

It was so odd for Randy to stand and glare at Caleb with Scar Nose returning he glare - truly surreal. They were like two cats posturing ready for a fight but without the accompanying growls.

Caleb must have sensed that Randy was going to bolt. He placed his hands on the rickety railing and vaulted over in an attempt to grab Randy.

Randy had turned to run at the same instant. Caleb landed an arm's length behind Randy. Caleb lost his footing on the water soaked ground. The thud of Caleb hitting the soft ground had the sound of a sack of flour thumping down on a soft surface.

Randy had just begun to place his front foot down in an effort to run, when Caleb hit the ground behind him. His footing was weak on the water soaked ground. He could feel the tips of Caleb's fingers grasping in desperately at the collar of his shirt.

Randy jerked forward trying to elude the reach of his pursuer. His lunge propelled him forward but caused him to stumble as well. Randy dropped his hand to the wet soil and righted himself with a stabilizing push. He dared a momentary glance at Scar Nose Fulton.

Caleb was not as fortunate as Randy when it came to keeping his balance. He lay face down on in the wet earth. He was pushing himself up off the ground while he tried to keep his eyes on his prey. He didn't say anything but his body language - even in his present awkward position - said all that Randy had to know.

As frightened as Randy was, the mud on Caleb's contorted face caused him to chuckle as he turned and ran down the narrow path in the direction that would take him to Helda's house by the milldam.

Chapter 29

Randy quickly took advantage of his fallen nemesis' difficulty in getting to his feet. He ran down the short path down to the creek's edge. Once he rounded the big oak tree that bordered Mr. Foster's property, he came to a split in the path.

Perspiration poured down his face. He had to decide which way to go. Either he would follow the shoreline, which was slick and uneven and exposed him to his pursuer or go up to the path and follow a trail up in the trees that bordered the shoreline. There was a twenty foot buffer between the shoreline and the trees most of the way to Helda's homestead. In fact the buffer grew wider the closer you approached Helda's property.

The trail in the woods was quicker but much darker and seemed to Randy to be much more perilous. Who knew what lurked in the woods. He tried to think which way would hinder Caleb more. He decided that he would take the path along the shoreline and sped off as fast as he could travel. The slippery uneven ground would be quite a chore for a half-sotted man.

The soft ground would prove to be a strong hindrance to Randy and slowed him considerably more than he would have imagined. He trudged forward with an occasional glance to the rear. He never caught a glimpse of Caleb and Randy hoped that Caleb was still trying to recover from the leap and fall from the porch or that he had given up altogether and had headed out of town.

These thoughts didn't slow Randy down. He moved forward with a marked determination. He didn't want Scar Nose Fulton to catch him. If he would smash Pup over the head with a shovel, Randy didn't want to think of what Caleb might do to a credible witness.

The pale moonlight illuminated the path in the more open areas, but cast ominous shadows as well. Randy's pace sometimes didn't allow for him to discern which objects were real or merely shadows as he approached them. He occasionally stumbled over sticks and roots that protruded from the ground and sometimes sank into the extremely soft parts of the wet sandy path.

The bugs attacked his face and exposed skin mercilessly. He swatted at the ones which bit him the hardest and merely waved at the gnats swarming over his sweat streaked face.

For a second night in a row, Randy was hauling ass from something pursuing him. Last night proved to be a clear product of his imagination, but tonight was different. Caleb was certainly real and very threatening. Randy wondered where Pony was tonight. Perhaps he would come and save him from Caleb- just like Rin Tin Tin did for his master.

Randy didn't think that he could stop and scare off Caleb with his shoe like he did Pony. He would need an object much larger and stronger. Although Caleb rolled over on his back with his arms and legs in the air, like Pony the night before was a vision that Randy would love to see just before he slugged Caleb with his shoe.

Randy trekked, stumbled and hurried his way along the uneven path towards Helda's house. He neither heard nor saw any sign of Caleb. He allowed himself to relax a small modicum, but he still was alert to any noise that he heard. He slowed his pace slightly and actually found that he could make better time, by moving a bit more carefully along the sandy path.

Randy's heartbeat pounded in his ears - his slowing down seemed to amplify the beating of his heart.

He stopped and turned to survey the path behind him. He took in a few deep breaths- breaths as deep as his overworked lungs would allow him. He tried to relax as much as he could. There was no sign of anyone or anything following him.

He stood motionless and concentrated on listening. He was trying to hear anything out of the ordinary. He could hear normal sounds of the chirping crickets, bullfrogs croaking and the slight rustle of the trees from the very small blowing breeze. The creek water rolled forward toward the milldam and Randy could discern the soft sound of the water rushing over the dam. He knew he must be close to Helda's house if he could hear the water tumbling over the dam.

He peered out over the water and watched the moonlight dance and twinkle on the ripples of the water. It calmed him and he turned to continue his journey to safety.

"RANDY, WHERE ARE YOU?"

A distant shout and a startled Randy peered in the direction of the shout. He saw a flashlight beam dance for a second or two and knew that he had foolishly thought that Caleb would give up so easily.

Caleb was up in the trees.

Randy hunkered down, squatting on the sandy wet soil. He stared intently at the spot that he had seen the bobbing light of the flashlight at a hallow distance in the woods.

The light beam had not been more than twenty yards behind him up in the stand of trees.

Was Caleb tormenting him? Did he really see him? Randy obviously didn't know.

He waited for more glimpses of the light. He was staring at the trees with a strained nervous glare. He rarely blinked to wet his eyes.

No more light. Caleb hadn't called out to him again. The few moments that Randy had taken to listen now seemed like hours.

Randy decided that he couldn't wait to see if Caleb had spotted him. He was committed to Helda's house, but he surmised that Caleb had guessed his destination.

Perhaps he should back track and throw Caleb off his trail. The problem was that if Caleb had actually seen him, he would follow Randy back down the path and then Randy would be trapped at the Foster cabin.

Randy wished that the Calvary would ride over the hill to save him. He hoped that Mary Jo and Picker had reached Mary Jo's house by now.

Yet even if they had garnered help, he couldn't be certain that they would be on the way down the trail to save him.

Randy quickly decided to forgo his planned stop at Helda's house. Going back the way he came was also out of the question. He would head straight to Piute's pig farm.

He would have to reach the milldam on the other side of Helda's property and traverse the road. He would also have to go by the \

Romo house on the hill in order to take the dirt road which led to Piute's homestead.

Randy despised taking the dirt road to Piute's place because of the small camp frequented by hobos and vagabonds that was set back off of the road on a small parcel of government land. The inhabitants had never bothered him, but he hated the way that they warily eyed him as he passed by the camp.

Occasionally the law would roust them from the camp, but they always filtered back to the makeshift houses undaunted by the hassle.

Randy felt that his choices were limited. He remembered Caleb talking to Mr. Romo at the rodeo last night. He didn't trust Mr. Romo.

Piute's place it was going to have to be; besides Randy was certain that Piute's dad had no great affinity for Caleb "Scar Nose" Fulton. He didn't know the circumstance of the friction, but it seemed that one either liked Caleb Fulton or one didn't like him - there was not much of a gray area as far as Caleb was concerned.

His heart pumped steadily faster as his anxiety grew. Randy surveyed the woods once more. He saw no visible sign of Caleb or the light flicker he had seen a few moments ago. He raised himself upright and ran as fast as he could across the wet sandy soil.

The run was treacherous and stumbled almost falling many times. He was determined not to let that drunken lunatic catch him.

Randy could see that the trees were beginning to thin out and the slope of the land was growing wider. He knew that he was almost on Helda's property.

He didn't slow down. He wiped the perspiration from his eyes. He was concentrating on the ground in front of him, trying to dodge shadowy obstacles that were illuminated by the moon hanging in the sky. If he didn't concentrate hard, he would ultimately fall and perhaps give his pursuer the opportunity to catch him.

As Randy rounded the small bend in the creek, he could definitely hear the water pouring over the small dam. The echo of the cascading water splashing on the rocks under the bridge gave off the impression that the dam was larger than it was in reality.

He was dragging in air, feeling it being sucked into his overworked lungs. The excitement and apprehension of the moment was causing his adrenaline to work his body hard. He listened intently for a sound out of the ordinary.

Caleb Fulton hadn't called to him in a while and Randy couldn't hear any rustling sounds behind him. The reverberation of the water increased the difficulty of hearing softer sounds.

Randy stopped and stood ten feet from the creek by a weeping willow tree. He leaned up against the tree in the hopes that Caleb couldn't see him as he rested.

Thirty yards up the slow rising slope Randy could see lights on inside of Helda's house. He was standing beside the tree that Helda used to hang her towel on when she took her nightly bath in the creek. She had finished her bath a long time ago.

He tried to calculate his chances of running up to Helda's house. Would he be able to reach the house before Caleb could grab him? Could he produce enough noise by yelling to have Helda come out of the house to see what the commotion might be? Probably not a good idea- Caleb had smashed Pup with a shovel. Caleb surely wouldn't have any reservations about bonking Helda's noggin as well.

Randy felt that he had regained sufficient breathing capacity and he didn't want to dawdle behind Helda's house any longer. He would break for the bridge to cross the road and head to Piute's house.

Pushing off from the tree, he ran toward the embankment that sealed off the dam on the side closest to Helda's house. His footing was much better as he traversed across the well manicured lawn that was a part of Helda's property.

He crossed over Helda's property line and was about thirty yards from the rise of the embankment when the grass had become longer and more unruly. The county maintained this area and wasn't quite as diligent as Helda in the upkeep of the grass. Occasionally, Helda or Caleb would mow the area if it grew too high in the summer.

The long grass slowed Randy's progress, but it also gave him some support as he powered his way up the incline. He would grab and clutch at the grass with his hands to support his way up the hill. The ground was slick and muddy.

He took a breather half the way up the steep embankment and peered at the property behind him to see if Caleb was following him.

He saw no sign of Caleb. He was starting to feel better about the situation. With a sigh of relief, he wiped his brow of the perspiration that was running down his face and swatted at the mosquitoes that were using his legs as an open air diner. He was itchy all over his body. He hoped that it was from the mosquitoes and not from a patch of poison ivy that he may have inadvertently traveled through on his journey to Piute's house.

A noise caught his attention and he looked up at the bridge. A car was thundering up the road and was about to stop at the stop sign across the way from the Romo house. Randy was elated. He would know that Thrush glass packed muffler sound anywhere.

As close as he was to the water running over the dam, the muffler's sweet song superseded the noise of the rush of flowing water over the dam.

It was his cousins Dennis' car. He must have picked up Karen and was on his way to take her home. Randy almost cried with relief. He wished that Scar Nose Fulton would show his face. Randy knew that Dennis would reduce the old scar-nosed drunk to a heap of skin and bone rubble.

Randy quickened his pace up the embankment. He wanted to wave his arms but the incline was too steep. The car engine was rumbling closer and closer to the stop sign and even closer to becoming Randy's salvation.

Randy began to yell. "DENNIS! DENNIS! WAIT! DENNIS!"

He tried to climb up the bank as fast as he could, while continuing to scream his cousin's name as loudly as he could scream. He had thrown caution to the wind and hoped to reach Dennis before Scar Nose Fulton could reach him.

The car engine and rush of water streaming over the dam all but preempted the desperate cry that Randy was projecting from the bank's incline. The tall grass grabbed his legs like thin ropes slowing his progress, but he trudged forward as best that he could.

Even with the car windows rolled down in the summer heat, Dennis and Karen, if she was in car, would have a hard time hearing Randy's calling out. The car radio would have only added to the din in the vehicle.

Randy was half the way up the embankment and the incline was beginning to level out as it sloped to the shoulder of the road. Even if he didn't reach the road in time to catch Dennis at the stop sign, he could stand in the middle of the road, hop up and down, waving his arms and hope that Dennis would see him in the rearview mirror, stop the car and return to retrieve him.

Randy was feeling a good sense of relief with his modified plan.

Then out of the blue or more appropriately out of the dark he heard, "He can't hear you, boy."

Randy stopped dead in his tracks. He was torn between running back down the bank to the creek or to try a mad dash to the road, which was infinitely much closer.

But close to the road was to Caleb Fulton and he was in between him and the road which led to Randy's sanctuary

The moment of indecision caused his heart to sink as Dennis gunned his car and roared off down the road.

The car zooming off toward town triggered Randy's flight reflex. He wasn't in any mood to banter with the shovel wielding drunk some ten feet away from him. Randy turned and ran down the incline to the water.

He would swim out a distance from the dam and swim over to the distant shore. If Scarnose followed him into the water, Randy calculated that he could swim around the dam to the other side and continue his journey to Piute's house. If Caleb didn't pursue him in the water, he would swim across to the distant shore and head down to the church. Mr. Dallie lived by the church and Randy would call the police from there.

If he had to swim to cross over to Mr. Dallie's house, he would try and swim underwater as much as he could so that Caleb wouldn't be able to follow his progress. Randy would try and not raise his head very far out of the creek's surface.

He hoped that Caleb wouldn't pursue him in the water. The man was older and drunk, but he could swim like a fish and that fish was as mean as a shark this particular evening.

Chapter 30

Randy power swam as hard as he could straight out from the bank. He needed to swim as hard as he could because he was so near to the curvature of the old milldam and he wanted a large lead over his adversary.

The water was cold versus the night air. His shoes weighed on his feet like anchors, placing a heavy drag on his progress, so he toed them off while he swam out into the creek. It wasn't easy to get the shoes off and frankly he liked those shoes, but he figured that it was better to live and get new shoes, rather than die with his beloved shoes still on his feet.

Randy underestimated the pull of the water cascading over the dam. The current moving in the dam's direction only added to the struggle that he had to escape the pressure of the water that felt as though it were trying to suck him in like a black hole. It was like a huge magnet drawing him into the rocks and that demented drunk was behind him. The only thing missing- regrettably to Randy - was the beautiful half-naked Sirens singing out to him to come nearer.

He decided to chance a quick stop to evaluate his position. He turned quickly while treading water and surveyed the creek behind him- no sign of Scarnose.

His brief stop moved him closer to the dam. Even treading water caused him to lose distance from the dam. It was sucking him ever closer. He decided to round the curvature of the dam and to exit on the other side. He didn't have enough stamina remaining to reach the other shore. He would have to chance running past Caleb.

While he was left to wonder which direction that Caleb had taken, Randy began to strong arm his way from the dam. Scarnose disappeared quicker than a soap bubble once it was popped. Randy would have to take his chance on the other side of the dam. He was nearing exhaustion and he was beginning to feel desperate.

He kicked evenly and steadily while he crossed his arms over on a strong controlled pace, just like Caleb had taught him. He could feel himself being propelled forward in the creek, but it was like three feet forward and one foot backward. He knew that he couldn't use his racing technique because the current and strength of the water falling over the dam would sap the rest of his energy.

Even at his current pace, Randy knew that he was going to lose the battle. He decided to angle out a ways from the dam and to work toward the diving board on the far side. He would hang onto the ladder that led up to the platform in order to catch his breath. He hoped that Caleb wouldn't be waiting for him at the ladder.

He stroked a hard steady stroke, his arms felt leaden and his muscles screamed from the fire that burned in them. Fortunately he had angled himself with near perfection from his perspective. He stopped swimming and began to tread water. He let nature begin to take over. The current and force of falling water over the rocks pulled him towards the direction of the ladder. He surveyed the distant shoreline and the bridge above the dam. The roar of the water splashing heavily on the rocks filled his ears. He didn't see old Scarnose, but he knew that the cunning drunk was around somewhere.

It didn't take long for the creek to move Randy up to the dam. He adjusted his position slightly and kicked his way over to the ladder and diving platform. He grabbed the bottom rung of the ladder and pulled himself around to the bank side away from the cascading water.

He rested, while holding onto the ladder, scanning with searching eyes for his pursuer. His breath was labored, he had no shoes on to protect his feet from the journey to Piute's farm and he was scared to death that Caleb might catch him.

He gathered his strength and held onto the metal rung of the ladder, so that he could move over to the concrete side wall of the dam. He would have to walk along the top of the wall to reach the bank, which led to the road. As he righted himself on the foot wide wall and stood erect, he saw his nemesis coming his way over the guardrail adjacent to the road. He was moving down the bank toward Randy.

With a deep sigh, Randy knew he was trapped. His strength was sapped from the run to the road and the swim in the creek; he was near to giving up and surrendering to Caleb.

He had no where to go but up the ladder and onto the platform. At this point jumping back into the creek was no option at all - so that's where he went. At least he would have the high ground. Perhaps he could rejoin Caleb in a conversation long enough to gather back his energy and he could try swimming out into the creek and over to the other side. He might even reach Dallie's house before Caleb caught him. Or maybe Caleb was intoxicated enough to fall over the dam into the rocks.

Randy had climbed up and turned to face the top of the ladder. He seated himself with his back to the creek and watched Caleb amble down the bank and onto the concrete wall. Randy noticed that Caleb was limping and seemed to have blood rolling down the left side of his face.

With a small iota of satisfaction, Randy chuckled out loud. The old fool must have fallen on the road and hurt himself that was why Randy hadn't seen him when he was in the creek.

Randy sat on the platform and swung his legs. He felt something irritating his legs and reached into his pocket to discover the rocks he had picked up to scare the wild cats away earlier that evening.

He nodded his head in a small revelation and was beginning to feel a little better about his situation once again. He was high up on the diving platform, so that a car could possibly notice him if they looked out over the dam, he had rocks to throw at Caleb and he could even kick the old fool if Caleb tried to ascend the ladder up to the platform. Things weren't so great, but they could've been worse.

Caleb reached the ladder and stood at the base glaring at Randy. He stood still and Randy could see that Caleb was short of breath, laboring to pull in oxygen. Caleb wiped his face with his sleeve to erase the dark trickle of liquid, which was rolling down his cheek He looked at the stain on his shirt and glared at Randy once more. The insinuation from the glare was that this mishap was Randy's fault.

With a sigh Caleb asked, "Randy, why are you running from me?"

Randy clutched a rock in his hand ready for firing and replied, "Caleb, why are you chasing me?"

Caleb rubbed his chin and blinked rapidly pondering the question. He rested one foot on the bottom rung of the ladder. "I'm not chasing you. I just want to talk to you for a moment or two. I need your opinion on something."

Randy laughed. "Caleb, it seems to me as if there isn't that much for us to talk about these days. I think if I were you I'd go into town and find out why the police are looking for you."

"Hell, boy, they're not after me anymore. Fact is…I'm not even in the county anymore."

Randy was puzzled and scared. What was this moron talking about? Where was all the traffic? Randy desperately wanted a car to come by the dam so that they could see him on the diving platform.

He said to Caleb, "What are you talking about?"

"Never mind, Randy…come closer. I can't hear you to well. Come down here. I want to talk to you."

Randy moved the pebble sized rock to his fingers, readying it for throwing. "Talk to me from down there."

Caleb cleared his throat and advanced one rung up the ladder. "How about if I come up to you and we chat a bit?"

Randy could feel himself beginning to feel more nervous at the advancement of Caleb. Caleb was attempting to speak in a calm even manner as if her trying to reassure Randy that he wasn't dangerous.

The pebble in Randy's hand was digging into his fingers because he was holding it so tightly.

As the standoff continued, the short silence was broken by Randy. "I don't think so. You stay there and I'll stay here. What do you want to talk about?"

Caleb stood on the bottom rung of the ladder with both feet. He couldn't reach Randy from where he was positioned and his head was just below the top of the platform.

"I need to be closer so that I can hear you over the noise of the water."

Randy said, "I hear you just fine."

"Randy, what's your problem? Why can't you just let things die?" Caleb's tone was a little less patronizing and more antagonistic.

"Caleb, I swear I don't have a clue to what the hell you're talking about…I don't have a thing to do with why the police are looking for you- if that's what you mean. I didn't burn down the church, I didn't paint graffiti on the walls of the town, and I didn't kill the dogs… that was you. You think you're some kind of God, who can control everything to your liking and now you're threatening me.

"Why? I don't know, but don't blame me for your predicament."

Randy didn't want to be specific about Caleb whacking Pup with the shovel. He wasn't sure that Caleb was cognizant of the fact.

Caleb laughed. "I don't know how to respond to that little speech of yours, but you've got me all wrong. I'm not threatening you. I…"

"Then get down off of the ladder and go away." Randy interrupted.

"What? I need to get closer. I can't hear you over the rushing water too well. I'm no spring chicken you know."

"That's too bad, because I can hear you just fine."

Quiet for a moment or two, Caleb sniffed in a breath of air with an irritated annoyed impatience. He eyed Randy with cold dead eyes. Randy could feel the evil penetration and battled the butterflies in his stomach. Caleb thoughts pushed through his mind and then returned a warmer friendlier demeanor to his face and eyes. He smiled at Randy and tested Randy's resolve by climbing up another rung on the ladder to the platform. Caleb opened his smile wider and was as close as four feet from Randy, who sat with his back to the water on the end of the diving platform.

Before Caleb could speak, Randy winged the pebble in his hand and plunked Caleb square on top of his head.

THUMP! The sound of a melon thumped for the hollow sound of ripeness.

Caleb dropped down a rung on the ladder. "Randy—don't do that again!" The words carried a deep ominous tone.

"Then stay where you are or go away."

Randy felt in his pocket and determines that there are only four pebbles left in his arsenal and one of them was very small. His ammo was running low. He needed a car to travel by soon if he was going to have any hope of getting out of this situation.

Caleb began to shake the ladder jostling Randy. Randy plunked Caleb on the top of the head with another rock. *THUMP!*

Caleb's melon must be getting sore. Randy had three pebbles left.

"I told you to stop throwing those rocks...you're pissing me off!"

"Then go away!"

Randy knew that he was pissing Caleb off, but he was also keeping him at bay, buying as much time as he could.

Another deep sigh from Caleb, "Look...let's talk this thing out. I know that you think that I burned down that old Negro church. Well...I didn't.

"That idiot Hammet says that I put him up to writing crap on walls in town...again—I didn't. And as far as those dogs of your uncles—why would I kill them? Some people thought they were a nuisance, but you never heard me say it, did you?"

He didn't give Randy a chance to reply.

"I was trying to learn from Pup if he had anything to with it and I think that he did. Why I bet you that he probably burned down that church you keep blaming me of doing. You know how bigoted his wife is.

"Randy, we were so close just a few years ago, but somehow you've turned on me like I'm some kind of devil...and you've done it without any proof. I'm thinking you've become delusional."

Randy interjected, "I think you're drunk and I'm sure I don't like your interrogation technique. I'll wager that Pup will attest to that." Randy had said the last part without really pondering it through all the way. If Scar Nose had any doubts about Randy knowing that he had struck Pup with the shovel, they were now confirmed.

Caleb smiled first and then he laughed a confused laugh. "That old fool, I know that he killed those dogs."

"Caleb, I think—"

Caleb cut Randy off. "Randy, there are many things you don't understand about this area. Things happen for the best.

"My bet is... even if Pup killed those dogs he was put up to it. People don't like their hands dirty. There are so many ways for people to get what they want. People are always looking for an advantage in life. Alliances change with the wind. Remember that everyone's into things for their own self interest."

Caleb slowly started to climb up the ladder as he was speaking.

Randy plunked him in the head again. *THUMP!*

"GOD DAMMIT, BOY! DON'T HIT ME WITH ANOTHER ROCK." Venom spewed from a very agitated and hostile Caleb 'Scar Nose' Fulton.

Randy had two rocks left.

"Then get down and go *AWAY!*" Randy was feeling the flight reflex very strongly and had to suppress it while he evaluated his dwindling options. He was having no luck with any passing cars. Where the hell was everyone and why were they staying at home?

Almost out of rocks, he would only be able to keep Caleb at bay and off the platform with two more tosses of his medieval ammo. He may be able to bluff for a few minutes but he didn't want to count on bluffing an angry, bumpy-headed drunk.

Randy was really trapped in a corner. His only decent option was to go back in the water. He had to decide which way to swim and he had to hope that he could out swim Caleb. But from his past experience, he knew that Caleb could out swim him even when he was full of beer.

Scar Nose shook the ladder with more vehemence. He nearly jostled Randy off. He held on tightly with one hand and squeezed his thighs like a vise around the platform. Randy threw one of his last rocks.

PING! Not *THUMP!* Randy had missed with a low throw and had hit the top rung of the ladder.

He had one rock left.

Randy reached into his pocket to retrieve the rock. He would have to be careful with his aim. With any luck he would strike Caleb in the eye and then he could dive into the water and escape from the drunken maniac.

There was a silence between the two adversaries. Water rolling over the dam was the only sound for a few minutes.

Randy readied his rock and prayed for a shot at Caleb's face. He was rolling it between his fingers when Caleb gave the ladder a short violent surprising shake. The rock fell from his hand and Randy tried to catch the falling rock. He could feel the edge of the semi-round stone as it eluded his grasp. Now he was out of ammunition and facing his nemesis with only his wit and guile.

Randy knew that he was defenseless, but fortunately Caleb didn't know that he was out of rocks—or did he?

Caleb was watching Randy very carefully. Randy tried to drive the notion from his head that Caleb was cognizant of his empty pockets, but with the Caleb's change in demeanor there was too much doubt in Randy's mind.

"Alright, Randy, I've had enough of this foolishness. Come on down from the platform. I'll go stand up on the road. We'll talk this out and I'll tell you why I think Pup killed your uncle's dogs."

"I think I'll stay right here and I think we're done talking. Just go away, Caleb. I'm not bothering you."

With a heavy sigh Caleb said, "Can't do it, Randy. Time isn't on my side."

Randy wondered what the meaning of that statement was but he didn't really want to know. He figured that he was the problem and that Caleb didn't want him around any longer.

Caleb tested Randy once more. He worked his way up the ladder by one more rung. His head was above the platform. Randy had no response.

With a knowing smile that was devoid of friendliness, Caleb said to Randy, "You've judged me without a fair trial, boy. The only dog that I'll admit to killing is that stray mutt that's been hanging around the area the past few days. He was acting like he was mad behind the cabin and I couldn't take any chances that he might bite someone and give them rabies.

"So I whacked him with the shovel and buried him on the spot. It was necessary and not evil…like many things that happen around here. Things need cleansing and I'm the cleaner."

Randy was stunned. Caleb had murdered Pony. He had only known the dog for a few days but he had grown extremely fond of the dog.

Randy felt fire come into his eyes. His upper lip twitched with anger. He glared at Scar Nose Fulton whose head and shoulders were above the top of the ladder inching his way toward Randy.

With his adrenaline surging and on the loose, Randy cleared his throat and brought a huge wet hocker into his mouth. He pushed his body up into a kneeling position on the diving platform and continued to glare at Caleb, who smiled malevolently back at Randy.

Randy reached his head back and spat the mixture of saliva and mucus with a mighty force and struck Caleb Fulton square in the face. He didn't wait for a response. He turned and dove into the water not listening to the expletives trailing behind him.

Chapter 31

Randy's dive into the water was as shallow as he could make the dive. With Caleb's deftness at diving and swimming, Randy's only hope was to produce an outstanding head start and to beat Caleb to the distant shoreline.

He threw one hand over the other and kicked with all the fury that he could muster. He drove toward the shoreline as fast as he could. He raised his head every fifth stroke to take in a fresh mouthful of air.

He could spy the reeds some thirty yards away, which told him that the slope of the creek would become shallower. He would be able to stand and be more maneuverable in the race out of the water. He didn't dare peer back to see if Caleb was there or even how close Caleb may have been to him. He knew that Caleb was following him and without his head start there was no way he would win a race against Caleb.

His heart pumping, Randy glimpsed at the dry land in front of him and saw a car's headlight beam bouncing down the road. A little too late he thought. He'd never reach to the road in time.

As he stroked with fervor, he felt something clutching at his feet. Randy kicked hard back at Caleb's probing fingers. He struck something hard and the tentacles fell away. Randy must have struck Caleb in the head with his heel.

The kick stopped the fingers from grabbing at him, but it also had broken his rhythm and slowed his momentum.

Randy's reservoir of energy was sapped. He struggled to regain his momentum. He relaxed the best that he could and kicked his feet trying to propel himself back on top of the water. He wanted to glance back to observe where his pursuer was located, but he couldn't risk the precious seconds.

His momentum restored, Randy drove as hard as he could toward solid ground. He was winded and anticipated that Caleb would be grabbing at his feet every time he kicked. The closer he was to the shoreline he neared the more confidence he was instilled with. Maybe he knocked the old drunk out with his kick.

Nope. As Randy turned his head to draw in a breath of badly needed fresh air, Caleb clutched onto Randy's left foot with an ironclad grip. He pulled Randy out of synch and drew him unexpectedly under the water. His fresh gulp of air was replaced with brown unsavory creek water.

Randy managed to raise his head and spit out the water involuntarily coughing the water that was filling his lungs. His head didn't stay out of the water very long; Caleb pulled him under once more.

Randy had sucked in a small amount of air. He struggled violently against the strong grip of his nemesis. He clawed, kicked and twisted his body. He broke free momentarily and even though he was underwater, he could feel his right toe touch the bottom of the creek briefly.

He knew that he was close to the shore. He may have been two or three feet underwater he assumed. What he did know was that he needed to bring in some fresh oxygen and he had to do it real soon.

He surfaced and gasped in a panicked breath. Caleb was going to drown him. He had to unleash that death grip on his foot and ankle.

Nope. Caleb dragged him under again. This time Caleb had grabbed Randy's arm. Randy swung his other arm violently and struck Caleb in the face. Caleb loosened his grasp and Randy tried to swim away. He was near tears and he was scared as he had ever been in his life.

He was almost on top of the water when Caleb jumped on him and hung onto Randy's lower torso.

Randy was almost done. He had no more strength no more air and no more fight.

He was underneath the surface of the creek holding the stale oxygen in his lungs. His mind turned to his dead cousin Scott, who he figured he would see any minute now. He thought of Mr. Foster and the bag that he would have to fill before he entered heaven. He hoped that it wouldn't too heavy. After all he felt as though he had lived a good caring life. He also thought of his father. Perhaps he would be in heaven as well or perhaps he was still picking up sticks of sin for abandoning him and his sister- that was if he was even dead, who knew.

Finally Randy saw the white light many people must see when they're about to die and speak about when they are revived to tell there stories. This must be the light that Mr. Miler from the movie theater must have seen at least twice. Randy's lungs felt like they were going to burst, he couldn't hold it in much longer.

The light wasn't a very comforting sensation to Randy. He had heard that there was a feeling of bliss after seeing the light. He only asked for a fresh gulp of life giving oxygen. He could hold out no longer, the pressure of the air must be expelled from his lungs. He felt the soft sandy bottom of the creek push between his toes as he tried to push up and out of the water. The struggle with Caleb had pushed them closer to the shore.

Randy only had to stand up to receive his life giving oxygen, but Caleb was too strong. The white light was shining through the water to Randy. No bliss. He couldn't control his lungs; he blew out the air with relief, but involuntarily sucked in a fresh lung full of creek water. He was going to drown.

Scar Nose had won. The dog killer, church burner, bigoted graffiti writer - old drunk Scar Nose had won. *Crap.*

Randy was closing his eyes when something grabbed his hair and pulled him straight out of the creek. Going to heaven kind of hurts he thought. He thought the angels would be gentler. He saw a large man with a flashlight and then the lights went out.

Randy awoke on the shore. He saw red and blue lights flashing all around him. People were moving in a chaotic manner. Directly above he saw old Doc Burly, who lived nearby and the face of his Uncle Harvey.

Harvey had that crooked smile that he smiled when he was relieved or amused.

Well it wasn't heaven, but it was good to be alive.

"How you doing, Randy?" Doc Burly asked.

"F…fine, I think," Randy managed to croak out. He was dizzy and his throat was rough. His chest hurt like hell. What he didn't know was that while he has passed out, the deputy had performed CPR on him to bring the water out of his lungs. He had really come close to drowning.

He didn't see Caleb anywhere, so he asked, "Where's Caleb?"

"In the patrol car getting ready to go to jail," his uncle answered. "You rest now, we'll talk later. The ambulance will be here soon and will take you to the hospital for observation."

"But I'm fine," Randy protested.

"Quiet, boy, we know what's best for you," his uncle rebuked.

With that Randy laid there and didn't say another word, he was too worn out to argue with his uncle.

Epilogue

Two days had past and Randy had been released from the hospital. His mom, sister and Harland had come to visit him in the hospital the night that he had almost succumbed to the creek water and drown. They had wanted him to come home, but Randy wanted to remain at his aunt's house for another week.

He was the talk of the area. He wanted to stay and be with Mary Jo for awhile longer as well.

As he sat in his stone chair and reflected upon the last two weeks events, it was quite remarkable for a small town boy.

Caleb Fulton and Sam Hammet were in jail. The Kearny dogs were dead. Lee's arm was sprained, Pup had a large lump on his head, but was still alive and Vern had become a man. But most importantly he had become Mary Jo's boyfriend.

He sat waiting wondering how it would all pan out, hoping that the law would keep Caleb and Sam in the slammer for a long time. He had overheard his aunt and uncle talking that Sam may be getting out soon by testifying against Caleb, but Randy hoped that Sam would have to spend some time behind bars. Vern's girl was long distance and not really his girl. Lee was as crazy as ever, feeling his oats now at least one girl had paid attention to him.

Thank goodness that Mary Jo and Picker had found help in time otherwise he'd have been a goner. Once the two of them had reached the canoe, Mary Jo went across to retrieve her father and they came back over to the cabin to check on Pup. Picker had high tailed it to the Kearny farm and gathered Harvey and Caroline and they had headed down toward the creek, driving slowly trying to spy Randy when they had headed around the bend and had seen the commotion in the water.

The police had been called and serendipitously shown up at the same time that Harvey had hauled his nephew out of the water by his hair. Caleb had been too exhausted to fight and literally had sat down in the water and held his hands out for hand cuffing.

Randy felt bad that he had suspected Picker of spying on him and of having something to do with the death of the dogs, but Picker had stuck by him and had not even mentioned anything about it. Picker was truly unique and a very good friend. Randy could only hope to be as loyal as Picker.

He shook his head and peered over at the Magurk dock. Mary Jo would be coming out of the house at any minute and would paddle her canoe over to pick him up for a nice float down the creek. He listened to the roll of the creek, the song of the birds in the trees and the leaves rustle above his head. The gentle wind formed into a dust devil just to his right and Randy thought of Pony. He would have been there to watch over Randy and perhaps he was watching over him now, sitting beside a smiling Mr. Foster. Randy knew that Mr. Foster must be his guardian angel and he felt safe and warm with the old man in his heart.

What a summer. It was tough growing up, but what choice did he have.